ANGEL FROM THE DUST

By Paul Kenney

KINVARA
PRODUCTIONS

ISBN: 1979734186
ISBN 13: 9781979734189

Rachel:

She held this truth to
be self-evident, that
All men _And_ women Are
Created equal!

To Reese

All the Best,
Paul

CHAPTER 1

I can remember my father lifting me up, while he stood on the ridge overlooking Hannibal harbor, so I could see a riverboat approaching under the blinding sun of a July morning. Beneath us, a gang of bare chested black workers were singing a haunting song while drenched with sweat in the broiling heat of the dockside.

They were unloading three wagons of hay bales on to a rusted barge bound for Baton Rouge, under the direction of a scarecrow like white foreman, who was armed with a pistol and mounted upon an aged grey mare. The foreman then removed his faded yellow fedora and wiped his brow with a red and white bandana, cursing his charges in a deep southern sort of way,

"You sons of bitches better get a move on and get this barge loaded or no food tonight. You can take a water break at midday. "

"Come, Mary, we will be late for Mass," my father warned, taking me by the hand up dusty Broadway road toward the hill upon which The Holy Family Church stood.

"Papa, I thought Mr. Lincoln freed the slaves?" I asked.

"He did, Mary but the old ways die hard around here. Here is your missal and a penny for the poor box. We'll say a prayer that the Good Lord blesses those men. Now come on, I don't want "Father" seeing us coming in late. Did you study your catechism?"

"I did, Papa. I'll pray to the "Blessed Mother" for those men. She will help. She will help mama too."

My father looked at me with those sad blue eyes. He had wavy chestnut hair and ruddy Irish cheeks. He was the loveliest men I ever knew and respected by all the others who worked as machinists in the rail yard behind the Hannibal depot.

He had escaped from Ireland on a coffin ship with the clothes on his back, fleeing the "Great Hunger", fleeing the landlords who did the bidding of the privileged, fleeing the fever and fighting all the way, toward the promise of America.

"I swear you're an angel," he said, while caressing my cheek. "Don't forget to say a prayer for me while you're at it."

"I do every day, Papa. I pray Mama will feel better and Timmy and Danny will find work so they can help you." The church bell echoed over Hannibal as we entered and blessed ourselves.

I was wearing the white cotton dress that Mama made for my First Communion. I loved how its fabric hugged my skin and the lace of its collar made me feel like the fine ladies I would see twirling their parasols on the riverboats that visited Hannibal. I loved to twirl and sashay in it, like the windswept petal of a lily of the valley. I remember old Sam Watkins calling me "my strawberry blonde butterfly" when I passed the steamship authority offices wearing it.

Mama was a seamstress in Cork City before her family made their way to America. She would marry Papa up in New Hampshire and together make a family and their way west with the building of the railroad.

I suppose it was 1870 or thereabouts. That was before the Panic caused the railroads to lay off its workers. That was before I heard Papa sobbing in the pantry because he couldn't provide for his family and before Mama took really sick.

Father Murray was the pastor of The Holy Family Church. There were a lot of people in Hannibal who didn't like us because we were Irish Catholic. They called us names and said we were fit for the gutter, or some such nonsense like that. Father Murray said that we should hold our tempers and turn the other cheek. Papa thought different.

I remember we were passing Montgomery's Dry Goods when one of the men who sat outside wearing a Confederate jacket and chewing tobacco called my brother, Danny, Irish scum. My father told Danny and me to keep walking and he would be right along.

Calm as could be he walked right back to that man and pulled his hat down over his eyes and kicked the cracker barrel he was sitting on out from under him. I don't recollect anybody ever calling us Irish scum in Hannibal after that.

Father Murray cared deeply for all of his congregation, which were mostly Irish railroaders and their families. He was a small man in his middle years with a head of red hair, silver wire eyeglasses and pale white skin. Although he was fervent in his beliefs, what he lacked was insight, as Papa would say. He preached that the Knights of Labor were a threat to the ways of the Church. That devotion to them was a turning away from the teachings of Jesus.

Papa thought different. He was a member of the Knights and an admirer of Terence Powderly. He believed that workers needed to band together to prevent being used up by the bosses. A lot of the Irish who fled the famine were against the bosses.

When I was a little older, I was able to go down to the Hannibal landing with my brother Timmy or my brother Danny and watch the riverboats gathering up passengers for a moonlight cruise. The minstrels would be playing their fiddles and banjos while singing *Camp Town Races* or some such song.

If we were lucky, we would see old Sam Watkins in the pilot's cabin and call up to him. I was always his favorite. If he wasn't too busy he would call us aboard and give us a licorice stick and maybe let me ring the golden bell outside his cabin.

I remember how his raven hair was like steel wool and his bushy mustache drooped over the corners of his mouth. He always smelled like Bay Rum and cigars and acted kindly to all, even to the ladies who worked the rooms at the old Butterfield Hotel.

The nuns at The Holy Family Convent School taught me my arithmetic and to write with a fountain pen in the Palmer method. They wore black habits that covered their bodies and black and white headdresses, leaving only room for their faces to squeeze through, like a tiny port hole.

They wore large black Rosary beads and a crucifix hanging over a starched white bib that covered their breasts. They made me do long division on the blackboard after school, because I just couldn't get the hang of it. Papa taught me to read before the nuns did, and to do it for the joy and adventure it could bring. I always said that if I had a good book and a nice cup of tea, I was in heaven.

CHAPTER 2

*S*ister Kathleen Mary taught me in the third grade. I never liked her and she wasn't too fond of me. There are some people I suppose who want everything done their way. Mama would say those people were spoiled brats or privileged characters.

I asked Mama once, whether a nun could be a privileged character. She just looked at me and said I better not bring disgrace on the family by disobeying the nuns. I never said anything bad about the nuns to her ever again.

I never told her how Sister Kathleen Mary used to punish Susie Rafferty with a rap from a ruler whenever she used her left hand to write. That poor girl would wet her pants from being so afraid. Once, when I asked her to stop hurting Susie, when all the others kept quiet, she slapped my face, called me a little urchin and told me to stand in the corner.

I didn't know what an urchin was, but I knew it wasn't good. Susie and I would become close friends after that. I swear it was Sister Kathleen Mary who caused that poor girl to stammer so terribly.

We were taught our Catechism almost every day. Mother Gabriel used to drill it into us like we were chirping parrots. Who is God? Why did God make you? I would go to bed on those nights and hear the answers of the class over and over in my head, like echoes in a canyon.

My brothers became altar boys and learned the Latin. I asked Mama why I couldn't become an altar girl. She just said that was the way things were and I should accept them. I didn't ever like accepting things that were, if I didn't think they were fair.

Back in those days, girls would only go to the fourth grade before being apprenticed out to work. It didn't matter whether you were bright and studious and wanted to better yourself by becoming an educated lady.

After I had my little run in with Sister Kathleen Mary, I just knew she had it in for me. Before that episode she promised that I would be promoted to the fourth grade with the others who were bright and had promise. I took her at her word and even got the hang of long division.

After I had the run in over Susie, everything changed. She didn't call on me like she used to. She didn't let me clean the erasers or carry messages to the other classes, like she used to. She thought I was a troublemaker.

When promotion day came and I read the note on my desk that I was being kept back, I just stormed out of the classroom during morning prayers. I didn't want to cry in front of the others, especially in front of Sister Kathleen Mary.

I told two girls in the hall that I was never coming back. They must have told Mother Gabriel. I just ran down the hill in the rain not knowing where to go. I was heartbroken and as angry as a wet hen. I decided I would go see if I could speak to Papa at his work.

As I mentioned, my father was a machinist by trade. He was a foreman for the Hannibal & Saint Joseph Railroad. The work was hard and the work day was twelve hours, Monday through Saturday. I don't ever remember my father taking sick or complaining about the working conditions in the Hannibal rail yard.

I do remember when young Sean O'Brien was killed while working in the rail yard. He was crushed to death between two rail cars. All the families of the Irish workers were in mourning after that.

I recall going to the funeral Mass and seeing Sean's poor mother, so overcome with grieving, her daughters had to hold her up to follow the pine box being carried by her husband and sons from the church.

Young Sean was a friend of my brother Timmy. They used to go to Ralston's fishing hole together. I still remember his golden hair with the cowlick. I can still see him barefoot in his overalls with the patches on his bottom, carrying his fishing pole and whistling a tune without a care in the world. He was twelve when he died. His body was too mangled to be shown at the wake.

I had never visited my father during work hours, before that morning. He worked mostly in the forge of the Hannibal rail yard. It was set back in the cinders in a building of brown brick. Through the top of its tarred roof protruded a long cylinder like brick chimney that spewed smoke and soot over the workers' village where my family lived.

When I arrived at the gate, the grey beard of a watchman, wearing a black duster and brown slouch hat, saw me through the window of his shack. At first he sat there, hoping I would go away, I suppose. When I stood there like a cigar store Indian in the pelting rain, he finally opened his door and shouted at me,

"What do you want, girl?"

"Could I please speak to my father? His name is Michael Kenney."

"He's busy at work. Why don't you run on home?"

"Please sir, I promise it won't take but a minute."

"I'll have to go and get him. Landsakes! Why ain't you in school?"

When I saw the worried look on Papa's face, I felt ashamed that I had come, but I really didn't know what else to do. He was wearing a leather apron over his bare chest. His face was covered in sweat and soot that was so thick, the rain rolled off it.

"Mary, what has happened, he asked. Is it your mother?"

"No Papa," I cried, "she promised I would be promoted to fourth grade and she kept me back because I told her to stop hurting Susie. Oh, Papa, I will never go to that school again. I know Mama wants me to be taught by the nuns, but I don't and I won't ever be taught by them again."

I suppose that was the first time I stood my ground against someone who had power over me. Although I was young, I knew my mind. When Mother Gabriel came by and said that I had sinned by leaving during prayers; Papa sided with me. He went up to the convent house and gave Sister Kathleen Mary a piece of his mind. I remember him saying that it was important to always fight for what I thought was fair.

CHAPTER 3

My father loved to sing. He had this beautiful tenor voice that would rise above all the others during Sunday Mass. I was so proud, just standing there beside him in the third row to the right of the altar.

He was so tall and handsome in his blue wool suit that Mama spent a month making, with its broad lapels and velvet collar. It was the only suit of clothes my father ever owned and Mama would clean and press it every week, so that her husband always looked his very best.

Mama and Papa were love birds. I don't ever remember an angry word between them, even after Mama took sick and could no longer take in the wash or scrub the floor of our cottage. I suppose my father knew that my mother was doing her best. I will always remember how she would struggle through her pain, saying that we should pity the unfortunate but never pity ourselves.

Unlike many of the other railroaders, my father never touched the drink. He told me once that his father was a drinking man and that made it hard on his family back in Ireland. When the famine came, my grandfather would pass away from the Typhus along with my grandmother and my father's two sisters.

Papa never spoke of the famine, nor of his passage to America. Not many of the Irish who came over, did. It was the same way with Seamus Egan and the others who fought in the "War between the States." I suppose some things are so horrid, they plague the mind and seal the lips.

7

I remember going to see Mother Jones speak in Chicago when I was living there. She was the first person I ever heard tell of the famine and all of its horror. She also told of the little breaker boys whose bodies were battered and broken from separating shale from coal in the mines, and how the Molly Maguires were betrayed by that Judas, McParland.

I remembered how the tears poured from her raging blue eyes. I would never ever forget that speech. It made me weep and it made me angry, just like I was on that day I was kept back at the Sacred Heart Convent School.

My father loved his garden. It was behind our cottage in the workers village. Before dawn, the men would pass by on their way to work in the rail yard. There would be Papa on his hands and knees, weeding and tilling its soil, then gently passing the green watering can with the painted shamrock over it, before joining the others.

He would speak and sing to everything that grew in the garden. He said they too were God's creatures, only from a different kingdom. Then after work, beneath the moon and the stars, after he had soaked and scrubbed the soot from his person in the tub within the outbuilding, he would return once again to tend to his garden. I tell you the meals that my Mama made from the harvest of that patch of God's green earth were like manna to the children of Israel.

My older brothers were my guardians when Papa wasn't around. I remember him telling them that they were the thorns and I and my older sister, Annie, were the roses, just like those in his garden.

Timmy was tall and strong like Papa with chestnut hair and blue eyes. His small straight nose turned up like that of a Spaniel and he was the fastest runner in the village. Danny was round like an apple with reddish hair and green eyes. He loved to laugh and to play jokes on me that were never mean. He would read to me before bed and tell stories of a beautiful fairy princess that could make all my dreams come true.

My older sister Annie was shy and sickly, since she was a baby. It seemed that she was always seated at the kitchen table with a towel over her head breathing into a bowl of hot water and a brew of plants and vegetables from Papa's garden. It smelled just awful but after a while it would seem to do the trick and allow Annie to get some rest from her coughing. I tell you, I miss my family something awful every now and again.

Family was what mattered most among the railroaders who worked in Hannibal. They were wage earners for sure and most were uneducated, particularly as far as monetary matters went, but they had dignity. There was a common spirit and a common cause among them. They all knew and looked out for each other, believing that they were blessed to be able to earn a living while living in America.

I remember summer Sunday afternoons at Riverside Park when there would be fifty, maybe sixty railroader kids playing baseball, or kick the can or follow the leader. On Saturday night the men would go into town on the wagons that left from Dickson's Livery Stable. There they would smoke their pipes, raise a pint or two or play checkers or dominoes at Slattery's.

Of all the young girls in Hannibal, my brothers used to say that I was the most daring. I don't know why, but I just wasn't afraid of a lot of things. Sure I wouldn't go into the caves that Mark Twain wrote about in "Tom Sawyer" all by myself, because I never liked bats and in the winter, when the river was half frozen, I knew enough not to go out on the ice.

Everybody in Hannibal knew about Jimmy Tomkins and how he drowned trying to rescue his dog who chased a jackrabbit out too far and fell through the ice. I remember them shooting off guns, sounding for Jimmy's body, before they finally found him and his dog frozen solid together, like two icicles.

Why they said I was so daring was probably because of the way I would ride Mr. Dickson's mules, Rube and Blue. You see, one Sunday a month, Mr. Dickson would let the village kids ride his two mules in the corral next to his livery stable, if they had the pluck.

They said that Mr. Dickson once rode with Bloody Bill Anderson and his "bushwhackers" during the war and that he knew Frank and Jesse James before they went bad and started robbing and killing folks. I just remember he had sand colored hair, the saddest hazel eyes and could spit chewing tobacco clear across his stable.

Those mules of his were cantankerous creatures, alright. They would buck and bite and not let nary anyone ride them around that corral, excepting me. If they could talk maybe they would call me their favorite, like Sam Watkins used to.

Papa once said that if you were afraid of an animal they could sense it and they would be afraid of you. I just never was afraid of those two mules. I felt kind of sorry for them. Mules aren't like horses. Nobody seems to ever be proud of a mule.

Well anyway, I could ride those two mules like nobody's business with my brothers watching in awe. They just thought I had some kind of magic, because I wasn't ever afraid to sit right up on either one and ride them around.

I suppose fear is something that stops a lot of folks from taking a chance on things. I just always believed that if I was good and brave, the Blessed Mother would look out for me. I believe that still.

Besides mule riding, I just loved to swim. I would go in swimming with all the boys wearing the cotton swimmer that Mama made. Of course, I would never go in swimming without either Danny or Timmy. I would swim in the river off the barge at Johnson's landing or in Swenson's swimming hole. I was never afraid, if the water was over my head. I just loved to swing out on the rope swing over Swenson's and fly through the air and down into the green glow of that swimming hole.

Mama used to be afraid that I would go in too deep and not get back, but I knew I was a strong swimmer and never was foolhardy with things that could be dangerous. Papa used to say that I must have been a trout before I became a little girl.

Years later, when I was living in Boston, folks would ask me about Hannibal and whether I ever met Mark Twain or knew any slaves, like Jim in "Huckleberry Finn." I would tell them that Hannibal was a happy place until the hard times came. I would tell them that I was once introduced to Mark Twain by Sam Gompers, after he delivered a lecture at the Boston Music Hall. It was called, "A Night with Mark Twain, World Traveler".

I would also tell them that we knew families of freed slaves who became share croppers on farms once owned by their masters, way out near Saunders Road. I would see them come in to town to pick up supplies and how they always looked so ragged and sad when they did. I never looked down on them or any other working people or thought that I was better than they were somehow. I just never understood people that did.

When I was nine years old, I started the fourth grade at the A.D. Stowell School. That was when everything began to change for us and all the other railroader families. That was when Papa had his wages cut and Mama began to get the rheumatism so bad, she could barely get out of bed.

The first I knew that we were in a fix was when I saw Papa and my brothers picking the vegetables from the garden until late at night and putting them in crates for storage in the salt bin behind our cottage. Papa used to make the best sauerkraut in the village and sell it to other railroaders for a penny a' pound.

Once the Panic took hold, it seemed that nobody had any extra pennies to buy sauerkraut anymore and Papa kept the cabbages so Mama could make cabbage soup, when there was nothing else for us to eat. I tell you I hate cabbage soup to this day.

I remember about that time seeing Papa at the kitchen table counting out the pennies and nickels he had managed to save in the tin box he kept on the top shelf of the pantry. I could tell by the way he ran his hand through his hair that he was worried. He was worried about how we were going to make ends meet and how we were going to get through the winter that blew in from the North and froze the river and Hannibal up tighter than a drum.

That was when my brothers, Danny and Timmy, left home in search of work and Annie, my older sister, took work in Saint Louis as a servant girl. Papa and I took her there on the train. That was where Papa took me to see Terence Powderly

It was inside Soulard Hall, a smoke filled place with a long wooden stage with a patched, rust colored curtain hanging down from the rafters. There must have been over three hundred in the crowd of mostly railroaders, seated on long pine benches, some carrying signs attached to wooden sticks with handwriting on them. I tried to read what they said but I was too young and too small to see them clearly.

Then a group of men came in and marched down the center aisle to the applause and shouts of the crowd. Then I saw him, standing with his hands behind his back. He was a small muscular man in a grey suit and green tie with a great big, brown mustache that curled up at the ends. His brown hair was coarse and barely covered his large head and curled around his large ears. The crowd grew quiet when he started his speech. His voice seemed to quake at first but then grew strong.

"My fellow workers, the time has come for us to join together and demand a living wage. The time has come for us to join together and demand an eight hour day. I say the railroad owners have been getting rich from your sweat and blood. Now they say that they can't afford to pay you what they did before. That they must reduce your wages and hours so that they can stay in business. I say that is robbery and not the way things should be in America."

The crowd stood up all at once and seemed to go wild. I never saw a crowd behave in such a way before that night. I tell you it made me believe that by joining together like that, we could make things better. We could change the minds of the men who ran the railroads. We could make them see that workers mattered and that if they just weren't so all fired greedy, we could work together with them to make things alright. I suppose that was the night when I came to believe that unity among workers was our only strength, our only hope for a fair shake from the owners.

CHAPTER 4

My mother, Mary, was a kind woman who didn't like to draw attention to herself or make waves. Although she never said it in so many words, she believed that women, like children, should be seen and not heard; that men should make the living and women should make the home, by cooking, cleaning and raising the children. That was the way it was in Ireland, before her family left there for America.

She was a real beauty, with reddish blonde hair, bright blue eyes and a fine womanly frame, before the rheumatism would take its toll from her. Like most attractive women, who see the desire in men's eyes while young, she was wary of men. She would warn me to turn my eyes away from a man who stares and to steer clear of a man who draws too close without a proper introduction.

She left her trade as a seamstress to marry my father when she was eighteen and became a cook for the men working on the railroad, as they made their way westward. She was content to be what she was, a simple woman devoted to her husband and her children.

I remember asking her if she ever wanted to change her life and find her own way, her own sense of herself, I suppose. She would just shake her head and smile that smile that rose from her loving heart and say with that Cork City lilt in her voice,

"Mary, I just don't know where you get these notions. I don't concern myself with such things, child. I believe in who I am and what I am, nothing more. I am the wife of your father, the finest man I know, and the mother of his children. That is what the Good Lord made me and that is what I am meant to be."

You know there were times when I would wish I was more like her. Times when I would pray for the strength she possessed, when fear and worry darkened my days. To her, life was simple and when it became a vale of tears as the years passed, she would never lose her faith. I suppose that was her salvation, the faith of a child.

That faith was instilled in me by my mother. I can see her still, kneeling upon the floor of our cottage with her four young children seated around her after dinner, saying the Rosary while her husband worked in his garden or read his books. That was the way it was back then. I always felt blessed to be born into a family such as mine.

When I was a little child, the men would meet around our tiny porch to smoke their pipes, sing in harmony and tell of times and heroes past. I would sit upon the lap of my father and soak it all in. My father wanted me to. He wanted me to become accustomed to the company of men and to grow strong among them.

When I grew a little older, he would tell me that I was blessed by the good Lord with looks and brains and that I should use both to help others. Friends of my father, men like Tim Flaherty and Seamus Egan, would say that I was pretty and brightened their day and that I would grow to be a great lady someday. My father would say that real beauty was beauty of the soul, the greatest beauty one could have.

When the hard times came, the talk among the men changed. I could see that they were worried and that they were angry. Seamus Egan was the one I most remember. My father told me that he had served under General Meagher in the Irish Brigade and had been taught by the Jesuits. My father said that he had been wounded twice and had come back from the dead twice more. Seamus would joke that he was born under the Dog Star but had the lives of a cat. He had been a rebel in Ireland.

Seamus was a rail gang foreman and as such would spend much of his time out on the prairie, away from his wife Nannie and his two boys, Liam and Brendan, laying and repairing track in the Indian Territory. He was what we call Black Irish, meaning that he had thick raven hair like a

Spaniard that tumbled to his shoulders and piercing blue eyes that almost became the color of indigo at times. He wasn't as tall as my father but his body was wiry strong like a steel cord.

The manner of his speech was what I most remember. His voice had a special quality that could carry above a crowd. He was one of those men who could lead other men, without them knowing that they were being led. I suppose he became that way from leading men in battle. He would become one of the leaders of the Saint Louis Workingmen's Party during their struggle with the railroad owners. He would pay dearly for that leadership.

Whenever Seamus would come to our cottage he would bring me a gift. He would tell me that his gifts were meant to make me imagine and make me remember. He gave me a Fox Indian bracelet on my tenth birthday that he said was given to the girl children of the tribe. It fit snugly over my hand and clung gently to my wrist. On it were the colors of the four seasons. There was green for summer, orange for fall, white for winter and light blue for spring.

Seamus said it was a bracelet meant to be the circle of life. He would give me other cherished gifts as well, poems written in his own flowing hand on colored paper from the teachings of Lao Tzu or Omar Khayyam and a handmade flute that he taught me to play, saying that if I played it once a day, I would be blessed with health and wisdom.

I tell you when I think of all of the people that I have had the good fortune to have known in my life, both good and bad; some that the history books praise and some that they condemn, I think most fondly of my father, Michael Kenney, and his cherished friend, Seamus Egan. They were my light bearers when I was a young girl. They showed the way for me to travel. There would be others along that way who would support me, guide me and even inspire me. I will tell you of them all. But they were the first to do so.

They were there for me in times of joy and times of sorrow. They gave me courage and they gave me comfort when I needed both desperately. Since so many have requested that I tell about my life and times and the struggle that continues, even now during this dreadful war, I have finally taken the time to do so. I hope that it will prove to be useful to others who take up the struggle. If that happens, I will be content.

CHAPTER 5

We should probably begin this story during the spring of 1877, when I was thirteen years old. My father and the railroad men of Hannibal had been laid off and "The Panic" had set in across America. In New York, Cleveland and Pittsburgh, men like Morgan, Rockefeller and Carnegie would grow wealthy, while countless others, including my family, would grow poor.

I had been apprenticed to Mrs. Tilden, the dress maker. She was a tall, aristocratic kind of woman with a long, narrow, powdered face that never seemed to crack even the hint of a smile. I would work at her shop located along Rock Road in the southern part of Hannibal from sunrise to sunset, six days a week, making patterns, cutting fabric, weaving and sewing, along with a dozen or so other young girls, including my good friend, Susie Rafferty.

We did our work crowded into three small rooms at the end of a second floor stairway with no windows and one door. Mr. Tilden would make certain that door would be locked and bolted daily, after we were counted and took our assigned posts. We would perform our duties while standing or crouching, but never sitting. In fact, if Mrs. Tilden saw you leaning against a wall or God forbid, sitting down, she would inform her husband and he would make it a point to watch you more closely, so that you wouldn't slack again.

I never liked the way he hovered so closely behind us when his wife wasn't around, or the way he called us "girls". He was a small ferret of a man with a balding head and a leer in his eyes. On top of it all, he ate sardines almost daily. I tell you as soon as we came through the door of that dust filled sweltering place, we were overcome by their odor. I will always remember the sayings that he placed on the walls surrounding our work space. "Idle hands are the devil's workshop. And my favorite of them all, "Work will set you free. "

The way it was for us as apprentice dress makers was that we received no pay, just two square meals a day and a chance to earn wages when our apprenticeship was through. Both Susie and I would save one of those meals to bring home to our family. That meant that we were always hungry while we were working.

Susie was a head shorter than me and a little on the plump side with dark brown hair and hazel eyes, when we first began working together. It didn't take long for her to lose that weight in that sweat shop of a place.

Whenever Mr. Tilden would speak to Susie, she would stammer just awful. I remember one time when he asked her if she had finished an order that needed to be shipped that afternoon. I was standing a few girls to her left.

"I am speaking to you," he shouted, above the whir of the spinning looms.

"I'm s. sorry, sir," she replied, turning toward him, "I c.couldn't h.he. hear y.you."

"Pity sakes, what is the matter with you, girl? We don't need morons working around here" he cried, while turning his back to her and storming out the door.

What a rotten little bully! I thought, while biting my tongue to prevent a battle royal from erupting and the loss of the apprenticeship that Susie and I so needed.

I will always remember the times when we would walk home from work down Sherwood road and see women and children of the village scavenging for food in the garbage heaps north of town. That is a sight you never forget, I tell you.

When you see people that you know, people who you always thought were like you, in such a state, it makes you afraid and if you are like me, it makes you angry. The one thing that scares the daylights out of me, even to this day, is the thought of slow starvation. The history books never talk about all the people who have starved during hard times in America.

During the Panic, the men who remained with their families, like my father, would take whatever work they could find in Hannibal or out on the prairie. There they would hunt for jackrabbits or gofers, so that they could bring some meat home to their barren tables. Some of the men would fish the river late into the morning, or tend to their gardens at all hours just to keep the hunger away.

In times like that, people grow desperate. The one thing that I have learned is that desperate people will fight and even die to have things change. At that time the men grew to despise the railroads and the banks that had failed through greed and speculation.

That was when men like Jesse James and Cole Younger became heroes to the people in Missouri. That was when other men, rich men like Thomas Scott, owner of the Missouri–Pacific Railroad, would rig the election of the President and have the blood of men, women and children on his hands. That was the time of the Great Railroad Strike.

I recall sitting at our dining table with Papa. Mama had taken to her bed by that time and he and I were reading the newspaper accounts of the railroad strike that had spread like wild fire from West Virginia to Pittsburgh to Chicago and finally to Saint Louis. I never heard tell of a strike before then. It seemed that the country was coming apart at its seams. Hayes had been elected President by Congress with the aid of the railroad interests in spite of the fact that Tilden had been elected by the people.

Later we found out that President Hayes withdrew federal troops garrisoned in Missouri and throughout the South to enforce reconstruction and ordered them to be used against striking railroad workers who were receiving slaves' wages. That night we found out that Seamus Egan was on the run from the thugs that the railroads hired to round up the strikers.

He came to our cottage before dawn to say goodbye. His face was battered something awful. Papa tried as best he could to dress his wounds. It was then that he spoke of what had happened in Chicago. Papa had told me that Seamus had been a hunted rebel in Ireland and received medals for bravery during his service with the Irish Brigade in Virginia.

It seems that he had travelled to Chicago for the Workingmen's Party to support the strikers because he believed that it was the city where the union spirit was the strongest. What he saw would make his blood run cold.

Chapter 5

Papa said I should stay and write down what he told us. I grabbed my pen and a bottle of ink while seated across from him under our kerosene lamp. I can still hear his words in that Donegal brogue.

"There was a spirit to the men on that day. It reminded me of the Brigade at Malvern Hill. I never saw workers so all fired up. I had received a telegraph that the army had killed women and children over in Pittsburg. I tell you I didn't believe it was true, so I counseled calm, stopping the men from arming themselves when we saw the troops appear in formation at the end of a cobblestoned street, bordered by brown brick warehouses."

"It was a hot and sunny morning and we could see the green of the lake behind at least two regiments of them, wearing Union blue and flying the flag I grew to love and bled for in battle. I was standing to the right, in the front ranks of the workers."

"That was when I recognized that bantam rooster, Phil Sheridan, on his black charger, with his coal black hair and pointed features. He rode up to the right of his men who were armed with Springfield rifles, as they rolled a Gatling gun up toward us and into position."

"Our men were screaming that their families were starving and that Lincoln had freed the slaves. There wasn't a rock or bottle thrown. They were mostly Irish workers of the Michigan Central whose wages had been cut to a dollar a day and their work week cut to three days."

"I tell you, I never thought they would do it. Then I saw Sheridan raise his sword and slash it down, commanding them to shoot us down in cold blood. They opened fire not fifty yards from us, making that street a slaughter house of dead and wounded workers. That was when I told those who could, to run, and we ran for our lives; all the while being chased and shot at by those murderers."

I will never forget the tears of rage that I saw in their eyes. Those two men who had made their way to America to escape from all that was rotten and wrong in Ireland. Two men who had seen what they never expected to see. Two men who had nurtured me and encouraged me to be a proud child of America the free. I tell you that was when I began to see that life wasn't fair for workers in America. It was then that I resolved to fight to make America a land where workers and their families could be free.

After Seamus made his way back to Missouri from that blood bath, he would travel to Saint Louis. At that time the railroad strike had spread throughout the country and the farmers and miners had joined the cause. That was the first general strike in America.

That was the first time that workers from different crafts and trades would band together and the owners would become fearful that a revolution was about to occur and their heads would roll. That was when the Workingmen's Party would hold a march in Saint Louis with thousands of workers and their families turning out in the street.

Seamus told me that a black man who worked on the steamboats and levies, maybe one of those men that I saw loading hay bales in Hannibal, stood up and shouted, "Will you stand with us in spite of our color?" Seamus said that they all stood together shoulder to shoulder and marched down that street. He told us that he was just so proud to be a worker in America at that time. They had done it. They had stuck together and stood up to the bosses. The Great Railroad Strike would end shortly after that march.

They believed they had won. The lesson would soon be delivered in blood that they were sadly mistaken. The Great Railroad Strike was just the first battle in the war for the heart and soul of America.

After the dust of that strike would settle, the railroads and the government joined forces to round up and punish the leaders who had dared to organize the working men of America and preach that they deserved a living wage with which to raise their families. That was when the rich and the powerful in America began to call men like my father and his closest friend, conspirators and agitators. That was when they became marked man.

You see, during that time, during the "Gilded Age", as Mark Twain called it, the rich and the powerful in America believed that they were chosen by God to lead and that workers like my family and friends were a lesser form of being, kind of like the mules in Dickson's stable, fit to be ridden and used up in any way their owners chose.

During that time, America became a different sort of country from what it had been. Industry and inventions changed things. The cities grew and men, women and children left their hopeless farms to work in mines, mills and manufactories, while men like Thomas Scott and Alan Pinkerton hired convicts and thugs to spy upon and prevent workers and their families from organizing and speaking up.

Seamus Egan was one of the first on their bloody list. They caught up with him when he got off the train at the Hannibal Depot earlier on that night. There were four of them. Like jackals they attacked him, using blackjacks and brass knuckles to bash him, in an effort to kidnap him to a jail house. They didn't count on him carrying a pistol for his protection. He had been pursued for speaking up in Ireland, by peelers who did the bidding of the British Crown.

He told us that he managed to retrieve that pistol during their attack, wounding three of those cowards and causing the fourth to flee for his life. I shall never forget him leaning over and asking me if I was afraid of him with such a battered face. I wasn't afraid of him ever, but I was afraid for him and his family. I was afraid for Papa and us too, knowing that it was no secret that they were members of the Knights of Labor.

Well, he gave me a kiss on the forehead and embraced my father like there was no tomorrow. He would leave Hannibal that morning and send for his loving wife, Nannie, and his two sons later on.

The Missouri-Pacific Railroad would put a price on his head and make of him an outlaw. I would see Seamus again after I had grown up and Papa was gone. That would be after I took up the bookbinding trade and made my way to the City of Chicago.

CHAPTER 6

*A*s I mentioned, I had a love for books and reading, since I was a little girl. I still do. I love the smell of their bindings and the crispness of their pages. I used to read every chance I could, in my bed at night under the light of a candle, at the kitchen table beside our kerosene lamp and down at Riverside Park under the spruce tree, on warm days when I didn't have to work.

When my father was laid off, there was nobody else who could help him but me. Danny and Timmy were gone, ending up over in Pittsburgh working as telegraph boys, while Annie left her position as a servant girl in Saint Louis to become a servant girl in New York City for a little more money.

It was just me and Papa with Mama laid up something awful with the rheumatism. That was when I heard him softly sobbing in our pantry when he thought I was asleep, and asking Jesus to help us make it through. I decided that I could make more wages as a bookbinder than I ever could as a dressmaker during those "hard times."

The Hannibal Printing & Binding Company was a brown brick two story place with both a front and a back door made of Kentucky hickory. Both were painted Confederate grey at first and then Union blue after the "war between the states." It had three large windows that faced the Sherwood Road and a second floor balcony that nobody ever used.

It became the place where I would go to work just before my fourteenth birthday in January of 1878. I would earn one dollar a day and work there from seven in the morning to five in the evening, six days a week. The

George Family from Lexington Kentucky owned it. They had twenty six employees, all but three being women and girls.

Mister Darryl George was the man who ran its operations. He was a tall, slender sort of gentlemen in his forties who walked with a slight limp and the aid of a long silver colored cane. He had salt and pepper hair with a broad grey mustache. He wore silver spectacles to assist his dark blue eyes when reading fine print. I never saw him dressed in other than a white denim suit, a white shirt with a grey frontier tie, and smartly polished brown boots. He had the bearing of an educated man, with a soft, syrupy southern drawl and a proper appreciation for both the written and spoken word. It was said that he despised slavery yet served as a Confederate officer. He was wounded in the Battle of the Wilderness and lost his wife and child to Yellow Fever.

He had great difficulty remembering our names but would greet each one of his female workers with a "good morning" when we arrived at work and a "good evening" when our work day was through. Truth be told, my heart used to flutter a bit when he walked by me, like most of the other women and girls who worked for him.

He did his best to run his business in an honorable sort of way. I suppose that was why we worked so hard for him and took pride in the work that we did. Working for wages paid by men such as him made me proud and helped me to help my father make ends meet.

After the "Railroad Strike" and the crack down on union men by the bosses that followed, my father wasn't able to work for the railroads anymore. He told me he had been "blacklisted" for his membership in the Knights of Labor and for being a close friend of Seamus Egan.

Instead, he took up working at Dickson's Livery as a blacksmith and down on the docks, if he could find work there. If he had to work late into the night or all night, he would do it. I used to see him dragging himself home at sunrise, so worn down from worrying and working all hours without much to eat, while I was headed off to the bindery. I tell you, it made my heart ache to see him in such a sorry state.

On the docks my father worked with a freedman by the name of Cyrus Washington. He was the loading foreman and he helped my father out after he learned what the bosses had done to him. Nearly everybody knew and respected Papa in Hannibal before those hard times came.

Cyrus was a giant, standing well over six feet tall. He had coffee colored skin and the largest hands and head I have ever seen on a man. He had bushy white hair and eyebrows that nearly knit together. I don't ever recollect seeing him without a smile, except once.

Cyrus told Papa that he bought his freedom in Delaware before the war, and that he used to live in Washington and make his living as a baggage man at the Willard Hotel. He said he was working there when Mr. Lincoln was shot by Booth across town at Ford's Theater. He told Papa that he preferred working outdoors and in open spaces and always wanted to ride on a riverboat on the Mississippi and finally did, after the war ended. He said he took a liking to Hannibal and its people, so he decided to stay.

I suppose I should tell you of that dark rainy night when my Papa left us. I came home from the bindery and I was fixing Mama some supper from the vegetables in Papa's garden when I heard a commotion outside our front door. I will never forget opening our door and seeing Cyrus standing with his hat in his hand and a sorrowful look on his giant face. I had spoken to him only once, but he remembered my name.

"Miss Mary, your father has been hurt real bad," he advised. "I and the boys wanted to take him to Doc Summers but he wanted us to take him home instead. I sent for the Doc and he should be here right quick. He been asking for you and your mama. Oh Miss Mary, I am so sorry."

I know that Mama was standing right behind me when we saw Papa lying in the back of the wagon that brought him to our door. His head was all broken and bloody and he was covered with a piece of tarp because of the rain. I ran to him and he reached for me with a shaking hand. I just remember climbing up into that wagon and burying my face against his heaving chest. I saw Cyrus tending to Mama who had collapsed on our porch crying and sobbing,

"Michael, oh Michael, please Mary, Mother of God, Michael!"

They took him from the wagon and carried him into our cottage. They placed him on the dining table. By then I don't really recall where mama was. I just know that I was standing right next to Papa, holding his bloody hand in mine and praying that he wouldn't die and leave us. All that I remember him saying, before Doc Summers arrived, was that he was so sorry. I kept saying that there was nothing to be sorry for and that he should rest. He fought to stay conscious but he had lost too much blood.

I remember old Doc Summers with his bowler hat and white beard coming to our cottage with Father Murray. I knew then that it wasn't good. He told the others who had gathered at our cottage to take mama and me into the next room, while he worked to keep Papa with us, all through the night and into the next day.

Father Murray prayed with us and told us that we must have faith. Then the doctor called for him, so that he could give Papa the last blessing. I remember Father Murray coming to Mama and me and saying that we should come and say goodbye. Papa was still lying on our dining table and seemed to be at peace. He knew his time was at hand.

I just couldn't believe that he was dying and I would never see him alive ever again; never hear his voice or have him walk with me, holding my hand. My mind was a jumble of thoughts as Mama went to him in tears and kissed his lips.

He then looked at me and I drew close. I just remember telling him how much I loved him and that he couldn't die and leave us. That I couldn't live without him. I buried my face in his chest for the last time and wept. He touched my head and whispered in my ear.

"Mary, darling', be strong. Be good, and take care of your mother. Please, give the others my love." Then he was gone. They took him from us that afternoon.

All of Hannibal would turn out for Papa's wake and funeral. Nobody from the railroad sent condolences. I recall sitting near the front of the Holy Family Church with Mama and the rest of our family, as Father Murray spoke of Papa in his sermon. I can't seem to recall what he said, I just sat there fighting back my tears and thought of him. Oh how I loved him and cherished the memory of him. I wanted to be strong like he asked, but I really didn't know how I could be strong, without him around.

What I remember most was that Tim Flaherty, my father's good friend, asked if he could have a word with me in private, after Papa was laid to rest in the Hannibal Cemetery. I always enjoyed hearing Tim tell stories of Ireland and its heroes and the way in which he and Papa would harmonize and laugh together on our front porch before the hard times.

"Mary Elizabeth," he said, "you know how much your father loved you and how much I loved him."

"I do."

"Your father always said you were the most like him. He was a great man, Mary Elizabeth. You go and be a great woman and make us all proud. "

CHAPTER 7

fter Papa died, certain people in Hannibal came to our aid in spite of the fact that the Panic was still raging. I suppose there are always those who have the milk of human kindness, no matter what may be going on all around them. Mr. Darryl George, my boss at the Hannibal Printing & Binding Company, was one of the first to lend Mama and me a helping hand.

You see, we never wanted any part of charity or a hand out. I suppose most people are proud that way, when times are harder than they can handle. We just needed a little assistance here and there to make our own way; that was all. That was the way Mr. George arranged it.

I remember that time he called me to his office, like it was yesterday. It was on a Saturday afternoon, just an hour or so before closing. He came to my work bench and asked if he could please have a word with me. I had never been to his office before that time and felt anxious as I followed him there. I remember I was still feeling so very sad and so very lonely without Papa.

His office was on the second floor up a winding staircase. It overlooked the Sherwood Road through two spacious windows with shades that could filter out the sun on hot summer days. It had a large white oak rocking chair, with a matching desk, two filing cabinets, and two cane back chairs for furniture. From its windows you could see across the road to where the riverboats and barges travelled up and down the Mississippi.

You could also see the green of the trees, fields and hills of Riverside Park over to your right. It was a smart and proper place for a gentleman like Mr. George to run his book binding business. He gestured for me to have a seat in one of his office chairs, before taking a seat in his rocking chair. My heart was beating like a drum.

"Miss Kenney, you have been with us for almost three years now, am I correct?"

"Yes sir, it will be three years this June."

"You are a fine worker, Miss Kenney, bright, cheerful and pleasant to all."

"Thank you, Mr. George."

"Now my records show you that you will turn fifteen this coming January, is that correct?"

"Yes sir."

"Therefore, in light of your good work and value to our firm, I intend to make you a supervisor with a raise in pay. How does that sound young lady?"

"Oh, Mr. George," I said, fighting back the tears that tightened my throat."

"I have decided that your wages should be raised to eight dollars and a quarter and that you will be allowed three days a year with pay to spend with your family."

"Oh, Mr. George," was all I could say, before breaking down.

It was like a break in a dam that held back my grief. When you are feeling lowly because life seems to be against you, little gestures or kindnesses can take hold and simply sweep you away. I just sat there sobbing, overcome by his gentle ways and his concern.

I tell you I had all I could do to stop myself from embracing him, like I did with Papa, and burying my face in his chest, just weeping away. I remember him approaching me and tendering his silk handkerchief. I remembered it had his initials, DKG, embroidered on it. He gently touched my shoulder and said,

"There, there, young lady, it will be alright. Now dry your eyes and take the rest of the day. You go home and tell your mother how much you mean to us here. We will see you bright and early Monday morning."

When I arrived home Mama was at the dining table sewing, hunched over like she was by then. She was wearing her little glasses and biting off a last piece of thread. She must have noticed right away that I had a spring in my step and stopped what she was doing.

I told her about my raise in wages and she began to cry. There we were the two of us, balling away with tears of gratitude. She then took me into the pantry and showed me another kindness visited upon us. There on the counter of our pantry were two plucked game hens, ready for the cooking pot, four ripened apples, one bottle of black molasses and one loaf of freshly baked bread.

Mama told me that Tim Flaherty and Cyrus Washington had stopped by in a buckboard wagon and in spite of Mama's proud attempts to decline their kindness, delivered this bounty to us. She touched my hand and said that we should give thanks to the Blessed Mother. Right there and then, we joined together saying three Hail Mary's and Three Hail Holy Queens.

I believe that was the very first time after Papa's passing that she and I shared a happy moment. I remember thinking that we might just make it through those trying times with the support of our faith and the friendship of others. There would be many times ahead when I would take comfort and strength from that memory.

After Mama and I had eaten the finest meal we could recall in the longest time, Mama surprised me with a request.

"Mary, why don't you play "Shenandoah" on the flute that Seamus made for you?"

I had almost forgotten that gift from what seemed so long ago. Then I remembered how Seamus taught me how to arrange my fingers to play Mama's favorite tune, while sitting together on our porch under the stars.

Papa believed that music brought you closer to God. Seamus said that if I played that flute once every day it would bring me health and wisdom. I knew what health meant, but wisdom was a word that I heard but never understood. I recall searching for that leather case that Seamus gave me three years before. I found it at the very bottom of our bedroom drawer.

There inside was the Fox Indian bracelet that I had stopped wearing after Papa's passing, the poems written on colored paper and the flute that Seamus had made. It took me a little while to do so, but I soon began to play it like I used to. I tell you that was a night I will never forget, Mama sitting there beside me, as I played a melody that she loved to chase our cares away.

The following week I would receive my first instruction on my new position as a supervisor for the company. I was assigned to proofread and check every McGuffey Reader that was printed and bound before sending them down to the first floor for shipping.

At first I was concerned that I might not be able to manage my new duties or that the other girls who had worked there longer would resent me somehow. I remember confiding these misgivings to Mr. George and he simply smiled and said,

"Miss Kenney, you are a very beautiful young lady. Please remember that beauty is as beauty does. I feel very certain that the others will follow your lead without concern or complaint. Simply stay true to who you are and that will be sufficient."

I would work for Mr. George and the Hannibal Printing & Binding Company for the next nine years. Their business and my duties would grow and lead Mama and me to move out of Hannibal sixty or so miles up the Mississippi to Keokuk Iowa.

During that time the Panic that plagued America ended and prosperity once again returned. Men like Morgan, Rockefeller and Carnegie would use their wits and their power to amass fortunes never dreamed of in America. Railroads consolidated and led the way westward, bringing the break neck growth of nearly all of the cities and towns along its web like course. They would change the land and the lives of the native people standing in its way, forever.

In the Old South reconstruction became a distant memory and a new brand of race hatred would spread its poison northward. While in the mills, the mines and the manufactories, men, women and children would toil for slaves' wages until they began to organize and fight for their fair share of America the free.

CHAPTER 8

*I*t was while I was working in Keokuk Iowa that I had my first romance. Like my mother, I had strawberry blonde hair and light blue eyes, along with a slender womanly figure that seemed to attract the attention of the boys, after I turned sixteen.

As I told you, my father wanted me to feel confident in the company of men and taught me to hold my own among them. I suppose having two older brothers as protectors and playmates was as good a way as any to learn about boys and to believe that I was every bit their equal. That set me apart from so many of the other girls. Truth be told, when boys began to notice me and to cater to me, I enjoyed it and used it to make my way, within the proper boundaries of my Catholic upbringing.

Keokuk was a hustle, bustle kind of town compared to Hannibal. It is at the junction of the Mississippi and Des Moines rivers and had its own hospital, medical college, a Civil War cemetery and a former professional baseball team. It had hotels galore on Main Street, a hydroelectric power station, a beautiful park for Sunday strolling and a great big statue of an Indian Chief, right in the center of town.

I would move there with Mama to work for Mr. George and his growing company. I would spend some of my happiest years there, before we made our way over to the City of Chicago.

The game of baseball would play an important part in my life from the time my father taught me how to throw a ball when I was no more than three, using my arm and shoulder, instead of my elbow, like most girls would do. I would play it with my brothers and the other railroader kids at Riverside Park and grew to love each and every part of its pace and play.

Most of all, I loved the fact that time didn't really matter in baseball. It was America's game. It was baseball that brought Seth Rogers to me. He would become my first beau.

I was seventeen and it was a sunny, summer Sunday, down at Rand Park in Keokuk when we met each other. I was, reading *Whittier's Evangeline,* seated upon a bench in my store bought blue and white cotton dress and my matching blue and white bonnet. I had placed my white parasol to the side. The shade of a wondrous elm tree was more than ample to keep me cool in the heat. That was when a baseball landed not ten feet away and rolled toward me. Seth Rogers came running after it and found me.

When I looked up, there he was, tall and handsome with golden hair, hazel eyes and a smile upon his dimpled face. His manner was shy but pleasant. I would find out later that it was more than happenstance that occasioned our meeting. He had seen me in the park on two previous Sundays and used the excuse of an errant baseball to make my acquaintance.

"What a beautiful day to spend in the park, wouldn't you say so, Miss?"

"It is indeed," was my reply.

"Do you come here often, Miss _?"

"Kenney, my name is Mary Kenney and no, I do not come to the park often. I work at the printing company down town and live nearby. What's your name?"

"My name is Seth... Seth Rogers, Miss Kenney. I'm a medical student. My family hails from Peoria, over in Illinois."

"How interesting, I recently moved here from down in Hannibal and just love everything about Keokuk. I understand they have a wonderful ball team. I would so like to see them play someday."

"Oh yes, the Keokuk Westerns are the best of the best. Maybe you would do me the honor of going to a game with me one Sunday afternoon, if that would be alright with your Father?"

I really didn't know what to say when he mentioned Papa. I suppose he took my hesitance as a rebuff. I liked the way he carried himself and showed an interest in me. He pressed on in a polite but persistent sort of way.

"I hope you don't think me too forward, Miss Kenney. My intentions are honorable. Do I have your permission to call upon you at your home and meet your parents?"

Suddenly my thoughts turned to his religion. You see, the way we were taught was that only Catholics could enter heaven. I remember feeling sorry for girls and boys in Hannibal, who weren't of our faith. I thought it was unfair that through no fault of their own, they would be denied salvation. Then I thought about how Jesus was a Jew and he was crucified for preaching that all men were his neighbors and should be loved. I decided that I would allow this nice young man to get to know me.

"You do, Mr. Rogers."

He would call upon me at my home the very next Sunday and meet Mama. He was so polite and caring, especially when he learned that Papa had passed. Mama and I talked afterwards about his religion. Mama cautioned me that getting serious about a Protestant boy would not be condoned by the Church.

I recall telling her that going to a baseball game wasn't exactly exchanging wedding vows. She just shook her head and told me to remember what she said. I loved Mama dearly but I saw no harm in going my own way on the matter of Seth Rogers.

Seth's father, Samuel Rogers, was a surgeon who served with the Illinois Infantry and spent some time convalescing in the Keokuk Hospital after the war. His uncertain state of health would continue to plague him and occasion Seth's devoted care. Seth's ambition was to follow in the footsteps of his father.

We would see the Keokuk Westerns play on a wondrous Sunday afternoon. The crowd was overflowing and the excitement was electric. They congregated on all sides of that emerald playing field while the teams in their different uniforms were warming up. It was like a picture post card that had come to life and would last for nine full innings. It was my first organized baseball game and I loved every minute of it.

Paddy Quinn was the Westerns' best player and a favorite of the crowd, with his dark hair, muscular frame and handlebar mustache. He was a pitcher and a center fielder who could throw with great speed, run like the wind and hit a ball clear out of sight. I watched him doff his cap from time to time and sign his name to the offerings of a handful of children and swooning ladies.

I was wearing my favorite green and grey dress without the bustle and a matching bonnet. Seth wore a striped grey suit with a white shirt, starched collar and grey cap.

Admission for two was fifty cents. The ticket taker wore a red, white and blue skimmer. Our seats were located in the middle of the center field stands. The aroma of roasted chestnuts caused Seth to purchase a ten cent bag of those delights. One bag lasted nearly the entire game.

The Podunk Robins were the opposing team. Their best player was Tommy Joyce, who would pitch a shutout until the sixth inning. That was when Paddy Quinn got a hold of one and sent it soaring in our direction.

The ball landed behind us and to our left, causing a near fist fight to erupt over its retrieval. That was the first home run I would witness, until I saw Babe Ruth play in Boston. What a wonderful day we had at that ball game.

After the game, Seth advised that his father had come for a visit and was staying over at the Medical College. He asked if I would like to meet him before making our way back to my home. I was uncertain that I would make a proper impression, after spending all day at a ball game.

He assured me that I looked simply stunning and that his father would be disappointed if he missed the chance at making my acquaintance. I remember thinking about Papa and somehow hearing him telling me to go ahead and make that day one that I would not forget. The nod of my head caused Seth to kiss my cheek. I blushed and so did he.

CHAPTER 9

*D*octor Rogers was a country gentleman who offered the warmest greeting when we met in a guest room at the Medical College. He resembled his son both in stature and appearance, except that his shoulder length hair and broad mustache were the color of sterling silver.

"So this is the girl that has captured my son's fancy," was his introduction in a deep, sonorous, voice.

I liked him right off and it was apparent that the feeling was mutual. His dignified manner reminded me of Mr. George. Perhaps their shared experience as officers in command was the reason. He had been told that I was a lover of books and a bookbinder by trade. He asked if I was fond of Dickens and I told him that *A Christmas Carol* was read by my father at our Christmas table.

"He must have been a wonderful man to have raised such a lovely daughter," he said, while gently touching my hand.

"He was indeed," was my reply.

"Well then, I must not keep the two of you from enjoying the rest of this day," he said. There was a sadness in his eyes that told me that his mind was troubled.

"I love September and its crisp night air. Please give my regards to your mother, Miss Kenney. It has been a pleasure making your acquaintance."

"Likewise, Doctor Rogers."

That evening I told Mama of my day at the ball game and my meeting with Seth's father. She soaked it in like a sponge, asking me to recite the day's events in detail. I suppose she could see that I was overjoyed and did not wish to dampen my mood by pestering me about getting serious with a Protestant boy.

I loved my Mama dearly and wanted to always be a credit to her and to Papa's memory. I do believe that she just wanted me to be young and care free when the occasion presented itself. She knew that my day with Seth was just such an occasion. That was my Mama.

When I returned to work on Monday morning, Mr. George looked troubled as he greeted me in an absent minded sort of way. As I said, he would always make it a point to say good morning and mean it, to each and every one of his employees, even after expanding his business to Keokuk.

It turned out that Mr. George had just received word that two of his company's most important customers had taken their business to a large Chicago printing house. J.M.W. Jones Company had promised to fill their orders in less time and for less money.

That was what large companies were doing all over the country at that time, from railroads to coal, to oil, to printing and binding. Like beasts in the wild, they roamed, scaring or devouring smaller companies.

At that time Charles Darwin and his text book, *On the Origin of Species* became accepted in certain scientific circles. An Englishman by the name of Herbert Spencer would use Darwin's teachings and seek to apply them to human beings. This came to be called *survival of the fittest.*

This teaching, along with John Calvin's dogma that man was predestined by God to be saved or damned, made it a virtue among certain of the rich and powerful to take advantage of the powerless in our society. This was the heartless way they would look at the world. This would be their justification, their excuse for the mistreatment of working people in America.

Besides large companies, there were other dangerous beasts that roamed throughout our country during the years following the Civil War. They were the beasts of race hatred and bigotry and they would threaten to destroy the freedom and liberty that so many had fought and died for in battles most bloody.

I had the privilege of knowing and assisting many courageous souls who devoted their lives to fighting these beasts in an attempt to make America a land where all men and women were equal.

For the next three years I remained in Keokuk working as a supervisor for a printing and binding company that was struggling to stay in business. Like those sad times when I watched Papa counting his pennies and nickels at the table worrying what tomorrow would bring, so too did I watch Mr. George, doing everything he could to care for the people who worked for him.

I recall many an evening when I would leave work and see the light in his office still burning, knowing that he would be working into the wee hours in an effort to help save the day. During that time he would confide in me and trust me to keep the books and ledgers necessary for our company to survive.

Slowly the uncertainty of it all began to wear upon him. As I told you, he had been wounded in the war and required a cane for walking. I would come to find out that there were more serious wounds that the war had visited upon him. Unseen wounds that slowly began to take possession of his spirit. Sadly, there are many whose wounds from warfare are unseen yet serious.

Because of his medical studies, I would not hear from Seth Rogers for weeks on end. When the weeks turned into months without a word, I grew concerned for his wellbeing. I took it upon myself to visit the medical college in search of him.

I remember walking among the chestnut tables and bookcases of its library, containing hundreds upon hundreds of medical texts. There beneath a table lamp I came upon him, fast asleep.

I thought it would be improper for me to awaken him with the touch of my gloved hand, so I simply sat across from him and coughed gently. When he awoke, there was a look of anguish upon his dimpled face.

"Oh, Mary, you are a sight I have longed to see," he whispered.

"I feared something had happened to you, Seth."

"Something has happened, Mary. It has made my days a misery and unfit to be in your company. Come let's go elsewhere to talk."

We walked from the library out to a rolling field. There we would take our seat upon a nearby bench and Seth would tell me of the ordeal that had caused him to separate from me. I could tell from the dark circles that appeared beneath his eyes in the sunlight that he was terribly troubled and had not been sleeping.

"Mary, my father has taken ill and it does not appear that he will recover. I did not want to burden you with it, in light of your own dear father's untimely passing."

"Friends should share both the good and the bad with those close to them," I offered.

"My father has gone mad, Mary. The war and the fate of my oldest brother, Edmund, has taken its toll upon him. He is confined to an asylum."

"Oh Seth, I am so sorry."

"My mother and sister are looking to me for guidance and my studies overwhelm me. I am in darkness Mary, and I too fear for my sanity."

I took his hand in mine, attempting to provide some solace for his suffering. Words were useless. His hazel eyes soon became filled with tears as he wept. I reached for him and he laid his head upon my shoulder. He would speak to me of his older brother's failed aspiration to follow his father into the field of medicine. A failed aspiration that would drive him into the life of a hopeless drunkard.

I could tell that Dr. Rogers' second son was fearful of a similar fate and that fear and his father's insanity had driven him to desperation. At that point I remember asking him whether he knew the Lord's Prayer.

"I do, Mary ", was his sorrowful reply.

"Then let's say it together."

There we were praying like children caught in a storm. I suppose we are all children from time to time, even as we grow old and infirm, caught in the storm of life. Faith is often our only way to weather the storm. It is faith that allows us to be as the little child of scripture.

I would never see Seth Rogers after that day. Years later I would learn that he was killed while storming Kettle Hill with Teddy Roosevelt and his Rough Riders. War is such a terrible waste of thorns.

CHAPTER 10

here are momentous days during the course of all of our lives. Days that stand out above them all. Days when you can remember just where you were and what you were doing when you received the news. Days that you knew would bring about dramatic change. The day following the Haymarket Massacre was such a day for me.

It was a cloud filled May morning in Keokuk with traces of dawn just beginning to break upon us. I had just finished making breakfast for myself and Mama and after a cup of tea was headed off to work. At that time we were living in a three story brick apartment building on Argyle Road, just down the road from the Lee County District Police station.

As I made my way along Main Street, I noticed three horse drawn police wagons outside the station house. As I drew closer, I saw a crowd of policemen in their blue uniforms and steel grey helmets standing out in front.

I recall suspecting that something was amiss and taking myself to the opposite side of the street. There I spied a newsboy selling the Keokuk Dispatch and asked him what the commotion was all about.

"A bunch of policemen was killed in Chicago, Miss, read all about it."

I bought a paper and remember reading the headline under a nearby street lamp. "Anarchist bomb kills police." I would learn later that martial law had just been declared and police stations across the country went on alert fearing that a revolution was about to break out.

That would be the beginning of a hysteria that would grip America and cause the rounding up and imprisonment of many innocent people with ties to the labor movement. After moving to Chicago, I would become a friend to one of these people, Lucy Parsons. She and her late husband would suffer terribly after Haymarket for organizing a peaceful protest. My father's devoted friend, Seamus Egan, would tell me the story behind those headlines.

At the time, Seamus was living in Chicago under the alias of Michael Duffy and serving as an organizer for the Federation of Organized Trades and Labor Unions, which would become the American Federation of Labor under Sam Gompers' leadership.

I would reunite with Seamus after I moved there. That would be two years after Haymarket had occurred. He was an eyewitness to both the massacre and the forgotten events leading up to it.

Twain has said that, "history is written with the ink of lies." After all that I have seen in my life, I believe that is the case. Freedom of the press is necessary for the protection of our liberty. It is one of the cornerstones of our democracy, set forth in the First Amendment to our Bill of Rights. Those of us who fought for workers' rights in America would learn that money and power often made the newspapers and news services far from truthful.

They would be bought and sold, like so many that held public office. They would portray our fight for workers' rights in false lights and as threats to America. Such was the case with the Haymarket Massacre.

Of course there were firebrands and anarchists who preached violence and revolution, given the ruthless nature of the forces marshalled against our cause, but most of us wanted to change the hearts and minds of the people through peaceful means with truth as our ally.

Seamus had made his escape from Missouri with a price placed on his head by the Missouri-Pacific Railroad. In Ireland he had been on the run and learned well the ways of those who were outlawed. Through old friends from his service in the Irish Brigade he was able to secure employment in the carpentry trade and make his way in Chicago under an assumed name.

To be safe he had changed his appearance with the trimming of his hair and the growth of both a manly mustache and beard. As an added precaution, he lost his distinctive Donegal brogue and developed the diction of a native born laboring man.

Although he would change his appearance and his identity, he would never change his heart. After sufficient time had passed, he would serve as a labor organizer and seek to bring betterment to workers through the union. Later he would become a trusted ally of Sam Gompers and an inspiring presence in the American Federation of Labor.

I would transcribe all that Seamus told me of those bloody events known to history as The Haymarket Massacre. I would also speak with my good friend and fellow organizer, Lucy Parsons, concerning the events that altered the course of her life and that of her beloved husband, Albert.

I have done this so that others who come after and take up the workers' cause can do so knowing of our ordeal. Scripture says that the truth will set us free. I say that the truth and the necessity of organization will make working men and women free.

As I sit here, an old woman, in my home in Medford, Massachusetts, re-viewing all of the notes and letters saved during those years of struggle and once again reliving the episodes that time and circumstance have caused me to forget, I know that there will be those who will doubt what I have to say. They will refuse to believe that the events and episodes that I describe oc-curred. I simply ask that those who read this story keep an open mind and ask themselves whether what I write has the ring of the truth.

CHAPTER 11

HAYMARKET I
(As told to me by Seamus Egan on October 4th 1888)

"May 1, 1886 was a Saturday without clouds in Chicago. Since sunrise, wage workers and their families by the thousands began to congregate for a peaceful gathering organized to support an eight hour work day. As few know, the federal government made the eight hour workday the law of the land way back in 1867. A law that business owners in America violated from the beginning."

"A law that the Mayor of Chicago, Carter Harrison, recognized and supported by the granting of a parade permit to the Knights of Labor and other unions, many months before. It was a wondrous day to behold, as we marched up Michigan Avenue arm in arm with bands playing and our banners flapping in the warmth of the breeze that made its way from the lake front."

"It was a day when both the promise and the power of organized labor flowered, sending the message that workers and their families mattered. A message that bestowed hope upon the powerless and fear upon the powerful. I remember thinking, as I had years before in Saint Louis, that this would finally be the day of our liberation as workers. Two days later the owners and their hirelings would deliver their message. It would be a most deadly response."

"Lucy and Albert Parsons were trusted friends of mine, as well as friends to all working men and women in America. I had met them at a Knights of Labor gathering, after they and I began living in the City of Chicago in 1880, three years after the Railroad Strike."

"Lucy was a beautiful young woman who was born a slave down in Texas, with raven hair, caramel colored skin and fiery green eyes. When Albert, set eyes upon her at a Freedman's Bureau dinner in Nashville, Tennessee, they fell in love and were married in a secret ceremony, forbidden by law and by most of society. They would bring three children into the world and devote their lives to making America free."

"In Chicago, Lucy would take up the cause of women sewing workers, forced to work for meager wages in sweatshops throughout Illinois and Iowa, while Albert would display his intellect and his passion for the cause of worker equality as the editor of *"The Alarm"*. Together, they would help to organize two peaceful marches by workers throughout Chicago in support of an eight hour day."

"I remember seeing them both parading with their young children up Michigan Avenue along with eighty thousand others on Saturday, May 1st. The following day, Albert traveled by rail to Ohio to rally workers there, while Lucy organized a second march which drew another thirty five thousand workers. Those were two unforgettable afternoons dedicated to the cause. As Dickens has written in his *Tale of Two Cities*," it was the best of times; it was the worst of times", during that first week of May in Chicago."

"The McCormick Reaper manufactory located at the junction of Western and Blue Island Avenues employed thousands of workers, both native and foreign born. All of them had been forced to sign a compact in violation of federal law that required them to work twelve hour days, six days a week. Those present will always remember that fateful Monday morning, May 3rd, 1886."

"From first light we stood in a picket line outside that factory's enormous iron gates, petitioning the men and boys employed there, to refuse to work under those conditions, and join our ranks instead. We were there to form a united front against a company that cared but little for their lives and the welfare of their families."

"We had strength in numbers and the union spirit was in the air. We cheered as the men and boys working for McCormick began to follow our lead and join us across Western Avenue in a more dramatic sort of peaceful protest."

I can still hear the organizers praising the workers in English, Polish and German, as they walked away from a gang of unbelieving and angry overseers who were crowded behind those gates, taking a tally of those who defied their authority."

"We were chanting and marching for an eight hour day, when six or so horse drawn wagons arrived on the scene, across from us on Blue Line Avenue, bringing at least two hundred cops in blue tunics, with gold buttons and grey helmets. I noticed that most were armed with nightsticks, while a handful were being armed with Winchester repeaters."

"When those with rifles began to assemble in the forefront of their formation, I remembered the bloodbath caused by Sheridan and his troops nine years before. I attempted to get the men to fall back, down Western Avenue and away from those armed cops."

"The English speaking workers heeded my warnings and started to fall back but the Polish and German lads did not. In defiance they peacefully locked arms and held their ground against those cops in the belief that they would not be shot down."

"Once again the streets of Chicago would run red with the blood of murdered and wounded workers when a trigger happy cop opened fire. This was followed in short order by a deafening volley from the others with rifles."

"Then the order was given and those with nightsticks attacked us, beating defenseless men and boys bloody. That was when we began to fight back, pelting them with rocks, bottles and paving stones. A peaceful protest was turned into a murderous riot by trigger happy cops."

CHAPTER 12

HAYMARKET II
(As told to me by Seamus Egan on October 9, 1888)

"On Tuesday evening, May 4th 1886, a protest of the massacre of the day before was scheduled in Haymarket Square. A pouring rain and the fear that another bloodletting would occur caused that protest to be delayed and the refusal of the scheduled speakers to attend. "

"Instead of a crowd of twenty thousand, there were less than three thousand that gathered in the rain amid that poorly lit section of the City. Less than a mile away, Lucy Parsons was at a meeting of her sewing workers when she received word that the crowd was growing angry and restless. "

"Her husband, Albert, had just returned from Ohio, bringing with him a Methodist preacher from Britain by the name of Samuel Fielden. They had come to meet Lucy for dinner, but were instead unexpectedly enlisted by her to speak to the crowd at Haymarket Square."

"I was standing in the crowd when they arrived. I remember Albert with his dark hair and mustache in a yellow duster. He was standing upon a wagon, trying to assure the angry crowd that the killings of the day before would be brought before a grand jury and justice would be meted out to those responsible."

"After he and Lucy left to attend to their children, Fielden climbed upon the wagon and began to preach to the crowd with a thick British accent. He was holding a bible in one hand as he screamed of the bloody injustice of the day before. He was crying that workers worldwide were being beaten and murdered."

"There were only a couple of hundred that remained to listen to him. That was when the police wagons came again, tearing down the cobblestone streets leading to the square with their alarm bells clanging. "

"I listened as he preached defiantly with his silver hair and flowing beard, that the workers of the world outnumbered the owners and their hired killers, and would one day, with God's might, vanquish them. I could tell that those rifle toting cops were out for blood, so I moved steadily beyond that speaker's wagon, bringing a handful of workers with me. I then watched as those cops fell in and moved what appeared to be one regiment each to either side of the crowd that stood listening to him."

"There were almost as many cops as there were workers in the rainy haze of Haymarket Square's gaslights when I noticed this burly Polish worker, wearing a grey woolen coat and hat, with flowing golden hair, throw a wrapped package into the regiment of cops gathered in front of him."

"The deafening explosion that followed shattered all the glass windows around and covered the square in smoke. It was a dynamite bomb that had been thrown in revenge for the murders committed the day before. It wounded and killed a handful of cops. The other cops soon opened fire in a panic, catching both workers and their own men in a deadly crossfire."

HAYMARKET III
(As told to me by Lucy Parsons on December 4, 1888)

"My husband Albert, a kind and generous soul, is dead. He was hanged on November 11, 1887 after a rigged trial, along with Adolph Fisher, George Engel and August Spies. I am utterly lost without him. My two sons and daughter are in shock still. They have lost their guiding light and guardian, a loving and devoted father. Why must the world be so cruel? Why must it be so unjust? Why should it require such sacrifice, in order to speak up for workers in America? "

"We fought a civil war so that men could be free, but sadly, we are not free. We are slaves to those who control production, in this, the land that Lincoln and so many others gave their last full measure of devotion in uniting. We are indentured to those who believe that it is their right to do so, for power and for profit. May God have mercy on them and make them see the light."

"My cherished friend Mary, a sister to all those who work for wages and yearn for equality, asked that I describe the aftermath of the Haymarket Square bombing. I have done so with a breaking heart."

"If a history is written of what we and others have endured, it shall be a bloody history indeed. America was and is a nation that has been bathed in the blood of countless martyrs. Martyrs whose hope was freedom and whose faith was equality. On May 4th, 1886 we had just arrived home to the love and affection of our children, when we heard the repeated alarms of the police wagons, followed by an explosion that shattered two of the front windows in our parlor, more than a quarter a mile from Haymarket Square. That was when we heard the sound of gun fire over and over again."

"Both Albert and I knew in our hearts that something terrible had happened and looked from our windows toward the rising smoke and the shimmer of fire coming from the Square. It seemed that alarms sounded all throughout the night with the dead and wounded being taken by ambulance to nearby hospitals."

"The next morning, while I was readying the children for school and Albert was shaving, a police wagon pulled up to the front of our building and a squad of armed policemen came running up our front and back stairs with their revolvers drawn. They then broke through our front door and seized first Albert and then me. I will always remember seeing my children screaming in terror, while we were beaten and arrested."

"They led us off in handcuffs, like common criminals, down two flights of stairs. I recall being hustled past our landlady, Mrs. Runyon, as she stood in her night clothes in the hallway among a group of other tenants. I pleaded with her to take care of the children; not knowing where we were being taken or whether we would ever see them again."

"I just remember the tears streaming down her wrinkled face, too terrified to protest the manner of our treatment. We were the object of racial oaths and murderous threats throughout that dreadful ordeal."

"They forced us into the back of a police wagon and took us to the Cook County Precinct House. Outside, the crowd jeered and spat upon us. They then locked us up in separate cells in the bowels of that damp, dark, awful place, while I just prayed and worried. "

"My beloved and courageous Albert attempted to provide some degree of comfort to me through repeated cries of love and devotion that echoed down that jailhouse corridor. These were soon silenced by the repeated blows of a police nightstick."

"Some have said that the Haymarket trial was a blood red blot on the history of justice in America. Like the Salem witch trial that came before, it was a sham with a foregone conclusion. It was a sideshow trial where the press was a conspirator in the murder of innocent men. Where the Chicago Tribune offered a reward to its jurors to return a conviction of murder in the first degree. It was a rigged trial, meant to persecute those who spoke up for workers. It was in fact premeditated murder, perpetrated by the owners of industry in America and carried out by spineless political hirelings who did their bloody bidding."

CHAPTER 14

*D*espite the very best efforts of all who were privileged to work at the Hannibal Printing & Binding Company and its sister company in Keokuk, we simply could no longer compete with the larger and more efficient J.M.W. Jones Company and were required to close our doors on December 31, 1887. It was a dark day for all concerned, but most especially for our benevolent employer, Mr. Darryl George.

The passage of time has not allowed me to forget my last conversation with Mr. George. We had both come to the pain filled conclusion that the company we loved and nurtured was to be no more. We were in Mr. George's office down in Hannibal, the site where he had made me a supervisor and saved Mama and me from the poor house, almost ten years before.

I was seated across from him and we had just reviewed the final tally for the year. I recall him standing without uttering a word, then going to the window behind his desk and gazing for a moment at the ships and barges traveling up and down the river. It was a cold winter's day.

I then watched as he dropped his head and slumped his shoulders as if in defeat. He remained there in that posture for several moments. I was at a loss for comforting words. Then he suddenly straightened up, turned to me and spoke in that cultured, southern, gentlemanly way that I had admired so much.

"We have come a long way together, my dear. I shall sorely miss the sunshine in your smile and the sweetness of your disposition. You have my undying gratitude for your service and your sacrifice over these last, difficult years. When I think of the uncertainty that lies ahead for you and the others, my heart breaks."

"You have done all that you could, Sir," I remarked. "I could not have asked for a kinder or more understanding employer, especially during the time of my father's passing."

"It will be necessary for me to bring everyone together for the announcement. I know that they have had their concerns about the future of the company."

I remember the day that he delivered the news to the others. There were seventy two employees of the company in total. Twenty six working in Hannibal and another forty six in Keokuk. We were called into the Hannibal printing room that we knew and loved as Mr. George entered and stood in the center of the printing floor.

He was wearing his customary white denim suit and white shirt with his grey frontier tie and polished brown boots. His hair and mustache were now a snowy white and his care worn face wore a pair of silver spectacles. He cleared his throat and delivered his final remarks to us all.

"My dearest friends, it is with the utmost regret that I must inform you that the operations of our companies will cease at the end of this year. The Hannibal Printing & Binding Company and The Keokuk Printing & Binding Company provided education and enlightenment through the printed word to the world outside their doors for seventeen years."

"Our companies have been run in the best interests of our customers and our employees. It is with a heartfelt appreciation that I use the term our, because those of us who managed the accounts; those of us who did the printing; those of us who did the binding and those of us who shipped our issue to our customers, have done so together, in unison, in harmony. It has been a privilege and an honor to know and work with each and every one of you. "

"Much is being said nowadays of the need for progress and change in all that we do in America. Progress and change requires a modern approach to business as the way of the future, we are told. "

"As the owner of this business over these many years, I bear full responsibility for failing to keep up with this "so called" progress; for failing to change our business practices and thus failing to keep our company's doors open. I am responsible for sending all of you out into an uncertain future. "

"I have had much time to measure my thoughts and words to you this day. Progress and change should never replace caring for one another. The truth is that we are all children of God, brothers and sisters of the same Father. As such, it does not avail any one of us to gain a fortune and lose our souls, by not caring for our brothers and sisters, by robbing our brothers and sisters, by killing our brothers and sisters."

"Our company is no more but the lessons we have learned from each other, the kindnesses we have bestowed upon each other and the love that we have for each other will remain, despite all the progress and change that swirls around us. May God bless and keep each and every one of you in the palm of His hand "

With that, Mr. George bade farewell and bestowed an envelope from the Hannibal Printing & Binding Company upon each and every one of us. Each envelope contained a personal note thanking us for our service to the company, a small golden colored pay envelope containing a month's wages, and a letter of recommendation for future employment made out" to whom it may concern."

Having an understanding of our books of account, I knew only too well that the company was without sufficient funds to meet a weekly payroll, let alone a monthly one. It was apparent that Mr. George was paying these sums from his own pocket. This realization only heightened my admiration for him.

I recall sitting with my children on a Sunday morning in Boston, many years thereafter. As was my habit, I was reading the obituary notices within the *Boston Globe*. They say that these are more popular than the sporting pages to the Irish. There before me was a notice that the right Reverend Darryl George had passed away at the age of eighty three years.

It told of his decorated service in the Army of Northern Virginia, where he attained the rank of Major. It mentioned his proprietorship of the Hannibal Printing & Binding Company and his dedication to the enlightenment of others. Lastly, it described his thirty years of devoted service as a missionary to the natives of American Samoa, teaching and showing them the blessings of God's love.

CHAPTER 15

CHICAGO

They say that necessity is the mother of invention. Necessity has certainly been a driving force in my life. After losing my employment with the Hannibal Printing & Binding Company and watching my mother's crippling rheumatism grow steadily worse, I became greatly concerned as to the course that our lives would follow.

Moving to Chicago without worsening Mama's delicate condition made it necessary to arrange her temporary lodging with my father's devoted friend, Tim Flaherty and his family, residing in Hannibal. This proved to be a Godsend that allowed me to make my way alone with a determination to succeed, despite my trepidation at being a young woman without station or protection in that overwhelming city.

It was in the dead of winter, shortly after my twenty fourth birthday, when I arrived by train at the snow covered Union Depot with the letter of recommendation of Mr. George and seventeen dollars within my purse. I had never felt the kind of cold and wind that greeted me as I made my way outside to the corner of Madison and Canal Street. Suddenly I was confronted by a scene of near pandemonium.

Despite the cold, there were scores of wagons and drivers, push carts and peddlers hawking their wares at that location. By sheer magnitude it was the most daunting spectacle that my eyes had ever beheld. Chicago, was a city fashioned by those who were seeking a new way of life. It was a raucous, rough house of a place, where work could be had for both native born and immigrant alike in its stock yards, slaughterhouses, factories, and shops.

It both terrified and thrilled me. It was where I learned to make my way as a woman of the world, while seeking a promising tomorrow. It would be where I resolved to organize other women of the workplace and demand an equal share for us all. It was where I would meet Jane Adams and partake of her caring and her wisdom.

My first lodging was at 857 LaSalle Avenue, a rooming house for single women run by Mrs. Ida Pudolski and her twin sons, Peter and Josef. They were Polish Jews who had escaped from Krakow and the oppression of the Russian and Hapsburg Empires.

They first took up residence in Cleveland, then moved to Chicago after Ida's husband was killed in an oil refinery fire. That episode made her a fiery adversary of the oil interests and John D. Rockefeller. She would be a guiding light to me and other young women.

Ida was a brawny women in her forties with the forearms of a long-shoreman. She had curled golden hair, bright blue eyes and broad Nordic features that she took pride in attributing to her Austrian blood lines. She insisted that the six young ladies who were permitted residence on the second and third floors of her three story lodging house be clean, punctual and respectable.

The rules of her house were posted on the notice board, located within the first floor hallway. The front and back entrance doors were locked at 9 P.M. and opened at 5 A.M. Lights were out by 10 P.M. Dinner was served at 6 P.M. sharp, within the first floor dining room. Room and board was two dollars a week and due on each and every Thursday.

Gentlemen callers were permitted, but their visits were restricted to Sunday afternoons between 1 and 3 P.M., within the first floor parlor. It was there that coffee, tea and Ida's apple strudel were served. I would re-ceive her strict but affectionate direction during the early months of my residence in Chicago.

Ida's twin sons worked as meatpackers for Armour & Company adja-cent to the Union Stock Yards. Although born on the same day, they were fraternal, not identical twins. Peter, like his mother, was blonde, blue eyed and brawny, while Josef was tall and slender with brown hair and blue eyes.

Both were twenty two and able guardians of their mother and all of us who resided within their lodging house.

During my first week in Chicago I remember poring over the newspaper, searching for suitable employment, when Ida politely made inquiry of me, with her Polish accent.

"How are you faring with job search?"

"I've narrowed it down to three prospects. I will visit each tomorrow, mam."

"How long have you worked in bookbinding trade?"

"Since the age of thirteen, back in Hannibal, Missouri, mam."

"Please call me Ida. I have some business in the Loop tomorrow, if you would like, I will go with you, so you don't get lost. Chicago can be confusing place. Besides, a young lady traveling alone can be target for undesirables out there. We leave by seven, yeah?"

"Yes, mam. I mean Ida. That is very kind of you."

"We women, we must look out for each other, yeah?"

"Yes, thank you very much."

CHAPTER 16

t 7 A.M. sharp, I headed off with Ida as my guide and guardian into the business district in the center of Chicago, known as the Loop. It was a bitter cold February morning. The biting wind made it difficult to walk upright. I wore my green woolen coat over a grey and black jacket and skirt. My hair was tied in a bun beneath a navy blue woolen hat and scarf.

As we walked together, Ida explained that in Krakow women would always walk arm in arm together, as protection against undesirables that might wish to follow with thoughts of theft or worse. In unity there was strength, since it required a tangle with two to take advantage. Besides, she explained, side by side walking on snow covered streets was good for safety, to prevent slips and falls on the ice beneath the surface

I was glad that she was there beside me to lean on, since the soles of my ankle high black leather boots made it seem that I was walking on ice skates. I do believe that I would have become terribly lost, had Ida not offered to accompany me on that morning. My first destination for prospective employment was the Thomason Printing and Binding Company, located on Wabash Avenue, a brown brick four story edifice with a gilded elevator located in its foyer.

A pleasant young man wearing a faded cranberry coat with gold epaulettes served as the elevator operator. When he smiled at me and asked where I was headed, Ida abruptly replied, "Thomason the Printer," causing him to attend to his duties without delay or distraction.

Once we reached the third floor and saw the Thomason name stenciled upon the front door, Ida advised that she would attend to her business and meet me back there within the hour. I thanked her for her assistance in helping me find my way and her concern for my welfare. She simply touched my cheek, smiled and left.

I gave my name to a male clerk in spectacles, then waited along with two other women who were seeking employment as bookbinders. Soon I was ushered into a small office and told that Mr. Travis would be available presently. I was asked to hang up my coat and have any references at the ready, since Mr. Travis was a very busy man. I waited for nearly an hour before he entered and sat down. He was a portly man, wearing a wrinkled white shirt and blue tie, with brown suspenders and grey striped trousers. His hair was sparse and combed over his expansive scalp, like a wave about to break upon shore. He was smoking a cigarette from a holder and appeared in desperate need of a bath. I would imagine he was close to fifty years of age.

"References", he intoned. "You have references, I assume."

"Yes, sir," I replied, tendering the letter from Mr. George.

"Ah, yes, The Hannibal Printing and Binding Company. They are defunct."

"I beg your pardon, sir."

"Defunct, out of business!"

"Yes, sir. They ceased operations after seventeen years this past December."

"I shouldn't wonder why, given their business practices."

"I beg your pardon, sir."

"Silence," he commanded, while displaying the palm of his hand.

After he perused my letter of recommendation, he looked up and soon began to stare at me like a vulture eyeing carrion. He then requested that I stand up, as he approached me, all the while puffing upon his cigarette holder.

"You're a fine figure of a young girl, aren't you?" he moaned, while drawing inexcusably close with a leering expression. "The wages are five dollars a week for sixty hours of work. Of course, for my favorites, there will be the opportunity for certain benefits. If you take my meaning."

"I'm sorry, Sir," I heard myself saying, "but I believe it's time for me to leave, my mother is waiting for me."

At that, I grabbed my coat and made a beeline for the door, leaving that portly vulture with an expression of rejection and disappointment. When I made my way toward the waiting area, I spied Ida. Suddenly, I burst into tears and she drew close.

"What has happened, child?" she demanded.

"Please let's just leave this place," was my reply.

Sensing that I had been the victim of an impropriety, she helped me on with my coat in that waiting area, which was busy with customers waiting for orders. She then turned and boisterously demanded that the clerk summon the manager of that establishment. The uproar caused a considerable stir and after a few moments the appearance of a tall, distinguished gentleman in a striped blue suit and tie.

"Yes Madame, I am Niles Thomason, the proprietor of this company."

"Well, Mr. "whatever your name", something has happened to this girl, just now. When I find out, I come back with police or worse, my two great big sons. They watch out for all my girls. You mark my words, mister. "

As we made our way outside, Ida handed me her handkerchief and told me to dry my eyes. I could tell that she was seething and had a sixth sense of what had taken place. She smothered me in one of her bear hugs and said,

"We must look out for each other."

"Yes," I replied, fighting back tears.

CHAPTER 17

I tried not to allow the incident at Thomason's to ruin my plans for that day, but I just couldn't. I was down in the dumps for sure. Here I was trying to find my way in an unfamiliar city, in the dead of winter, and secure a position that would provide a living wage for me and Mama. I didn't need lecherous old men trying to rob me of my good name.

I recall wishing that Papa was around, so I could cry on his shoulder. That was when I became angry and resolved to restore my pluck, no matter what. Thank the Lord for Ida. It was as if she could read my mind, knowing my spirits needed lifting. She asked if I would join her for a bite to eat and a cup of tea.

McNeil's Restaurant on South Wabash served as the location for our heart to heart talk. From that day onward McNeil's became associated with a most memorable conversation between two working women, determined to make their way and keep their self-respect in a man's world.

Ida began the conversation by warning me of the dangers that a young woman such as I faced, when attempting to secure employment in Chicago. She advised that she could escort me through sections of the city with brothel after brothel full of young women, forced to sell their bodies and their souls to make their way.

She confided that in many instances captains of police precincts received payoffs from those who ran these enterprises and many of the city's

57

leaders visited them regularly. She described in pitiful detail how abandoned children, both girls and boys, were bought and sold into human bondage through a criminal underworld

She told me of courts of law that never gave a poor or working person an even shake, and political and religious figures who wrapped themselves in Old Glory or the Holy Bible, while lying and cheating their fellow man. It was an unforgettable lesson, taught to me by a woman who had endured the oppression and murder of her people, and the death of the man she loved.

"What can be done to change this, to make things better?" I asked.

"We must fight," she answered.

"But how, they have the power. They have guns. They have armies."

"Is true," she remarked. "But we have truth and we are many and they are few."

Now I will tell you of that unforgettable Saint Patrick's Night when Ida took me to see Mother Jones speak at the Columbia Theatre. It was after I had secured a position as a bookbinder with the J.M.W. Jones Company.

Perhaps it was the loss of all that was near and dear that made Mother Jones the force of nature she became. In the years to follow she would become renowned as a fiery labor organizer, enlisted to swell the ranks of the United Mine Workers Association. Later, she would be denounced as "the most dangerous woman in America" on the floor of the United States Senate.

The Columbia Theatre took my breath away, when I first laid eyes upon it. It reminded me of a magnificent French palace, standing six stories high with a pyramid shaped tower on top. Its first story appeared to be constructed entirely of iron, while the rest of its façade was the most finely polished white stone.

As we entered into a lobby area where two enormous ivory statues of personages from Greek mythology stood vigil, we tendered our tickets to a formally dressed young man who directed an usher to show us to our seats in the second balcony. There we observed a capacity crowd assembled. At that time Mother Jones was known simply as Mary Jones. She was a fervent supporter of the Knights of Labor.

Since it was Saint Patrick's night, there were pipes, fiddles and drums being played by a formally dressed orchestra, followed by the high kicking straight backed reels of six Irish step dancers, dressed in a lovely rainbow of cloaks and dresses.

Then a handsome gentleman, dressed in an emerald coat and tails with silver hair and a ruddy complexion appeared on stage to a rousing ovation. He was none other than Robert Maloney, a Dublin born vocalist and disciple of the Great Liberator, himself, Daniel O'Connell. He was to provide the musical introduction to our featured speaker. The pipes soon commenced with a stirring melody that invited our vocalist to soar in a resounding tenor voice with the strains of that rebel anthem *"The Wearing of the Green."* That overflow crowd soon began to clap and sing its chorus while standing.

> For the wearing of the green,
> For the wearing of the green
> They are hanging men and women
> For the wearing of the green

The next selection was a piece entitled *"Bold Fenian Men"* with its haunting, sorrowful melody. It was followed in short order by an indelible rendition of *"Wayfaring Stranger."* This was a song that my father and his friends sang in harmony on our front porch in Hannibal. Its lyrics always make me cry, especially the ones that say,

> I am a poor wayfaring stranger
> While traveling through this world of woe
> Yet there's no sickness, toil or danger
> In that bright world to which I go
> I'm going there to see my father
> I'm going there no more to roam
> I'm only going over Jordan
> I'm only going over home.

After receiving the standing applause of the crowd, Mr. Maloney raised his hand, soon achieving a respectful silence. He then cried out, "Ladies and gentleman, please give welcome to the inspirational Mary Jones. "

The crowd applauded and whistled as a small round woman in her middle years with snow white curled hair and silver spectacles appeared and took center stage. She wore a plain black dress flowing from her neck to the floor. It appeared to be a dress for mourning from a decade before. She stood perfectly still with her eyes downcast, as if afraid of the crowd that came to hear her speak.

When complete silence was achieved, she raised her pale Irish face, and began sobbing uncontrollably while falling to her knees. When her attendants approached to render assistance, she waved them away. Then ever so slowly she rose and cried at the top of her lungs with a distinct brogue. Her address would ring to the rafters of that majestic theater.

"I saw the landlords driving starving families into the road in the land of my birth. I saw children whose tiny bodies were sacks of skin and bone, their mouths stained emerald from trying to survive the famine by eating grass to fill their empty bellies. I saw piles of dead from the fever, being burned to prevent that fever's spread. On a coffin ship I came from across that cruel sea, in search of freedom, with the promise of equality for all. This is what I am in America."

"I am a mother who cries these tears for the dead and the dying. I have come to bring light into the darkest pits of hell, where the little breaker boys labor, coughing and choking, their tiny lungs turning black. Losing fingers, hands, toes and feet, while separating coal from shale in the mines of America."

"I am a mother who cries for the shop girls who toil day and night in the sweat shops, the mills and the manufactories of America. Behind locked doors in rooms without windows, without decent air to breathe, they work for slaves' wages, huddled together beside their looms and their machines. There the foremen hover, like beasts, commanding them to work faster, work longer, without rest, while lusting for their bodies. They draw close, moaning like devils with desire, clutching, grabbing, wanting to use them, wanting to corrupt them and turn a generation of innocents into harlots for hire."

"I am a mother to the men who go down into the hole to mine coal, who split the rails to make the railroads run, who refine the crude to turn greed into gold in America. Men who have been betrayed by paid informants, like that Judas, McParland. Men, blacklisted, beaten and shot down by paid thugs with badges. Men whose only crime was to band together in the hope of a decent wage and a decent way of life, with dignity for themselves and their families in America."

"For all of these and generations of workers to come in America, I shed tears. Will you shed these tears of sorrow, these tears of outrage with me? Will you join the righteous ranks of workers unions with me? Will you march to the drumbeat of worker equality with me? Will you become foot soldiers in the cause of freedom with me? Will you help make America keep its promise and become a land of liberty for men, women and children, both native born and immigrant, with me? "

I remember standing, crying and shouting out to her that I would. Through the tears that filled my eyes and ran down my Irish cheeks I observed that crowd standing and shouting as well. I remember Ida turning to me and hugging me as if there was no tomorrow. Two women who had been inspired by one of our own. Mary Jones was both a mother and a sister to all of us who were searching for dignity and equality in America.

CHAPTER 18

As we made our way from the second balcony amid the overflow crowd, Ida asked if I would like to meet the featured speaker at a reception for her friends and supporters. I couldn't believe my ears and told her that I would be thrilled to do so.

Ida advised that she had always been a supporter of workers joining together to improve their lives, since she was a young girl in Poland. She said that her father and brothers were worked like slaves in the coal mines. I then spoke of Papa and how the railroads blacklisted and beat him down for his membership in the Knights of Labor. I told her of the time I saw Terrance Powderly speak when I was a little girl. She then spoke in a heartfelt manner.

"You and I are much alike. I all times pray that God give me daughter after twins were born. My Stephan, he wanted little girl to come along, before Rockefeller and his oil company make me widow. I think maybe you be like daughter to me."

"You have been like a mother to me, Ida. I am so grateful for all that you've done."

"This will be night to always remember."

"Yes it will."

At the time I was introduced to Mother Jones, she was in a spirited conversation with a distinguished looking stocky gentleman with a

Scottish accent, whom I later learned was Peter Arthur of the Brotherhood of Locomotive Engineers. At that time his union had gone out on strike against the Chicago, Burlington & Quincy Railroad run by that crusty old curmudgeon, Charles Perkins, a sworn enemy of labor unions.

Beside Mr. Arthur was a tall slender gentleman in his middle years by the name of Eugene Debs. He had a high forehead and the kindest eyes and gentlest manner of any man I had met. On that night Ida and I sat down together beside him and discussed the strike that was taking place and the fact that the railroad had gone to court and obtained an injunction. He seemed almost heartbroken by this. When he left the table Ida seemed to grow angry and turned sullen. I asked her what an injunction meant.

"Like Poland, they get government to make outlaw of worker. Then soon the thugs and the scabs come. They don't care if work-er and his family starve. They care for business and to hell with workers."

It was close to ten o' clock as Ida and I, along with fifty or so others, were leaving the theatre. That was when we heard a terrible commotion coming from across Monroe Street. As I looked over, I saw a gang of ragged men carrying clubs and what appeared to be paving stones. To my shock they were directing their venom toward those of us leaving, calling us foul names and threatening to do us harm.

I remember grabbing Ida's arm and holding on to it like a frightened child when I saw five or six men and women in our group suddenly struck down by the stones that these men hurled. Blood was everywhere and the police were nowhere in sight. Then these men ran across the street at us with their clubs raised.

All I can remember is running for my life and Ida suddenly fall-ing behind me. She must have stumbled and fallen. I turned and saw a burly man in a dark coat approach her and strike her twice with a club. I screamed bloody murder and he looked up at me like a wild animal then ran off. All I could hear were the screams and oaths of those engaged in that awful melee.

I saw that Ida's head had been spit wide open and was spurting blood. I was in shock that all this was happening. I just remember grabbing her and trying to stop the bleeding with my gloves, when a kindly middle aged man wearing a tweed overcoat with salt and pepper hair, came to our aid, helping Ida to her feet and directing us to the shelter of his nearby doorway.

Inside there were a dozen or so others. They were beaten and bleeding, and seeking a refuge from those men. The man in the tweed overcoat, it turned out, was Dr. John Osborn, a physician whose office was located around the corner from the Columbia Theatre. He was like a battle surgeon, tending to those who had become the victims of that violence.

He placed Ida in a sitting position on the floor and gave her a sip from a small, dark, blue bottle. I was advised later that it was laudanum. He directed me to place a white towel against her head wound, assuring me that he would be back to stitch her up and that she would pull through. I remember asking him who the men were who attacked us. He said in a matter of fact manner, "Criminals hired by the CB&Q to break the strike."

Later that night, Ida's two sons found us there. I tell you, they were beside themselves with concern upon seeing the condition of their beloved mother. There they were, shedding tears of outrage and vowing to make those who had attacked us, pay with their lives. It was the indomitable Ida who counseled them toward a wiser response, with her head wrapped in a bandage. Her wound and the laudanum made her speech slow and halting,

"You do just what they want with vengeance and killing. Then they call us criminals. Then all will be against us. Use the heads God gave you. We fight them with union. We fight them with truth. I and your Papa came to America for promise of being more than what we could be in Poland. In America, if we work, if we learn and stay together, we will win. Now we go home."

As we were leaving, I saw three men arranging for the wounded to be taken home or to hospital. I heard what I thought was a familiar voice from my childhood. He seemed to be the man in charge and he was speaking to all those who were gathered nearby, collecting their names and addresses.

As we drew close, I recognized Seamus Egan, despite his efforts at changing his identity. His shortened hair and beard made him appear more youthful, but his eyes and his voice were unmistakable. He was standing directly in front of a saddened Eugene Debs and an outraged Peter Arthur. Mr. Arthur was at that time pounding his right fist into his left hand shouting to nobody in particular but to everybody.

"Where were the police when all of this was going on? Where in God's name were they? If we wanted a workers' parade, they would be here alright, keeping the peace in force, making sure no railroader spat on the bloody street. The injunction wasn't enough for the likes of him. No, he had to order the blood of innocents spilled to try to scare us off. The blood money of Charlie Perkins and his railroad was behind this, make no mistake. If they think we are beaten, they don't know Peter Arthur and they don't know our Brotherhood."

I was just about to call Seamus by name when I remembered that he had been on the run with warrants sworn for his arrest. Instead, I moved up next to him and touched his elbow. When he turned in my direction, I said,

"I still play that flute you made for me."

The warm expression on his handsome face was a sure signal that he knew me. I tell you I had all I could do not to wrap my arms around him, just like I used to do with Papa. He spoke affectionately, while looking into my eyes.

"Mary, it gives me great joy to see you all grown and looking so well. "

"So good to see you as well, Mr. _?"

"Duffy, Michael Duffy, please allow me to attend to those in your company."

CHAPTER 19

After that evening Seamus Egan, now known as Michael Duffy, took me under his wing once again, introducing me to friends and acquaintances involved in the labor movement. At that time, he and his lovely wife, Nannie, were living on the south side of Chicago.

Their two sons were now grown men who were making their mark in the world. Their oldest son, Liam, was a year older than me. We used to play kick the can and follow the leader together, back when we were kids in Hannibal. He had grown into a tall and very handsome young man. He was a journeyman carpenter in business with his father. Like his father, he was a member of the Workingmen's Party and The Federation of Organized Trades and Labor Unions. He too was a stalwart advocate for workers' rights.

His younger brother, Brendan, who was two years my junior, had studied for the law and was on his way to becoming a criminal lawyer. True to his heritage, he would go on to represent working men and women who had run afoul of the law throughout Illinois. He would later become a powerful alderman from Cook County and introduce me to the likes of Peter Altgeld and Clarence Darrow.

Michael Duffy & Son Carpenters was a going concern and a contractor to many of the companies that were engaged in the building boom taking place throughout Chicago. Their horse drawn wagons could be seen all over the city, with their distinctive green and gold lettering above a golden harp and a green shamrock. I was told that this insignia was similar to that on the flags that the Irish Brigade carried into battle. It was his brothers in arms, who aided Seamus in his escape and helped him get established in the Chicago carpentry trade under the name of Michael Duffy.

As I mentioned, I had secured employment with the J.M.W. Jones Company. It was a far cry from my previous employment for Mr. George and his companies. The reason for this was the manner in which the Jones Company was managed.

Hiram Jones was a stocky, grey haired, skinflint of the highest order, who was of the unshakeable belief that it was a distinct privilege to be in his employ and subject to his wiles and his whims. Although an outwardly devoted father and husband, he treated his hired help like they were a lesser form of being, particularly the women.

There were three separate locations in Chicago from which the J.M.W. Jones Company did a booming business. I worked at the Michigan Avenue site. It was a musty, dusty, place without sufficient light or ventilation for myself and almost one hundred other binders and printers. The work week was Monday through Saturday, ten hours a day. The weekly wages for women, no matter what their experience, was 7 dollars.

When the workday commenced at 6 A.M. the foremen would lock the doors to the rooms in which we worked and would not open them, until 9 A.M. for a water and bathroom break; then again at Noon for a lunch break and once again at 3P.M., before the workday ended at 4P.M. Our work was tightly supervised. Sitting and talking except for work matters was forbidden. It did not take long for me to become noticed by Hiram Jones.

From time to time he would grace us with his presence, usually in the company of his oldest son, Benjamin, a small, gargoyle of a human being, with an enormous head of unruly auburn hair and sloped shoulders. He would often wear a monocle along with a grey fedora and a black cashmere overcoat, when making his rounds. His heir would follow behind in similar dress, like a devoted pet.

He was a man in his sixties by then and his son was probably half his age. The similarity of their appearance and manner confirmed to all in their employ that the apple had not fallen far from the tree.

My father and mother taught me to be a hard worker and to be honest, polite and respectful to my elders and my employers. These traits, they would say, were proper and lead to success. I had been working since I could remember, in one manner or another, and couldn't really imagine what it would be like to be one of the idle rich. I was a working woman who wanted to make my own way. I was also outspoken, meaning I would stick up for myself when circumstances demanded it

Such a circumstance presented itself at the J.M.W. Jones Company during the second week of my employment. Since both male and female printers and binders used the same bathrooms and those bathrooms were always disgusting and unsanitary, I remember asking Mr. Rich, the nice enough second floor foreman, what could be done about this. He seemed totally taken a' back that I even brought up such a concern, probably choking off a surly reply that I should be thankful that I had a paying job. Instead, he simply shrugged his shoulders and suggested that I put my concerns in writing.

I firmly believe that he thought I would never do it, but I did. I sat down at my writing table that very night, and composed the letter. I showed it to Ida and she approved it with a broad smile. I still have a copy here somewhere. Oh, yes, here it is.

April 17, 1888

To: Mr. Hiram Jones, President.
From: Mary Kenney, Second Floor binder, Michigan Avenue Site
Subject: Health and well-being of your employees.
Dear Mr. Jones:
I am a dedicated lady worker in your company and want to be able to remain that way for a long while. Would you please see that the bathrooms we ladies use are cleaned regularly and that they are restricted for ladies only.
Yours truly,
Mary Kenney

The following morning just before the work day commenced, I handed my note to Mr. Rich, asking if he could be so kind as to tender it to Mr. Jones at his earliest convenience. I swear you could have knocked him over with a feather. I remember him standing there, holding the note and then reading it. He just looked at me and shook his head. I simply smiled my most beguiling smile and went about my business for that day.

Two days later I was summoned by Mr. Rich to come with him across the bindery yard to the offices of the man, himself. I was almost struck speechless by this at first, but screwed up my courage and resolved to put my best foot forward.

I remember being ushered into his spacious office with the heads of buffalos, lions and bears festooning its walls. It was apparent that Mr. Jones fashioned himself as some sort of big game hunter. I myself could never appreciate hunting God's creatures for their heads or their skins. Hunting or trapping animals in order to eat and survive was for me the only justification for doing so, not for the so called sport of it.

All of a sudden from a side door appeared Hiram Jones and his son, each of them similarly attired, as always. They were wearing black coats, amber vests and grey striped trousers topped off by impeccably white shirts and tasteful black and grey ties with jeweled stick pins in their center.

I can remember almost every word that was spoken between myself and that captain of industry on that occasion. To my dismay, this man I resented, because of the shoddy treatment of his work force, was altogether charming. He requested that I take a seat in the ornate velvet armchair facing his enormous desk and leather upholstered chair. His son was standing to his right.

"May I offer you a glass of water, young lady?" he began.

"No sir, but thank you for your kindness," I replied.

"I received your note from our foreman and must say that I was taken by your pluck. May I ask your age, young lady? "

"Twenty four."

"I suppose a young lady like yourself will not be in our employ too much longer, with all the eligible bachelors arriving in Chicago every day. I daresay that you will make yourself a doting wife and mother in the not too distant future. "

Not knowing what to say to this inquiry, I simply smiled and nodded my head slightly, not in agreement but not in disagreement either. I dreamed of being married one day but had not as yet met the man of my dreams. Besides, I was the caretaker of an invalid mother and her care was my chief concern at that time in my life. I decided I would press on with the matter that had occasioned our meeting.

"I greatly appreciate your taking the time to meet with me."

"Nonsense young lady, we have been blessed to be the beneficiaries of the Good Lord's bounty and it is our obligation to look out for those who work for us. We will consult with our staff and see what can be done to address your concerns. "

At that point he abruptly stood up, signaling that this was the end of our meeting, while his dutiful son showed me the door. I remember thinking afterwards that I should have persisted and inquired when the matter would be addressed, but I didn't and it wasn't. I resolved to do better the next time such an occasion presented itself.

CHAPTER 20

At this time in my story I should introduce you to two people who entered my life through the influence of my father's devoted friend, Michael Duffy, formerly known as Seamus Egan. I should also describe my romantic interlude with his son, Liam. The occasion was a Saturday evening dinner party located at the Duffy home during the month of June of the year 1888.

The dinner was by invitation only for myself and a guest. It was hosted by the ever gracious Nannie Duffy, whom I had loved and admired since our days back in Hannibal. I came there in an emerald evening dress of silk that Mama had made for me before I left for Chicago. I wore a matching cameo choker around my neck and a pair of heeled silver shoes made of kid's leather.

I came there, accompanied by Ida, my devoted ally. She wore a royal blue velvet evening dress and a tasteful white stole. Her golden hair was arranged in a French twist complemented by a pair of royal blue earrings. She had completely recovered from her head wound by that time and was as feisty as ever. I had confided in Ida the true identities of the Duffy family, knowing that wild horses couldn't drag that secret from one such as her.

We were met at the door by the host and hostess in formal attire and escorted to a sumptuous table by Liam Duffy who cut a dashing figure indeed, in a charcoal coat and tails. He was a tall, handsome young man with black hair and piercing blue eyes. I could tell when he saw me coming through the door that I made a favorable impression. He approached and tendered his white gloved hand with the warmest of smiles.

"Could this be my playmate from long ago? You look beautiful this evening, Mary. It is a pleasure seeing you after so many years. I have been asking my father if you were going to appear."

"You are making me blush, Liam. I was looking forward to seeing you as well. This is my dear friend, Ida Pudolski."

Ida tendered her hand like royalty and smiled, advising that it was a pleasure to make his acquaintance and to be welcomed into his family's lovely home. I could tell right off that Ida liked him and was prepared to enjoy both his company and the evening to the fullest. I thought for a moment about Mama and became a bit melancholy. Ida once again seemed to sense what I was thinking and took my hand, saying,

"Your Mama will be with you soon. Let's make most of a special night."

Together we made our way toward the dining area where a delightful crowd had gathered and then to a small table where punch and an array of delicacies were served. When dinner was served, Nannie Duffy rose from her position beside her distinguished looking husband, welcoming everyone.

She was wearing an evening dress of red silk. She respectfully introduced Doctor Edward McGlynn to bless our meal and ourvening. I had been introduced to Dr. McGlynn by Brendan Duffy, earlier in the evening.

He was a gentleman of great stature with grey hair, and an infectious brogue. The devotion and eloquence with which he delivered the blessing led me to the belief that he had missed his calling as a member of the clergy. Brendan would later inform me as to the accuracy of this impression.

At that time Brendan was a smaller version of his father with black hair and the bluest of eyes. He had a small straight nose and an expressive mouth with perfectly white teeth and a manicured dark mustache. Like his father, he possessed a wonderful speaking voice In the future he would use that voice in addressing many a jury.

The meal was a delicious preparation of roasted chicken with scalloped potatoes and green beans. Doctor McGlynn was seated to our left and Elizabeth Morgan, a tall, refined woman in a white chiffon evening dress, wearing a pair of small tortoise shell eyeglasses and a tiny silver tiara in her luxurious dark hair, was seated to our right, beside her husband.

The dinner conversation and the series of toasts that followed told one and all that this was a gathering of labor union activists and sympathizers who had no intention of being cowered by the powerful men and the political machinery that ran Chicago. I remember Doctor McGlynn asking me what I thought as a working woman of the wealth and treatment of workers, exhibited by men like Rockefeller and Carnegie.

I was reluctant to express my sentiments with my lack of education, but two glasses of that delightful punch seemed to loosen my tongue and bestow an unexpected eloquence upon me. Besides, when Ida heard the name of Rockefeller, I thought I had better reply before she launched into a salty tirade on the subject, as only Ida could.

"I think that they are acting against the teachings of Our Savior, by doing so," I heard myself saying.

"You're a young woman of faith, my dear. Our Lord and Savior has taught us "what you do to these the least of my brethren, you do to me." I pray that they will be given the grace to see the light and to do what is right, before the workers of America are forced to rise up and smite them down like the Philistines. "

"The battle for worker's rights must be fought with our heads and our hearts" Elizabeth Morgan offered. Her confidence and beauty shining through to all.

"Unless the rich and the powerful recognize the dignity and worth of workers, both male and female, a revolution will be visited upon them, like that in France and heads will roll."

"In Poland, they jail and murder workers who try to make change for better. They do same here, if we let them," Ida added.

"I agree," Elizabeth replied. "That is why we must fight with our heads and our hearts. Look what happened at Haymarket. They will jail us and kill us for trying to make them change. We must not give them the excuse to do so by violence. We must organize and demand that workers be treated fairly. If we need to, we must go out on strike and stay out to get what we deserve. All the while, we must spread the message that what is good for workers will be good for America. "

"How do you make your living?" I remember asking, taken by the way she spoke.

"I'm the President of Local 2703 of the Ladies Federal Labor Union."

"I've not heard of that union."

"We just received our charter. Are you a working woman?"

"A bookbinder, I work for the J.M.W. Jones Company."

"We need young women like yourself to join us. To help us make a difference. We should talk later and maybe you and your friend will join us. We need all the help we can get."

That would be the evening when I resolved to take an active role in the representation of women in the workplace. Here I was, seated between two people whose beliefs would shape my life from that date onward.

Doctor Edward McGlynn, it turned out, was a Catholic priest, in fact, the defrocked pastor of Saint Stephen's Parish in Manhattan. It seemed that his fervent devotion to the poor had caused him to vigorously support Henry George's candidacy for Mayor of New York. Like Mr. George, Father McGlynn preached humane ideas with regard to the acquisition of private property in America and the funding of public schools through the taxation of the wealthy.

His advocacy of these ideas rankled his Archbishop and resulted in his temporary excommunication by the Vatican. It is said that Father McGlynn was responsible in part for the Pope's Encyclical, *Rerum Novarum*, and the Church's less than zealous support for the rights of working men and women in America.

Betty Morgan would later take me under her benevolent wing and instill in me the courage and conviction necessary for labor organizing. I always admired her devotion to the cause of working women. She possessed an unshakeable belief that loving service to others would one day win out over all the power, all the greed and all the violence of those pitted against us.

I dare say that there was many a time in the years ahead when I questioned whether her nobility of spirit was out of step with what was taking place around us. Whatever wisdom I would attain in these matters would be conferred by the experiences that would follow.

As frosting on the cake of that unforgettable evening, Liam Duffy sought me out as Ida and I were preparing to leave and asked if he could have a word with me in private, within the foyer of his family's home.

I must confess that I was smitten by his manly bearing and his gentlemanly ways.

"Mary, once again it is such a pleasure seeing you looking so lovely after all these years. I regret that I was not able to spend more time in your company."

"It is a pleasure to see you as well, Liam," I whispered, with my heart beating a gentle tattoo.

"Would you allow me to take you out for dinner in our fair city? Please tell me that you are not already spoken for."

"I would enjoy such an occasion and no, I am not already spoken for."

"Oh how wonderful, would Saturday next be too soon an occasion."

"That would be grand."

With that, he caressed my hand and gently kissed my cheek. All the way home in our carriage Ida held that hand, with a womanly understanding that our evening at the home of the Duffy family was one that I would not soon forget.

CHAPTER 21

*B*etty Morgan, true to her word and her calling, dropped by my residence the following afternoon in an effort to enlist me as a delegate of The Ladies Federal Labor Union, local 2703. We met in the sitting room adjacent to Ida's dining room over a cup of tea and a helping of her delicious apple strudel.

It was a warm Chicago Sunday afternoon and Betty was particularly striking in an embroidered white blouse and navy blue cotton skirt that accentuated her long slender figure. Once again she wore those distinctive tortoise shell eye glasses with her lovely brown hair worn long to her shoulders.

She had been married for nearly ten years and was the mother of three young children. She advised that she would turn thirty five that December. Her winning manner and impressive knowledge of the labor movement, along with a passionate belief that organization was absolutely necessary for securing a living wage for both men and women, won me over completely.

She advised that the LFLU was affiliated with the Chicago Trade and Labor Assembly and the American Federation of Labor. Following the example set by the Knights of Labor under Terence Powderly, the preamble of LFLU's constitution was to secure equal pay for equal work. When I told her that Papa was a Knight, she smiled and said that was probably the reason our paths had crossed.

She told me that if I wished to join, I would have to appear before members of the Assembly and be voted in as a delegate. She said that our membership would be drawn from the female clerks, typists, candy makers, bookbinders and dressmakers of Chicago. As a delegate, I would be called upon to enlist other women bookbinders at my present place of business and elsewhere. I would also have to attend monthly meetings.

When I questioned her as to how I would find the time to do this, given my need to work six days a week, she said that I would receive a monthly stipend of twenty dollars from the Union that would allow me to work less hours. Thus began my involvement with Women's Bookbinding Union # 1 and my career as a labor organizer in America.

I should tell you at this point of my whirlwind romance with Liam Duffy. He appeared at my residence the following Saturday at six sharp in a shiny black and silver carriage drawn by a regal chestnut mare, named Polly.

He brought as gifts a bouquet of wild flowers and a small blue and gold box of confectionary delights. If his intention was to sweep me off my feet during our first dinner engagement, he had succeeded.

He was stylishly attired in a blue suit with a carnation in his lapel, a white shirt and striped red and white tie. His ebony shoes were shined to the point where you could almost see yourself in them and the smell of his Bay Rum cologne brought back fond memories of old Sam Watkins and summertime in Hannibal Missouri.

Our first night together would begin with a carriage ride along the shore of Lake Michigan on a golden June evening. Liam advised that he knew Chicago like the back of his hand and would show me the sights before a delicious dinner at Demetri's, a cozy Hungarian restaurant, within walking distance from the Chicago River.

Our conversation was without awkward silences as we each traced the course that our lives had taken since our play dates at Riverside Park. It was a delight to converse with a handsome young man who actually listened and appreciated what I had to say. The fact that I had secured a position with the LFLU earlier in the week that would afford the opportunity of working less hours and would allow me to bring Mama to live with me, made that night a most delightful affair.

The manner in which Liam was greeted by the suave maître de and escorted to a favored table for two made me want to pinch myself. I was actually in the company of an up and coming young gentleman and the object of his considerable affection. During a delicious meal of Beef Stroganoff followed by a delightful desert of strawberry shortcake, I can remember coming to the unmistakable conclusion that the spirit of Papa must be watching over me and making my way both straight and sure.

The finale of that first evening was a band concert at Grant Park with the two of us seated in Liam's carriage holding hands. The moon and the stars seemed to be perfectly in place above us and the melodies that were played would secure that evening in the chest of my memory. That unforgettable evening would be sealed with a most unforgettable kiss. Romance, is a wondrous thing indeed.

By that time I had been recognized for my energy and experience at my place of work with additional supervisory responsibilities being placed upon my shoulders. These would not be coupled however by any addition to my weekly wage.

It was about that time when my foreman, Mr. Rich, advised that I had made a most favorable impression upon Mr. Jones. That was why he had chosen me to assume the duties and responsibilities of an experienced male bookbinder by the name of James Timilty who had suffered an unfortunate injury when his right hand was caught in a printing press.

The request was made for me to stand in his stead for the remainder of that week until a suitable male replacement could be brought in from an outlying branch of the company. I recall feeling a sense of pride from this recognition and feeling that it was an opportunity to prove my mettle in the trade.

Well, I worked like I had never worked before, binding, printing, sorting and packaging products for transit for the booming business of the J.M.W. Jones Company. On at least two occasions I would look up from my labors and see Hiram Jones, himself, looking on with a smile upon his approving countenance.

It was the following Friday when I received my wages for the week before, fully anticipating that I would find 21 crisp dollars in my pay envelope, which were the weekly wages that would have been paid to Mr. Timilty for the identical duties I fulfilled so diligently.

Much to my disappointment, contained within that envelope was a measly 7 dollars, the standard weekly wages for a female bookbinder, not a single cent more. I soon resolved to take this matter up with my supervisor on the following Monday.

All the following Saturday and Sunday I simmered, wounded by the injustice of my employer, angered at the plight of working women in America and determined to be that someone, who would make it change for the better. That was my quest and that would be my calling as a labor organizer in the Chicago of 1888. I harbor neither regret nor remorse for choosing that life to lead.

CHAPTER 22

efore I requested another meeting with Hiram Jones, I sought the counsel of my mentors, Ida and Betty Morgan. I also asked Liam Duffy if I could speak with his father concerning the matter. Throughout my years as a labor organizer, it was the counsel of others of like devotion that would help guide my decision making.

Both Ida and Betty advised that an immediate audience with Mr. Jones would probably not occur but that I should bide my time, while respectfully requesting another opportunity for a face to face meeting. I remember Betty saying that my work as a bookbinder should continue to be exemplary and that I should make an extra effort to be cordial and cooperative with all the supervisory personnel of the J.M.W. Jones Company.

It was Papa's closest friend who would remind me of the teachings of Lao Tzu in the parlor of the Duffy home. A gentle but steady flow of water can transform even the hardest of stones, was his way of describing the manner in which I should proceed.

It was Ida who suggested that I simply deliver a note to my supervisor, asking Mr. Jones for the opportunity to speak with him, when convenient with his busy schedule, then simply await a reply as before. Should I not hear back within two weeks, then I should ask again.

Betty advised that it would be left to me as to what I should say to Mr. Jones, if the opportunity arose and Women's Bookbinding Union # 1 would stand squarely behind me. She said it was a golden opportunity to learn how to bargain with an owner of "the means of production." I recall that was the first time I had heard that phrase and asked where it originated. That was when Betty mentioned Karl Marx and Frederic Engels and *"The Communist Manifesto."*

In the years to come in America, many of those who called themselves Communists were in the forefront of the quest for worker equality, while fighting and dying so that the workers of the world could unite and by that unity be freed from the bondage of their chains. The philosophy behind Communism and its notion of a society without class, where all men and women could be equal, was certainly a noble one. As someone would later say, after the Russian revolution shook the world, the road to hell is often paved with good intentions.

It was on September 6th in the year 1888 when a meeting was finally arranged with Mr. Jones. Once again I was summoned by my supervisor to accompany him to Mr. Jones' office. This time Mr. Jones had dispensed with the companionship of his copycat son and met me by himself, while seated and smoking a foul smelling cigar. I received the distinct impression that this meeting was an inconvenience by the abrupt nature of his introduction and his failure to offer me a seat.

"What can I do for you, this time?"

"Sir, I greatly appreciate your seeing me once again. I was wondering whether you knew that I worked Mr. Timilty's hours during his absence and received only my normal wages as my pay."

"What do you want me to do about that?"

"I have been advised that male bookbinders receive 21 dollars per week."

"That is my understanding as well. Surely, you're not requesting that you should receive pay equal to that of a working man, young lady? "

"Yes, Mr. Jones that is what I am requesting."

"Balderdash!"

"I beg your pardon "

"Nonsense! That will never occur while I run this company. You know you have quite the nerve waltzing in here and suggesting that a wisp of girl like yourself should be paid the wages of a male breadwinner."

To be honest I was on the verge of tears upon hearing that obstinate old polecat talk to me in such a way. I was tempted to advise him that I was a member of Ladies Bookbinding Local #1 and maybe a strike would be more to his liking, but I thought twice about doing so and about the shedding of tears. I took a deep breath and attempted to compose myself, all the while thinking of Papa.

"Sir," I began uncertainly, "I am the sole breadwinner for my family. When Mr. Rich asked that I take Mr. Timilty's hours, I was determined to work every bit as hard as him. I believe I did just that, and that I deserve the same pay as him. It is my hope to marry some day and to be blessed with children, but that day is not now. With your permission, I will, return to my labors. Thank you for your time."

I left his office as quick as I could because my knees were shaking and my heart was in my throat. It was only later, while at my workbench, that I felt proud that I held my own against the likes of Hiram Jones. To tell the truth, I expected to receive my dismissal from Mr. Rich before the close of business that day.

When I arrived home both Ida and Betty were waiting, wondering how my meeting went. When I told them all about it, they each gave me a sisterly hug. There would be one last time when we would show Mr. Jones what working women could do, before I moved on.

Someone once told me that the business of politics in the Cities of Chicago and Boston, two cities where I resided and plied my trade of labor organization, was like that of ancient Athens and Sparta, more of a blood sport than a contest of respectful rivals. Chicago's municipal elections for mayor, city council and other less exalted offices in November of 1888, were bitter fights to the finish. In nearly every ward and precinct, the printing of thousands of lengthy, uniform ballots as well as distinctive pieces of campaign literature was required.

In the midst of this political free for all stood the mostly female work force of printers, binders and distributors of the J.M.W. Jones Company. Our task, it seemed, was to paper each and every inch of "The City of Big Shoulders" with an array of printings that provided access to a political process and the exercise of a right, denied to the adult female population by the male power structure of America. I suppose it was the twin denials of the right to vote and that of equal pay for equal work that moved the women of the Jones Company to rise to the challenge.

Around the clock from 7 AM on Friday morning until 4PM on Saturday we worked, printing, binding and packaging for distribution, with a bare minimum of respites. Our determination to get the job done and our sisterly concern for each other throughout that 33 hour interval would later become the cornerstones for my organizational efforts on behalf of Ladies Bookbinding Local #1.

Despite being a wisp of a girl, as Hiram Jones had described me, and the company's youngest forelady at age 24, I shall never forget the look of satisfaction on the weary, soiled faces of my sister workers lying upon that filthy floor, strewn with the remnants and refuse of that election.

There they are and there they will remain in my mind's eye, bone weary from their labors. Lying exhausted beside their work benches and machinery. As I passed among them, dispensing water, I congratulated each and every one of those working women for an inspired effort in a job well done.

CHAPTER 23

$\mathcal{L}$ater that month, before the snow began to fly and the Chicago River became frozen solid, I was able to send a telegram to Tim Flaherty, Papa's devoted friend back in Hannibal, and make arrangements for Mama's coming to live with me at long last.

By that time I had managed to attend four or five delegate meetings of Local 2703 in the basement of The Green Briar Saloon over on Wabash Avenue. I also saved two months of my union stipend in order to secure a two bedroom apartment in a section of the city that would later become part of "Little Italy", at 690 South Halsted Avenue.

With the able assistance of Peter and Josef Pudolski, and a wagon borrowed from Michael Duffy & Sons, Carpenters, we moved into this sunny, spotlessly clean, second floor residence on November 18th, 1888, one week before Thanksgiving.

This would be mine and mama's home for the next year and a half. This would be the time of my apprenticeship as a labor organizer and my coming of age and emergence as a woman of the world. It was also the time when my devotion to mama became an impediment to my romance with Liam Duffy.

Mama's health had grown steadily worse while I was living apart from her in Chicago. Although I used Western Union to communicate with her twice a week, her replies were few and far between. I later began to send my telegrams directly to Tim Flaherty, asking him to provide a candid assessment of her health.

I would find out later that Mama had persuaded Tim to paint a more optimistic picture of her condition, so that I would not fret about her while attempting to make my way in Chicago. When Tim and his son brought her over from Hannibal by wagon and I saw her for the first time in so many months, I was speechless.

She appeared so much older with her hair turned completely gray and her mobility almost completely gone. She could make her way for short distances or climb a flight of stairs with the assistance of a cane, but longer trips required her to be pushed in a wheeled chair. The pain of her rheumatism must have plagued her terribly but she never uttered a complaint in that regard. Her faith was the cornerstone of her coping. She would remain an inspiration and my strongest ally throughout the remainder of her life.

As a child, I learned early that life on this earth is unfair for so many, without any rhyme or reason. That was when faith came into the picture, a faith instilled in me by Mama, most of all. A faith that caused me to ponder; a faith that caused me to believe.

Like the atom, electricity, gravity or the blowing of the wind, there is much that is and has being that is invisible or untouchable. There is much that is above and beyond the world as we know it. During the course of my life, first Edison and then Einstein would discover invisible spheres and bring light to our world. In a sense they were men of faith in an unseen world of energy and power. So too were those who believed in the mercy and love of the Almighty.

The Thanksgiving of 1888 was a mixture of blessings and bewilderment for me. There was the blessing of being reunited with my mother. The blessing of a profession where I could serve others by organizing them into our union. The blessing of my good health and the blessing of Liam Duffy's love and affection. The bewilderment arose from being unable to balance these blessings with the fulfillment of my duties as a devoted daughter and caretaker.

Liam and I had been keeping company since our first evening alone together. I knew that he was a man of integrity and strength, as were his father and his younger brother. I knew that he wanted to care for me and to one day make me the mother of his children. That became evident soon after our first dinner engagement when he and I spent a joyful July Sunday together enjoying a picnic lunch along the shores of Lake Michigan.

There we were on a hillside reclined upon a red and white checkered table cloth with my head resting gently upon his shoulder. We were bathed in the shade of a magnificent chestnut tree while watching sailboats glide through those bright green fathoms with the caress of a summer breeze. Lovers and young families were strolling about, while we took a welcome break from our working lives.

It was at that moment that Liam turned his face toward mine and kissed me with passion and desire. His touch and embrace thoroughly captivating me. He had brought out the woman in me. I was twenty four and he was two years my senior. I was his and he was mine and the world was simply wonderful.

"Mary, my darling" he whispered, "I want and need you to be my wife."

"Oh, Liam", I heard myself saying, "Is this a dream?"

"No darling girl, it is true love and it will last forever."

During that Thanksgiving meal I was seated between Mama and Liam with the Duffy family all around. I could see Mama giving her very best to conceal her pain from one and all, not wanting to be a burden to anyone. That brought a sadness and a certain consternation. I then began to realize that my duty to care for my mother must take priority over my devotion to Liam. That balancing my happiness with my duty was not to be.

I must confess that there was a melancholy that came to trouble me because of this, despite the joyful circumstances of that celebration. At that very moment I observed the eyes of Liam's father focused upon mine with the selfsame realization, clouding them with the selfsame melancholy. He knew that Liam's love for me could not be returned in kind, and my pain was his pain as well. I suppose loving service to others always requires sacrifice.

As was the case with most decisions that changed the course of my life, it was made in solitude and only after prayerful meditation. I would like to tell you that the noble course was like a beacon light, revealing a rocky shoal to be avoided, making my life's voyage safe and clear, but that simply was not the case. I suppose that you can always look back on your life and reflect on paths not taken, wondering what might have been.

Following that Thanksgiving celebration, I wrestled with the choice I had to make to forsake the love being offered so completely by Liam.

Being noble and giving of oneself is not without reservations. Did I love Liam Duffy and would I have made a devoted wife and a mother to his children? Perhaps, but my duty to my mother kept me from falling in love completely and that allowed me to break free from his devotion. It was a painful experience when I told him of the decision I had made.

It was December of 1888, December 8th to be exact, a holy day of obligation in commemoration of the Blessed Mother, that brought Mama and me to the six o' clock Mass. I recall praying fervently that I had made the right choice and that the right words would come, so that Liam would be able to understand my reasons for forsaking his love. The intention of my prayers was that Liam and I would still remain close friends.

A recent snowfall had spread a blanket of white over Chicago, causing Liam to arrange for a driver to take us by horse drawn sleigh to Demetri's, the location of our first dinner engagement six months before. I had not had the heart to break the news to him before that occasion. I have always wondered whether his father had given him advance warning. That he should not be heartbroken over my need to reject his marriage proposal.

To my relief, he would appear both gracious and understanding. We were seated at the very same candlelit table as that of our first dinner engagement, shortly after an aged violinist in coat and tails had completed a Hungarian rhapsody. That was when Liam commenced his overture.

"Mary, I trust you understand the depths of my love and devotion for you. When I first set eyes upon you after so many years, you enchanted me completely. It is my heartfelt wish that you and I spend our lives together. Tell me, darling Mary, will you marry me?"

"Oh, Liam, my heart is full of love for you, but our marriage cannot be. My mother's care must come first and foremost, I am so sorry. "

"But Mary, I will love and care for you both. Love will find the way."

"No Liam, such would not be fair to you or Mama. My mind is made up."

For three months afterward I continued to have regrets about the choice I made. As an antidote for my anguish, I rededicated myself to caring for Mama's every need and the organizing work of our Local. I purposely would avoid all social occasions that might cause our paths to cross and revisit more hurt upon us both.

Ida and Betty Morgan counseled me to turn the page on this failed love affair. That was when I ran into Brendan, while Betty and I were leaving McNeil's. I asked her to give me a minute to speak with him in private. It was a frigid February morning without snow.

"Brendan, will you give Liam my fondest regards."

"Would that I could, Mary dear, but he is abroad."

"Oh Brendan, my heart aches. Please don't hate me."

"Noble courses can be painful ones, it seems, Mary, dear."

"Oh Brendan, please give your father and mother my love."

That April the newspapers ran a notice that Liam Duffy had become engaged to one Anne McCabe, the daughter of a Dublin solicitor from a fine Dublin family and she and Liam would be married that autumn. The notice caused me to conceal my tears from Mama.

I would never see Liam again. I would continue to see Brendan Duffy and watch his rise to prominence, while his father would remain a guiding light in my life until he met his ending. Life is often like the sea, it seems, an endless series of ebbs and flows.

CHAPTER 24

*S*trikes would be common place occurrences during the following two years. In Chicago and many of the other Northern cities, carpenters, machinists, dock workers, bricklayers and railroaders would attempt to gain a greater say in the course of their working lives. A say that those who were in control of those industries would oppose.

The captains of industries like rail, coal, oil, and mining would use all manner of means, both fair and foul, to keep a tight grip on what they had built through the sweat and blood of working men and women. All the while believing that they were well within their God given rights in doing so. They would use the newspapers to compliment and portray themselves as doing good, while demonizing those like me who fought to organize workers to speak as one.

In January of 1890 the pressmen working for the J.M.W. Jones Company went out on strike, seeking higher wages and shorter working hours. Their union knew that The Jones Company had signed contracts with certain customers that required the work to be completed near the beginning of the year. A timely strike would be to their advantage in negotiations. That strike would be a peaceful one.

I can remember reading it in the *Voice,* one of the weekly papers that supported the workers' cause, that the agreement reached was an important victory. It seems that Hiram Jones had agreed to a modest increase in pressmen wages and a 2 hour reduction of their Saturday work hours.

Having firsthand experience with Mr. Jones, I remember wondering to myself where and when the other shoe would drop. I didn't have to wait long for it to occur. It was during the signing of the agreement reached. Mr. Jones had summoned the scribes of the *Tribune* and the other daily papers to take down what he would say. It was a warning shot across the bow of the pressmen's Union and a sign of things to come.

"There will always be trouble of this kind until the legislature passes a law against conspiracies of this kind. We had important contracts on hand and didn't think the few extra dollars a week should be considered. I told the boys, however, I would get even with them. I think girls should feed the presses and a few laborers should be employed to bring them the stock."

I can remember sitting, reading the news of the signing with Betty Morgan and a few others from our union and seeing her shake her head and explain to us all the sinister nature of the response that Jones had delivered. He would lead others of his kind toward the same approach in the months and years ahead.

They would use female workers and their need to help make a living wage for their families to keep male breadwinners' wages low and their hours less, throughout the country. Nobody ever said that those who controlled the so called "means of production" in America weren't resourceful as well as ruthless.

That was the time when I would meet many who were dedicated to the cause of unionism and the betterment of workers lives. Some preached for peace, others for violence. Some would have their names written in the history books of America, while others would be forgotten or live on only in the memories of their friends and families.

As I learned the ropes of organizing female wage earners, I realized that there were different approaches and dangers to doing my job. The first order of business was to find a safe and secure location for union meetings that were free from spies and thugs hired by the owners to harass and scare away our membership.

I would always remember that terrifying attack outside the Columbia Theatre, after Mother Jones' spoke. From then on I would begin carrying a knife in my purse and wearing a very long and lethal hatpin in my hair for protection, when travelling to and from our meetings.

The first location for the meetings of Local I of the Women's Bookbinders Union was the cellar of the Green Briar Saloon down on Wabash Avenue. Our meetings were held between five and six thirty on Sunday evenings, a time when the saloon was usually quiet.

Most of our membership were women in their teens and twenties and most often of Irish or Polish heritage. It didn't take long, given the location, for criminals and assorted other riff raff to take notice that young women were about and potential prey to their dark designs. The month before, two of our girls were followed by three hooligans belonging to a local gang as they left our meeting. If it wasn't for the intervention of a courageous young Chicago patrolman, making his rounds in the area, and the timely application of a nightstick to the head of that gang's ringleader, I shudder to think what could have happened.

It was shortly after that occasion when I ran into Ida and told her what had occurred. Without batting an eye, she offered the services of her two sons as both our protectors and our carriage drivers. To say that her boys would become quite popular with our ladies and a magnet for new members in the market for a gainfully employed husband, was an understatement. I should tell you of an occasion involving Ida's sons that still lingers in my memory.

It was during the month of June in 1891. It was a time when both spring and baseball had a firm grip upon the City of Chicago. Almost every bar and beer hall had its own baseball team and Sunday afternoons were reserved for games to be played and beer and whiskey to be drunk.

We were in the middle of our union meeting when a crowd coming from the game that had just finished up at Saunders Field began making its way into the Green Briar. From the sounds of the commotion they made upon entering, they were feeling no pain.

As I recall, there were twenty to thirty of our members in attendance when a player using the outbuilding in back, spied our congregation through a cellar window and gave notice of our presence to the others. His calls brought a flock of his friends from the saloon above.

As the leader of that meeting, I was uncertain as to what to do. I didn't want to open our door and risk the entry of that rowdy bunch into our midst in confined quarters, nor did I want to force my girls to exit through the upstairs saloon. I must admit that some of our girls complicated matters by flirting with some of that lot, gathered near the rear door.

This, in turn, caused the others joining in that crowd to begin hooting and hollering then pushing their way forward toward the attention of those girls. I suppose it was this pushing and shoving that caused a donnybrook to erupt in that alleyway and pandemonium to reign.

It was while we were huddled together looking out that alley window when the Pudolski bothers arrived to escort us home. I tell you those twins were something to behold during that melee. The next thing I recall is seeing the blond, blue eyed Josef with his massive shoulders and hands take two of the rowdiest of that lot by the scruff of the neck and bash their heads together, knocking both of them senseless.

Next it was his brother, Peter's turn. I remember him scaling a nearby stairway, his brown hair flowing over the collar of a striped shirt and his steel blue eyes ablaze, launching himself upon a half a dozen of them. We watched in awe as those brothers joined forces and proceeded to batter those still standing with a grim determination. They were like a couple of powerful threshers, slashing their way through ripe wheat, in reaching our refuge.

Ida's sons came to our rescue on that night, and reigned victorious, while their adversaries were either unconscious or in flight before them; no doubt regretting that the drink and desire brought on the wrath of our stalwart guardians. I would learn that a few of our girls bestowed their grateful charms upon their gallant protectors, during their carriage rides home.

The upshot of that exercise in fisticuffs was that our local could no longer use the cellar of the Green Briar as a place for our union's meetings. We now needed to find another gathering spot that was free from hooligans, spies and other assorted riff raff. Through the support and generosity of the Royal Order of Hibernians we were able to secure the top floor meeting room at the Hibernian Hall over on North LaSalle Avenue on Tuesday nights.

Beyond finding a suitable location to hold our meetings there was also the constant need to find new members with the courage and willingness to join the ranks of our local. This was a daunting task indeed.

By that time I had managed to gather twelve girls from the Jones Company to join our ranks. I began first by speaking to them during our morning and afternoon breaks and then followed up any interest expressed with the distribution of one page fliers. Fliers they could conceal upon their persons, describing how joining our union would be the key to better working conditions, higher wages and shorter working hours.

We informed them that an eight hour work day was supposed to be the law of the land, passed by Congress years before, yet violated by almost every shop and factory in America ever since. We did not mention the use of slowdowns or strikes as weapons of choice, for fear we would be labeled agitators or conspirators against commerce. For that we could be carted off to a jailhouse as so many others had been. More than anything else, managing to persuade a girl to attend one of our monthly meetings was the best way to get her to join our ranks.

By October of 1891 I was prepared to leave my position with the Jones Company and begin my career as a roving bookbinder, traveling from shop to shop in order to spread the word. Only through organization could working women gain control of their lives. I remember my last day at Jones as if it were yesterday.

I had asked Mr. Jones to allow female workers to have separate and sanitary bathrooms, nearly a year before. As you would guess, nothing was ever done to respond to these requests. If anything, those conditions worsened, calling for more drastic action on my part.

On my last day of working there, I carried nearly one hundred fliers with me and proceeded to place one on each and every work bench within our bindery. I then sought to speak one last time with Mr. Jones and was abruptly told that he was unavailable for any further meetings with me. Before leaving that bindery once and for all, I stood in the middle of the work floor during the morning break and shouted at the top of my lungs,

"I am Mary Kenney. I've worked in the bookbinding trade since I was a young girl. I have spoken with Mr. Jones about correcting the unhealthy conditions that exist in this company and nothing has been done. I will leave here and head straight to the Chicago Board of Health and request an inspection of this and every location where The Jones Company conducts its business. The health and safety of its workers should be this company's first order of business."

"The eight hour work day is the law of the land and Mr. Jones and other employers throughout America have been violating that law on each and every day since it was passed. The slaves' wages that are being paid by the Jones Company are not sufficient for you and your families to live with dignity. Instead, you have little more than the beggars in the streets of this city. "

"I am proud to say that I am a member of Ladies Bookbinding Local # 1 and I welcome all of the women working in that trade to come to our meeting on this coming Tuesday evening at The Hibernian Hall over on North La Salle Avenue. "

I can still see most of my fellow bookbinders looking upon me fearfully. There were a few however with admiration on their faces. A few was all we would need.

CHAPTER 25

I received a written dinner invitation that December from Jane Addams, shortly after the story of my farewell to the Jones Company became a back page item in the *Tribune*. In it, I was mentioned by name, labeling me an agitator and troublemaker. Unexpectedly, this was music to the ears of a certain segment of Chicago society that would soon become unlikely allies in the workers' cause.

Of all the people whose lives were devoted to fostering understanding to make America a land where freedom and equality would be our birthrights, Jane Addams stands out above them all. I was blessed to come under her influence when I was young. As I sit here in the winter of my life, I must say it was her love and goodwill toward others that would make me see the light and follow her example throughout my life.

I knew nothing about settlement houses before entering Hull House on that Saturday evening. It was a stately mansion that resembled an Italian villa, located on South Halstead Avenue in the "Little Italy" section of Chicago. I remember telling my mother that I would be returning home shortly, since I didn't know what someone who lived in a mansion would want with me.

The lowly wages I had received at the Jones Company, even with the monthly stipend from the union, had forced Mama and me to scrimp and save on everything, in order to keep the wolf away from our door. I suppose I was suspicious and had my guard up when the, well-dressed, attractive woman who answered the door bell, asked for my name and whether she could take my coat and hat.

I was wearing my most fashionable and warmest outfit. It was an emerald and black checked woolen coat with a high collar and a pleated bodice that reached the tops of my high buttoned brown leather boots, together with a matching woolen hat. My reluctance in delivering these precious articles of clothing to a perfect stranger must have seemed most peculiar to someone of her class.

Her cordial manner and the warmth of her smile unsettled me. She showed me into a spacious drawing room and requested that I have a seat before the warmth of a granite fire place. Years later I would remember my first meeting with the lovely Florence Kelley with great fondness. With her flowing auburn hair, azure eyes and finely attired womanly frame, she sought to make me comfortable in those strange surroundings.

"Miss Addams and Miss Starr will be with you momentarily. We are all proud of the work that you are doing. May I get you a glass of Sherry?"

"No I am fine, thank you," was my nervous reply.

I recall Jane Addams and her companion, Ellen Gates Starr entering shortly. They were women of wealth and privilege in their early thirties. They had become acquainted while attending college over in Rockford Illinois.

Miss Adams was the shorter of the two, with closely cut brown hair, somber green eyes, a prominent nose and a clef in her chin. What I remember most was the fact that her gait was marred by a pronounced limp, which I would later learn was occasioned by a bout with childhood tuberculosis. Miss Starr was taller, with a slender frame, brown hair, a winning smile and a very refined manner. She spoke first.

"Good evening, Mary, we are so glad that you could take the time to meet with us, with all that you are doing for female workers. You can call me Ellen. It is my pleasure to introduce you to my dear friend, Jane Addams."

"Good evening," Jane Addams said with a shy smile. Her voice was barely audible, as if she was anxious to be in my presence. "Won't you come and join us for dinner. I take it you have already had the pleasure of meeting our sister, Florence," she said, while directing me to an adjacent dining room where Florence Kelley and two servants were waiting.

The notion that these well to do women, only a few years older than me, from a far different class than my own, seemed to care about who I was and what I was doing, was shocking to me. After partaking from a delicious buffet, the four of us became better acquainted.

"You are probably wondering why we invited you here this evening, Ellen Starr began. "We learned of your work on behalf of female workers when we read the recent piece in the paper. I must say the three of us support your efforts wholeheartedly. We were wondering what we could do to help your cause."

"Why would the cause of working women be of interest to women of your___?"

"Station", Jane Addams offered, with an understanding smile.

"Yes," was my curt response, not wanting to be pitied or patronized by them.

"That is exactly why we asked you to drop by Hull House, Mary", she explained. "We are women whose upbringings have been privileged but that does not make us unmindful of the unfairness of the world outside our door. If you would be so kind as to give us the benefit of your experience as a working woman and your insight, perhaps we can lend a hand in the struggle that concerns us all. Our mission is to create a home here at Hull House for people of all classes and nationalities to gather together, in order to teach and learn from one another, so that Chicago and eventually all of America can become a better place to live and to work, for both men and women."

"How old were you, Mary, when you first began working? Florence Kelley asked while seated across from me. Her face and her manner were so warm that I soon became her admirer. She displayed a beauty and a grace of spirit that was unmatched.

"I apprenticed as a dress maker at the age of thirteen, then a bookbinder."

"I'm sure you're aware of children working in the mines and factories of this country as young as seven years of age, she continued. I for one will not rest until this is no longer the case. That is why I've come to Hull House to live and to work. Won't you give us the benefit of your experience, Mary? Won't you come and join us here and together we four can begin to change the way things are for so many."

"I will think it over," was my uncertain response.

On the carriage ride home, I sat alone with my thoughts. It was a cold and windy Chicago night. I can remember looking from that carriage window out into the streets of that impoverished neighborhood, seeing ragged men, women and children hustling about to escape the bitter cold. The alleyways, the dilapidated dwelling houses, and the snow covered fire escapes all painting a chilling picture.

I remember feeling a deep resentment against those wealthy do-gooders, wanting to make me an object of their charity, seeking an insight into my life and that of others who worked for wages. And yet they seemed so sincere, so committed to the cause of equality that try as I might, I could not dismiss them or Hull House from my mind. I decided that I would speak to Mama and get her thoughts on the subject first, and then go to see Ida and ask her what I should do.

By that time, Mama's crippling rheumatism had confined her within the four walls of our tiny apartment. She continued to sew and to knit, whenever able, but those occasions became less and less. When I told her about my meeting at Hull House, she detected my hostility and my suspicion and sought to show me the error of my ways in her always loving manner.

"Remember the words of our Savior, Mary darling." "Judge not lest ye be judged." "Just because they are educated or wealthy does not mean that they are bad people. You should pray for guidance and not close the door to their kindness. Talk to Ida, she will know what to do."

That Sunday evening I visited with Ida and told her about my meeting with the women of Hull House. Her advice, as always, was wise and practical.

"If they want to help, without looking down their nose, you let them. Remember pride can be a fault for rich and poor. You go back without a chip on shoulder, listen and learn."

Following the advice of Mama and Ida would prove a saving grace in my life.

CHAPTER 26

I would return to Hull House again and again over the next weeks and months. All the while remembering to not let my pride or my distrust of the wealthy stand in the way of my mission.

As an organizer, I was required to speak before crowds. I was always fearful of becoming tongue tied while standing before them, stammering or seemingly struck dumb. I suppose it was the fact that I was poorly educated, that caused these fears, particularly in front of those who were better off than me and better educated.

As I mentioned, I became an admirer of Florence Kelley. She was one of the most beautiful women I have ever met and yet she was gentle in manner and kind and caring to all who would make their way to that now famous settlement house. It was she who encouraged me and helped give me confidence before a crowd.

I recall many an evening when we would talk together like devoted sisters. We would sit in the spacious parlor and discuss our hopes and our dreams for the future and the future of America. She would tell me how truly special I was, how courageous and pretty. She advised me to say a little prayer and just let my spirit speak through me, assuring me that if I did, the right words would always come. I can still hear the sound of her voice and see the warmth of her smile.

Gradually, through her encouragement, I began to believe in what she had to say and grew more confident in the company of educated and refined women and men. I suppose it was my admiration for Florence Kelley that drew me closer to Jane Addams.

At first sight, Jane's pronounced limp seemed to diminish her. In coping with this difficulty she would become both uncommonly caring and uncommonly courageous. She lacked an effective speaking voice, and her small stature and plain appearance, almost always attired in a long black dress with a cameo broach fastened to its collar, made her almost unnoticeable in a crowd.

It was only later that I grew to appreciate both her intelligence and her love for others. It was she, more than any other, who made me understand that all of us have shortcomings, all of us have difficulties that we must endure in this life. It was she who made me realize that it was the manner in which we coped and overcame the difficulties of life that made us who we truly were.

At first she offered to provide financial help to print up pamphlets for our union and to help pass them out. After meeting Mama and getting to know me better, she made me a totally unexpected offer.

"Mary, we were wondering whether you and your mother would come and live with us here at Hull House. We have plenty of room and you can use the third floor for your union gatherings. That way you can care for your mother and still do your work."

I remember sitting there speechless with Florence and Ellen Starr looking fondly upon me. My first thought was to decline their offer because of my pride and a refusal to accept any type of hand out or charity. That was when Florence spoke,

"We thought that our offer to you and your mother might pose a problem, knowing how much you prefer to make your own way in this world without the assistance of others. Please understand that you and your mother will be providing Hull House with a great service by living here."

"The women of this neighborhood are in need of women like you and your mother as examples of dignity and courage," Jane added, with a benevolent smile. "You have been forced by circumstance to make your own way. You can ` inspire them, Mary, and you can inspire us while doing so. Help us make Hull House the home that it needs to be? Please Mary, come and live with your mother, here at Hull House. "

Mother and I would take up residence at Hull House during the second week of March in the year 1892. Soon the mission of Hull House began to spread, causing others, both well to do and without, from different occupations, nationalities and social stations to visit and congregate there. By doing so, making it a center for learning and development.

On the second Tuesday of each and every month I held organizational meetings for Ladies Bookbinding Union # 1, while spending my days travelling from shop to shop as a so called "tramp bookbinder" throughout the Chicago area. At each and every location I would make note of the hours being worked and the wages being paid as well as the working conditions under which the young ladies labored.

More often than not, I would find that these were the worst of workplaces, with poor ventilation, unrestricted, unsanitary bathrooms, and confined work areas behind locked doors and windows.

Often I would be required to assume an alias in order to obtain employment at these shops, since the name of Mary Kenney had been blacklisted in Chicago after my notorious run in with the J.M.W. Jones Company the year before.

CHAPTER 27

I should tell you of a particular episode that occurred at the Thayer & Jackson Printing House that has remained with me these many years. I obtained employment there under the alias of Mary Cullen. To my surprise, the working conditions of this shop located at 126 La Salle Avenue were considerably better than most of the others that I visited. The bathrooms were separate and sanitary. There was adequate ventilation. There seemed to be a proper appreciation for the work being done by the twenty three female bookbinders employed there.

As a "tramp bookbinder" I would often spend no more than a couple of weeks at each bindery, all the while observing its day to day operations and getting to know my coworkers. As a finale to my stay, I would leave organizing pamphlets at various locations throughout the bindery, finish up my work and most often send a postcard to the Chicago Board of Health describing the health concerns that needed to be addressed.

Through my contacts at Hull House I had learned the name of a Deputy Health Inspector whom I would address these postcards to, knowing that he was conscientious and would almost always follow up on my complaints with an unscheduled inspection.

At Thayer & Jackson my only complaint was the lack of an afternoon break that I sought to remedy by simply going to the washroom, then sitting in the lunch room for fifteen minutes before returning to my duties.

There was a young foreman by the name of Fremont Jackson who observed me do this without making a fuss. I was advised that he was a nephew of the owners.

He displayed a pleasant disposition to all of the ladies who worked under his supervision without crossing the line by taking liberties with them, as so many others would. After the first week of my employment, he stopped by my workbench and advised that there would be rush orders coming through the following week and could I plan on staying late to get the job done.

I remember him commenting upon the thoroughness of my work and that it was equivalent to that of three others. I remember joking that he should seriously consider paying me three times my wages. A good natured smile accompanied by a jaunty salute was his response. I must admit that he was quite a handsome man. He appeared to be in his early thirties, with a fine head of auburn hair, brown eyes and a robust mustache.

The following week after two hectic ten hour days, we managed to finish the rush orders and send them off for distribution. As I was leaving, he invited me to have dinner with him at O'Hare's Restaurant, within walking distance of the bindery. Up until that point he had always addressed me as Miss Cullen.

It was customary in the bookbinding trade to refrain from using first names between workers and management. At first I was reluctant to accompany him and then I thought to myself, why not. Besides, I was famished. As I recall, it was a lovely April evening and spring was in the air.

Shortly after being seated at a table for two, the waiter, an older gentleman with a distinctive brogue, asked whether he could bring us something from the bar. Before I could respond, my dinner companion spoke with a gentlemanly assurance that caught me off guard.

"Shall we order a bottle of the house wine?"

"I am fine with a cup of tea, no cream or sugar, thank you."

"In that case, I'll have a Scotch and water."

As the waiter departed, he leaned over and whispered, "May I call you, Mary, Miss Cullen? My friends call me, Monty."

"Mary would be fine, Mr. Jackson."

It had been too long since I had been in the company of an attractive young man and I must admit that I was anxious at the prospect of carrying on a meaningful conversation with someone I barely knew. After I received my tea and he, his scotch and water, the conversation turned to my experience in the bookbinding trade.

"You know what I first noticed when you began work at the firm?"

"The quality of my work?"

"I have already complimented you on that. No, that wasn't the first thing I noticed. It was the way in which you hummed while working. There was a joy in it. It no doubt aids in making you such a good bookbinder. How long have you been working in the trade?"

"Since I was a young girl in Hannibal Missouri. I worked for Mr. George at the Hannibal Printing and Binding Company there, and later in Keokuk Iowa. I came to Chicago when their business closed. I have always been partial to reading and the bookbinding trade allows me to spread the joy of reading to others. "

"I am not a big reader, myself. The bookbinding business takes too much of my time. Besides books, what else interests you?"

"Um, I am very fond of baseball and I enjoy good music," I replied, avoiding any mention of my organizing activities, yet feeling uncomfortable at not being truthful with him.

"Is there a man in your life?"

That was when the waiter mercifully arrived with our meals. I took that opportunity to avoid answering what I thought was too personal a question. I noticed that he had nearly finished his drink and asked the waiter for another. I recall examining the prices on the menu and ordering a meal that I knew I could afford with a decent tip for the waiter. I remember being concerned about making my way back to Hull House after dark. I was wondering how to make mention of these concerns when he spoke.

"I really don't make it a habit of socializing with women who work for me. To be honest, my uncles frown upon it. But you're such a good bookbinder and very pretty too. I thought I would make an exception this once. By the way, dinner is my treat and I will escort you home."

"Thank you, that is very decent of you. If you could escort me to the nearest trolley stop, I can make my way home from there."

"Whereabouts do you live?"

"Not far, over on South Halstead."

"That can be a rough area, why don't you allow me to at least pay for a carriage. That way you can relax a little and maybe have a drink with me."

"I'm not partial to alcohol."

"Just one drink wouldn't hurt. Unless you're a member of the temperance union?"

"No, just a lady who prefers not to drink."

"Well I apologize if I have overstepped my boundaries. I just thought we could get to know each other and enjoy ourselves after a couple of long days at work. Enjoy your dinner."

"Thank you," I said, while noticing that he had begun to stare at me, while smoothing his mustache between his thumb and index finger.

We barely spoke during dinner. I remember becoming concerned when he ordered another drink, sensing a change in his mood and manner. After the waiter brought his drink, I recall him making quick work of it and abruptly excusing himself and engaging the waiter in conversation in private, handing him what appeared to be payment and glancing over his shoulder in my direction. The nod of the waiter's head and the slight smile on his face made me strangely uneasy. He returned to the table and advised that he had arranged for a carriage and it would be arriving shortly.

I found it curious after we left the restaurant when he said that the carriage would meet us down the street. As we walked together in that direction, he drew close, suddenly placing his right hand upon my lower back.

"Like I said," he slurred, "my uncles frown on fraternizing with the help. I thought that I would show you a good time and you would appreciate the kindness, but not you. You know how many working girls would jump at the chance to dine with someone like me."

As we came upon an alley entrance to our right, he grabbed my neck and forced me down it. I can still remember the smell of whiskey on his hot breath. I tried to wriggle away from his tightening grip but he was too strong. I recall him groaning,

"How about a kiss? You know you want it, you pretty Irish muck."

"You're hurting me. Let me go," I screamed, managing to escape from his grasp.

He was facing me now and beginning to undo his belt buckle. My heart was pounding as I screamed from the top of my lungs. I recall my hair tumbling down as I removed my hatpin. It had the shine of steel and it was six inches long. I recall pointing it toward his face and hearing myself saying,

"I will drive this into your eye, if you don't let me go."

Fear was in his face at that point. He stumbled backward. I remember brushing by him and running down the street toward a gathering of carriage drivers congregated on a nearby corner. When I told them what had happened they ran into the alleyway and took hold of Fremont Jackson and gave him the beating of his privileged life. On the carriage ride back to Hull House I was afraid and ashamed. It took me weeks before I would mention this episode to anyone.

CHAPTER 28

As I mentioned, survival of the fittest would be the philosophy that most industrial capitalists followed in exploiting wage earners during the so called "gay nineties in America.

Many working men and women, who were pushed to the brink of ruin and starvation by employers, rose up and sought a redress of their hopeless working conditions. Most would do so through peaceful means of strikes and boycotts but some through guns and bombs. In desperate times people are willing to perform desperate acts.

I was an eye witness to these times in our country's history. I must confess that I contemplated the use of violence on more than one desperate occasion, only to recognize that its use was contrary to the teachings of Our Savior. Besides, it was most always contrary to achieving our ends.

Since my aim is to present a truthful history to you all, I will describe episodes where workers rights would be taken away to purposely provoke a violent response, so that those rights could be eliminated altogether. Episodes not often taught in American history classes.

The episode that stands out foremost is the Homestead Strike of 1892. It will introduce you to Henry Clay Frick, Andrew Carnegie, The Pinkerton Detective Agency and The Amalgamated Association of Iron and Steel Workers. It began at the Homestead Steel Mill owned by Carnegie Steel near to Pittsburgh and it would lead to an assassination attempt and the notoriety of Emma Goldman.

It would become a memorable example where union demands played into the hands of industrialists in control of the means of production. It would allow those industrialists to instigate union violence which eventually led to their complete control of the entire industry.

Henry Clay Frick met Andrew Carnegie while on his honeymoon in New York City. That meeting led to a partnership between their two companies and put Frick in charge of Carnegie Steel's operations.

The Amalgamated Association of Iron and Steel Workers known as the AA, was formed in 1876 and became the most powerful craft union west of the Allegheny Mountains. It had succeeded over the years in winning concessions from Carnegie Steel through strikes and contract negotiations.

Concessions that Carnegie and Frick believed prevented increased production and profit for Carnegie Steel. Their plan was to use negotiations for a new agreement to break the AA in June of 1892.

I would like to say a little bit about Andrew Carnegie, an immigrant from Scotland who came to America with next to nothing. Through hard work and native intelligence he built an empire. His public face would however camouflage a ruthless heart.

For those who may want to investigate, the catastrophic Johnstown Flood of 1889 which destroyed an entire Pennsylvania city and killed thousands, was caused in large measure by the failure of a private club of steel industrialists to make needed repairs to an earthen dam up river from the City. An earthen dam meant to create a private lake for the club's fishing excursions.

Membership in the exclusive South Fork Fishing and Hunting Club included Henry Clay Frick, his closest friend and banker, Andrew Mellon, and Andrew Carnegie. After this catastrophe, the club would contribute to the nationwide relief effort organized by Clara Barton to minister to the displaced and bury the drowned. The club would also successfully defend its membership against all of the lawsuits that were brought to compensate the victims of their neglect.

After the Johnstown Flood, the courts were forced to change the law to provide for a strict recovery without the proof of fault in certain extreme cases. It could be said that behind every safety measure there is a martyr. It could also be said that behind every great fortune there is a great crime.

Behind the murderous occurrences of the Homestead Strike was the decision making of Andrew Carnegie and Henry Clay Frick.

The steel industry was doing a booming business in the spring of 1892. The AA in turn sought a wage increase during negotiations for a new agreement with Carnegie Steel beginning on the first of July. Carnegie would direct Frick to seek an across the board wage decrease of 22%, as well as the elimination of hundreds of jobs at the Homestead mill, while he and his wife sailed to Europe on vacation.

Frick advised the AA that he would negotiate for thirty days and if an agreement was not reached by then, Carnegie Steel would no longer negotiate. On June 28 Frick ordered the AA locked out of the mill, and arranged for the arrival of hundreds of replacement workers, protected by the Pinkerton Detective Agency, armed with Winchester rifles.

Over the next two weeks pitched battles would take place around the town of Homestead and sixteen lives would be lost. Under Frick's direction, Governor Pattison would declare martial law, calling in eight thousand members of the Pennsylvania State Militia. The strike and the AA were broken by July 15, 1892. From that time onward, Carnegie Steel would control the entire steel industry.

Before that July of 1892 I really didn't know who the anarchists were or what they wanted. Emma Goldman was one of their leaders. She had immigrated to New York City from Russia. She arrived just before the Haymarket Massacre.

As Lucy Parsons has told us, those were times when workers and those who supported them were being rounded up and imprisoned, sowing the seeds of the anarchist movement. It is my belief that violence only fosters more violence and two wrongs never make a right.

Emma Goldman believed that the actions of Henry Clay Frick during the Homestead Strike had been so awful that his murder would be justified and a victory for the anarchist movement in America. She and her fellow anarchist and companion, Alexander Berkman, decided that he would do the killing and she would spread the word to the country that the revolution had begun.

On July 23, 1892 Berkman broke into Frick's office, armed with a gun and knife. Frick was behind his desk when he saw Berkman enter. Berkman opened fire hitting Frick three times. Despite his wounds, Frick managed to wrestle Berkman to the floor of his office. Berkman then used his knife to stab Frisk in the leg.

At that time Frick's associates came to his assistance and subdued Berkman, who was placed under arrest. Frick would return to work within two weeks while Berkman received 22 years in prison. Emma Goldman was not charged but the plot to assassinate Frick was condemned by unions and anarchists alike throughout the country. After years of vainly preaching revolution, Emma Goldman would be deported back to Russia.

Emma Goldman was a misguided sister of all those seeking equality in America, but a sister nevertheless. The anarchists believed in freedom from all government and societal restraints. They did not preach violence, except in extreme cases, where life and liberty were at stake. They believed that capitalism and religion were hostile to the basic freedoms that human beings needed to fulfill their lives. Like the communists, they were idealists without a proper understanding of America.

Our nation was born under God's law. A law written into its sacred documents and sealed with the fire and the blood of revolution and civil war. In America, all men are supposed to be created equal. In America, its governments, its businesses and its unions are supposed to protect that equality from those whose greed, whose power and whose prominence threaten it. That is the promise of America.

In the America of my lifetime I would make my lot with those who believed in that promise and in the dignity of workers and their yearning to be free and equal, like Mother Jones, Eugene Debs and even Emma Goldman.

We were opposed by those who believed that workers were simply a resource to be exploited by a chosen few who would later become philanthropists. Men who would go on to build concert halls, museums and universities across America in order to wash the blood of workers from their hands, men like Andrew Carnegie, John D. Rockefeller, and Henry Clay Frick.

CHAPTER 29

*I*n July of 1892 there would be a grand celebration sponsored by the Chicago Trade and Labor Assembly which took place at the Central Music Hall. It was an unforgettable event that brought out thousands of labor's supporters. I would attend this gala occasion in the company of my close friends and associates, Betty Morgan and Florence Kelley.

After moving into Hull House with my mother, I was able to conduct organizational meetings for the bookbinders' union in earnest. As a result, our ranks would swell to 450 women and girls over the next three months. That was when Betty Morgan suggested that I expand my efforts to other working women in Chicago, all of whom were under paid and overworked.

Advertisements, paid for by Hull House, were placed in various newspapers and we soon began to attract cloak, garment and carpet workers to the LFLU. Through these efforts I would become the foremost female labor organizer in Chicago. That was when the Trade and Labor Assembly celebration took place.

It was a whirlwind of a day as I recall it. I remember being asked to deliver an address in the afternoon on the subject of organization to a congregation of working women who filled that theatre to capacity. By then speaking in front of a throng of people had become almost second nature to me.

As Florence had suggested, I prepared my remarks the night before and said a prayer before retiring for the night. The next day, I remember simply surrendering myself to the spirit. When the curtain rose, I walked confidently out into the middle of the stage, being greeted by polite applause, and simply soared away.

Ladies and Gentlemen,

"I am a working woman meant to make my way through this world by the sweat of my brow. Alone, I am just a voice crying in the wilderness. Together, in the company of my working sisters, lending their voices and their support to our cause, we can be a force to be reckoned with in America. "

"The objects of our union are to make each individual feel that she is not alone in her daily efforts to make a respectable livelihood. To make her look upon herself as a part of that entire body of workers who acting together are an important element in the commercial interests of the great city of Chicago."

"I have a fourth grade education and I have been poor for my entire life. But poor does not mean that I am powerless, without a voice to speak up when I see ignorance and selfish behavior toward workers. When I see insensitivity and cruelty being used to wield power in America, by those who should know better."

"In my labors as a bookbinder I have seen employers who have cared for their workers and other employers who could care less. I began to understand that in coping with employers who could care less, I must be that someone who will go from shop to shop to observe and record their behavior, meant to deprive my sisters of their dignity, and speak up about it."

"Not as a solitary female, told again and again that I had no meaning, but as the member of a union that spoke in unison. A union committed to the cause of working women. A union that can teach employers that we women have meaning, not just in the homes as wives and mothers, but also in the workplace, as qualified, capable, dependable workers who deserve to be treated as equals."

"This is why we organize. It is our only means of making them see the justice of our cause and making them change their ways of doing business in Chicago and throughout America."

It was as if some sort of an epiphany had occurred by the uproar that shook that theater on that afternoon. I recall looking out across that standing, cheering audience of mostly working women and marveling at the magnitude of their response.

As I was making my way from the rear of that stage, I was congratulated by Betty, and Florence. They were so genuinely moved by what I had said, that they were actually shedding tears. Tears that told me of their love. I knew then that they would be my sisters in spirit for the remainder of their lives. At that moment, I recall coming to the realization that my life had more meaning than I had ever imagined. In the service of working women, I had finally found my salvation.

That evening there was musical entertainment and a dinner held in honor of the Trade and Labor Assembly with some twelve hundred invitees. I remember wearing a dress of red satin that my mother made especially for that festive occasion. Before I left in the company of the always beautiful Florence Kelly and her close friend from Cornell University, Frank Fetter, I bid goodnight to Jane Addams and thanked her once more for all that she had done for Mama and me.

I recall her saying that she and my mother would enjoy a cup of tea and converse about my wonderful speech before going to bed, and that I would have the time of my life that evening. I wondered later whether she had the gift of prophecy, for that was exactly what that evening would become.

I fully expected to see my father's best friend on that occasion, since he had assumed a prominent role as an organizer for the American Federation of Labor under the leadership of Sam Gompers. I would learn later that he and Sam were attending to important business in New York on that day and regrettably could not attend that soiree. I did however run into Brendan Duffy and two acquaintances.

The first man who was introduced to me by Brendan on that evening was a slight, bearded gentleman in his forties with a sickly pallor and kind grey eyes, who spoke with the hint of a German accent.

"Mary, I would like you to meet Judge John Altgeld, formerly of the Cook County Superior Court, and now the Democratic Party's candidate for Governor of Illinois."

"So pleased to make your acquaintance, Miss Kenney ", he said respectfully,

"Very nice to meet you."

Angel from the Dust

The second man to be introduced, looked upon me with just a hint of desire in his riveting blue eyes. He was wearing a wrinkled grey suit and a faded green tie. He appeared to be in his thirties, with a shock of uncombed greying hair.

"Say hello to Attorney Clarence Darrow, he is quite the admirer."

"How do you do, Mary. That was quite the speech you gave this afternoon. It rendered the audience spellbound. I was smitten by it and by you. "

"You're too kind, Mr. Darrow."

"We are in need of your passion for the equal treatment of women,' John Altgeld pressed. "Everyone is talking about your speech. Perhaps, later on, you could give me your insights, so I can help make Chicago a progressive city for us all."

"It would be my privilege," I heard myself saying.

"I sent a telegraph to my father in New York and told him that you're the talk of the town," Brendan offered. "I told him to hurry and enlist you as an organizer for the AF of L."

"It sounds like you're making a name for yourself," Darrow added. "I hope with all this adulation you'll still be able to honor me with a dance."

"We shall see", was my reply to a man who had an unmistakably roving eye. "I hope to see you all of you a little later on. I must attend to my friends."

Just as a violinist began to play within the spacious, green carpeted lobby of that theatre, I saw him standing all by himself, observing the crowd intently.

CHAPTER 30

$\mathcal{J}$ ack O'Sullivan barely noticed me at first, since the reason for his attendance at our assembly was to describe the events of that evening in his weekly labor column in the *Boston Globe.* I would later learn that his focus, when engaged in his profession, was very intense. It was probably this intensity that drew me to him.

I knew that I was the subject of considerable attention and conversation on that occasion, some of it due to my speech and some of it due to the fact that I was a single young woman in a red velvet dress. I, on the other hand, was concentrating upon Jack O'Sullivan's attractive appearance, as well as his lack of attention to my standing purposefully nearby.

I remember wanting to take the bull by the horns and make my introduction, but thought better of it and simply passed him by in search of my companions of that evening.

There was a full orchestra of brass and strings, all dressed in black tie and tails that provided the musical entertainment on that evening. There were two bartenders at either end of a spacious ball room dispensing an assortment of beverages and three silver punch bowls situated on tables in strategic locations, containing a rose colored liquid that I must confess sampling and enjoying immensely.

During the first hour, the musical entertainment created a refined atmosphere for discussions of the plight of workers throughout America. In the company of Florence Kelly and Betty Morgan and their male companions, I was situated at a prominent table where I would converse with an impressive assembly of luminaries of the Chicago Labor Movement. The influence of the punch and my encounters with so many memorable personages made that a night to remember.

Dinner chimes were rung promptly at Seven Thirty and we were directed to another ballroom where hundreds of tables adorned with sky blue table cloths and bouquets of flowers in their center. I recall that there seemed to be waiters and waitresses everywhere to cater to our needs, while serving a three course meal of soup, salad and the most delicious roast beef and mashed potatoes I have ever tasted.

I swear I was inclined to pinch myself to make certain that the entire affair was not a delightful dream from which I would soon awaken. That was when Florence Kelly introduced me to the man whom I had attempted to attract earlier in the evening, Jack O'Sullivan.

He was even more handsome up close with thick ebony hair and a robust mustache along with the most delightful sky blue eyes. He was tall with sinewy long legs and broad shoulders, and his smile and voice were nothing less than magnetic. He had been the subject of considerable curiosity and conversation during the evening, especially from the females in attendance.

"Mary, I would like to introduce you to John O'Sullivan from Boston who is a friend and ally to our cause," Florence said, while gently directing him toward me.

"How do you do," I responded, tendering my hand in his direction.

"Pleased to meet you, Miss Kenney. "Florence has been telling me about your speech and I am so sorry I missed it. I would like to speak to you at some point about the cause of women workers. I am the labor columnist for the Boston Globe and our readers would be very interested in your views and your efforts at organizing them."

"I would like that very much, Mr. O'Sullivan. Has Florence told you? We reside at Hull House. That is where we do most of our organizing. Maybe we can arrange a time when you can attend one of our meetings and see the challenges we face, firsthand."

"I have heard a good deal about Hull House and I would be thrilled to visit you there and witness your organizing skills I can't tell you how important your work is. My mother was a seamstress who recently passed away after years of work for low wages in terrible working conditions. It's my belief that women workers are the most oppressed workers there are. Something must be done to meet their needs and I commend you for your efforts."

I was impressed by the apparent sincerity of his feelings. There was a light that appeared in his eyes when he spoke about matters that brought forth the passion of his soul. That light soon mesmerized me.

I mentioned earlier about the lessons that Mama taught me about men and the desire in their eyes that spoke of a lesser form of passion, a passion that was sensual in nature. I had seen that look of desire in the eyes of many men during my twenty seven years on earth and grew almost to expect it.

That was the difference that so intrigued me about Jack. His was a passion for justice first and foremost. It was this that would make me fall in love with him, a love like no other, a love for the ages. I recall him leaving the table to speak with others as part of his duties for his newspaper and my wishing that he would return shortly.

It was after dinner that the orchestra changed their selections to more popular waltzes and melodies that we knew and could dance to. My father and I would dance together in our house in Hannibal on many an occasion, swinging and swaying with Irish melodies that warmed the heart and made any cares that we shared, drift away.

I remember accommodating Clarence Darrow with a dance, despite my misgivings about his intentions. To my relief he was the perfect gentleman, although an ungainly dancer, who smelled too much of cigar smoke. All the while I was waiting and hoping that Jack O'Sullivan would find his way into my arms.

I was standing near the table where punch was being served, deciding whether I should enjoy just one more glass of that refreshment, when he tenderly touched me upon the shoulder and said in that tender voice of his,

"Would you do me the honor of this dance, Miss Kenney?"

"By all means, please call me Mary. What shall I call you?"

"Call me Jack."

I remember spying Florence Kelly and her companion as they drifted by us. The look of love that Florence displayed toward us, told me that she knew. She knew that after so many years of waiting and wishing, after so many lonely nights wondering whether I would ever find it, I had found true love in the person of a truly wonderful man from Boston.

CHAPTER 31

*J*ack would visit with me at Hull House the very next day, before taking the train back to Boston. We were sitting alone at a table in the rear of the second floor meeting room when he took hold of my hand and looked tenderly into my eyes. My heart was racing.

"Mary, I couldn't wait to be with you once again. Do you feel the same way?"

"I do. "

"Let me tell you about myself," he began "My parents come from Ireland. They met and married in New York before moving to Boston and raising a family. I am the fourth of their five children. I went to the eighth grade and then to work in a shoe factory before joining up with the seaman's union when I turned seventeen."

"Have you been to many far off places? "

"I've traveled all over the world and have had many wild and wonderful times. When my father passed away four years ago I was out to sea. When I returned, I promised my mother that I would stay and look after her. I joined the Car Man's Union and became a trolley driver about three years ago. I just became a member of their bargaining committee. I'm a union man through and through."

"My father was a member of the Knights of Labor."

"How do you like that? My father was a Knight as well. I wonder if they ever met. He must be very proud of you, Mary. I would like very much to meet him."

"Sadly, he has passed as well. I would like you to meet my mother. She lives here with me."

"I would be honored."

"When did you start writing for the Boston Globe?"

"Just last year, I've always liked writing letters and such. I read constantly.

The head of our bargaining committee suggested I apply, after reading some of the proposals I submitted. His uncle is the Editor."

"We have so very much in common."

"Oh Mary, I must tell you how much I want to see you, to be with you.

I have never felt like this about someone I've just met. I've just turned thirty. This is the time when I want to settle down and find a partner to share my life. I know that it may be too soon to tell you of these things, Mary, but I don't care. Will you think of me while I'm in Boston?"

"Oh Jack, I will think of you every day."

That day I would introduce him to Mama and Jane Addams. He would make an indelible impression upon them both. He promised that he would write to me every week and he would find a way for us to be together soon. When he kissed me for the first time, I knew. He would be the man in my life.

Almost like a thunder bolt, the very next day I received a telegraph message from New York. It was from none other than Sam Gompers inviting me to travel to New York City to be interviewed for a position with the American Federation of Labor as its first female organizer.

My life was changing dramatically for the better I believed, and I would embrace that change with all of my heart and soul. I kept remembering the words and the lesson that they taught me. "To those who give all, all is given." Those were words that I would live by for the remainder of my life.

I had heard of Sam Gompers from Betty Morgan. He was born in London before his family immigrated to America and settled in the Lower East Side of New York City. His father was a cigar maker who ran his business from the family apartment.

When Sam was fourteen be became a member of the Cigar Makers' Local Union and rose to become one of the vice presidents of the Cigar Makers International Union. Through his skill in organizing and his passionate speeches, he would seek better wages and working conditions for the members of his union.

He then began to believe that a federation of craft unions, like the cigar makers, the carpenters and the stone masons would have greater power to improve the wages and working conditions of their members through collective bargaining and electing candidates to local and state offices that understood the needs of workers. He was a man for that moment in the history of our country. He would form and lead the AF of L.

It was a sweltering August afternoon when I made my way toward the offices of the American Federation of Labor, located on Delancey Street in New York City. That part of the city was full of tenement housing, overflowing with impoverished men, women and children, seated upon stoops, suspended from fire escapes and congregating upon its sidewalks. Everywhere pushcart peddlers hawked a multitude of wares, while horse drawn wagons made their deliveries and trolley cars ferried passengers back and forth. The activity and raw energy of it all overwhelmed me.

I remember taking a rickety elevator to the third floor which opened its doors into a long, dark, narrow hallway with a small group of what appeared to be working men waiting at the end of it, in front of a wooden door with a smoked glass panel in its middle that read in bold black stenciled lettering,

AMERICAN FEDERATION OF LABOR
SAMUEL GOMPERS, PRESIDENT

As I approached the men stopped and stared. There were the usual remarks that I had grown to ignore as I made my way by them and opened the door. Inside was a hubbub of activity. There was a crowd of male clerks of all shapes and sizes working intently.

They were seated and standing, amid tables, chairs desks and filing cabinets within a spacious office, cluttered with an avalanche of paper and files. When I stepped forward and announced, "Mary Kenney, here to meet with Mr. Gompers. " There was a hush that fell over that entire place.

There I stood like a wilted flower in my pink and white cotton dress with a matching bonnet for what seemed like forever. That was when Peter McGuire, a small man with salt and pepper hair and mustache, came forward and politely introduced himself. He then turned to that speechless crowd of men and boys and said,

"Boys, this here is Mary Kenney, the best labor organizer in Chicago. She has an appointment with the boss. Come forward and introduce yourself, once you stop admiring her, that is. Don't worry, Mary, they won't bite. Mike Duffy told us you would make a great first impression and was he ever right. "

One by one, each of them stepped forward and politely introduced themselves as if I was some sort of royalty. I quickly managed to disarm them by announcing that I was pleased to make their acquaintance and that I hoped they would forgive me if I didn't remember each of their names, since I was quite overwhelmed at that moment.

As I mentioned, Papa had taught me to be comfortable in the company of men. He also taught me that a smile and a humble approach would work wonders when being introduced to others. I tell you I grew to love the energy and the companionship of all those boys and men who worked in that unforgettable place, that would soon become the home of the American Labor Movement.

CHAPTER 32

*I*n August of 1892 Peter McGuire and Sam Gompers were both in their early forties and intent upon building the AF of L into the most powerful association of craft unions the world has ever known.

It was Peter who escorted me down the hallway behind the clerks' office to the office where Sam and Peter conducted the business affairs of their recently formed federation. The door was open and Sam was seated behind a stack of papers and files smoking a cigar, when we entered. He rose politely and smiled warmly. It was apparent that he had been anxiously awaiting my arrival.

He was a small, stocky man with thick black hair and an enormous mustache that spread across his broad, manly face. He had an English accent when I first met him. He would lose that accent later, from speaking before endless crowds of workers at home and abroad. His voice had the resonance of an Irish tenor and he loved to sing Irish melodies, even though he was a proud member of the Jewish faith. He was as tough as nails but as tender as a lamb when you got to know him. Like Jane Addams, he would become another unforgettable influence in my life.

"Boss, this is Mary Kenney," Peter announced.

"Pleased to make your acquaintance, Miss Kenney, our good friend, Mike Duffy, has told us all about you. My understanding is that he has known you since you were a little girl."

122

"Seamus or rather Michael was my father's best friend back in Hannibal Missouri. I would so like to see him once again, is he around?"

"He is up in Buffalo on some business and should arrive in town later tonight," Sam replied. "I am sure that you'll have the opportunity for a get together before your return home. Peter will show you around and escort you to the hotel. That will give you time to freshen up after a long train trip.

We have made reservations for an early dinner. Afterwards, we can discuss how you can play a part in our plans for the future. I will see you then."

Sam and Peter McGuire, a carpenter by trade, had been close friends since childhood. They shared the belief that unionism and political power were the only means by which workers could secure their rightful place in America. They had fought their way up together from the streets of New York's Lower East Side. They would rise to prominence as able stewards to the craft workers of America.

I had heard so much about New York City that I was afraid I was going to be disappointed when I went there. To the contrary, it was a city like no other. Its people, its politics, its vibrant rivers, its spacious avenues and parks, all of it would entrance me.

Following a nap and a refreshing bath in a porcelain tub with silver faucets and hot and cold running water, I waited in the foyer of the Lexington Avenue Hotel for a carriage to arrive and take me to my dinner engagement with Sam Gompers and Peter McGuire.

As I recall the name of the restaurant was Ahearn's and its menu offered a selection of meals that would please even the most demanding of customers. It was a crowded place with ornate grey and green windows and a series of tables adorned in silver and white linen.

The waiters wore black waist coats and trousers with starched white shirts and collars, complemented by red bowties. Peter and Sam were waiting near the door when I arrived. Each of them was attired in a navy blue suit with a white shirt and a tasteful red tie. I had saved my green and gold cotton summer dress with the scalloped collar and grey heeled shoes for that occasion.

Before leaving Chicago I had discussed this meeting with Betty, Jane and Florence. It was an important opportunity for a working woman such as myself and I wanted their advice and approval for any decision or commitment I would make. To say that I was treated with the utmost consideration and respect by my hosts was an understatement. They were two gentleman who seemed to recognize that I could become an important addition to their organization.

"Mary," Sam began, "we've been hearing so many good reports about your organizing skills that Peter and I were wondering whether you would consider working for our Federation. Since you have done so well in Chicago, the plan would be for you to work at increasing our rank and file there first, and then eventually moving on to Boston and New York. "

"You want me to help organize male workers?" I recall asking.

"Yes of course, our organizers lack your energy and your dedication It would be a positive thing to have a woman with your qualities as part of our organization," Peter replied.

"I was under the impression that you wanted me to organize female workers and bring them into your federation. That way I could continue our fight for equal pay for equal work. "

I remember them looking at each other at that point and having the distinct impression that I appeared to be a little bit more that what they were bargaining for.

I was just about to elaborate on my position when a smile made Sam Gompers' broad black mustache turn up on both ends. He seemed to be pondering what a federation of crafts that included working women would mean for the future of the AF of L and appeared to be receptive to that development. It was then that he said these words,

"Mike Duffy has told us you would be something special, Mary. It may take some getting used to, but you appear to be just the type of organizer that we need to bring both working men and working women into our organization. Please think it over and we will as well. We would be honored to have you as our first female organizer."

After speaking at length with Betty Morgan and Florence Kelley and receiving their approval, I telegraphed Sam Gompers and accepted his offer of employment. Betty graciously agreed that I could continue on for the LFLU, organizing female bookbinders, cloak makers, shirt makers and carpet makers at Hull House, unless and until my organizing for the A F of L interfered with those duties.

With the added income, Mama and I were able to move to a spacious two bedroom flat located within walking distance of Hull House. My first assignment for the AF of L was to organize male cloak and shirt makers who were some of the lowest paid workers in Chicago.

There were maybe sixty men who came to hear me speak on that first night. It was the first time that Sam had visited Chicago and he was suitably impressed by the size and the spirit of the city.

I had been in correspondence with Jack O'Sullivan on an almost daily basis since the occasion of our meeting and he agreed that my organizing male workers for the A F of L was a noteworthy and positive development that his readers would find of considerable moment.

He managed to persuade his editor that another trip to the "City of the Big Shoulders" would be a worthwhile one in order to cover the event first hand. I was simply thrilled when his telegraph arrived advising that he would be in attendance with pen in hand.

It was a crisp September evening. It seemed that the stars were aligned to make it a memorable occasion. I recall Jane Addams visiting with me before I began to speak in the company of my mother. Perhaps it was their shared ordeal in coping with a crippling disease that drew them so close together. They were like devoted sisters. Both of them were so very proud and supportive of me on that evening that I soon began to cry.

That was when my father's devoted friend, Michael Duffy, appeared with a bouquet of roses in the company of Sam, wishing me well and telling me that we were all playing a part in a memorable occasion that would begin a new chapter in the history of the American Labor Movement. A new chapter that would be described in eloquent and glowing terms within the pages of the Boston Globe under the byline of Jack O'Sullivan. Here is an excerpt of that report which I recently found in one of my scrap books.

MARY KENNEY, AN ANGEL FROM THE DUST, SPEAKS TO WORKERS.

"They await within the spacious second floor meeting room of Hull House, located in the "Little Italy" section of Chicago. They are men and boys of many nationalities who have come there to hear a young woman tell them why they should become members of a workers' union in the America of 1892."

"Suddenly she appears in a radiant dress of pink, a woman in her twenties. Her golden hair frames a face of strength and beauty. Her bright blue eyes shine forth across this crowd of working men and boys of all shapes and sizes. They sit there in rapt attention, as if under the spell of an angel. An angel who has risen from the dust of the American workplace to deliver her message, seeking to make their lives better. The name of this angel is Mary Kenney. Remember that name and listen to what she had to say."

"America made a promise in the beginning. A promise that was written in our Declaration of Independence and Our Constitution. A promise written with the ink of blood, the blood of those who fought and died in the hellfire of the American Revolution and the American Civil War. A promise that we must make America keep. A promise that brought many of you here to our shores from across a treacherous sea. A promise of a better day of freedom and equality for all Americans, both male and female."

"Since Adam and Eve were banished from the Garden of Eden, man has been required to work, to toil, to make a living for himself and for those he loves. Down through the ages, there have been those who seek to enslave others. There are still those men in the America of today. They are the bosses, the owners, the wealthy and the powerful who believe that their privilege entitles them to make workers their slaves, their mules, to carry their burdens and do their bidding. To such men as these, workers and their families are of no matter."

"That is why I come before you tonight with these truths. Truths that I have learned as a child of the workplace, a daughter to workers, a sister to workers, poor, uneducated and underserving in the eyes of those in control of industry in America. Only through unity will we possess the strength to overcome their power. Only through membership in a union will we obtain dignity within the workplace. Come join in our union. Join in our cause to make America keep its promise to you, your children and your children's children, a promise of freedom and equality for all workers in America."

They stood and cheered and lined up to a man to join the union. There was so much enthusiasm, so much support for my message. I remember thinking that it seemed so much easier to organize and unionize men than it was to organize and unionize women.

This was a lesson I would remember and relate to Sam Gompers, to Mike Duffy and most especially to Jack O'Sullivan. In the years that followed I fully understood that women in America were molded from birth to follow; not to lead. They were raised to become wives and mothers, beholding to their husbands, not leaders.

CHAPTER 33

*J*ust when things were beginning to look up for workers in America, another panic struck in 1893. A panic that would cause the failure of banks and businesses and the unemployment of tens of thousands throughout the country.

In my new position as an organizer for the A F of L, it was a time of challenge and change. It was a time when men like Sam Gompers, Clarence Darrow and John Peter Altgeld rose to power, while women such as Florence Kelley, Leonora O'Reilly and Susan B. Anthony rose to prominence.

In the second floor conference room of Hull House I would lead numerous organizational and strike committee meetings. They would include female bookbinders, garment workers, carpet workers, as well as male and female shirt makers, cloak makers, retail clerks, clothing cutters and last but by no means least, male carriage drivers who were a particular challenge to organize.

I was returning home after a particularly long and hectic day when my carriage driver, an impish man wearing a top hat and a frock coat, inquired whether I could give him and his coworkers a hand in getting a better shake from the carriage owners. The man's name was Jimmy Hogan, known to his friends and many of his customers as "Mouse."

Mouse Hogan had once been a welterweight prize fighter with a hair trigger temper that caused him to put up his dukes at the drop of a hat. He stood just over five feet, with narrow shoulders and a large head. His high pitched voice made his nickname eerily appropriate. With flaming red hair and chin whiskers, he appeared much younger than his forty seven years. He was the devoted father of six children. He would become one of my favorites.

The carriage drivers had never heard or been a part of any type of union or association that could help them get a square deal from the companies that owned the carriages they drove. They were little more than serfs, required to work all kinds of hours in all kinds of weather, oftentimes seven days a week, ten to fifteen hours a day. If they had the misfortune of taking sick or becoming injured in the all too common traffic mishaps that occurred, they would summarily be replaced and their families were left to starve or rely on charity to survive.

Their wages were the worst part of their working conditions, consisting of gratuities, garnered from the good graces and generosity of their passengers. When the panic of '93 hit, gratuities became even harder to come by for Cook County's carriage drivers. Because of their impossible work schedules, the only time Mouse could manage to bring his coworkers to Hull House was on a Sunday night after ten. They appeared a very tired and beaten lot.

It became crystal clear to me a few short minutes after hearing their list of grievances what needed to be done. They needed to come together as a union and petition the carriage owners for a forty hour work week and an hourly wage to augment their gratuities. If the owners refused to listen and bargain to make things better, they had to strike.

I knew full well that my gender and youthful appearance would be an obstacle to their accepting my advice for resolving their difficulties. A lesson I learned early on was that organizers were required to know their audience. The other lesson was that there was more than one way to solve a labor problem. That was where Florence Kelley and Carter Harrison, the Mayor of Chicago, would come to the rescue.

I had watched Mouse closely from the time that we met and understood that he possessed the qualities to be a leader of men. He was physically tough as well as tough minded. More importantly he was committed to every worker getting a fair shake.

From my reading of Lao Tzu, first taught to me as a young girl by my father's best friend, I understood that a leader should be fair minded, humble and above all courageous. That was why I asked Mouse to remain after our first meeting was concluded. I could tell that he was disappointed that I had not been more outspoken on that occasion.

"Well, what did you think?" was how I began our conversation on that night.

"You want the truth?"

"Of course."

"I thought you were going to speak up and tell them what they needed to do. "

"They're not ready to listen to me, but they will listen to you," I replied.

"You're the labor organizer, not me. I'm a carriage driver, "he argued.

"No, Jimmy, you're so much more than that. You're one of them. They listen to you and they follow your lead. You're the one to tell them that they have to organize and if needs be, strike to get a fair shake."

"They are barely making ends meet now. How are they going to strike?"

"You have to tell them that they can live on their knees or die standing up to the owners. The AF of L and Hull House will help with getting their story out to the public. I will see what can be done at City Hall. Next Sunday will be the time for me to speak, after you've spoken to each and every one. That is the way we'll do it Jimmy."

"I'll give it a try, Mary."

The following morning I spoke with Florence and Jane about the carriage drivers and they were appalled at their meager wages and oppressive work hours. It was Florence who suggested that each and every carriage for hire was required to be inspected and licensed by the City. Florence had developed a close working relationship with the Mayor and Jane had been a significant contributor to his reelection. As I mentioned there was more than one way to solve a problem and the politics of Cook County would help us to do just that.

During this conversation it dawned on me that the wealthy patrons of Hull House who were devoted to social reform should put their money where their good intentions were. Not with handouts or charitable giving but contributing to a health and welfare fund for union workers. This could be used to assist the families of injured or sick bread winners and also as a strike fund, when a living wage was not being paid.

It was Ellen Gates Starr, a co-founder of Hull House, who provided our union health and welfare fund with a most generous first donation. This would be followed in short order by other donations from her well to do friends and acquaintances. I recall thinking that an alliance of sorts was being formed in Chicago, between social reformers and workers. An alliance that would allow us to fight the good fight.

I would learn soon afterwards that the newly elected democratic governor, Peter Altgeld, had requested a meeting with Florence Kelly to discuss what could be done about the prevalence of sweat shops in the state of Illinois. It was in the worst of times, during the panic of 1893, when the seeds of the Progressive Movement were sewn.

That following Sunday night I spoke before a meeting hall full of carriage drivers. As he promised Mouse had sought out and spoken with each and every driver in Cook County. With the assistance of a printing press purchased by Hull House, he handed each driver a flier that we had written. It read as follows:

CARRIAGE DRIVERS OF COOK COUNTY
I. Are you working more than eight hours a day?
II. Are you working more than forty hours a week?
III. Are you tired of your families suffering while carriage owners get rich?
IV. Do you believe that workers should be paid a living wage?
V. Will you come to our meeting next Sunday to fight back?

Before our meeting took place Florence and I met with Mayor Harrison in his office at City Hall. It was apparent that this warm, bearded gentleman in his late forties was a friend and supporter of the working man. In fact, he told us that on the night of the Haymarket Massacre he had walked through the crowd of workers who had gathered there, asking them to remain calm and telling the police to not make arrests, unless it was absolutely necessary. What a pity he had left before tragedy struck.

The mayor was a staunch supporter of the eight hour work day and the forty hour work week. When Florence told him about the plight of the carriage drivers, he told her that he would call upon the men who ran the carriage companies and encourage them to listen to the grievances of their drivers or their licenses would come up for an immediate review. It was apparent that Florence possessed a persuasive charm with men. A charm that I would try to emulate in the cause of working men and women from that day forward.

As I stood before that crowd of drivers, I was mindful that a strike fund had been established and that political power was on our side in our dealings with the carriage owners. Mouse had introduced me to them as a champion of workers' rights and a national labor organizer who would show them the way to a better tomorrow. I don't remember what I said but it met with their applause and approval.

Over the next few weeks meetings were arranged where Mouse and a six member bargaining committee presented their proposals to representatives of the owners. The owners' response, no doubt influenced by the mayor's veiled threat, resulted in the establishment of a decent hourly wage and a forty hour work week. There would be no carriage driver strike in Cook County in 1893.

From that day onward I was required to insist when taking a carriage ride in Chicago that my driver accept not only the payment of my fare but a gratuity as well. The appreciation of those carriage drivers warmed my heart. Mouse Hogan would go on to own a fleet of carriages that proudly displayed the label of the United Carriage Drivers Association on each and every one.

CHAPTER 34

There were many notable occurrences that took place during my time with the AF of L. The three that I most remember were when Sam Gompers and Governor Altgeld addressed a desperate crowd of thousands of unemployed workers in Grant Park. The next was when Jane Addams sought to improve the living conditions of working women throughout Chicago and the last was my face to face meeting with the legendary Marshall Field.

During 1893, I would engage in three major strikes involving the clothing cutters, the shoe makers and finally the shirt makers. In addition to negotiating the demands of these workers with their employers, oftentimes late into the night, it was also my responsibility to organize food and clothing deliveries to their families during the day. The hardships suffered by the families of workers on strike would always pierce my heart.

Hearing the cries of hungry children as I climbed the stairs of the dilapidated, filthy tenement buildings where these workers lived, was a commonplace occurrence. I remember that the winter of '93 was a particularly brutal one, where thousands would freeze and starve to death, making our merciful deliveries of food and clothing often lifesaving endeavors.

Jack O'Sullivan, who had become the Labor Editor for the Boston Globe by that time, would work tirelessly through his contacts in the newspaper industry to help publicize the plight of these desperate working men and women. That publicity would hasten the appearance of Sam Gompers at an enormous labor rally in August of that year. That was the occasion that brought together an impressive assembly of most of the leading lights of the social reform and labor movements in America.

We sat together on a platform facing a sea of faces under a blazing sun. A blessed breeze from Lake Michigan gave a degree of relief from the day's tropical temperature. It was the bareheaded and bearded Mayor, Carter Harrison, who ably addressed that standing crowd first, telling one and all that the rampant unemployment of that time was a national disgrace that merited action on the part of Congress to remedy it.

That was the first time in "The Gilded Age" that the mayor of a major American city called upon the federal government to intervene and improve the lives of workers in America by ending unemployment. The approval of the crowd for just this type of bold action was evident from their uproar of applause and hurrahs.

Soon afterwards Sam Gompers was introduced, wearing a straw hat to shield his large head from the sun and a striped grey suit that fit his squat muscular form snugly. His broad black mustache bestowed his diction with a manly flair, while the gestures of his enormous hands were in concert with his tenor voice. He was in rare form on that memorable occasion.

"Why should the wealth of this country be stored in banks run by the idle rich who have once again squandered and speculated their way into this present financial disaster? Why should able bodied workers, seeking a living wage to raise their families be without a place to live, a place to work, and food to eat, while wandering the streets, as the well to do pass by in their fine carriages looking down their noses at them? Why should the controllers of capital and the titans of industry and finance look out on peaceful meetings such as these and call them riots? They do so to cover up their guilt for causing these circumstances to occur."

As that crowd of thousands roared their outrage and their support, I remember fearing that the desperation of those workers and their families might soon reach a boiling point and explode into mindless violence, bringing with it another wave of retaliation and repression. That was when the newly elected Governor Altgeld wearing a white shirt with its sleeves rolled up and a blue frontier tie spoke with just the hint of a German accent.

"My dear friends, these are desperate times in this city, this state, and this country. It seems that certain of our people who have had the good fortune to succeed in business have forgotten the source of that success. That source is the hard work of people like yourselves. It is the worker who matters most of all, for without the worker there is no wealth, there is no prosperity, there is no progress in the America of today."

"There are some of you within the sound of my voice who may be losing the hope of a brighter tomorrow. There are some who may be willing to resort to the brick, the gun or the bomb to prove a point or to settle a score. That is not the way to win the day, my dear friends. "

"The way to win is to organize into unions, and peacefully petition the owners and managers in control of production that your cause is just and your demands are righteous. The way to win is to wield your power in the market place through lawful strikes and boycotts and at the ballot box by electing representatives who speak and work in your best interests."

"Here today on this very stage are those who will represent your interests, defend and protect those interests, whether on a factory floor or in the halls of government. The way to win is for us to stick together and work tirelessly to bring about a brighter tomorrow. That is the way we will win in America. That is the American way. "

It was not long after his speech that the Governor, with the able assistance of Clarence Darrow, showed the world a courageous concern for justice. After a complete review of the transcripts of the Haymarket trials he determined that a miscarriage of justice had occurred and granted clemency to all those who had been falsely convicted.

It was on that occasion that I was first introduced to Susan B. Anthony, a cantankerous, plain Quaker woman in her seventies with greying hair arranged in a bun, wearing a long black dress in that infernal heat. She had traveled to Chicago to speak at the Columbian Exposition on behalf of women's suffrage. She confronted me while I was descending the stairs of the platform in the company of Florence Kelley. She could hardly hold back her rage as she approached me.

"I suppose you're proud of what you've been doing. I've been reading about you and all your organizing."

"I'm sorry," I replied, attempting to be cordial, "have we been
introduced?"

"I am Susan Anthony and I know who you are. You should be
ashamed. Luring ingrate workers into unions to bite the hand that
feeds them."

"Arranging for strikes and boycotts against commerce, when there
is a panic endangering the country. You and your unions should be
thrown in jail and they should throw away the key."

I suppose it was her passion and conviction that made her a prominent
voice in the movement to abolish slavery years before, and caused her to
become the prime spokeswoman for women's suffrage at that time. That
same passion and conviction was now directed squarely at me and to the
cause I would devote my life.

I remember Florence attempting to intervene between us, but I would
have none of it. I had heard of Susan B. Anthony alright, and actually
agreed wholeheartedly with her pursuit of female suffrage, but I had also
read of her anti-union sentiments and her fervent belief that strikes and
boycotts against employers were nothing less than criminal behavior, mer-
iting a lengthy imprisonment. It was neither the time nor the place for a
battle, but I was never one to back down from an attack.

"Maybe you would change your tune, Madame, if you saw the starving children of workers when visiting the hovels where they live.
I am not one bit ashamed of what I do for a living. I too believe
that women are denied their lawful rights in America. My fight is
for the right of equal pay for equal work. Your fight is for the vote.
Rather than fighting with each other, we should be joining forces
to make America the land it should be for everyone. "

I remember turning my back upon her at that point and walking away
with the distinct belief that I had succeeded in having the final word. A word
that would make her think twice about the plight of workers in America.
It was the irony of ironies when later that month she and I were the featured speakers at a meeting of the World Confederation of Representative
Women during the Columbian Exposition.

We were to speak to an enormous crowd of women from all over the
world and the rotund, bearded janitor of that lecture hall had refused to

open the doors and windows in the sweltering heat, for some unknown reason. Maybe he took offense at all of those females being told about their rights.

In any event, Susan Anthony agreed to my proposal that we would simply refuse to continue, unless all of the windows and doors were immediately opened to the cool of the night air. Word was promptly sent to that obstinate janitor who had no choice but to comply; much to the vocal delight of that gathering. At that point, I remember looking straight into those steel grey eyes of my former accuser and crowing, "Congratulations on your first successful strike, Madame."

I have told you of my love and admiration for Jane Addams and the lifesaving benefits she conferred upon my mother and me in allowing us to live at Hull House. I remember when Jane announced that Hull House had recently purchased two vacant buildings on Ewing Street and they were to become future rooming houses for single working women in Chicago.

To my delight she asked me to be in charge of making these new tenants feel at home when they moved in. That was the beginning of what would later become known as The Jane Clubs of Chicago.

We were a congregation of working women whose love and understanding for each other, and whose dedication to hard work and equality would become an inspiration to women throughout America. Within those safe, and spotlessly clean rooming houses, hundreds of young ladies were protected and nurtured to succeed in a Chicago that would otherwise have been a hostile environment for them all.

As I told you I had organized three major strikes that year. I remember the cloak makers and the shirt makers most of all, for very different reasons. The male cloak makers went out first and it was a long drawn out battle over wages and working conditions, mainly because the female cloak finishers had refused to strike and were swiftly transformed by that decision into scabs who did the jobs of the men out on strike.

This was a terrible circumstance that played right into the hands of the worst of the anti-union forces, wanting to drive a wedge between male and female workers in America. Divide and conquer has always been the way that tyrants rule. There was only one factory where the men had not gone out and that was Remington's. I applied for a job as a cloak finisher there under the alias of Mary Dolan.

I recall working in the basement of that stifling, filthy place learning that trade on the fly. It was during my lunch break when I noticed an older cloak maker looking at me with a paternal smile.

I took the chance and made his acquaintance right there and then. His name was Joe Bojarski and he had been making cloaks since the age of twelve. He was a small muscular gentleman in his fifties with a bald head and a thick Polish accent. I got right to the point, since I didn't want to spend any more time than was needed working in that dungeon of a place.

"I'm told that all the other cloak makers in Chicago are out on strike.

Does Remington's pay so much better than those other shops?"

"Hah,' that's joke you make, right? We don't strike since the women will take over our jobs and strike will fail."

"Did anybody talk to the female steward to see what she thought?"

"Why do you think all the women are in the basement? We see each other maybe once during the day. There is not enough time."

"Let me see what I can do, Joe. Don't tell anybody."

The female steward's name, it turned out, was Nannie Clougherty and she was receptive to meeting with me and Joe at Hull House later that week. It was my thought that we could beat the bosses at their own game and give them a dose of their own medicine, if we played our cards right.

It was resolved that the men of Remington's would strike the following Monday and at that point all of the female finishers would demand a raise to that of what the men were receiving, which was twice what they were making. When the managers refused and called us "ungrateful shrews" among other names, that was when all the female finishers proceeded to pack up and walk out, right there and then. Within two and a half weeks the strike of the cloak makers of Chicago was settled and both males and females in the trade returned to work with an across the board raise in pay.

As to the strike of the shirt makers, the biggest factory in Chicago at that time was Marshall Field. When the shirt makers struck for a sizeable raise from the $4.85 a week being paid, Field not only refused to meet with our union but ordered an immediate lock out, telling the newspapers that the shirt makers should be grateful they were employed during those troubled times. I remember examining a photograph of Field in the Tribune and observing the distinct light of kindness in those pleasant features of his.

I always tried never to speak out against an employer in public without first giving him a chance. The face staring back at me from that newspaper seemed to tell me that here was a gentleman who might listen to reason, if I could only have a face to face meeting with him. As I mentioned, there was more than one way to achieve a successful result if you took the time to think it through.

I decided that I would go to The Home for Working Women down on Michigan Avenue and speak to its manager, Katie Holmes, to see if Marshall Field had donated money for it. It turned out that he had been quite generous the year before but had not as yet made a donation for 1893. I asked Katie if I could take a subscription book to Marshall Field directly and help two worthy causes in the bargain. She said yes and I was off to the races.

I can remember my trolley ride on that beautiful September morning across town to Franklin Street, between Quincy and Adams and stepping up on to the sidewalk to take a gander at that seven story architectural marvel created by the legendary H.H. Richardson, known to history as the Marshall Field Wholesale Store.

Upon entering I boarded a crowded gold and glass elevator to the sixth floor, where the executive offices of the company were located. I entered suite 606 and was immediately greeted by an attractive young woman from behind an enormous desk. After advising her that I was from the subscription section of the Home for Working Women there to see Mr. Field, I was ushered into the office of the wealthiest man in America.

When he came through the door, I thought he was the handsomest older man I would ever meet, tall and dignified in stature with a magnificent head of snow white hair and a broad mustache to match. What I recall most was how incredibly clean he appeared. It was as if he had spent a week being soaked and scrubbed in a Turkish bath. His skin was flawless and without a single wrinkle even though he was a man in his sixties. His teeth were straight and as white as the finest pearls. He was wearing a perfectly tailored three piece grey wool suit and a radiant white shirt with an elegant cranberry colored tie and matching lapel handkerchief.

His smile beguiled me at once, with a manner that was refined but not one bit stand offish. I was completely captivated and fought to retain my senses and return to the business at hand. Even though he had the appearance of an aristocrat, I had discovered that he hailed from western

Massachusetts and had made his fortune at a young age in the cut throat competition of the dry goods trade.

"Good morning, Mr. Field, thank you so much for taking the time to meet with me. My name is Mary and I am working with the subscription service at the Home for Working Women. We are hopeful that you can match your very generous donation of last year."

"Would you kindly refresh my memory as to what we gave in '92, young lady?"

"Our records show a two hundred dollar amount."

"Well the times are uncertain, as you probably know. America is in a fix right now. Nonetheless, I would not want to disappoint a confident and lovely young lady such as yourself. Put us down for three hundred this year. That should put you in good stead with your superiors."

"Oh, how wonderful, the Home will be so very pleased. You know I was speaking to a very nice young gentleman just last evening about the fix that the country is in. He is a shirt maker by trade and he is out of work from your factory. He told me that his weekly wage of four dollars and eighty five cents was barely enough to put a roof over his head and to buy food, The poor young gentleman wants to marry one day, but doesn't know how he could ever do so on the wages paid to shirt makers. "

"What's that you say?"

"You know what else he told me? That the foreman in your factory charges him twenty cents a week for the ice that he puts in the glasses of warm water he gets from your faucets. He says he needs that ice to prevent heat stroke while working in those stifling conditions in such close quarters."

"What is the name of this young gentleman?"

"Oh, Mr. Fields, I don't want to get him in any trouble. He also told me that the same foreman refuses to wash the factory floor unless he is paid one dollar per shift by the shirt makers working that shift. What with all the soot and the dust, he says they can barely breathe unless that floor is washed regularly. So they pass the hat to pay him off. He says none of the men want to take sick or contract tuberculosis from being forced to work under such conditions."

"This is the first I've heard of all this," Field protested.

"You know that is exactly what I told him. I said if Mr. Field knew about all of this I am certain he would not tolerate it."

"Young lady, you tell your friend Mr. Field will look into this."

Within two weeks of our meeting, representatives of Marshall Field reached out to the bargaining committee of the shirt makers local and negotiations soon began. Within what seemed to be a matter of days, a new contract was agreed upon and the strike of the Chicago shirt makers was ended. Although Marshall Field would never become an ally, it was good to see, at least in that one instance, that the man at the top was willing to right the wrongs being done to workers, once he realized what they were.

It was not long after that when I would learn that Marshall Field had become wise to my ruse in coming to his office. I was making my way toward Hull House one day when an elegant carriage pulled alongside me and the distinguished and impeccably dressed Mr. Field suddenly alighted in front of me. As I passed, he deliberately doffed his Homberg hat and held it high above his head, exhibiting a broad smile from beneath his snow white mustache.

"Wishing you a blessed day, and congratulations, Miss Kenney," were the words he spoke in a very cordial tone of voice."

"Likewise Mr. Field," was my reply.

As I mentioned, there was more than one way to achieve successful results if you took the time to think them through.

CHAPTER 35

he Chicago World's Fair was a coming out party for the City, celebrating the 400ᵗʰ anniversary of the voyage of Christopher Columbus and his discovery of America. It was one of the most spectacular occurrences that I would ever witness and the setting of an unforgettable weekend interlude with Jack O'Sullivan.

Its architecture, its landscaping and the inventors, artists and musicians drawn to it from all over the world would put Chicago on the map of great cities. It would also put America in the forefront of great nations, where science and art could combine as never before to create a new age.

There were more than two hundred buildings constructed for the exposition. Fourteen of these were of a grandiose scale that bordered a lagoon and a reflecting pool.

These would become known as the White City for their alabaster painted cement exteriors. The grounds were designed by Frederick Law Olmstead, the first of America's landscape architects, who would go on to design many of the public parks across the country, including those in New York, Saint Louis and Boston.

It was Olmstead's vision that cities should contain public parks that would provide a refuge of beauty and serenity amid all the hustle and bustle. Years later I would take the grand children to the Public Gardens in Boston, one of his many creations, to have a ride upon the swan boats that meandered through its picturesque little lagoon.

Electricity was on display throughout the Exposition. I have always had a fascination with this mystical force of nature that was just beginning to turn the darkness of night into the freedom and opportunity brought about by electric light. I actually had the good fortune to be introduced to one Nickola Tesla on that occasion and to witness firsthand his amazing discovery and usage of electricity's alternating current.

The exposition was spread over an expanse of some six hundred and thirty acres in the Jackson Park section of the city. Some 46 countries had contributed exhibitions to the majesty of it all. I remember spending three wondrous evenings strolling throughout its fair grounds and amusements, arm and arm with my handsome Labor Editor, who had come to spend that October weekend in my company.

On a lovely Saturday night we were seated outside the most magnificent structure within the White City, known as the Liberal Arts Building, admiring its architecture, when we heard a piano being played in the distance. I remember us crossing over the midway and seeing a nattily attired black pianist on an outdoor stage in the distance, accompanied by three nattily attired bandmates.

It was none other than Scott Joplin from Texarkana Texas and his trio was performing *The Maple Leaf Rag* to the joyous delight of an enthusiastic audience. That was the very first time I heard Ragtime music being played. It would be the beginning of my lifelong affection for the music of America, now known to the world as Jazz.

The date was October 21, 1893. The location was within car 16, perched at the very top of a gargantuan Ferris wheel, revealing a breathtaking view of Chicago. It was the most popular attraction of the entire world's fair. That was where the dashing Jack O'Sullivan, stylishly dressed in a green and grey sweater over a sky blue shirt and brown trousers looked into my eyes and asked me to marry him. I recall saying yes again and again as my heart fluttered within my breast.

An impassioned kiss, that curled my toes, soon followed, bestowing pure bliss upon me. A bliss that I had never felt before. We would break the news to Mama and the residents of Hull House the following afternoon, much to the genuine delight of all. A wedding date of October 10, 1894 would be announced within the nuptials section of The Boston Globe and The Chicago Tribune. It would prove to be a marriage made in heaven.

Following our announced engagement, Jack surprised me with two tickets to Buffalo Bill's Wild West Show which was taking place in an arena within walking distance of the White City. I first read about this mythic figure in American lore in the dime novels of Ned Buntline. Bill Cody was a Pony Express rider, a Union scout during the Civil War, and an Army scout during the Indian Wars.

He had received the Medal of Honor and was a dear friend to Wild Bill Hickok and Sitting Bull, the great chief of the Sioux nation. I remember reading about his beliefs that the Indian Wars were caused by the broken promises of the government and that women were entitled to equal pay if they did the same work as men.

These beliefs were probably why Jack bought the tickets in the first place, making the event the frosting on the cake of our engagement. I would venture to say that anybody who saw Buffalo Bill and his legendary Wild West Show will never forget the parade of horsemen from all over the world that began it and the hair raising Indian attack on the wagon train that was its grand finale.

Sadly, those wonderful events would soon be followed by a most tragic one. Carter Harrison was serving his fifth term as Chicago's mayor and had always enjoyed great popular support for his compassionate administration of the City. He was wildly popular among working men in particular who voted for him in droves in all the wards. His genuine concern for the City's carriage drivers was a perfect example.

When it was announced that he had been assassinated in his home by a mad man who believed he had been misused, just before the end of the Columbian Exposition, the entire city was thrown into the darkness of grief. What would prove most astonishing to me was that the mayor's close friend and political associate, Clarence Darrow, would attempt to save his murderer from the gallows by asserting that he was insane and not responsible for his mad act. In that instance, Darrow would suffer a defeat. Years later he would manage to save two wealthy Chicago murderers, named Leopold and Loeb, from being executed with a masterful summation lasting nearly two days.

I should tell you at this time of our efforts to legislate the ending of child labor in Illinois during that unforgettable year. Once again the dauntless energy of Florence Kelley would be in the forefront of this worthy cause. In those efforts she would receive the enlightened assistance of the Governor.

Because of our close relationship and our common concern for workers, Florence enlisted me to travel with her out to Springfield on many the occasion to lobby the legislature around the clock.

She made no bones about the method in her madness, telling me to select my most attractive outfits for these efforts. After all, I can hear her saying, "with brains, good looks and a peck of courage, we will surely succeed."

It was a truly astounding instance of political organization. The residents of Hull House and the members of the newly formed Jane Clubs fanned out across the state obtaining endorsements for this legislation from every social and civic organization. They also enlisted the support from the president and secretary of each and every union.

These endorsements were printed on the Hull House printing press and sent to each and every senator and representative, urging their vote. Never had the Illinois legislature witnessed such an overwhelming demonstration of political will, so expertly organized by the lovely Florence.

I remember a particular instance when she and I encountered one of our most vocal and determined adversaries in the corridor outside the senate chamber. It was just before the pivotal vote would be taken in the wee hours of the morning. His name was Augustus Warner and he made no bones about doing the bidding of big business within the state.

I recall Florence giving me the heads up as he walked toward us. His rotund figure seemed to be testing the stitching of his striped grey suit, while his irritated expression and perspiring countenance signaled his concern that we were about to make history.

"Senator Warner won't you consider a vote on behalf of Senate Bill 603,?" Florence asked, while tendering our listing of supporters to him as he passed. At that point, in a fit of exasperation he paused, addressing us both,

"You young ladies have certainly been making a nuisance of yourselves. I will never vote for this bill. I went to work at the age of seven, making strawberry baskets. As you can see, hard work never hurt me. I'm the youngest senator in this legislature."

Before Florence could register a reply to his response, my contempt for his self-importance caused me to utter,

"Senator, that's probably what is addling your mind right now."

To my utmost satisfaction and that of all of those who worked tirelessly on its behalf, Senate Bill 603 was passed by an overwhelming majority of the Illinois Senate. It was placed upon the Governor's desk for his signature, just before Christmas of 1893.

The following February I received the news that the Governor had appointed Florence, as the State's first female Labor Commissioner. I in turn was appointed one of her ten labor inspectors, whose duties were to enforce the new law and help assure that the evils that I had witnessed and endured during my own childhood would be prohibited within the land of Lincoln.

CHAPTER 36

I would travel to New York and Boston during the early part of 1894 to organize working men and women on behalf of the A F L. During those sojourns I would meet victim after victim of the economic turmoil that was plaguing our country. Almost daily, I would hear tell of fathers being thrown out of work, while mothers and children were being forced by poverty and starvation to do whatever they could to survive.

In stark contrast, bankers like J.P Morgan and industrialists like Rockefeller, Schwab, Edison and Carnegie would be securing new avenues for the electrical, steel, rail, oil and coal industries to consolidate and grow in stature and influence. A stature and influence never contemplated by the likes of our Founding Fathers.

While I was working to organize workers, Jack was doing all in his power to do the same and to publish articles about their plight in the pages of the Globe. Very often we felt like voices crying in the wilderness. A wilderness where workers and their families were of little consequence, except to those whose minds were focused upon a more equal division of the fruits of their labor.

Four months before our scheduled marriage and our much anticipated honeymoon in the village of Niagara Falls, the Pullman Strike would commence, causing us to postpone that joyous occasion and lend our support to the unskilled railway workers of the newly formed American Railway Union.

During that episode we would once again become the allies of some old acquaintances, namely Eugene V. Debs, Clarence Darrow and Governor Altgeld. During the Pullman Strike those three would unite to defy President Cleveland and by doing so step to the forefront as defenders of the most disadvantaged of American workers

Pullman Illinois was a town located on the South Side of Chicago, created and controlled by George Pullman, the president and owner of the Pullman Palace Car Company. That was where workers employed by the company and their families lived. It was a company town in every way. Its residents paid company rents for company housing and purchased their food and clothing at company owned stores with company issued script.

When the Panic of 1893 decreased the demand for Pullman manufactured trains, George Pullman ordered workers' wages reduced by nearly thirty percent. His edict was not accompanied by a reduction in company rents and fell most heavily upon the unskilled, mostly immigrant members of the American Railway Union.

My life has taught me that hard times are all the harder on those who are without. Such has been the nature of economic downturns in America then and now. Shortly after notice of the wage reduction was issued, Jack and I would attend a contentious Union Convention at the Columbia Theater.

A suitable response to Pullman's edict became the foremost subject on the convention's agenda. I was there as a representative of the AF of L and Jack was there to report that memorable evening's events in the pages of his paper.

It would soon become apparent to us, who knew labor history well, that competing interests between skilled and unskilled workers would be used by Pullman to divide and conquer. Competing interests based upon levels of skill, gender or even where workers were born, would continue to be available means of winning labor disputes by those in power.

I remember being introduced once again to Gene Debs. It had been near to six years since our first encounter at that very same location on that eventful evening when Mother Jones spoke. His appearance had changed remarkably since then. He had lost most of his hair and a good deal of weight. He was now a gaunt and lanky man in his forties who oftentimes exhibited the demeanor of an eccentric college professor.

He was there as the leader of the mostly immigrant membership of the newly formed American Railway Union. The word we received was that the drastic reduction in wages ordered by Pullman would leave that lowest paid rank and file in desperate straits making a desperate response inevitable.

Jack and I were seated in the front row of the first balcony along with various leaders of the craft unions, as we heard speaker after speaker address the crowd that filled the theater to its rafters. The sweltering heat and the outright hostility of those in attendance was near to overwhelming.

That was when Clarence Darrow took center stage, with his signature shock of grey hair, notifying one and all that the recent actions of George Pullman had caused him to resign his position as legal counsel to the Railroad interests. He would take up the cause of railroad workers from that day onward, he promised. His change in allegiance was met with a lukewarm response.

Then suddenly, he seemed to rise to the occasion with a fiery recitation of the trail of abuses visited upon workers in America by the so called "Robber Barons", from the Johnstown Flood, to the Haymarket Massacre to the Homestead Strike.

With riveting eloquence he soared, urging us all to close ranks and unite in the cause of worker equality. He then introduced Gene Debs as the champion of the unskilled railway workers of America and the leader of the American Railway Union. Debs, was direct and to the point when he spoke,

"I have met with the membership of the ARU and we are in agreement as to the course we must take in response to the Company's decision to reduce wages. On this date, we shall go out on strike and we ask all of you to join us and to boycott all trains with Pullman cars."

I recall sitting there stunned, along with Jack, while watching as the leaders of the skilled railway workers stood up and angrily filed past us in protest. They were furious with the course of action called for by Debs and his ARU. As a crescendo of opposition fell upon him and Darrow on the stage below us, both Jack and I could read the tea leaves and see the handwriting on the wall.

The Unions representing skilled, mostly American workers, would oppose both the strike and the boycott and thereby set the stage for its bloody defeat. When push came to shove, my AF of L, as well as all the other craft unions of America, failed to close ranks with their fellow workers during the Pullman Strike. They made the choice not to bite the hands that fed them, even when those hands became bloody.

Within a week, thousands of unskilled workers from nearly thirty different railroads, west of Detroit, would walk off their jobs and refuse to handle trains that contained Pullman cars.

In response, the railroads began hiring replacement workers and strikebreakers to evict striking workers from railroad company towns. Murder, mayhem and arson were the fruits of that response. Nearly a quarter of a million workers would join in that doomed strike and boycott.

The Railroad Interests would soon persuade President Cleveland to seek an injunction against Debs and the ARU to end the strike, on the basis that the delivery of the mail was being hampered. Cleveland would eventually call in the army to restore order and to break the strike.

Governor Altgeld on the other hand, vigorously defended the ARU by opposing the army being sent to Illinois. Darrow would be called upon to defend Debs on charges of contempt for refusing to abide by the injunction and end the strike. Debs would be sent to an Illinois penitentiary for his activity during the Pullman Strike, serving six months. After his release, he would continue to speak out for working men and women in America and for freedom with repeated, unsuccessful campaigns for the Presidency.

After breaking the strike and abolishing the ARU, President Cleveland would seek to soothe his conscience and repair burned bridges with a certain segment of his fellow Democrats, by making Labor Day a national holiday. The Pullman Strike was one more tragic instance where big business and governmental power would join together in denying workers an even shake in America.

CHAPTER 37

BOSTON

The winds of change would soon transform my life after my thirtieth birthday and my engagement to Jack O'Sullivan, causing me to take up residence in the City of Boston, a city I grew to love like no other before it. I suppose the opportunity to change the circumstances of my life was a blessing, bestowed upon but a few women of my heritage and my class during that age, and one for which I was eternally grateful.

It all began with my beloved Jack and his resolve to become both a family man and a labor leader. His courage and his confidence were only surpassed by the warmth of his disposition. He had seen much and done more before we met and our love for each other was something to behold and to describe in some significant detail in this, my life's story.

It was his devotion to me and my mother, along with his insistence that the three of us live under the same roof in his beloved Boston that would lay the foundation for my future as a wife, a mother and an advocate for the cause of working women. Our first residence would be a third floor walkup on Saint Botolph Street, a working class section of Boston.

It bordered the Back Bay, where the well to do Brahmins resided and hobnobbed. On any given Sunday you could observe them in formal attire and the latest Paris fashions boarding and alighting from carriages on Marlborough and Beacon Streets or taking Sunday strolls among the brownstone mansions on Commonwealth Avenue.

One of these Brahmins was Miss Hannah Parker Kimball, a woman I first met in Chicago when she came to Hull House to learn about my organizing efforts. We would meet later in Boston at the Denison House.

She was blonde, pretty, petite and stylish, often wearing an impressive orchid colored hat with a swooping goose feather above a fashionable jacket and skirt. The warmth of her smile and disposition was endearing. She was refreshingly sincere and unusually sympathetic to the workers cause.

After describing my occupation to her and the dire need for working women to organize, her inquiry was right to the point, in light of the success of her family's manufacturing business.

"Do you think my father got his money honestly?"

"Miss Kimball, employers daily and yearly get all the labor possible from humanity, just as they get it from their machinery. Yet when the machinery breaks down they take care of it. May I ask you, do you think your father takes care of his workers as well as his machines?"

"There is much justice and right to your question," she replied. "I take it that your answer to my question is no and that is why you organize."

"Yes," I answered.

Sam Gompers and the boys and men who worked at his offices were extremely disappointed when I advised them of my intention to resign, advising him that my engagement to Jack and a desire to start a new chapter in my life in Boston required my leaving. He had become aware of my disappointment in his decision to not support the ARU during the Pullman Strike but chose not to ask me whether it played a part in my decision making. In truth, it was a major reason behind my resignation.

Before a tearful farewell, where I received three rousing cheers, Sam asked me if I could complete a last assignment for his AF of L. That was to help organize as many working women in the Boston area as I was able into trade unions. In gratitude for all he had done for me, I agreed. My efforts would bear fruit and be some of my proudest achievements.

Like Chicago, Boston had a large immigrant population with a history of opposition to the privileged and the powerful of their homelands. It would soon become a fertile field for the seeds of trade unionism. Besides, its heritage as the birthplace of the American Revolution ran deep within the hearts and minds of many of its wealthiest citizens, causing them to be sympathetic to the downtrodden and to support the reform of government and commerce.

My organizing efforts there would bring me into contact with many others seeking to improve the lives of their fellow human beings, both in and out of the workplace. Many of them were residents and visitors to that hothouse of the reform movement known as the Denison House, a three story wood framed rooming and meeting house for women, located at 93 Tyler Street in Boston's South End.

I first visited the Denison House in the spring of 1894. It had been founded two years earlier and it was sponsored by the College Settlement Association, a group of recent graduates from women's colleges like Smith, Radcliffe, Bryn Mawr and Wellesley. It was modeled after Hull House and its first proprietor was Vida Scudder.

Like my mentor, Jane Addams, Vida was a woman determined to make a difference in her lifetime. Like Jane she was small and unassuming in appearance but powerful in her impact upon the lives of others. She would become a lifelong friend and a loyal ally during some of the most difficult times of my life.

She, and Hannah Kimball would be present at my very first organizational meetings held at the Denison House. There they witnessed firsthand the plight of women workers in their native city.

The first shops I went to were the binderies. I always tried to organize in the trade I knew best. I would, as I had done so many times before, secure a position at the lowest level of bindery work, for it was there that I could observe the disregard of the bindery owners in a most particular detail.

It was as if the entire industry had never heard tell of worker safety and sanitary working conditions. It was my practice to work for a period of time at a bindery without uttering a word of protest, while diligently cataloguing the dangers and abuses that occurred there on a daily basis.

Just as before there was the locking of doors and the herding of workers into confined areas with little ventilation. There were ten hour work days with breaks of ten minutes in the morning, a half hour for lunch and another ten minutes respite before the last hour of the day. The forewomen were cold and disinterested in the welfare of their workers, oftentimes ruthlessly demeaning them for minor infractions, like leaning against walls and asking for bathroom breaks beyond those allotted.

What was more is that there was a disposition on their part against Catholic workers that I had not witnessed either in Missouri or Illinois. It was at the Kenmore Printing Company, which employed sixty three women and girls, where I was forced to emerge from my role as a passive witness to that of the passionate advocate.

It arose when a saintly young Irish girl named Nora Connelly, with the most beautiful red hair and alabaster skin, was saying the rosary during her lunch break. The foreman, a Mister Dobbs as I recall, observed her doing this and advised the forelady to monitor her work more closely, inviting her to find fault and impose a discipline upon her. I was both in the lunch room and working across from her when I witnessed those very deliberate acts of abuse. I remember seeing that grey haired shrew approach Nora minutes after her return to the bindery.

"Nora Connelly."

"Yes, mam."

"There's been a report about you slacking and taking liberties at lunch. You're going to be watched from now on. If another report is received, you'll be let go. "

"Excuse me, Madame," I cried. "She is a very capable binder and you're picking on her for being a Catholic. You should be ashamed of yourself."

"What is your name, she sputtered, shocked by my outburst. "

"Mary Kenney and I am a national organizer for the AF of L. "

"I'm going to take this up with Mr. Dobbs right away," she threatened.

"You go right ahead. I'll be waiting right here to give him a piece of my mind about the working conditions in this God forsaken place. I think a visit from the Board of Health is in order."

Soon afterward an indignant and perspiring Dobbs came with two other men to escort me from the bindery. Before leaving, I told all within earshot that they did not have to put up with the working conditions of that bindery and they should come to an organizational meeting at the Denison House on the following Saturday night.

That was the meeting that Vida and Hannah would attend. When we saw the women and girls who came there on that evening, we were all moved to tears by their sorry state. When I invited each of those workers to speak up about their lives and the abuses that they endured, you could have heard a pin drop.

At that time my Jack was a delegate of the Boston Central Labor Union. Even before our marriage he had become a favorite of the women who lived and congregated at the Denison House.

In the spring of 1894 he and his close friend, Frank Foster, a two fisted hydrant of a man in his forties with a magnificent head of white hair and eyebrows to match, had organized Federal Labor Union 5915 to be made up mostly of unskilled working women, shut out from the male dominated craft unions.

Its open membership would allow the reform minded women who resided at the Denison House to join it in an official capacity and form a bond with the working women I would help to organize. My work at Hull House had taught me how to reinforce that bond through monthly meetings, as well as educational and child rearing services meant to enlighten and uplift working women in the City of Boston.

It was then that the silk weavers in nearby Newton Upper Falls were told that their wages were being cut in half because of hard times, allowing Jack and me to persuade them, both male and female, to join local 5915 and go out on strike. With the support of organized labor and the publication of the hardships those workers were suffering, the strike would settle favorably within two weeks.

On the heels of the silk weavers' strike, the garment workers were soon advised of a similar across the board cut in pay. This put Garment Workers Local # 53 in a bind, since it had a long history of not permitting women to join its ranks. The fact that the clear majority of garment workers in the Boston area were women would make the chance of a successful strike much more difficult.

That was when Jack met with their leadership and through much straight talk it was agreed that I would form the all-female Local # 37 and an industry wide strike would then take place. Our slogans and platforms were "equal pay for equal work and no reductions in that pay." Closing ranks like that would both settle the strike and make labor history in Boston.

I remember delivering the good news of that settlement to a crowd of mostly ragged young girls. Sadly, most were turning old before their time, with fingers that were gnarled from weaving and teeth that were broken from biting through fabric in the dreadful conditions of their employment.

Amid a sea of tears along with a series of hugs and kisses, I looked over and saw my beloved Jack sitting there beaming with pride beside Frank Foster and a sobbing Hannah Kimble. That was two weeks before our marriage in New York City and an unforgettably romantic honeymoon at Niagara Falls.

CHAPTER 38

*I*t has been written that true love is a many splendored thing. For someone like me who had waited and saved her love for so long, wondering whether being alone and lonely would be my lot in life, the love between Jack and me would bring the two of us a fulfillment beyond our fondest dreams.

Jack was a man's man, as they say, who had gone to sea at the age of seventeen and traveled the world, both near and far. Never one to be confused with a choir boy, he had once served sixty days in a California House of Detention. He had earned money as both a prize fighter and a numbers runner for an Irish gangster named O'Malley in his youth. He would join the Carmen's union in his twenties and eventually become a member of its bargaining committee.

He was, as I probably mentioned, tall and dark featured with the most beguiling pair of azure eyes. His father's death while he was at sea and the remorse he felt in not being at his bedside would cause him to return home to stay, and to mend his ways to the straight and narrow. I tell you in our prime, when we walked together arm in arm along the streets of Boston, we were two of a kind that could beat a full house.

I remember one occasion, early on before our marriage, when Mama and I were waiting at South Station for Jack to arrive from a trip to New York. I had been missing him something awful and plans had been made for the three of us to meet and have dinner at the Union Oyster House.

I was dressed to the nines in a matching outfit of green satin. I was checking the clock above the concourse, while Mama was resting on a bench nearby. That was when two British sailors on shore leave, feeling no pain and up to no good, entered and made straight toward me.

Their manner was surly and their talk was sprinkled with slurs and swears. I attempted to ignore them but they were having none of that. That was when I saw Jack approaching, just before one of them tried to paw me. The next thing I knew, Jack was right beside me and proceeded to address them both in a manner they both deserved.

"You blokes better get a move on or you're in for a beating."

"What's that you say?," the burlier of the two replied in a cockney accent.

When he raised his fists, Jack knocked him to the ground with one punch, while his pal thought twice about becoming involved. That was when Jack smiled at them in a steely eyed sort of way and spoke in a menacingly low tone of voice,

"Pick up your friend and get going, while you can still walk.

Remember this, we look out for women here in Boston. Now get."

To see those two hooligans leave with their tails between their legs was a joy to behold. What was even better was that it occurred without Mama even knowing what had happened. After giving us his warm embrace, off we all went to dinner.

Jack loved my mother and she simply adored him. While living on Saint Botolph Street he would often sweep her up in his arms and whisk her up three flights of stairs like she was a sack of feathers, all the while serenading her with song.

As I mentioned, *"Shenandoah"* was her favorite. She was also partial to songs from her childhood in Ireland like, *"The Parting Glass"* and one of my favorites, sung on the evening that Mother Jones spoke at the Columbia Theatre, *"Wayfaring Stranger."*

Like my father before him, Jack simply loved to sing and had perfect pitch that caused him to never miss a note in a melody, even if he had heard it but once. I suppose you would call his voice a tenor, even though he could traverse both high and low octaves without any difficulty at all.

Back in Hannibal my father would dutifully deliver his pay envelope to Mama as a sign of affection and respect for all that she did in caring for the family. So too would Jack tender his pay envelope to "Mother Kenney" as he called her, on each and every pay day with both a smile and a kiss on the cheek. He was like a tonic to her that seemed to lift her spirits and help her cope with her crippling illness.

I hadn't heard of Niagara Falls as a honeymoon destination before the two of us read a brochure about it at the Boston Public Library in Copley Square. Jack and I would go there often when I wasn't organizing or he wasn't working a shift as a streetcar driver or performing his duties in his position at the Globe.

We just loved it there and looking through the catalogues for our favorite authors' latest efforts. Jack was partial to biographies, while I was partial to stories of adventure and romance. A mutual love for reading was another of our common bonds.

The wonders of nature were not something I knew much about before taking the train to the picturesque village of Niagara, New York. A village that Frederick Olmstead would make into a place of beauty, with rolling hills, beautiful vistas and water views. We each delighted in the breathtaking power of Niagara Falls.

I can remember like it was yesterday, the two of us walking hand in hand, lost in love's embrace during that week long excursion, with those magnificent, thundering cascades roaring in the background. Evenings were spent dining and dancing to the melodies of a handsome ragtime quartet, dressed in ties and tails within the hotel's spacious ballroom. It was all so perfect, so joyful. It caused our passion and love for each other to take wing like never before. True love is a many splendored thing indeed.

During the early part of 1895, I would continue with my remaining obligations as a labor organizer for the AF of L and become a frequent lecturer at the Denison House. That was when I was asked by Mary Kehew, the married sister of Hannah Kimball, to join the Board of Directors of the Women's Educational and Industrial Union (WEIU).

Meanwhile Jack and I would move to a more spacious first floor apartment located at 37 Carver Street in the South End of Boston. It was a quiet side street with a cozy little park nearby. It would allow us to take Mama outside to get the air and to feed the sparrows that gathered there. It was at that address where we received many visitors from Chicago. They would include my three mentors, Ellen Gates Starr, Betty Morgan and Florence Kelley.

Jack invited all three over for dinner on a beautiful spring evening. Mama was concerned that our guests would think less of her when they found out that Jack had prepared our meal. He would be the master of the moment, using that occasion to display both his charm and his sense of humor, announcing,

"Ladies, after much protest from Mother Kenney, I finally convinced her that I would cook our meal this evening. How is it, by the way?"

"Just delicious," all three replied.

"I was hoping you would say that. Now you can be told where I learned to cook for such an illustrious group. Where was that Mother Kenney?"

"In jail," my mother replied, while blushing and shaking her head.

That was just one of the memorable moments of that lovely evening. I can recall their leaving and the genuine warmth of their gratitude and congratulations for inviting them to our household. We would put Mama to bed and curl up together as man and wife, firmly believing that Boston would be the city where we would live happily ever after.

CHAPTER 39

I learned that I was pregnant on New Year's Day of 1895. My diary says that I spent the morning over in Hyde Park meeting with a group of rubber workers about organizing, then met with two of the directors of the WEIU at the Denison House before going to see the midwife on my way home.

Her name was Mildred O'Keefe and she was a great big woman with long grey hair and spectacles. She had been delivering babies in the South End of Boston for some twenty years. She told me that I was due during the latter half of August. I asked if she were certain and she said that she most assuredly was.

Even though it was a blustery cold evening, I can remember feeling like I was walking on air and I was the luckiest woman in the whole wide world, as I made my way home along snow covered streets. I couldn't wait to break the news to Mama and then to Jack. Mama was in the kitchen cutting tomatoes for her special brand of vegetable soup when I broke the news to her.

"Mama, I'm going to have a baby, can you believe it?"

"Oh, Mary dear", she yelped, while hugging me like there was no tomorrow.

"Your Papa would be so happy." Then both of us burst into tears.

I was sitting at the window in our front parlor when I saw Jack turn the corner on Carver Street under the street lamp. He was wearing the green herring bone overcoat I had given him for Christmas with a bright red scarf. I just couldn't hold myself back and ran from our front door while Mama yelled for me to put on my coat. I tell you, the warmth of my joy and love for the father of my child made it seem like the Fourth of July outside. Concerned he ran towards me. We drew together within the Carver Street Park.

"Oh Jack, Jack darling, we are going to have a baby," I shouted, while throwing myself into his arms. All I can remember is him calling my name over and over while smothering me in kisses. I remember thinking later that evening that I wished Papa was there to receive the wonderful news. Just then I received the warmest reassurance my faith could provide that Papa was right there among the three of us, smiling away with tears of joy in the corners of his wild Irish eyes.

My pregnancy did not prevent me from continuing my efforts to convince the board of directors of the WEIU that the organization of working women and equal pay for equal work were essential to industrial democracy in America. With Jack's support I organized the Union for Industrial Progress. We would arrange for speakers from all over the country to come to speak on important matters. These would include the health and safety of working women and the need for frequent and regular inspections of their workplaces to prevent them from being injured and killed.

At first these lectures were at the Denison House then a new location had to be found to accommodate the crowds that came to attend. As a goodwill response for my efforts, the directors of the WEIU voted to approve the use of the elegant Perkins Hall on Boylston Street in the Back Bay for these lectures to take place.

Their vote came with certain offensive restrictions, to my way of thinking. The Union for Industrial Progress was prohibited from sending any advertisements concerning these lectures, mentioning either Perkins Hall or its address, but they were permitted to mention its rear entrance and its address of 96 Providence Street.

I can remember mentioning to Hannah Kimball that these restrictions were like telling the domestics of the mansion that they could only use the servants' entrance. When I began to fester and get my Irish up concerning this, I can remember her counseling me "give milk to babes."

In other words it was more important to forget my pride and to be patient in doing what was right for working women. I had learned back at Hull House that my way wasn't the only way to solve a problem or handle a situation. Being humble, harmless and true to my mission was a lesson I would learn and one that would almost always serve me well.

The very first lecture held at Perkins Hall was on a Sunday afternoon in April of 1895. Its subject was industrial safety and its featured speaker was the unforgettable Mary Richardson.

She had been a laundry worker since she turned eleven years of age and she was now twenty three, yet looked so much older and beaten down by life with all the marks of hard labor. She was just skin, bones and wrinkles. She told how she was working the night shift at the Pilgrim Laundry in Chelsea beside a fifteen year old girl by the name of Margaret Dobbins. In gruesome detail she related what occurred when Margaret's hand and entire right arm became caught in the laundry mangle before the engineer could shut off the power in the cellar.

That poor creature's blood curdling screams were finally silenced by a loss of consciousness from a massive loss of blood. She died in Mary's arms on the way to the hospital. She had begun work at the laundry the week before.

It became Mary Richardson's mission and that of the Union for Industrial Progress to get legislation passed requiring a kill switch on all laundry mangles. It would take all of our efforts and that of the directors of the WEIU, who attended that lecture in stunned silence, to finally succeed in getting that legislation passed, seven years later.

Boston was a fertile field for trade unionism and social justice concerns during those weeks and months of 1895. It was likewise a place where safeguards were being put in place to protect the health and safety of its people.

These would include the elimination of faulty gas jets, a citywide building and sanitary code, and legislation assuring that our meat, poultry and vegetables were marketed and sold without spreading contamination and disease.

During that time, visitor after visitor would come to our modest home from all over the world. There our dinner discussions would almost always last into the wee hours. They would concern the rights of workers and the responsibilities of owners, as well as the ways and means of protecting our people from illness, injury and death.

Two men and one unforgettable woman stand out in my mind as having visited with us there. First there was the Englishman, John Elliot Burns, whom Jack had met in New York. He was a bright eyed, self-educated, intelligent man in his thirties with a manicured beard and mustache who had been imprisoned by the British government for his part in the "Bloody Sunday" labor strike. He was at that time a member of the British Parliament and the leader of the Socialist Democratic Federation.

Since Jack and I had vocally opposed the inclusion of Socialist Plank 10, calling for the public ownership of industry at the previous year's AF of L convention, the fur flew during that dinner and beyond. John Burns was a thoughtful, persuasive gentleman of deeply-held beliefs who never allowed our disagreements to detract from our lasting friendship.

The next on the list was Andrew Furuseth of the Seaman's Union of the Pacific.

A Norwegian by birth, he spoke four languages and became a legendary labor leader to all those, like my beloved Jack, who had gone down to the sea in ships.

A manly handsome man with a magnificent head of salt and pepper hair and steel blue eyes, his life would be devoted to the cause of organizing seafaring men and improving their lives. Since coming ashore in San Francisco, he was determined to make America his home and to lead the way in eliminating brutal punishments aboard sailing ships. He was also a moving force in eliminating the injuries and deaths that were a matter of course in the seafaring trade.

I can remember just listening in awe as he spoke to us of his adventurous life with vivid descriptions of exotic peoples and ports of call. I recall telling him again and again that he should collect all of his stories and publish them for posterity. As I mentioned, I simply loved tales of adventure and romance and could read them over and over to my heart's content. To that, Andrew simply replied in his thick Norwegian accent,

"Mary, Mary, there are far more important things for me to do, before this life is through."

The last of the three would have the most telling effect upon my life in the years to come. That would be the loving, caring, strikingly beautiful, Elizabeth Glendower Evans. At the time we met, she was already a widow in her late thirties, having been married to the Harvard educated Glendower Evans, a partner in Oliver Wendell Holmes' Law Firm.

She was a stunning woman with luxurious golden hair, green eyes and the most beautifully shaped nose and mouth. Her endless variety of memorable hats would become the signature elements of her attire. I became enamored of her when we were first introduced at the Denison House. Although an aristocrat, she had the heart and the soul of an underdog.

The first time that Mrs. Evans came to dinner she had taken up the cause of penal reform, particularly as it applied to youthful offenders who were often the victims of the most abject poverty and the brutality it caused. At that time, juvenile reformatories in Massachusetts were little more than dark and dismal dungeons where young people were confined in conditions that were repugnant to a Christian society.

She had recently used her political influence to become one of the directors of the Lyman Reformatory for Boys and immediately set about bringing compassion and enlightenment to its administration. She believed that young people would most often chose the straight and narrow path to that of the crooked course, if only they had the chance to do so.

Through education, industrial training, better food and fresh air, she would make the Lyman School a model for reform throughout the country. I can remember her sitting at our kitchen table, her green eyes blazing in the gaslight, describing her commitment to saving those unfortunate young boys from turning into hardened criminals.

Jack had been one of her admirers, since her name was brought up at a Beacon Hill dinner he attended as an editor of the Globe. It was there that the hostess, a former director of the WEIU, informed the gathering that the pickets who had been arrested during the Carmen's strike had been bailed out by none other than her neighbor, Elizabeth Glendower Evans.

"Just think, she was once a lady," she remarked.

"Madame," Jack replied while standing up to leave, "as a card carrying member of the Carmen's local, who has known the suffering of such a strike firsthand, it would be an honor to meet such a lady and congratulate her."

Our Carver Street home was like the cradle of a new born movement and our life there expressed the joy of youth finding comrades in ideals; then fighting for those ideals while growing closer together, in order to make those ideals a reality.

CHAPTER 40

*D*uring the spring of that year the rubber workers employed by the Gossamer Rubber Company in Hyde Park, both male and female, went out on strike after a forty percent across the board wage cut. What was the worst part was that there had been no decline in the sale of their products, it was pure and simply a selfish and greedy power play by ownership to reduce their costs and increase their profits.

The explanation provided by Henry Klous, the owner's son, was that the wages of rubber workers had to be brought in line with those of other trades in the city, never bothering to mention which trades he was referring to. That was when I was asked to get involved in organizing those rubber workers into unions.

Jack and I went out to meet with these workers and soon had all of them signed up as members of two unions, one male and one female. Then we organized a strike committee of three men and three women and sought the backing of the BCLU and the WEIU at a raucous gathering at Perkins Hall.

It was during that gathering that I spoke with the lovely Mary Morton Kehew. A stylish woman of grace and rectitude, her family had the advantage of great wealth. She and her sister, Hannah Kimball, had become social reformers and union supporters of the very highest order.

We were in need of a more public forum to publicize the injustice of the Gossamer Rubber Company. They had not only refused to meet with a delegation of their own rubber workers but had begun the hiring of immigrants from Italy and Armenia at slaves' wages to take over their jobs.

It was Mary Kehew who suggested that we hold our gathering at Faneuil Hall where the Colonists would often meet to publicize their grievances against British rule. She said using that historic place would be symbolic of right against might. When I asked her how we would raise the funds for such an event, she simply replied, "Just send me the bill."

That ancient hall was something to behold for both Jack and me. It was a rainy June evening that we hoped would not diminish the crowd invited to attend. To our delight the rain subsided and a magnificent rainbow spread its beauty and grace over the City where the American Revolution took root, an hour before our gathering was to begin.

There I was, six months pregnant and beaming, while seated on the stage beside Frank Foster, the head of the BCLU and Mary Kehew, the executive director of the WEIU. That was when Jack, wearing a stunning blue suit, white shirt and striped green tie, rose to speak to that capacity crowd. Through his contacts, a congregation of newspaper reporters were there with pen and ink at the ready to chronicle what occurred. My notes from that night detail most of Jack's amazing speech.

"Ladies and gentlemen, the need of working men and women for a living wage must no longer be disregarded in order to satisfy greed. There was no justification for the Klous family to slash the wages of these loyal and diligent men and women who have given their all for Gossamer Rubber, since it opened its doors in 1891. Their faithful service has made a fortune for the Klous family yet their reward has been the back of a hand and a kick to the teeth."

"Workers such as these have allowed men like Vanderbilt to build railroads and make millions, Carnegie to build steel mills and make millions and Rockefeller to turn crude oil into a mountain of gold. All of them have done so without any real regard for the workers who have enabled them to. The same applies to the Klous family."

"That is why we organize. That is why we publicize what Gossamer Rubber has done and what we will do to remedy it. That is why we strike. That is why we come here tonight in this hallowed hall where Adams, Hancock and Revere once gathered, to resist and rebel against tyranny."

"We come here to tell all the greedy, selfish owners of industry that the unions are here and here to stay. That the unions will resist and rebel against all manner of tyranny in the workplace. That they will not rest until workers, both male and female, are paid a living wage and are not used up, cast aside and replaced by others the owners can enslave and later cast aside when their greed demands it."

In the crowd on that unforgettable evening was a beautiful young lady from Brooklyn by the name of Leonora O'Reilly and her devoted mother Winifred. Both had been told of our gathering by Father Edward McGlynn with whom I continued to correspond since meeting him at the Duffy household in Chicago years before.

Leonora was at that time in her mid-twenties with strawberry blonde hair, vivacious hazel eyes and a slender womanly figure. Like her father and her mother, she was a proud member of the Knights of Labor and an avid believer in the cause of working women. A seamstress and dressmaker by occupation, both she and her mother resided at a settlement house in Brooklyn and regularly attended lectures on matters of union organization and social justice at the Cooper Union.

During her organizational activities on behalf of seamstresses and cloak makers she became acquainted with Sam Gompers and my father's devoted friend, Michael Duffy. In fact she brought me letters penned by both, congratulating Jack and me for our efforts on behalf of working men and women and pledging the continued support of the AF of L in all that we were doing in Boston.

The notoriety of our Faneuil Hall gathering had the desired impact upon the business of Gossamer Rubber. It would cause the Klous' family to offer a restoration of the wage cuts and a reduction of the workday to 9 hours. With the assistance of the Massachusetts Board of Conciliation and Arbitration a settlement was achieved that was satisfactory to all.

In August, just before I was to give birth, we received the news that the garment workers had received a totally unexpected notice of drastic layoffs and wage cuts, industry wide, that resulted in what would prove to be a prolonged and bitter strike.

Again and again we received visitors and messages seeking our advice and assistance, while that strike was initiated and intensified. I can remember going into labor amid all of this and advising Jack that we should call Mildred O'Keefe, the midwife, and forget about me giving birth at the New England Hospital.

Poor Jack, he was a nervous wreck and we had quite an argument as he hustled me into the waiting carriage, protesting all the way that the demands of that strike required our staying home. I would later find out that the carriage driver assumed that the baby was out of wedlock and tried to extort hush money from Jack as a result. His payoff would be a punch in the nose.

Well the baby was born after a prolonged labor and the doctor demanded that I take my rest while protecting me from the committees of garment workers that came to the hospital again and again seeking advice and direction.

Mama always told me that the pain of childbirth would soon be forgotten with the presentation and nursing of a thriving child. I would like to say that was the case with me, but I've promised to tell the whole truth and nothing but in this recitation.

Child birth was the single most painful occurrence I ever endured and each time I endured it, it seemed to be even more painful. Yet, as Mama counseled, when I set eyes upon that beautiful blonde haired infant that we would name John Kenney O'Sullivan and began to nurse him, there was nothing that would ever surpass that intimate, serene act of motherhood.

CHAPTER 41

The garment workers would reach an agreement with the manufacturers in October. The strike had brought out the best and the worst among the rank and file, as did most strikes.

The best was that a settlement was achieved and male and female garment workers received better wages for less hours of work as the result. The worst was that many of the male workers and their leaders had mistreated their female counterparts in often rude and insulting ways that demeaned their skills and their womanhood.

As a woman who grew up holding her own in the company of men and most often gaining their respect, it was this behavior on the part of certain men that would continue to inspire me to fight for equality in and out of the workplace throughout my life.

When it came time to execute a contract between the garment workers and the manufacturers, which included a nine hour day and an increase in wages, A.S. Shuman, one of the foremost cloak makers in New England, refused to do so, asserting that once his word was given it would not be disavowed and a written contract was unnecessary.

I demanded otherwise on behalf of the female garment workers of Local 37 but was soon overruled by Frank Morgan of The Garment Workers District Council No. 2. In a patronizing manner, that blustering walrus of a man asserted that I would soon be out of the organizing business and assuming the full time duties of motherhood. His men wanted to end their hardship and go back to work and were willing to do so without an agreement in writing.

Not three months later, Shuman and the other manufacturers reinstituted a ten hour work day and payment under the old wage scale in total disregard of our agreement, after discovering that there was dissension in our ranks. It was another instance of divide and conquer by the owners of industry.

I can remember Frank Foster of the BCLU, at the behest of District Council No. 2, coming to our home seeking to mend fences. Jack took the baby out for a stroll to blow off steam and not display his Irish temper for the way I had been treated by the leaders of District Council No.2.

"Mary," Frank began, "I told Morgan and the others but they wouldn't listen to me. With Christmas coming he wanted to get the men back to work. They just didn't have the stomach to continue and grasped at straws. "

"What do you want from Local 37?" I replied, without saying I told them so, or mentioning that women made up nearly half of the work force and their interests should have been considered as well.

"We need your women to join with the men once again and strike."

I suppose it was the lessons that I learned at Hull House that caused me to swallow my pride on that occasion and agree once more to assist, despite what Frank Morgan and all the other ignorant men said or believed about working women and my representation of them. Our cause was too important.

I succeeded in securing the support of Local 37 and a strike was called. In addition, Local 37 began a letter writing campaign publicizing what A.S. Shuman had done in breaking his word and deceiving us all.

Soon the manufacturers responded by dragging me into court for conspiring and counseling an illegal boycott. After I testified in the United States District Court in Post Office Square, that case was dismissed and the strike was settled favorably for all, both male and female.

As a telling footnote to that episode I decided to set the record straight with The United Garment Workers of America, District Council No. 2 on behalf of the women I represented in Local 37. I wanted to deliver a lasting message to all those who believed that women were second class citizens who could be disrespected and abused, both in and out of the workplace, once and for all.

I insisted that our position and protest be read into the official record of The Boston Central Labor Union by Frank Foster, its president. Frank was only too happy to do so. This is what was entered on May 3, 1896.

"Because of insulting and abusive treatment, our delegates have refused to attend any more meetings of District Council No.2. We are called insulting names and the worst kind of language is used towards our delegates. We believe that this behavior is an attempt to break up Local 37 and to deprive us of the means of earning our living in the clothing trade. "

Respectfully,
Mary Kenney O'Sullivan, President.
Helena Dudley, Vice-President.
Local 37, Ladies Garment Workers Union.

CHAPTER 42

I suppose that tragedy and loss are essential parts of our lives upon this earth and the manner in which we cope with them determines who we are and who we become. Since my marriage to Jack, my life had been full of joy. He was all that I had ever hoped for.

Through our love for one another we had brought the most beautiful child into our world. Our darling Johnny would become our focus and our hope for the future. His golden curls, his bright blue eyes, and the healthful blush of his skin were as if an angel had come to dwell among us. An angel who would be called back to Paradise before the age of two.

Diphtheria was the name of the disease that stole our baby from us. It began with a sore throat and progressed all too quickly to the point where there was no hope. In a shocked and saddened state Jack, Mama and I sat by his bedside watching him fade away, as the doctors at the New England Hospital summoned the chaplain to provide what solace he could, along with the last blessing of the Church. Our fervent prayers were to no avail on that tragic occasion, testing our faith like no other circumstance before.

My beloved Jack took charge as Mama and I wept and wondered why this tragedy was visited upon us, robbing us, we believed, of all our hopes and dreams. I would not recover from such a loss, I feared, while watching the priest anoint Johnny's golden head with oil and recite the Lord's Prayer.

It brought back the awful memory of my father lying upon our kitchen table, his head broken and bloody, being anointed by Father Murray while Mama wept and I begged that he not leave us.

Just as then my pleas were in vain and only sadness and sorrow would remain. It was as the scripture says, a vale of tears. I suppose our youth and our love for one another would allow Jack and me to recover from that indelible loss and to go on. The same would not hold true for Mama.

She took sick three months from the date of Johnny's passing. It seemed that an old injury to her left leg shortly after her marriage to Papa became infected and brought on the fever. She had never regained the lightness of her spirit after Johnny's death in spite of my Jack's loving attempts to brighten her days with song and stories of his time at sea.

She resisted our taking her to the hospital, no doubt wishing to pass on in her own bed, surrounded by her loved ones. What we will never forget is that in assisting a window washer by opening her hospital room window to the cold and holding his ladder to prevent him from falling, she brought on the pneumonia that claimed her life.

Perhaps it is a superstition that is peculiar to the Irish that causes us to believe that tragedy will often rear its horrid head three times before passing on to plague some other family. Such was the case in the fall of 1897 after Mama's recent death.

My sister, Annie, had come to visit from New York, bringing her two children, Moira and Brian. She had been married for almost twelve years to Bob Muldoon, a carriage driver and night watchmen from Queens who meant well but never made his mark at anything he did. His battle with the drink was no doubt a stumbling block in that regard. A stumbling block that would cause his family much suffering.

As Annie related it to us, Moira and Brian were out in the back of our home on Carver Street frolicking on a hammock that Jack had suspended between two oak trees. That was when Moira tumbled to the ground, causing a nasty gash to her forehead. Fearing an infection, Annie brought Moira upstairs to the bathroom and administered rubbing alcohol to her cut.

Jack was out of town at the time and I was delivering a lecture at Wellesley College to a class of freshmen girls concerning the work of Mother Jones and the recent massacre of workers in Lattimer, Pennsylvania. In any event it seems that Annie's children soon returned to play and she was determined to watch them more closely by accompanying them into the back yard this time.

Forgetting that she had left the bottle of rubbing alcohol next to the bathroom's gas jet, the explosion that followed caused a fire that consumed nearly all of our living quarters and almost all of our belongings.

I will never forget turning the corner on Carver Street and seeing the smoldering wreckage of our cherished home and that sorrowful, guilt ridden expression of my sister, who had just been advised by the Fire Inspector of the cause of the blaze.

I recall simply standing there in disbelief across the street in Carver Park then falling to my knees under the weight of another misfortune that would compound the darkness that Jack and I were living through.

From the time I was a little girl I discovered that coping with tragic loss and the difficulties of life can often be made easier by focusing upon the loss and difficulty of those who are less fortunate than we and counting our blessings by contrast. I suppose that I was looking for a specific instance where this held true when I learned about Helen Keller and her enrollment at the Cambridge School for Young Ladies.

It was while Jack and I were staying at the Denison House following the fire. It was Elizabeth Evans who told us about the Perkins Institute for the Blind located in Jamaica Plain and the work that they were doing with the blind through the use of braille. That was when she mentioned this young girl from Alabama who was determined to attend Radcliffe College despite her being deaf, dumb and blind.

Both Jack and I were astonished by her story and wanted to learn more about her. We soon discovered that her teacher, Anne Sullivan, was the person to speak to and resolved to reach out to her through the Perkins School. It was our intention to arrange for her to deliver a lecture on the needs of the blind, at the Denison House.

Anne Sullivan was living in Cambridge at the time with her pupil, Helen. Both were attending classes at the Cambridge School for Young Ladies in order to prepare Helen for her lifelong dream of admission to Radcliffe College. I remember first meeting Anne in Harvard Square over coffee and being struck by her beauty and confidence. She was two years younger than me at thirty one.

She exhibited the distinctive features of the Black Irish, like many of the Sullivan heritage. Her hair was the most exquisite shade of black. Her indigo eyes shone through a pair of darkened spectacles. Her skin was the shade of alabaster and her figure stood strong and erect. I recall congratulating her on the work she was doing for those afflicted with blindness and her complimenting me for my efforts on behalf of working women.

To my surprise, she advised that she was legally blind and it was only though her affiliation with the Perkins School that her condition was improved through an advanced form of eyeglasses whose lenses allowed her to recognize faces and read sparingly without the use of braille.

When I proposed that she come and speak at the Denison House she was enthusiastic concerning the prospect, while unexpectedly requesting that she be allowed to bring Helen along with her.

I tell you, when I told Jack about our meeting I remember him looking into my eyes and saying it was good to see the light of promise in them once again. How wonderful it was that the blind would allow me to see my way beyond tragedy and loss and become hopeful once again in the future.

The overflow crowd that wanted to hear Anne Sullivan speak and to see the inspirational Helen Keller required the scheduling of two separate lectures on that November Sunday. At that time, Alexander Graham Bell and his invention of the telephone had focused attention upon the deaf among us. His work with the Boston School for the Deaf had received considerable notoriety as a result. It was the miraculous story of Anne Sullivan and Helen Keller that would focus attention upon the blind among us and the wonderful work being done at the Perkins School.

Both Jack and I were mindful of not making a spectacle of Helen's affliction and sought Anne's guidance as to the appropriate manner in which her story could be presented. To our surprise Anne advised that Helen wanted more than anything else to be treated like any other student at the Cambridge School for Young Ladies with the ambition of securing a college education. We soon learned that Anne was dead set against treating Helen with either pity or preference.

The second floor of the Denison House had a spacious room that could accommodate a crowd of seventy five. Jack and I had arranged the seating so that Anne and Helen would be situated on a small platform stage in the center of the room with seating and aisles on three sides.

I remember asking Anne whether she was fearful of public speaking and her replying lightheartedly that her near blindness in that instance was a distinct advantage, since she would be unable to readily decipher whether the crowd was quietly attentive or merely asleep. After an introduction by Vida Scudder, Anne and Helen entered arm in arm to a standing ovation.

What was readily apparent much to the surprise of those in attendance was how lovely Helen Keller was in appearance, with flowing auburn hair, bright blue eyes and a flawless complexion. She was in her eighteenth year. She and Anne were stylishly attired in the fashion of the era, wearing tailored wool jackets and skirts complemented by starched white blouses topped with distinctive cameo broaches.

Once the applause subsided, Anne brought Helen to her seat on the stage and soon held the crowd in rapt attention as she described her journey from being almost totally blind and shunned as a child in Agawam Massachusetts to becoming an instructor at the Perkins School.

She then proceeded to describe traveling to Alabama at the request of Helen's father to see what could be done to educate his daughter, after a menacing fever had deprived her of both sight and sound. What we thought would be a personal account of overcoming adversity became a lyric lesson in courage, compassion and the cause of childhood education. I have included three of my favorite quotes from that afternoon.

"Keep on beginning and failing. Each time you fail, start all over again, and you will grow stronger until you have accomplished a purpose; not the one you began with perhaps, but one you'll be glad to remember. "

"It is a rare privilege to watch the birth, growth and first feeble struggles of a living mind; this privilege is mine. A miracle has happened. The light of understanding has shone upon my pupil's mind, and behold all things are changed."

"The immediate future is going to be tragic for all of us unless we find a way of making the vast educational resources of this country serve the true purpose of education, truth and justice."

The finale of those lectures was when Anne brought Helen to the center of the stage and proceeded to demonstrate their means of communication with the use of sign language. Then with a braille version of Cicero's Orations, she had Helen read passages aloud, much to the tearful amazement of that overflow crowd.

CHAPTER 43

*D*uring 1898 there was a shoe workers strike out in Marlboro Massachusetts. I was asked to assist with the strike committee. At that time I discovered I was pregnant and the thought of bringing another "little one" into our world to be loved and cherished gave me new found energy. Jack, on the other hand, became especially protective, assisting like never before with the cooking and the cleaning, while discouraging me from taking on too much of a burden with my lecturing and organizing.

I can recall him saying that it wasn't necessary for me to become Joan of Arc, especially when I was "in a family way." I remember telling him that the blessing of another child was bestowed upon us because we were committed to serving others and with that we should continue. As always, Jack listened to what I had to say and agreed to work together as before. His only reservation was that I should be more careful, given my condition.

I tell you I almost gave that loving man a heart attack when I traveled out to Marlboro by train on a frigid February evening for an emergency bargaining session. I would soon become caught in a blinding blizzard that caused the trains to stop running in Framingham and required my traveling by an open sleigh to my destination. It took me close to an hour in front of a blazing fire place before I could feel my feet and hands.

I am certain Jack was beside himself when the bargaining committees became snowbound over that weekend and a telegram was finally sent to advise him of my safety. I will always remember him meeting me at South Station on that following Tuesday and embracing me like there was no tomorrow. The good news was that memorable snowfall forced the parties to bargain through the night to iron out their differences and reach a satisfactory agreement.

It was shortly after that occasion when Jack and I moved to a two bedroom apartment on Harrison Avenue in the South End. What with moving in and getting ourselves situated, we were temporarily removed from the day to day involvement in public affairs required by our occupations. This absence caused many of our closest friends to inquire whether they could be of assistance during that difficult time of transition.

I recall Elizabeth Evans in particular, dropping by unexpectedly one evening and insisting that she take us out for dinner at Jacob Wirth's. I had just taken the clothes in from the line and was just about to spend the evening sprinkling and ironing them. To my amazement that charismatic creature of wealth and prominence proceeded to do all my sprinkling and ironing in short order, while Jack and I got ready for an unforgettable dinner at one of Boston's most storied eating establishments.

That was the night we would be introduced to "the People's Lawyer", Louis Brandeis, and his lovely wife Alice. That was also the night that we would learn of the sinking of the U.S.S. Maine in Havana harbor as war clouds gathered over America.

On the carriage ride Elizabeth advised that we would be meeting a lawyer who was committed to the cause of serving the public. His brilliance in legal matters and uncommon wisdom would make of him an unparalleled leader both in Boston and throughout America. What was more, he had wanted to make our acquaintance since reading about the strike of the Gossamer Rubber workers and Jack's speech at Faneuil Hall.

Just before the turn of the century there was much reflection among the compassionate and the caring of this country as to the course America should follow. The industrial revolution was still in full swing and new inventions were bringing about revolutionary changes in American industry. Immigration was supplying an almost limitless source of human labor that would help transform corporations into conglomerates and conglomerates into trusts of unprecedented wealth and power.

On the other side of the ledger there was an increased interest in matters of the spirit. These included a renewed interest in traditional religion with the building of church after church in our cities and towns. There were also newer brands of mysticism and spirituality derived from Buddhism and Hinduism that focused on the transcendental and the expansion of the human mind.

Fortunes were being doubled and tripled among the wealthy and powerful while workers continued to be used and abused in the American workplace. Survival of the fittest was still the philosophy of the Captains of Industry while do unto others was being preached in places of worship and union halls.

Many were becoming more callous as poor houses and prisons were filled to overflowing, while an increasing few were becoming more concerned with the plight of their fellow human beings. That was when Louis Brandeis, a man of wealth, privilege and erudition, would step forward and show America where its soul should be.

At the time of our introduction Louis was a bespectacled, soft spoken, stocky man in his early forties with a fine head of silver hair, a prominent nose and steel blue eyes that seemed to see into your mind. He was wearing a starched white shirt, a red striped tie and a grey three piece suit of Harris Tweed.

He was a partner in the law firm of Brandeis, Dunbar and Nutter which specialized in all manner of litigation. He was accompanied on that occasion by his devoted wife, Alice, a personable, attractive woman of grace and bearing who was stylishly attired in a cashmere coat and skirt of royal blue.

Jack and I became enamored with this illustrious pair. Despite the divergence of our backgrounds, an abiding concern for the cause of the less fortunate and the future of our country made us near instant allies in the quest for equal justice under law. It was Elizabeth Evans whose introduction and conversation guided us from one subject of mutual interest and concern to another during that unforgettable dinner engagement.

His eloquence, and his depth of understanding of the motivations and methods of the commercial elite was only surpassed by Brandeis' desire to balance the scales for those who were without privilege or prospects for the future. Those who would never partake of the bounty being created by industrial capitalism, the disadvantaged, the destitute and the deserving, who went to work twelve hours a day, six days a week.

On that evening Brandeis proclaimed that the have nots must be given greater attention and an even shake in the twentieth century or an America with liberty and justice for all would never be. It would become like so many other failed states and societies where a select few steals from and subdues everybody else. Jack and I sat in awe as his nimble and caring mind soared over the landscape of American society and proposed controls and reforms that would assure the pursuit of happiness for every American. At first he spoke of the elimination of poor houses and debtors prisons in this country, where the impoverished, the infirm and the insane were heaped together in a Dante's inferno of indifference and inhumanity.

He then touched upon penal reform and the crying need for integrity on the part of our elected officials and the elimination of graft and corruption through legal oversight by an Attorney General. He then touched upon public education and the need for taxation and teacher training to assure literacy and equal educational opportunity for all of our children.

Last he spoke of instituting committees of public control for our water and gas supplies. He also predicted that public transportation and the public dispensation of electricity would require public control in the next twenty years.

Never would Jack or I encounter a man of such supreme intelligence and an abiding belief in the future as Louis D. Brandeis. He would later become the light bearer of the Progressive Movement in America, leading the way for others who believed in compassion and the promise of America.

It was while we were seated within the spacious dining area of that popular emporium when we heard a newsboy within the adjacent bar crying out to one and all that the battleship Maine had been sunk in Havana harbor and that we should read all about it.

Jack hastily purchased a newspaper and read aloud the still sketchy details of that momentous event. Both Jack and Louis Brandeis had been following international matters and it was their belief that the American sugar interests had been stirring up popular support for a revolt in Cuba against Spain, in an effort to foster an American intervention. I recall Brandeis declaring that war was an extension of industrial capitalism and warned against America being stampeded into a war with the Spanish Empire.

CHAPTER 44

As Brandeis cautioned, a stampede toward a war with Spain began even before the circumstances of the sinking of the U.S.S. Maine were investigated. Within weeks Congress passed legislation allocating fifty million dollars to build up military strength while the New York World published so called eye witness accounts of the torture and murder of Cubans by the armed forces of Spain.

Mark Twain spoke of a Spanish American War as being "a jaunty little adventure" while Theodore Roosevelt, the Assistant Secretary of the Navy, declared that Spain should be evicted from Cuba to support the spread of democracy and to enforce the Monroe Doctrine. After a hasty determination that an underwater mine had blown up the Maine by a U.S. Naval Court Of Inquiry, war was declared on April 25th of 1898.

It had been thirty three years since Lee's surrender to Grant at Appomattox Court House. All who had been born during the bloodletting of The Civil War, could remember the sight of destitute widows and fatherless children being the poison fruit of fathers lost to war. Or the presence of forlorn young men growing old before their time after losing limbs or their minds during that horrid conflict. I don't remember who it was that expressed the feelings of most Americans when he said that "war is all hell."

I suppose that three decades without war had caused memories to fade among those in power in America as to the real costs of warfare and their effects upon our people. During that three decades, American industry had grown and prospered beyond all expectation. Those in power in America began to believe that our might made right. A war to further American economic interests and open overseas markets would help eliminate future panics and focus attention away from the struggle between workers and owners.

These matters were the subject of our discussions as we sat in the Beacon Hill parlor of Louis and Alice Brandeis on the evening after war had been declared. It was Louis who brought up one of that war's foremost advocates, Theodore Roosevelt, who had been the focus of an avalanche of publicity.

"I have high hopes for Roosevelt. His reforms with respect to Civil Service and his work in trying to root out corruption in the New York Police Department were commendable. I've met him at Harvard functions. He's a bantam rooster of a man with a fine intellect and unmatched enthusiasm for his chosen undertakings. "

"He and Leonard Wood, President McKinley's Doctor, are assembling an expeditionary force to fight in Cuba. At least he doesn't want someone else to do the fighting for him. It is well known that American sugar interests have purchased large plantations in Cuba that cannot turn a profit while Cuba is under Spanish rule. I fear that the spoils of this war may see Cuba trading Spanish rule for one much closer to home. "

"Have you read "The Art of War" by Sun Tzu, Louis?" Jack asked.
"I've not."

"I'll lend you my copy. I'm told it is required reading at West Point. Sun Tzu teaches that as long as a war is seen as moral and it's brief, it will receive the support of the people. From what the Hearst papers are telling us, we are going to war because our battleship was sunk, most likely by agents of Spain, and to free the Cuban and Philippine people from the oppression of Spanish rule."

"Their papers also insist that the war will be over in a matter of months. Maybe the Hearst editors know a little something of Sun Tzu's teachings and want to publish those reasons in order to avoid questions about good old fashioned greed and the quest for power causing this war. From what we've seen in our lifetime, Louis, neither Mary nor I have much faith in our present government or those who speak on its behalf."

"Let's just hope and pray that this will turn out well for America and its people," I recall saying, as the four of us gathered together. All of us suspected that we were about to be led into war under false pretenses and it would set us on a course from which there would be no turning back in the upcoming twentieth century.

My diary tells me that Jack and I attended a patriotic rally on the Boston Common after word had been received that the Spanish fleet had been destroyed by Commodore Dewey in Manila Bay. It was a warm, sunny Sunday in May of 1898 as Jack and I strolled along the outskirts of that festive crowd while thousands listened to a rousing rendition of Souza's *"Stars and Stripes Forever."* from the bandstand.

There I was, seven months pregnant, walking arm in arm with my husband, as a series of chants of "Remember the Maine" and "Down with Spain" arose from that festive crowd of thousands. I remember the sight of children at play, while peddlers hawked bars of ice cream, swirls of cotton candy and miniature American flags. It was a red white and blue occasion. I must admit that despite our terrible misgivings, it was almost impossible to not become caught up in the fervor of that day's display.

Then we watched speaker after speaker take the megaphone and recite the virtues of America the beautiful and proclaim its destiny to bring democracy to the world beyond our shores. I remember looking forward afterwards to returning home day after day, after spending my time organizing or lecturing, to catch up on the latest news accounts of American heroism under fire and the thrilling victories that were being achieved.

All of these stories were written to proclaim America's unselfish dedication to the freeing of oppressed peoples from the clutches of tyranny. It was organized labor that saw through that illusion and spoke up again and again about the real reasons for that "jaunty little adventure."

I remember Jack publishing an article entitled, *"War, the other side of the Coin."* in the labor section of the *Globe* that was vigorously condemned by the powers that be. In it, he discussed the policies put forth by President McKinley on behalf of big business interests and the war mongering of Massachusetts Republican Senator, Henry Cabot Lodge. He concluded that article with a direct quote from the *"Craftsman"*, the official publication of the Connecticut AF of L.

"A gigantic scheme is being worked ostensibly to place the United States in the front rank as a naval and military power. The real reason is that the capitalists will have the whole thing and, when workingmen dare to ask for a living wage; they will be shot down like dogs in the streets."

That June American Marines captured Guantanamo Bay and seventeen thousand U. S. troops landed on the outskirts of Santiago. Later that month more troops landed at Daiquiri. Just before the fourth of July, Teddy Roosevelt and the Rough Riders would make household names of themselves in the battle of Kettle Hill, while General Jacob Kent would storm San Juan Hill and inflict seventeen hundred Spanish casualties.

Finally in December of 1898 a peace treaty was signed in Paris that pretty much annexed Cuba, The Philippines, Puerto Rico and certain islands in the Pacific to the United States of America. Expansion and foreign entanglements were now an essential part of our country's foreign policy. Expansion and entanglements that would cause American forces to kill thousands in Cuba and the Philippines who were fighting to be free. All the while American business interests prospered like never before.

It was just before New Year's Day, after the birth of our beautiful baby boy, when I was reading a listing of all of the American boys who had made the ultimate sacrifice in that "jaunty little adventure" and would never return home to their families again.

That was when I came across the name of Seth Rogers from Peoria Illinois, the same Seth Rogers who had taken me to a baseball game in Keokuk. The same Seth Rogers who wanted so badly to follow in his father's footsteps. I recall wondering how his mother would remember The Spanish American War.

Would she be like so many other mothers who had suffered the loss of their loving sons and be left only with memories that would fade and medals that would rust? Or would she believe that her indelible loss was a tragic but worthwhile sacrifice for America. An America whose history would continue to be written with the ink of lies.

CHAPTER 45

Over the next five years the O'Sullivan family would grow to five, with the birth of our sons, Mortimer and Roger, and the arrival of that lovely little bundle of joy and apple of her father's eye, Mary Elizabeth. While raising our two boys in the home on Harrison Avenue, it became apparent that neighborhood was not the place to do so.

I remember many an evening when the boys were awakened by the sounds of drunken men screaming and fighting after a night out on the town. While their days were spent playing in our back yard, amid the stench of rotting garbage or the smoke of cigars from the idle men who congregated on the back porches of nearby tenements.

I mentioned to Jack that I would very much like to move and try living near the ocean, if it could be arranged. In short order, he told me of a friend he worked with who lived over in the City of Revere. He would ask him to keep an eye out for a suitable apartment for our family.

Within a matter of weeks, we would move kit and caboodle to a sunny, spacious three bedroom apartment in Beachmont, a close knit community near to Revere beach and the Atlantic Ocean. We moved there in June of 1900.

The next two years were the best of times for our family. As I mentioned, I became a strong swimmer during my early childhood days back in Hannibal. Since Jack had learned to swim long before becoming an able seaman, we would spend that first summer coaxing our sons to shed their fear of the water. They soon became accustomed to submerging and swimming amid the salty green waves of picturesque Revere beach.

I can see Jack still, gathering his "morning glories", the nickname he gave the boys, and carrying them out of the front door and down the street to the beach, while I trailed after, pulling a little wagon loaded with sandwiches, towels, pails and shovels.

It was an invigorating and romantic setting for him and I to be together while sitting and strolling upon the beach in our bathing attire that modestly shielded our Celtic skin from the blaze of the summer sun.

In the cool of the evening, after the boys were in bed, we would cuddle on our front porch swing, while I played the flute and Jack sang the lilting refrains of his favorite melodies, between sips of fresh squeezed lemonade from two mason jars.

Before Mary Elizabeth came along, and the boys were enrolled in school, they grew straight and strong, collecting sea shells, cavorting in tide pools and watching ships and sailboats pass us by. I remember all four of us sitting upon a sea wall, eating ice cream from sugar cones and observing Irish and Italian working men engaged in the construction of an amusement park that would attract adults and children from all over and make Revere Beach, its penny arcades and terrifying roller coaster world famous.

Like our cozy little home on Carver Street, our home in Beachmont became a meeting place for friends and associates from varied backgrounds to gather and discuss strategies for the betterment of working men and women and our country.

The number and variety of our visitors would soon cause a nearby busybody to inform the local parish priest that I was a fortune teller and he should take steps to prevent me from doing the work of the devil.

When the congenial Father Hitchens, whose father was a member of the Knights of Labor, stopped by and Jack advised that we were labor organizers and not disciples of the dark arts, we all enjoyed a good laugh and soon became the best of friends.

It was during this time that two old friends, Sam Gompers and Michael Duffy, invited us to accompany them to a lecture given by Mark Twain at the Music Hall in Boston. By that time, Twain had undergone a change of heart, transforming himself from an ardent supporter of the war with Spain and American intervention in foreign affairs to the Vice President of the Anti-Imperialist League.

On that occasion he had just returned from a world tour and was at the very peak of his popularity. Having become an early supporter of the AF of L, he arranged for four tickets to a luxurious balcony box overlooking the stage. I can remember that evening as if it were yesterday.

There he stood, with his luxurious white hair and mustache, attired in his customary suit of white with a grey frontier tie, in the center of that spacious stage. Under a flattering spotlight, he captivated that audience in a melodious tone of voice with his rapier wit and homespun wisdom.

Sam would take us backstage to meet the famous author afterwards. The entries of my diary on the following morning contain a number of references to his novels, which became classics of American literature. They also include the most illuminating of quotations. Here are some that I will always remember.

"The fear of death follows from a fear of life. A man who lives fully is prepared to die at any time."

"Age is an issue of mind over matter. If you don't mind, it doesn't matter."

"Loyalty to the nation all the time, loyalty to the government when it deserves it."

"Humor is mankind's greatest blessing."

"Kindness is the language that the deaf can hear and the blind can see."

Jack and I invited Sam and Michael over to our home on the following Saturday afternoon and they were more than happy to oblige. After a simply delicious dinner of steak, and French fried potatoes prepared to perfection by my darling Jack and a setting sun stroll along the beach, we put our sleepy little boys to bed and sat down for a final interlude with my father's closest friend and the world renowned President of the American Federation of labor. It was the evening of June 8, 1901 according to my diary.

"What a wonderful spot to raise your boys," Sam remarked, as the four of us sat in our parlor, becoming reacquainted over a serving of tea and my chocolate cake. The golden rays of the setting sun embraced us in its glow.

"I'll bet your father is looking down on us right now, just thrilled to see you faring so well after all those years of struggle," the Seamus Egan of old offered. "You two are like the hands of a clock, each clearing the way for the other as time passes by. By God it is good to spend time with you both. How goes the battle?"

We would spend some time telling them of our lecturing work at the Denison house and the strikes that we had successfully concluded. We also mentioned our encounters with Anne Sullivan, Helen Keller, Elizabeth Glendower Evans and Louis Brandeis.

That was when Michael Duffy began to relate certain episodes of his life in Ireland and his service in the War Between the States for the first time that I can remember. I tell you I had never seen him so swept up by that reminiscence, first folding his hands almost in supplication and then wringing them with the anguish of his recitation.

It was as if his memory suddenly ushered him into an altered state of consciousness, as he slowly rose and stood before us. There was a fire in his wild Irish eyes. His speech displayed an unmatched eloquence and eerie resonance that would have made his Jesuit mentors proud. I tell you the three of us became spellbound by the blaze of his recollection.

"In fear, the Crown would dispatch their hirelings and informants among us, like jackals, as our fields yielded another harvest of worms, bringing famine and fever that killed untold numbers of our people, like the plagues of old. Village after village became so many graveyards, where many would survive by eating the flesh of their family members. Some few would rise up, it is always a few, and rebel against the cruel indifference of the landlords who drove their starving tenants from their land and into the road, while their tables were stocked with the fruits of our countryside. "

"That was when Meagher of the Sword threw off the cloak of privilege to lead us in a doomed rebellion that would make of him an exile to a land beyond the seas and me an outlaw. Hunted and wretched I would make a harrowing escape in the hold of a coffin ship bound for the promise that was America."

"Then Meagher would be resurrected and reappear in the City of New York and once again lead his brethren in another quest for freedom, a quest to set all men free. In battle after blood drenched battle we would answer the call to arms under the green flags of The Irish Brigade. At Malvern Hill, bloody Antietam and the butcher's yard of Fredericksburg we would make our passage through the fires of hell itself."

"Then upon the fields of Gettysburg, men would fight and die as never before or since on American soil. It would be three horrid days of slaughter under an unforgiving sun. Three days where I fought and feared death would take me at each and every turn. It was like unto a crucifixion that rose from the original sin of human bondage. From it the promise of America was resurrected. A promise of freedom and equality for all. "

I can remember us all just sitting there speechless when he finished. In an instant my mind was flooded with all that my father and he had been and done for me over the course of my lifetime. I suddenly began to shed tears that I could not stem. . Tears through which I could only say, "I just love the three of you, oh so very much."

On Friday evening, June 14, 1901 the Staten Island Ferry, Northfield, was leaving the port of Whitehall with 995 passengers aboard. In the fog it would collide with another ferry and sink almost immediately. It was reported that Michael Duffy, a labor organizer from Chicago Illinois, was lost and presumed drowned while attempting to save the lives of a mother and child.

He was sixty nine years old, the devoted husband of his wife Nannie and the father of two sons, Liam and Brendan Duffy. What was not contained in that obituary was that his real name was Seamus Egan and he was the most wonderful friend my father and I would ever have.

There is that old quotation that says 'he that lives by the sword, dies by it.' That may have been the case in September of 1901 when President McKinley, a veteran of the War Between the States, who zealously led the country into its War with Spain, was assassinated in Buffalo New York by a crazed anarchist who was later executed.

Theodore Roosevelt, the former Rough Rider from New York, would soon be sworn in as the country's youngest President and America would never be quite the same ever again.

CHAPTER 46

Mary Elizabeth was born on February 8, 1902 at the New England Hospital. It was one of the coldest days of that frigid, snowy winter, where the Charles River and all of the state's lakes and ponds became frozen solid since shortly after Christmas.

Jack brought the boys in from Beachmont bundled up like Eskimos on the following day to visit with us. They were simply thrilled to see and say hello to their lovely little sister.

We thought she was the most beautiful baby we had ever seen and Jack and I were overjoyed that the Good Lord had bestowed a whole and healthy daughter upon our family. I remember him inviting both friends and co-workers to stop by to see his "beautiful little queen." He was always so very proud of his family.

That spring I stayed at home to nurse and spend precious hours with the two boys before Mort began school that September. Every morning, weather permitting, our routine would be the same, a quiet breakfast of fruits and milk then putting Mary Elizabeth in the baby carriage and going for a nice long walk along the beach with the two boys on either side.

Along the route we would most often meet and speak to the grocer, the ice man, the rag man, and the shop keepers and laborers that lived and worked in that close knit section of the City of Revere. By midmorning we would stop by the brand new branch of the public library where I would use my freshly issued library card to obtain books to read to the children, a biography for Jack and the works of Dickens, Dafoe, London, or Twain for me.

Theodore Roosevelt's becoming the President and what it would mean for working men and women was the primary focus of our concerns during that time. There was never a president quite like him and truth be told, given his privileged upbringing and his pronouncements, we were very afraid that his term as president would prove to be more of the same or worse for those we cared about.

Roosevelt's early life was lived among the ruling class of New York City. After attending Harvard he won a seat in the New York legislature and became interested in political reform. After his wife passed away suddenly, he suffered profoundly from her loss and took refuge from the public eye by becoming a cattle rancher out in the wilds of the Dakotas. When Jack and I learned of this history we felt he would certainly be no ordinary occupant of the White House.

As Brandeis counseled, after his second marriage, Roosevelt reentered public life and soon became a moving force for reform in his role as one of the Commissioners of the New York City police force. He would fight vigorously for the elimination of its graft and corruption and work with a Civil Service Commission in a sincere attempt at hiring qualified candidates, instead of unqualified cronies to compose its rank and file.

Not long afterwards, his lifelong interest in the history of America's navy would propel him to become the Assistant Secretary of the country's Naval Department. Then came his sojourn as a Rough Rider in Cuba and then his election as the Governor of New York. It was from there that he was selected as a running mate by McKinley. When he became President and spoke of a square deal for unions, we began to look with favor upon him.

On September 22, 1902, a day I will never forget, my husband, Jack, was killed by a streetcar over in Everett, Massachusetts and my life and that of our three children entered a valley of darkness. It took me years to come to grips with that awful occurrence and its impact upon our lives. I cannot say, even at this late date, that time has healed its wounds completely, but it has eased their pain.

I can remember putting the baby down for her nap and preparing lunch for the two boys when two police men and Father Hitchens came to the door. I tell you it was as if it was a terrible nightmare from which I prayed to awaken. All I can remember is crying "no" over and over, as the boys buried their little tear stained faces into the folds of my skirt. It was only later that I learned of the details of Jack's passing.

It seems that he was returning from an organizational meeting of shoe workers in Everett, Massachusetts when he smelled smoke and saw the flames of a four alarm fire raging nearby. The blaze was threatening to engulf a row of tenement houses and all of the tenants were in need of being evacuated.

From what I was told, Jack assisted in these efforts and then assumed his accustomed role as a Boston Globe reporter who had arrived first on the scene of a noteworthy event. He would take out his notebook and secure statements from eye witnesses and others in the know on the cause and the effects of that conflagration.

He soon learned that Michael Moriarty, a close friend and Revere fireman Jack had helped to get on the force, had been killed in a fall from a rescue wagon. It was believed that Jack was on his way to inform his widow when he stepped into the path of that streetcar.

You know, I really can't remember who told me about all of that, whether I read it in the paper, or whether I heard it at the wake, where so many came to stand in a line that stretched through the pouring rain from the funeral home.

What I do remember most vividly, is the visit I received from General Charles Taylor, the distinguished President of the Boston Globe, who came to our home on the evening before the funeral. There he stood with his sterling silver hair and beard in a charcoal grey overcoat, his hat in hand. With tears in his eyes, he reached for my hand and kissed it. He expressed his deepest sympathy for my loss, telling me that I should not worry about the future, since Jack O'Sullivan's widow and children would be under his personal care and protection from that day onward.

Just before he left, I recall him taking me by both hands and whispering, "Jack was one of a kind, Mary. I loved him dearly." All I could say in response was, "I know General and I did as well." I recall Father Edward McGlynn delivering a stirring eulogy to a standing room only crowd at the Mission Church, and giving us all his blessing.

After Jack's casket was lowered into the ground. After the mourners had gone. After the funeral carriage departed from our home. I remember sitting there among my children and coming to the anguished realization that I was now a widow and I would have to fend for myself and them for the rest of my life. I never felt so alone and afraid as I was on that day.

I must confess that the remainder of that year and the first three months of 1903 are a blank page in the history that I recite. A blank page occasioned by the profound and overwhelming nature of my grief. It would cause me to lose all hope and drag me down into a dark spiral of depression. I cared not, whether I lived or died. If it weren't for the intercession of Elizabeth Glendower Evans, I would have been lost.

She would visit with me almost every day, consoling and counseling me to keep my faith and not succumb to the demons of my circumstance. If it had not been for her, I do believe that I would have either taken my own life or been committed to an asylum and a far different ending to this story would be written.

It is indeed a dreadful circumstance to be laid so low by darkness that you are unable to find your way back to the light. What is more difficult is the stigma that accompanies an illness of the mind that causes one suffering so awfully from it to become ashamed, anxious and afraid of everything and everybody, even those closest to you.

Perhaps the very worst part of that terrible ordeal was the despair that I felt and the blame that I felt God deserved for forsaking me. From the time that I was a little girl I had always prayed to The Blessed Mother on those occasions when the struggles of this life surrounded me and obtained a certain solace. Such was not the case during that horrid instance. A new avenue, another approach was needed. Vida Scudder and Elizabeth Evans would help me find it.

Vida was teaching at Wellesley College when she came to see me and tell me of this man that she had met at a meeting of the Massachusetts Society for the Prevention of Cruelty to Animals some years before. He was a scholar who had studied the teachings of Lao Tzu, Buddha and Emerson. A philosopher who was an influential member of the "New Thought Movement". An author whose book entitled *"In Tune with the Infinite"* had changed her life for the better, Ralph Waldo Trine. She and Elizabeth took me to see him speak at the Denison House on the night of April 18, 1903.

I can remember desperately trying not to fidget or attempt to flee during that carriage ride. My nerves were almost getting the best of me. They were like angels of mercy on a mission to save a lost soul. They were sitting on either side of me, holding each of my hands and telling me that I must believe. That the wisdom I was about to receive would bring me back, give me hope and help me to regain control of my life.

There it was. Its mention was like unto a beacon shining forth from my childhood, the word wisdom that I had wondered so much about. My desperation made me receptive to their entreaties. For the first time in months I whispered a prayer that all would be well as we arrived at the entrance to the Denison House.

As I climbed those familiar stairs to the second floor meeting room and felt the press of the crowd, after so many months of malaise, I somehow began to feel that I was about to undergo some sort of revelation. An epiphany that would help me set a new course in my life without Jack's love and affection to support me.

Doctor Trine was a dignified, handsome gentleman with auburn hair and piercing green eyes, two years my junior at thirty six. He was dressed in a grey coat and tails. His manner was gentle, almost reverent, like that of a clergyman. His voice was soothing and his speech was eloquent and inspired.

It was his gentleness that beguiled most, as he began to weave his spell over all in attendance with an unmistakable goodness. His message was profound yet simple. As I sat there, I could feel a warm, refreshing, reassurance suddenly come over me.

I can hear him still and see him standing there with his hands folded before him, as if he were praying. These are the words I remember most.

"The optimist and the pessimist are both right, since each creates their world from within. Their thoughts have the power to make either a heaven or a hell of their lives. Here is the wisdom. Taught to us long ago. "

"If we open ourselves to the influence of the Light Divine we can in turn become that Light, limitless, creative and courageous. The same holds true for opening ourselves to the darkness, we can in turn become dark, barren and fearful. It is our conscious choice to live a life that is full or a life that is empty.

"The Master, Jesus, spoke of this on the shore of the Galilean Sea when he said I and the Father are one. In order to enter heaven ye must be as a little child."

CHAPTER 47

I suppose if I had thought at length about the adversity of raising three young children and once again being the only breadwinner for our family, I would have given up and become another forlorn recipient of the charity of others. My epiphany on the night that Trine spoke and the reassurance of General Taylor's promised assistance would return the wind to my sails and begin a new and different course in the voyage of my life.

America in 1903 was on the verge of historic developments. There was Marconi's invention of the radio and the usage of its invisible waves to communicate across great distances. There was Edison's continued success in using the light of electricity to dispel the darkness of our cities and towns and his first promising attempts at moving pictures.

There was Ford's refinement of an automobile powered by an internal combustion engine that would usher in a new age of travel and mass production. There were the beginnings of subway systems in Boston and New York that would speed the pace of life in our cities. And there was the first instance of prolonged flight, inaugurated by the Wright Brothers down in Kitty Hawk, North Carolina.

Roosevelt's presidency and his cock sure confidence in the promise of America, became a stirring example of the power of positive thought. His sincere endeavors to bring about a square deal for each and every citizen, both immigrant and native born was a welcome change from business as usual in Washington.

His controversial speeches recognized the positive part that unions were playing in advocating for American workers and the negative part that monopolies and trusts such as Standard Oil were having on the country as a whole. He would herald in the Progressive Movement and its use of the golden rule to oppose the rule of the jungle.

His efforts to preserve and protect the wonders of nature from their mindless destruction and to create a canal in Panama that would link the Atlantic and Pacific oceans were visionary and beneficial to America and the world at large. It was pure and simply a time of momentous change both in my life and in the life of our country.

After much soul searching and prayerful meditation, I came to the conclusion that dramatic changes must be made in my means of making a living for my family. First and foremost, it was essential that I achieve a proper balance between my need to work and my family obligations.

It was on the last Sunday of that October when the lovely Mary Kehew came to visit and over a cup of tea strongly suggested that I look into employing a live in nurse maid to help care for my children, while I went back to work. Maybe it was my heritage, my pride or my distaste for domestic service that caused me to fail to see the forest from the trees.

Mary's gentle approach allowed me to come to grips with my new found reality. Feeling guilt ridden by the thought of having another woman involved in raising my children had to be overcome and forgotten.

Her name was Moira Doyle and she was a gift from God. She had been the older sister to five brothers in Galway before the sorry state of her country caused her to board a steamer for a turbulent voyage to Boston during her eighteenth year. At first, she took a job in a twine factory over in Roxbury that nearly robbed her of her health. Then she tried her hand as an apprentice book binder.

It was there where her raven hair, peaches and cream skin, blazing blue eyes and fine womanly frame brought the unwanted attention of a night foreman at the Huntington Printing Company, who attempted to take liberties on the second floor stairwell. This caused her to tender her resignation there and then. That was when she came to the Denison House in desperation, looking for a safe place to stay. That was when she found her way to me.

I can see her still, coming up the street toward our home, a note in her hand bearing our address, wearing her only warm coat of red and grey wool, along with a stocking hat of blue on that blustery November day. She was an immigrant girl who had been bruised and battered by life, but just proud and tough enough to make her way alone. I had a feeling right there and then, that she and I would become a matched pair and would work together to overcome the shared challenges of our circumstance.

By that time I was resolved to pursue certain avenues of employment that would combine to make up for the loss of Jack's salary. These would include taking a position as a rental agent for a real estate company in Boston, taking a positon performing periodic factory inspections for the State, submitting featured articles to the Globe on social issues, and last, organizing on behalf of working women. This would lead to the formation of the National Women's Trade Union League.

After interviewing Moira and her agreeing upon a weekly wage, along with room and board within our domicile, I advised her of my hopes and plans for both of our futures. Her experience in keeping a house and raising children along with her wholesome demeanor and eagerness to work and please, convinced me that she was the right choice as a housekeeper and nanny for my three children.

Phillip Cabot had introduced himself to me at Jack's wake. At that time, The Cabot Real Estate Company was making a name for itself in the renovation of run down rooming houses and apartment buildings through-out Boston. I had heard Jack speak highly of Mr. Cabot, a silver haired gentleman of Brahmin heritage and Ivy League pedigree, and the quality of his company's work in turning eye sores and dens of iniquity into safe and affordable residences for working men and women.

After interviewing with him and recognizing that he, like our President, was bent upon offering a square deal to all with whom he did business, I became the rental agent for a three story rooming house at 88 Warrenton Street in Boston. That position would prove to be an adventure for sure.

When I first visited the property, I discovered that the previous owner had illegally turned an office building into twenty four apartments for rent by the week or the month. There were blackboards on almost every wall and shabby, make shift residences hewn from former office space. It was a pig sty where derelicts congregated and prostitutes plied their trade. I remember speaking with the policemen on the beat, as to what I should do first. He advised half-jokingly "purchase a gun."

For the next few weeks I would travel by train and trolley from Revere into Boston, while the children became familiar with their very capable nurse maid. Her love and affection for her charges and their obedience to her commands reassured me that my need to make a living would not detract from their proper upbringing.

During that period I made observations of all the tenants and their living conditions and presented a listing to Mr. Cabot as to who should stay and who should leave. With the assistance of John Baron, a two fisted, red haired, construction superintendent, and Martin Lomasney, an alderman and ward healer from the Third District, we were able to discourage undesirables from congregating there.

I recall taking considerable satisfaction when Mr. Cabot and John "Honey" Fitzgerald, who would soon become the first Irish Catholic Mayor of Boston, appeared at a ceremony of sorts for 88 Warrenton Street's grand opening in March of 1904. It was attended by all the grateful tenants who had been selected to remain and those whose tenancy had recently been approved.

It was shortly after that event when Martin Lomasney sought me out and asked that I meet him one Saturday afternoon over in South Boston at the Ellis Memorial Building. It was an apartment house containing fifty six three room tenements, where recently arrived immigrants and their families were living.

It gives me great satisfaction to this day that I was able to enlist the assistance of General Taylor and his Boston Globe in publishing articles detailing the lives, the hopes and the dreams of these immigrant families that would lead to their improved living conditions. Through my contacts I was able to secure union jobs for most of the families' breadwinners and in many instances the education of their wives and children. The frosting on the cake was a ceremony at that location where almost all of those residents became naturalized citizens.

CHAPTER 48

When I lived in Chicago and Florence Kelley was appointed that state's Labor Commissioner, I became involved in performing factory inspections to safeguard the health and safety of workers. After moving to Boston, while organizing for the AF of L, I became painfully aware that hazardous working conditions in Massachusetts mills and manufactories were rampant.

It may seem difficult to believe, but it was a common occurrence to hear of workers being killed and maimed back then, with dire consequences befalling their family members. In the spring of 1904 I received my appointment as a factory inspector for the Commonwealth of Massachusetts and became a vigilant watchdog for worker safety.

Initially it was a twenty hour a week position and I could visit any factory within the state, as long as I provided a notice of forty eight hours to each factory owner before my first inspection. Once my visit was completed and a list of violations issued, the owners would be given from ten to thirty days to remedy each violation. As was the case in Illinois, my contacts with the board of health and the building inspectors of the cities and towns gave a bite to my bark and most often proved effective in eliminating most of the worst hazards.

The fact remained however that I was only one inspector and there were hundreds upon hundreds of work places in the state that I could not inspect. Once again I resorted to articles published in the Boston Globe and other newspapers to spread the word of the most common of the violations discovered.

Through my organizational efforts and my contacts with shop stewards and other workers representatives in the know, a system began to be put in place. A system that encouraged workers to be the keepers of their brothers and sisters' welfare, and help to prevent lives and limbs being lost due to owner carelessness and greed.

Although I assisted Florence Kelley in having legislation passed prohibiting child labor in Illinois, its evil dimensions had never really become a primary focus of my reform efforts until Sam Gompers enlisted me to look into its practice within the State of New York in the summer of that year. Like any evil, focusing upon it from afar allows for a certain detachment to occur, that avoids the anguish of delving into its darkest depths. I would venture into that darkness in July of 1904, only this time attired in widow's weeds.

It was always a joy to see Sam. He wanted me to help him bring an end to child labor in America and asked whether I could get the ball rolling in the City of New York. In light of the fact that children were doing work for paltry wages that union men and women could be performing for a living wage, he could justify paying me a generous salary. His ambition was to help expose and eventually eliminate this evil through the able assistance of his political associates in Albany.

I can recall him handing me what appeared to be a large brown and gold diary like book with the names and locations of businesses in Manhattan, Brooklyn and the Bronx where child labor was taking place. He then introduced me to a sandy haired giant of a man in his late twenties to serve as my body guard. Thus began my association with Michael "Moose" Mahoney.

Moose was an orphan who had been abandoned and left on the doorstep of a convent when tuberculosis took the lives of both his parents. At the age of fifteen he would be introduced to Peter McGuire and begin an apprenticeship in the carpentry trade. By age twenty eight he had become a card carrying member of the American Federation of Labor. Moose was tough and fearless with a knight's sense of obligation toward the weak and the less fortunate.

Sam had advised that laundry work was an occupation where children were being used and abused in New York. We were given the names of five separate laundries, where children, as young as seven, were supposed to be working twelve hours a day, six days a week.

The first and wickedest of these offenders was the Blue Star Laundry located in the lower East Side. Our practice was to arrive early, often before the sun came up, and take up a position where we could observe the arrival of the work force. What we observed was enough to make us weep.

As the orange traces of dawn began to dispel the darkness, we saw them. There they were, a dismal assortment of ragged, malnourished little wretches, both male and female, without joy, aging before their time. They were the product of an industrialized America, built upon greed and a careless indifference to the interests of the young.

I was outraged by what I saw and wanted to take whatever steps necessary to punish and even imprison those responsible for that state of affairs there and then. It was my protector who counseled patience until our inspection was complete. I can remember him reaching out his gigantic paw of a hand and directing me to the Blue Star Laundry's front entrance.

He proceeded to ring its front door bell repeatedly until a young ferret of a man opened the door. Moose flashed what appeared to be a badge and advised him that he and I were New York Factory Inspectors and we were there to conduct an inspection. When he protested, Moose summarily grabbed him by the collar and said,

"Listen little man, you can allow us to look you over, right here and right now, or you can appear at a hearing at City Hall to show cause why your place of business should not be shut down. What will it be?"

Needless to say, he let us pass and observe firsthand what we had suspected. It was an enormous, unventilated sweat shop where little children were engaged in scrubbing, washing, pressing and folding mounds of laundry from shirts and trousers to table cloths and towels from the finest of Manhattan's hotels and restaurants.

When I asked their overseer the age of the children employed by his company, he attempted to tell me that nobody who worked for the Blue Star Laundry was without a working permit. Since a working permit was only supposed to be issued to children fourteen and older, I demanded to see all of the working permits for the children standing right in front of me. His silence spoke volumes. We counted thirty six in all. None appeared older than the age of ten.

After finishing up with an inspection of the laundries listed and documenting each and every one of them as employing young children for slaves wages, we moved on to The Wilson Braiding Company in the Bronx. There we discovered a work force of females under the age of fourteen attending to dangerous machinery that could kill and maim.

It was at that location that the owner attempted to resist my inquiries by enlisting two threatening brutes to show us the way out. When one of them shoved me from behind and called me a profane name, Moose intervened on my behalf, beating both of those bullies bloody. In the aftermath I can remember him standing outside that dismal, windowless edifice in the pouring rain and asking me,

"Did he hurt you, Mrs. O'Sullivan?"

"Not at all, Michael."

"My friends call me Moose, mam."

"My friends call me, Mary, Moose."

"I get really upset when I see a woman being treated poorly."

"You're a good man, Michael, I mean Moose."

Perhaps the most heart rending places that we visited were located in the borough of Brooklyn. One was a twine factory whose dust, filth and odor were turning its work force of young boys and girls into a sorry congregation of ancients, soon to be plagued by tuberculosis and other assorted maladies that would cut their lives short. The other was a third floor factory of three rooms, without windows and a means of egress.

There we witnessed children as young as five in the company of brothers and sisters, seated at a series of work benches. Amid the very dimmest of lighting, they were working their little fingers bloody from morning to night, while fashioning scraps of metal into various bouquets of multicolored artificial flowers.

I remarked to Moose how so many of those babes were wearing spectacles before discovering that the paint they were using would coat their hands with a chemical that would eventually cause blindness when it came in contact with their sorrowful little eyes.

Many of these children were the sons and daughters of Italian immigrants whose parents had been forced to work for slave's wages and needed the income that their children could earn in order to survive in their new homeland. I can remember taking the most adorable dark featured little boy aside and speaking with him. He was no more than ten years of age. His name was Marcello.

"How many hours do you work a day, Marcello?"

"Twelve, Senora."

"How many days a week?"

"Six, Senora."

"Do you ever go out to play in the fresh air?"

"No Senora, no work, no eat."

I would like to tell you that my experience investigating and documenting these horrid instances of child labor at the behest of Sam Gompers bore fruit and soon resulted in the removal of its scourge from the American work place through laws passed and enforced. Sadly, that was not to be the case. Child labor in America would persist for decades.

CHAPTER 49

Over lo these many years of my involvement with the cause of working women, it has been a common occurrence that their hours of work and wages were always the first to be placed on the chopping block when the market for goods and services diminished. That was the harsh reality of the situation and crying about it would only make a bad situation worse. One of the first lessons I learned in my life was that nobody likes or listens much to a cry baby.

What was needed was a response to this reality that would turn a negative into a positive. It is remarkable how one circumstance can somehow lead to another down the road. I had begun to take my children to a summer camp over at Point Shirley in nearby Winthrop, which gave Moira, their nurse maid, some well-deserved time off. That was when Helena Dudley came for a visit and observed my preparing breakfast and then lunch for my children. I recall her remarking at that time,

"Wouldn't it be wonderful if the working women at Denison house could come here with their children and observe how you care for your children, so they could do the same when they return home."

It wasn't long after that when Elizabeth Evans mentioned that she had been speaking to Helena and the two of them were about to purchase a home at Point Shirley. When she and Helena came for a visit in the spring of 1904 they began to discuss turning that property into a camp from June through September where working girls who had been laid off could come and spend a week to rejuvenate themselves.

Since I had become quite used to lecturing and instructing, it became one of the distinct joys of my life to travel over to Point Shirley with my children in tow and meet with a host of working girls. They were of Polish, Irish, Italian and Syrian heritage who had come there for a respite from their labor. Under the direction of women who had their best interests and that of their children at heart, they would enjoy those occasions and improve their lives.

Our vacation retreat was located on Cottage Hill with magnificent views of both Boston Harbor and the Atlantic Ocean. After all the necessary renovations were completed, it could receive up to forty vacationers at a time. It was readily accessible by the railroad train from Boston.

During the warm weather months it would also be the only location we knew where large groups of working girls, as well as mothers and children could make their way to the beach and receive instructions on proper swimming techniques. There was also advice as to taking in the sun without becoming as red as lobsters.

I tell you there is nothing quite like the sun, the sea and the salt air taken in moderation to make you feel that your life is well worth living. It was a welcome change from the usual course of those vacationers' lives and one that they would look forward to repeating year after year.

How the girls loved their freedom. The camp was their home. The news of it soon spread throughout the factories and stores where they worked. We were flooded with applications. I soon became one of the camp's directors. In that position I did all the buying and hired a cook who would help me instruct our guests on the proper preparation of healthy meals on a modest budget.

We would set aside separate weeks during the season for mothers and their children, since young mothers most often want to have their children with them rather than worrying about them being somewhere else. Since most of the children came to the camp from congested tenements and streets, their little heads often needed to be inspected for little crawlers. Once disinfected, they could enjoy their vacation without spreading unwanted guests to the other vacationers.

Many of these children would grow up straight and strong while visiting our camp year after year. I know that I saved several grateful letters from vacationers who described their stays on Cottage Hill as some of the most memorable and enjoyable occasions of their lives.

I should probably tell you at this time of my involvement with the Women's Trade Union League and my association with a kind and committed young gentleman by the name of William English Walling. It began during the convention of the American Federation of Labor held at Boston's Faneuil Hall when Sam Gompers asked me to address the gathering on the benefits to be derived from the organization of women.

I remember this tall, handsome, smartly dressed, young man seated in the front row, diligently taking notes during my speech, then asking the most perceptive questions afterwards. After Sam introduced him to me as a disciple of Jane Addams and a devotee of the cause of working women, I agreed to meet him for dinner that evening at Boston's Revere House.

William English Walling was born into a wealthy Kentucky family. When he was ten years of age he was an eyewitness to the Bloody Sunday demonstrations in London. The bloodshed he witnessed of workers desperately seeking to improve their lives would never be forgotten and would inspire him to take up the workers' cause. He resided at Hull House after his graduation from the University of Chicago and came under the direction of Jane Addams and Florence Kelly.

He would then work for a time as a factory inspector and seek to correct conditions that were claiming the lives and well-beings of working men and women in Illinois. He was pure and simply a man after my own heart and one with whom I enjoyed a sisterly bond. I should tell you of our memorable first dinner engagement.

The Revere House was the foremost hotel in Boston, located in Bowdoin Square. It was where Charles Dickens and Ulysses Grant stayed when they came to town. That would be my first and only occasion to have dinner in its luxurious restaurant. A widow like myself, forced to watch her every expenditure, could never have afforded to dine there, had it not been for the generosity of the well healed Mr. Walling.

There he was in his late twenties, seated across the table from me, resplendent in a tailored grey suit, complemented by a formal collared white shirt and grey striped tie. He was there seeking my experience and views on a host of social topics, while humbly offering his own experience and views that revealed a wisdom and compassion far beyond his years. He soon came to his reason for coming to Boston.

"Mary, what do you think of a national union for working women?"

"I think it would be a great challenge."

"Would you help me put the pieces in place to form the National Women's Trade Union League?"

"We will need the support of the A F of L."

"I've already spoken to Mr. Gompers about it and he told me to speak with you first. He said if you're in, he will need to run it by Mr. Duncan, his Vice- President, but he doesn't see that as a problem."

"So that was the reason Sam insisted on my speaking at the convention."

"He said if he was going to begin such a union, you would be the first woman he would enlist. I have already spoken to Jane Addams and Florence. They both said the same thing."

"Do you understand what you're getting yourself into? Equal pay for equal work is a noble ideal, but very far from being realized."

"Then there's no time to waste, is there? Let's roll up our sleeves and get started."

"First things first, we must begin with a Constitution and a designation of officers."

Over the next three hours we soared from nuts and bolts to mission statements to our dreams for a new day in the quest for female equality. Our waiter finally asked that the check be paid. When William discovered that he lacked sufficient funds, he excused himself and after a short interval returned with payment in full but without his watch.

CHAPTER 50

he textile workers strike in Fall River, Massachusetts began in July of 1904. It would become a baptism of fire for the newly created Women's Trade Union League. It would bring to the surface all of the disputes and differences that made our quest for a fair shake for female workers so difficult. It began, as most strikes begin, with the decision of the owners to enact an across the board reduction in wages for all workers, blaming the price of cotton and competition from down south as its reasons.

When I was first notified that a strike was imminent, I remember asking William Walling to find out how many mill workers were union members and how many workers were not. To my chagrin, I was advised that there were 72 mills employing more than twenty thousand, mostly female, cotton mill workers in Fall River. There were less than five thousand who were members of craft unions, and they were men.

I knew right away that the decision of the mill owners was made at that point in time because their inventories were fully stocked and they could endure a loss of production without experiencing a loss of income. In fact, a work stoppage by the mill workers would be of benefit to the owners, since their expenses would be reduced by not paying workers out on strike, thus increasing their profits. It was cutthroat capitalism at its worst, without conscience or concern for workers and their families.

The first order of business was to not break ranks and allow the owners to use poorly paid, unskilled female workers who had not been organized to replace the higher paid craft workers who had the benefit of savings and a strike fund to fall back on. Meetings were held in union halls, church basements and public parks to stress the importance of hanging together through thick and thin.

Fliers were distributed in French, Portuguese and Polish inviting workers to join together by joining the WTUL. Just as before with the Pullman Strike, there was a conflict in interests between organized craft workers and disorganized industrial workers that the owners would seek to exploit to gain greater control of the entire industry. In addition, there was the usual difference between what a male worker was receiving as a weekly wage and what his female counterpart was being paid.

The last division that would complicate the Fall River strike and was its most sinister was the prejudice that existed between the more experienced French Canadian textile workers, both male and female, and the less experienced non-English speaking Portuguese and Polish workers. This hampered their joining together for a common purpose.

I can recall an open air meeting held in a Fall River ball field shortly after the strike began. There were close to four thousand female mill workers in attendance on that blazing hot day. The open hostility and crude comments that I heard from the French Canadian women concerning the dress and hygiene of their Polish and Portuguese coworkers was appalling. It was a prejudice that needed addressing right away. I had brought three translators with me to deliver our message loud and clear.

On that occasion I was accompanied by William Walling who wanted to attend a labor rally where labor organizers spoke to a gathering of mostly female, non- English speaking workers. With the assistance of an enormous megaphone I was the last to address the crowd. I recall that I had forsaken my widow's weeds of black on that occasion for a white cotton blouse and skirt that I had purchased in a Fall River thrift shop before the strike began. I would await the translation of each segment of my speech before pressing on. Here is a portion of what was said.

"Have you had enough of being treated as slaves of the work place, sisters?

Have you witnessed the firing of your fellow workers who gave the best years of their lives to the owners, only to be discarded and replaced once they reach age forty, so they can heap more work on the shoulders of younger women? Have you seen more modern machinery increase production and owners' profits while your hours and your wages are being slashed and your families suffer? "

"The only way that we can be treated as equals by men in this world is to treat each other as equals, as sisters with the same heritage of want, with the same yearning to break free, with the same need to organize and speak up for justice. If you want to fight and succeed against the oppression that surrounds us all, we must unite as sisters, having the same hearts and the same souls that will lead us to our salvation."

The Fall River textile workers strike would become a case study of ruthless owners seeking once again to divide and conquer workers who were very often victims of their own lack of organization and concern for their fellow workers. At first it was expected to be a strike lasting but a few weeks in warm weather but became one that would last into the frigid winter of 1905 resulting in the untold suffering, starvation and even suicide of all too many desperate workers. It was an experience that William Walling and I would never forget and a supreme test of the mettle of our newly formed WTUL.

What came to light as the strike dragged on was the indifference of the AF of L to the legitimacy of the Women's Trade Union League. I was convinced that my trusted friend and mentor, Sam Gompers, believed in his heart of hearts that women should receive equal pay for equal work but his rank and file membership simply did not. This was evident from their repeated refusals to confer the right to vote as delegates to any member of the WTUL, including myself.

It was a back handed slight that was orchestrated by Frank Foster, once a devoted friend of my late husband, who had presided over the Boston Central Labor Union for years and still wielded enormous influence in Massachusetts labor circles. I should tell you of our confrontation after I learned about his role in all of this.

I took the train in from Revere to his office located on Congress Street in downtown Boston. It was in late October of 1904. By that time Frank had developed the appearance of Father Christmas with his shock of white hair and florid complexion. He was a stocky man in his fifties. My diary recounts our discussion almost word for word.

"What can I do for you, Mary?"

"I've been told that you've opposed making any WTUL member a voting delegate to the AF of L."

"That's correct."

"Why?"

"Because it's a union in name only, full of wealthy do-gooders and settlement house proprietors that have no understanding of trades or trade unionism. When push comes to shove, they will make a run for the door. You're an exception to them of course, but I just don't believe that they are deserving."

"Are you aware that there are roughly twenty thousand women down in Fall River right now, who have braved utter poverty and imminent starvation to stay out of work in support of the WTUL and against the greed of the mill owners? Don't you believe that makes them deserving?"

"My heart goes out to them, Mary, believe me, but my first obligation is to our rank and file membership and not to them. If you want change, you should seek to secure the right of women to vote and make your power felt at the ballot box. Stop being a thorn in the side of organized labor with your female union."

"Organized old men, set in their ways, is more like it, Frank. If my Jack were alive, he would be ashamed of you. He would have believed in the WTUL. He would have done all within his power for worker equality. Good day to you."

I had been involved in the distribution of food and clothing to striking workers and their suffering families before in Chicago, but the pathetic scenes of poverty and starvation that I sought to remedy during the Fall River Textile Strike made me weep.

Day after day the situation seemed to worsen as I visited the tenements where these families lived. The cry of starving children is a pitiable sound like no other.

On repeated occasions the WTUL would seek the assistance of both public and private sources of charity to help alleviate the suffering. The Cities of Fall River and New Bedford did what they could. The churches, synagogues and soup kitchens did what they could, while sympathizers with and without means put their money where their noble sentiments were. Still, it remained an endless ordeal of distress with the cruelty of winter fast approaching.

That was when I once again reached out to Sam Gompers for his advice and his aid. He would send a telegram in response, inviting me to put forth our cause at the A F of L convention in San Francisco that November. He likewise forwarded sufficient funds for train fare and lodging for myself and a traveling companion. It would be a journey of mercy that I would not soon forget. It would be a journey I would make with Leonora O'Reilly, that truly courageous angel of mercy.

As I mentioned earlier in this narrative, I had met Leonora and her mother, Winifred on the night that Jack gave his stirring speech at Faneuil Hall during the rubber workers strike. When she arrived from Brooklyn to lend her support as a member of the WTUL's Executive Committee during the Fall River strike, I had just received the telegram from Sam and inquired as to whether she would want to accompany me on my cross country mission to speak at the A F of L convention.

She simply stated, "When do we leave?" I tell you, she was a young woman cut from the very same cloth as myself and devoted to the cause of working women. We would depart from South Station on November 7, 1904, a blustery grey day. Two women of common purpose who were about to embark on a most memorable excursion across America.

CHAPTER 51

I had been hearing about Leonora and her commitment to the cause of equal pay for equal work ever since our first encounter. As I may have mentioned, she was an attractive young woman who was six years my junior with lovely chestnut hair, a flawless complexion and the most vivacious azure eyes. As long as we knew each other, I never saw her downcast or dressed in other than the latest style, despite the fact that she and I had lost our fathers at a very young age and as a consequence entered the work force under difficult circumstances.

Our similarities did not end there. Her devoted father was also a member of the Knights of Labor and famine Irish with an abiding distrust of the wealthy and the powerful. In addition, Leonora was absolutely devoted to her widowed mother. She had been a disciple of Father Edward McGlynn and her and her mother had recently resided in a New York settlement house. It was as if the fates had determined that we were meant to be two sturdy branches of the same flowering tree.

We left South Station at eight in the evening on the first leg of our journey. We would avail ourselves of a freshly painted forest green Pullman Sleeper on that cross country sojourn, heading west on the New York Central Railway through the farms and fields of western Massachusetts. Thereafter, we traveled out through the Mohawk Valley and on to Albany, the pastoral capital of New York State.

Along the way I remember thinking of the Pullman Strike ten years earlier and all the water that had passed under the bridge since the completion of the transcontinental railroad after the Civil War. I couldn't help but think of my father and mother and the parts they had played in helping to build what would become part of the Union Pacific Railroad, after fleeing the land of their birth.

Both Leonora and I had grown up reading the works of Irving and Cooper and thrilled to the sights and sounds of historic places that played a role in tales like that of the sleepy Rip Van Winkle and the fearless Hawkeye and his blood brother Uncas attempting to rescue the Munro sisters from the Huron Indians. I tell you, we were like two sisters ourselves, thrilled to be in each other's company and thrilled to be playing a part in our own American adventure story.

Neither of us had experienced traveling within a sleeping car before that occasion and marveled at the speed in which George, our silver haired black porter, transformed our carriage seats into top and bottom bunkbeds an hour into our journey and then enclosed us both within the privacy of a dark green curtain. I tell you I can still see his face and remember the soothing sound of his cordial voice as he patiently answered all of our questions. He would address our concerns and minister to our every need, like some sort of guardian angel.

That was a tumultuous time in the country. Teddy Roosevelt would be elected to a second term in office. Progressives were popping up everywhere to remedy the evils of industrialization, urbanization and the flood of immigrants coming to America. Work would begin on the Panama Canal and America would ascend beyond all expectations toward becoming a worldwide power.

In response came the "Muckrakers", as Roosevelt called them, and a brand of journalism that would expose the schemes, shoddy behavior and darkest secrets of successful companies and their owners, whom other compromised publications had canonized.

I can remember both Leonora and I buying the latest issue of McClures from the delightful little man that traversed the train with his overflowing cart. He was also selling Cracker Jacks, Hershey Bars, and sundry merchandise. We both read Ida Tarbell's latest installment of *The History of Standard Oil,* as we made our way west.

From Albany we traveled toward Buffalo with the rhythmic rumble of the rails rocking us toward our destination. Leonora was a marvel at conversation. Her infectious Brooklyn accent and expressions made me smile and chuckle with the very fondest admiration.

I remember when the conductor shouted that Niagara was the next stop growing suddenly sullen with memories of my husband and our honeymoon flooding my mind. I must admit that I soon began to cry, causing Leonora to simply lean over and whisper, "It will be alright. He is here with you in spirit, Mary dear."

She and I grew closer and closer as the miles of our journey passed. For hours on end we conversed about our lives and the places and people that had played a part in them. With the assistance of a young, coffee colored porter, who likewise advised that his name was George, we secured a pack of playing cards and a tiny red and black checkerboard with tiny red and black checkers to play upon it.

It turned out that Leonora was a pretty fair card and checker player, telling me that Winnifred, her worldly wise mother, would play for pennies with the men who lodged in their boarding house. She would often bestow a bag of penny candy upon her daughter the next morning, while advising that she had "cleaned up last night".

At each stop we would observe passengers depart and passengers coming aboard, sometimes striking up acquaintances; other times simply wondering about the lives of those who were playing their parts in a changing America. Leonora was an amateur artist of sorts who possessed a small sketch book in which she chronicled the landscapes and people encountered. We would travel along the southern shore of Lake Erie on through Pennsylvania, on to Ohio and Michigan then up through northern Indiana toward Chicago. The Lake Shore & Michigan Southern Railway was a small but very efficient rail line at that time.

Some of the stations that we saw were like cathedrals or museums of remarkable architecture that spoke of the artistry and sacrifice of those that had designed and built them. For someone such as myself who had seen the dark side of the railroad interests first hand, I began to develop a grudging appreciation for those whose foresight and skill had bestowed the freedom to travel upon countless Americans across our great land.

I should mention one episode that brought another aspect of the American experience home to both Leonora and me. As I mentioned, on that portion of our trip we had a courteous young porter named George attending us. I would watch him assisting others on board and noticed that he always maintained a cheerful servility that seemed on certain occasions to be less than genuine, especially when unthinking white passengers were rude or even insulting in the manner in which they treated him.

I believe we had just left the stop at Gary Indiana when three men entered our railway car who had a certain air about them that caused both Leonora and me to become uneasy. The elder of the three, a bearded bear of a man in his fifties in a white fedora, would soon become loud and obnoxious, while drinking from a silver flask. When he began to bother the other passengers aboard, our conductor intervened, telling him to please behave himself or he would be put off at the next stop. For a while he seemed to heed this warning.

I overheard their conversation at one point about a gathering that they were on their way to in Chicago, and the mention of a certain grand dragon who would be in attendance. I recall leaning over at that point and whispering to Leonora "I think those men are members of the Ku Klux Klan." It was clear to me that Leonora had heard of that sinister organization, which had risen to power after the Civil War.

I remember both of us beginning to eavesdrop more closely when George, our porter, unfortunately entered the car, inquiring whether he could be of assistance to the passengers aboard. That was when that white haired bully began calling to him.

"Hey, what you want, boy? Checking in to see if you can sneak a peek at some white women in their night gowns? "

I could tell that George heard what was being said but tried to ignore it. I felt awful for him and ashamed that he should have to endure such insults, while just trying to do his job and earn a living. Still that bully persisted,

"Did you hear me, Sambo? I think my shoes need shining. Come on over and let me rub your head for good luck."

From the time I was a little girl in Hannibal, I had seen white people mistreat black people as if the Civil War had never been fought. Racial hatred was an evil to be despised and fought against. That was probably what got into me when I suddenly rose and flew into a rage, while making a bee line toward that hooligan and his companions.

"You leave that man alone. Do you hear me? You should be ashamed of yourself and know better at your age. If I were a man, I would punch you right in your nose. You're just a bully and a coward. That's all you are."

To my astonishment, he offered not so much as a word in response. He simply stared at me with hatred oozing from every pore. Then he took another drink from his flask and curled up toward the window, as if to fall asleep. That was when I heard it. It was the sound of applause and hoorahs from the other passengers on board.

I remember blushing and returning to my seat beside a smiling Leonora O'Reilly.

Before we changed trains in Chicago, she would give George a flattering portrait that had been drawn in charcoal. She had been working on it since our stopover in Cleveland. Beneath his image was the notation, "Keep the Faith."

We thanked him for all that he had done for us. Words were not necessary as he silently accepted our gratitude with a humble nod and a smile. Tears of appreciation were brimming in his eyes.

As an old woman, I am of the considered opinion that greed and prejudice are the twin evils that have plagued America from the start, and caused untold pain and suffering to so many, even here in 1944, during this Second World War.

CHAPTER 52

There was a seven hour delay in Chicago before we were to board the Union Pacific "Sleeper" onward to our destination in San Francisco. I sent a telegram from Indianapolis to Jane Addams, advising of our anticipated arrival and to our delight she and her closest friend, Mary Rozet Smith, were waiting for us when our train pulled into the Union Depot. It was a frosty cold November morning, as we made our way by carriage through familiar environs to Hull House. After a nap and a bath, Leonora and I would become reacquainted with two close friends and supporters of the women's cause.

Mary Smith was a delightful woman of means, in her late thirties, with a giving heart and a devotion to music, juvenile justice and the cause of women's suffrage. She had become one of the primary benefactors and trustees of Hull House after nursing Jane Addams back to health following a bout with typhoid fever.

By 1904 Hull House had become a complex of several buildings that included a residence for up to twenty five women, a kindergarten, a gymnasium, an art gallery, a book bindery, a gigantic kitchen and a flourishing night school where mostly immigrants from the surrounding neighborhoods came to receive a higher education.

After a guided tour of the grounds and facilities and Mary's spirited rendition of the *Battle Hymn of the Republic* on a magnificent Hook and Hastings pipe organ, a scrumptious dinner was served. It was then that a fateful discussion would occur that would chart the course from our past accomplishments toward our future endeavors.

It was the now silver haired Jane who began the discussion and graced us with her special brand of gentility and wisdom. With the years, she was no longer as small or as frail as she had been. Her affliction still persisted but her face was that of an aging matriarch.

"To see you and our lovely Leonora faring so well and carrying on so courageously on behalf of our sisters in Fall River is one of the satisfactions of my life," she began. "I understand that you're off to San Francisco on a mission of mercy. "

"Mary is the one in the lead, as always. I am just along for the ride," Leonora offered, displaying an affectionate smile.

"I would not have been able to come, if it hadn't been for you, Leonora. Your companionship has made this journey a joy. I must say that the challenges facing the Women's Trade Union League and the cause of female equality seem to be steadily increasing. I wonder whether there is another course we can follow to make our cause a reality."

"Miss Smith and I have been mulling this over and we are of the notion that our cause must proceed along several separate but interlocking channels in order to succeed," Jane declared. "Why don't you explain it to them, Mary."

"I certainly am respectful of all that you and Leonora have done in organizing working women and I firmly believe that your efforts must continue in earnest," she began, with the most marvelous diction.

She was an educated lady in her middle years with an attractive face and style. It was her ability to offer comprehensive solutions to pressing problems that impressed me most and made her a godsend to our cause and our movement.

"A unified approach is the only way to achieve our objective of real and lasting equality," she continued. "Beyond organizing, we must move simultaneously to secure women's suffrage by an amendment to Our Constitution. This should be followed by the organized exercise of that suffrage to elect progressive candidates for elected offices. These should coincide with our becoming vocal and visible advocates of legislation meant to protect and promote the public welfare. We must also eliminate child labor and hazardous work-places that maim and kill."

I was impressed by the depth of her understanding and wisdom on matters that I had made causes in my life. I sat there with my cup of tea in hand, reflecting upon my life and once again coming to the realization that I was truly blessed by the people who assisted and inspired me throughout it. I recall offering this measured response.

"You know ladies, when I first came to Hull House as little more than a working girl and the caretaker of an invalid mother, I was reluctant to listen, let alone accept the different viewpoints of others who were not cut from the same cloth as me. It was first and foremost, our sister Jane, then our sister Florence and now you, Mary, who helped to show me the way."

"I wholeheartedly agree with you. From now on, we must proceed along several separate but interlocking channels to achieve our goal, both in and out of the workplace. I'm always ready to be inspired whenever I come for a visit to Hull House."

On the next leg of our journey westward we traveled through vast stretches of America. These made us marvel at the courage and sacrifice of those who made their way westward in covered wagons and those who braved misery and death to build the railroads.

On we rumbled through Saint Louis and over the great Missouri. Across the sandy plains of Kansas and through the frontier towns of Abilene, and Topeka we traveled, then up along the majestic mountains of Colorado with stops in Denver and Boulder. We then made our way down through Ogden Utah, where the transcontinental railroad was first completed. Finally, we traveled across the desert of Nevada and onward into California.

Throughout it all, we were observers and chroniclers. I was taking detailed notes, while Leonora continued with her memorable sketches. All the while we acquainted ourselves with all manner of people and places that would become the heartland of America and a veritable promised land for native and foreign born alike.

After our arrival in San Francisco, we took a short carriage ride to the Saint Francis Hotel as the delegates were just beginning to arrive for this, the second AF of L convention to be held there. It was a day of bright sunshine and crisp salt air that soon turned overcast and stormy in what seemed a matter of minutes.

As we were making our way through the hotel's spacious lobby, we saw our old friend, Sam Gompers, holding court amid the crowd, while acknowledging our arrival with the wave of his hand. Suddenly, a distinguished looking Clarence Darrow approached us in the company of a giant of a young man wearing an eye patch. His name was Bill Haywood and he would prove to be one of a kind.

CHAPTER 53

Clarence Darrow had taken up the cause of the Pennsylvania coal miners during the anthracite coal strikes of the previous two years. Through President Roosevelt's dogged efforts those strikes were finally settled and a new era in labor relations was begun. It was apparent by the way he gazed at the lovely Leonora and tenderly embraced and kissed my hand that he had not changed his flirtatious ways.

"It is a joy to see you once again, Mary. Your Jack would be thrilled, if he could witness this gathering. Tell me, who is this captivating creature? "

"She is a very special lady and devoted to our cause. Leonora O'Reilly meet Clarence Darrow."

"Pleased to make your acquaintance," Leonora offered. "I'm an admirer."

"Let me introduce Bill Haywood to you both. If you've not heard of him, you most certainly will. Bill and I have just come from Chicago where we have made plans for a brand new union for all the workers in America."

"Pleased to meet you." Haywood responded shyly.

We met with Sam Gompers that evening for dinner. Through his countless travels, and tireless work he was well on his way to creating a federation of labor whose reach was worldwide. He was in his mid-fifties then with silver hair and thick bifocals. Despite all he had to attend to in running that convention, he still managed to take the time to dine with us.

It was there that he provided advice in appealing for assistance from that mostly male rank and file.

Sam had appeared at a rally in Fall River the month before and delivered a stirring speech to an audience of strikers to continue to stand up against the degradation of wage slavery. That speech would inspire a renewed dedication on the part of those strikers to persevere. We thanked him for all that he had done in making our cross country pilgrimage possible. I recall him telling me,

"Mary, you came to our attention long ago because of a speech you gave in Chicago. A speech that only you could deliver because of your experience and your passion. I have arranged that you will be the last of the speakers at the convention. "

The magnificent second floor ball room of the world renowned Saint Francis Hotel was illumined by a dozen enormous chandeliers. Leonora and I had saved our very finest outfits to act as the sole representatives of the Women's Trade Union League. I had worked on my address for hours on end, refining and rehearsing it with the inspired assistance of my lovely sister in arms, before retiring in the wee hours of the morning.

As I mentioned, I had grown accustomed to speech making over the years and had pretty much lost my fear of the stage and the moment. Yet I wanted that speech to be special, to stand out as the very best I could deliver. I remember looking through a cloud of cigar smoke into the enormity of that mostly male crowd, as speaker after speaker before me delivered their appeals on a host of needy causes, too plentiful to recollect.

As Leonora and I sat side by side on that stage, I suddenly had the most vivid recollection of Mother Jones speech on Saint Patrick's Night in Chicago. I tell you it was as if she was right there with us. As I was introduced, I whispered a final prayer and surrendered to the spirit within me and began to soar.

"Men of the American Labor Movement, I come to you first and foremost as a worker who has suffered the privation of paltry wages, while providing the sole support for an invalid mother. I come to you next as the widow of a labor leader, whose inspiration and love remains with me still. I am the mother to three young children whose company I currently long for across the reach of America."

"I come to you in the company of my sister, Leonora, cut from the same enduring cloth, daughters of fathers who fled from the famine and fever that plagued their homeland. Fathers who died before their time. Fathers who were overworked and underpaid by bosses and owners who grew rich from their labors. Fathers who taught us that only through organization and an abiding concern for one another will we one day overcome injustice and attain the freedom and equality that are our birthrights as Americans. "

"We come to you as workers, daughters, sisters and organizers so that you can accompany us back across America to the Massachusetts Mill Town of Fall River. So that you can hear the terrible, anguished cries of starving children, ragged, cold and without hope in a world of darkness, a world dominated by the greed and the power of the textile mills. A desperate world where winter fast approaches and a prolonged strike continues without end or mercy."

"Come with us and meet two working women who have chosen to join our union in order to make a better life for their families. They are working women who fled from their homelands to the promise of America. One is Maria Rezendes, the other is Katrina Kowolski, wives and mothers both. One comes from the Azores of Portugal and the other from Warsaw in Poland. They are in their twenties, forced to take up the textile trade along with their husbands in order to survive."

"See the terror in their eyes and the eyes of many thousands more, as day after day passes without a resolution of their fight for a living wage and less hours. Feel their pain, as they look into the eyes of their loved ones, while living in dilapidated tenements, where vermin abound, without food, without heat, without help. "

"They are part of one great sea of workers, forced to become little more than beggars, at the mercy of those who control their workplaces. See them struggle to stave off starvation and the hopeless release of suicide. Witness their agony, their humanity and their identity as fellow workers in need of your compassion and your assistance. Please, don't forget or abandon them."

Clarence Darrow's friend, Bill Haywood, was the first to approach and thank me, his enormous face stained with tears. The next morning as Leonora and I were leaving the hotel, to head back across the country, there was Frank Foster. It was contrition that I saw in his florid face as he drew near, offering his hand and speaking tenderly,

"Mary, your speech made us want to lend a helping hand to your membership.

Here is a check for twenty thousand from the BCLU and my solemn promise to do whatever we can to bring an end to the suffering in Fall River. Please accept my gratitude for making me see the light."

With the funds provided by the BCLU and those to follow, the WTUL mustered through a bitterly cold December and a vain effort by the textile mill owners to reopen just before Christmas in a sinister attempt to break the unions that had called upon them to strike.

As I mentioned, the anthracite coal strike of two years before was resolved through the intercession of President Roosevelt and had a ripple effect throughout the country. For the very first time the federal government did not side with the owners and recognized the legitimacy of unions and that of the workers cause. The Progressive movement was now in full stride.

The adverse publicity generated by the prolonged Fall River strike caused the newly elected, democratic Governor of Massachusetts, William L. Douglas, to step into the fray on the same day that the Boston Globe reported upon the suicide of one hopeless striker and the attempted suicides of three others.

On January 18, 1905 it would be reported that through the mediation of Governor Douglas, a settlement of the cotton mill strike had been achieved and all mill workers were to return to their labors forthwith. Alas, it was a day of jubilation and thanksgiving for both Leonora and me, as well as that of the rank and file of our Women's Trade Union League.

CHAPTER 54

espite a more enlightened approach toward unions and the plight of workers on the part of the President and a smattering of governors and mayors, strikes and violence resulting in death and destruction were still common place occurrences throughout 1904 and 1905 in America.

These included transit workers strikes in New York, packing house workers strikes in Chicago and continued bloodshed in the coal fields of Western Pennsylvania, with Mother Jones in the forefront. Meanwhile out west, Bill Haywood's Western Federation of Miners would engage in pitched battles with private detectives and scabs in the blood drenched Colorado Labor Wars.

Perhaps the most notable of these violent strikes was the sympathy strike of the Chicago Teamsters that began in April of 1905 arising from a clothing workers strike against Montgomery Ward. It would result in 21 deaths, hundreds being wounded and the destruction of property in the millions of dollars.

Upon our return from San Francisco, there was a shoe workers strike in the mill town of Haverhill Massachusetts. That would be where Leonora and I on behalf of the Women's Trade Union League succeeded in winning concessions from the mill owners as to wages and hours of work. Our victory was the direct result of the perseverance demonstrated during the prolonged Fall River strike.

It was at that time that the O'Sullivan family along with our indispensable housekeeper, Moira Doyle, moved from Revere to a spacious three bedroom apartment located at 351 Dudley Street in Roxbury. That was when an old friend from Chicago came calling with a proposition that would play an important part in my future and that of the movement.

When she appeared at our front door, Lucy Parsons was then a smartly dressed distinguished looking woman in her fifties with silver hair and a regal bearing that belied the untold difficulties she had endured after the execution of her husband. She had read of my speech in San Francisco and sent a telegram in care of the WTUL advising that she would be traveling back east and wanted to arrange a meeting to renew an old friendship with a sister in arms.

After introducing her to the children, Moira took them down to a nearby variety store, allowing Lucy and me the opportunity to become reacquainted after so much water had passed beneath each of our bridges. She was one of the editors of the *Liberator* at that time, a publication of anarchists and socialists. She remained a fiery advocate in the cause for women's rights. The front room of the Dudley Street apartment on that sun splashed May afternoon gave us a panoramic view of a Boston being transformed by the engines of industrial progress.

Along with a recently constructed trolley line there was a building boom of apartment buildings, shops and factories taking place along Tremont Street. Over a delightful cup of tea and a delicious helping of Moira's coffee cake, we conversed like sisters with much in common.

"When I read about your speech I couldn't help but remember our first meeting in Chicago," Lucy began. "You were just a young girl back then. Now here you are, a mother with children but still speaking up for workers. Tell me whatever became of Michael Duffy, I've just lost track."

"He drowned trying to save a mother and child after a ferry collision in New York. He was one of my father's closest friends. He and my father were members of the Knights of Labor. "

"In a way that is why I've come. I understand that you've become acquainted with Bill Haywood. He asked me to enlist women I knew and admired into our organization. He has asked me to enlist you in particular. We will be meeting next month in Chicago and he wanted you to come and join us. It will be called the Industrial

Workers of the World and it will become the most powerful union that the working class has ever known."

"I have my hands full right now with the Women's Trade Union League and want to see it progress to where it should. That is where my allegiance is right now, Lucy. Who else is involved with your group?"

"Gene Debs, Bill Haywood, and Mother Jones, are some of its leaders and we expect a rank and file in the hundreds of thousands, since our object is not to organize a craft or a shop of workers but entire industries of workers. This is the only way that the workers of the world will become truly united and secure the means of production. It's a class struggle, Mary. Come join with us. We need you. You can continue with your group and still be one of the leaders of the IWW."

I remember looking into the flame of her green eyes as she spoke so fervently and wanting to assist her so badly. She was truly an inspiration. I knew that the course ahead for the WTUL and female equality would be an uncertain one, marked by frustration and failure but it had to be a righteous course, without resorting to violence.

"Lucy, what you're telling me may very well be true. But you must know that the means of production will never be turned over to workers voluntarily. It will require violence and bloodshed that will destroy everything good and decent in America."

"And Lucy, there is much that is good and decent in America.

I appreciate you coming here to meet with me but I owe it to my kids and I owe it to America, to stay the course with the WTUL."

On June 27, 1905 at Brand's Hall in Chicago, Bill Haywood opened the first convention of the Industrial Workers of the World. In the crowd on that occasion were Gene Debs, Mother Jones, Lucy Parsons and Clarence Darrow, along with two hundred delegates representing the interests of socialists, anarchists, miners and industrial' workers.

In fiery words, fashioned in the darkness and inhumanity of the Colorado coal mines, he prophesied that conflict between capitalists and workers in America was inevitable. He predicted that the only way in which workers could gain their freedom was to gain possession of the means of production by whatever means necessary.

I remember reading that speech and gathering my children around me, just as my mother had gathered us around her, and praying fervently that love not hatred would bring freedom and equality for all in America. I say those prayers still.

The presidency of Theodore Roosevelt gave many of us in the labor movement cause for hope. He continued to speak of a "square deal" for all Americans, rich and poor, owner and worker. It was at that time that he used the Sherman Anti-Trust Act to take on John D. Rockefeller and the industrial octopus that was Standard Oil. That was where he would win his well-deserved reputation as the *"Trust Buster "*. It was shortly thereafter when he would step upon the world stage and mediate a peace treaty between Russia and Japan and win a Nobel Prize.

During that time, I remember dining once again with our old friends, Louis and Alice Brandeis in their Beacon Hill home and listening to Louis speak of the philosophy of Aristotle and the necessity for achieving balance between competing forces to achieve unity and goodness in all things. He was convinced that the same balance was needed between the interests of capital and labor.

It reminded me of the sayings of Lao Tzu and the words of Trine. Despite all that I had witnessed and endured in my life, I still had hope for the future, when so many around me had none. I suppose it was a hope that stemmed from my experience and my faith. It has made me continue on with the struggle.

Living in the Dudley Street apartment made it easier for me to care for my children and ease the feelings of guilt that plague working mothers that their most important responsibilities are playing second fiddle to the need to earn a living. With the access to trolleys from Roxbury and the new subway line between Boylston and Park Streets I could make sure the boys were off to school with a kiss and hug and Moira's day with little Mary was mapped out. Thereafter, I could still manage to be at my desk in the State House by 8 A.M.

My duties as a State Inspector for the Department of Labor and Industries would often result in my giving testimony in court. I always loved the pageantry and the drama of court trials. I can say that I never brought a violation to court where I didn't give the offending factory or business ample opportunity to remedy the situation beforehand, and thus avoid both the bad publicity and the public punishment that often resulted.

I recall one instance where I was leaving the Boston Municipal Court when a court officer approached and asked me to accompany him to Judge Murray's chambers down the hall. He said not a word as we walked together down that corridor through a crowd of claimants and criminals, congregating there to have their cases heard. I must say I felt anxious as I waited outside Judge Murray's office, before he summoned me to enter.

"Mrs. O'Sullivan", he began, as he rose with a smile and the tender of his hand, "I want to tell you that because of the fair play you give all the Defendants you bring to our Court to enforce the laws, you are a first class public official. Thank you for your dedication."

"Thank you, Judge, for your kind words and your fairness," was my sincere response.

I suppose everybody needs a pat on the back and a compliment now and again to keep them going, especially an unsolicited one. If circumstances were otherwise in my lifetime, I would have loved to become a trial lawyer. Then I would have been able to use my training and my wits to try cases for the common good.

Trial lawyers like Louis Brandeis, Clarence Darrow and others, whose names are now forgotten to history, were often scorned and attacked by the powerful during those times in America. In many instances they would become the solitary guardians of our liberty. That was the way it was and that is the way it continues to be.

CHAPTER 55

*I*n the early morning hours of April 18th of 1906 a devastating earthquake would rumble through the City of San Francisco and its environs, killing thousands. It was the greatest natural disaster to ever hit America. In its aftermath, whole city blocks were destroyed and hundreds of thousands were made homeless.

I remember completing a lecture at Wellesley College in the late afternoon and stopping at a nearby newsstand, as was my custom, to pick up the late edition of the *Boston Globe*. It was then that I saw its startling headline in bold letters, crying, DISASTER.

The San Francisco earthquake would generate worldwide interest and sympathy for months to come and provoke some misguided souls into believing that the end of the world was coming soon. I still have that edition of the *Globe* in my files at home and I still read it from time to time in appreciation of its expert journalism.

Since I had recently visited that beautiful City by the Bay and become acquainted with certain of its more illustrious avenues and architectural accomplishments, I felt personally saddened by the detailed descriptions of the loss and devastation that had been visited upon it. I can recall seeing an advertisement from Austen's Nickelodeon Theater telling of a series of five minute films that depicted the enormous destruction and utter desperation that followed.

The magnitude of the catastrophe and the wholesale displacement of the City's populace would cause the mayor of that city to make a plea for immediate assistance from the rest of America. I remember how the membership of the WTUL lent a helping hand to the victims of that disaster through repeated clothing drives and fundraisers and did so, not for the recognition derived, but based upon a genuine concern for those less fortunate. The worst of times can often bring out the best in us.

The Governor of California would soon be forced to enlist the army to provide food and shelter to tens of thousands of those sorrowful survivors. When they arrived, their first order of business was to restore order to prevent looting and to help stop the raging fires that stemmed from ruptured gas lines by dynamiting whole city blocks of dwellings to prevent the complete conflagration of everything left standing.

Publications throughout the civilized world focused squarely upon San Francisco. Writers like H.G. Wells and William James would chronicle what had occurred and the lessons to be learned from such a profound loss. Tales of misery and despair were counterbalanced by tales of courage and hope, all arising from an indelible, natural catastrophe.

As you may remember I left school after the fourth grade to be apprenticed into the dressmaking trade, in order to help put food on the table and keep a roof over the heads of our household. It was my father who recognized that ignorance can be readily exploited and wanted me to be as independent as those times allowed. That was why he taught me to read by age six, before the nuns set eyes upon me and to do so for the education and enjoyment that reading fostered. Truth be told, if I never loved to read, I would never have become the woman I am today.

The reason I am telling you this is that there were two novels that I would read in 1906 that had a profound impact upon me and likewise upon a significant portion of America. The first was written by Jack London, a young man who led a life of hardship and adventure that would take him from California to Alaska, through a war ravaged Cuba, and back and forth across America before his untimely death.

He would, like me, actually read the Communist Manifesto and the Constitution of the United States and like me, hoped and worked for a better world. He had become a dyed in the wool socialist and a vocal supporter of the IWW when he wrote the *"Iron Heel"* about a socialist brotherhood arising from open warfare between capital and labor.

Although I was opposed to the violence that it condoned, there was much that I found in that novel that was based upon fact and written with insight and eloquence. It would inspire me in my own efforts to bring about a better America by peaceful means. One of its passages that I would often use during my lectures was as follows:

"In the face of the facts that the American worker lives more wretchedly than a caveman and his producing power is a thousand times greater, no other conclusion is possible than that the capitalist class in America should be held accountable for the most reprehensible sin of selfish mismanagement."

The second novel was written by Upton Sinclair, a son of wealth and privilege who attended the City College of New York at age fourteen and devoted his life to writing and working for the creation of a better America. He wrote hauntingly about the inhumane, unsanitary conditions of the meatpacking industry in Chicago, through the eyes of Romanian immigrants.

It was called *"The Jungle"* and it would result in the enactment of laws to protect Americans from contaminated meat and poultry. My close friendship with the Pudolski twins and their own descriptions of the work they did in the Armour meatpacking plant brought Sinclair's vivid depictions of those conditions very much home to me.

As an experienced factory inspector, I would keep abreast of working conditions not only in Massachusetts but in New York as well, due to my work for Sam Gompers and my continued correspondence with Leonora O'Reilly. She would write the most heartfelt letters to me during that time about the conditions she observed, particularly within the garment industry of New York and Brooklyn. Next to outright slavery, it was the most heartless, criminal exploitation of men, women and children in America. Here is a passage from a letter she wrote to me on May 13, 1906.

"In the Lower East Side you see them, if you rise before the sun. Men, women and children of mostly immigrant stock, spilling from squalid tenement houses by the hundreds. A ragged, hapless sea of abject humanity, they are on their way to work for the next ten hours in hazard filled factories, full of unforgiving machinery that can maim or kill at each and every turn. Or they are headed to the sweat shops, those dark, unventilated, dungeons, to fetch and carry under the thumb of merciless overseers for slave's wages. This is how the other half lives and works in the America of today.

Oh, Mary what must we do to end such dreadful drudgery in our lifetime? "

Leonora and I were playing our parts in trying to make things better. Despite the working conditions that we had personally endured and continued to observe, we would seek to reinforce each other during that time through our monthly organizational meetings and our correspondence. Those were the ways we kept hope alive for a better tomorrow for workers in America. Without hope, all can soon be lost.

Through our work with the WTUL, we moved forward slowly but steadily in the march toward female equality, while understanding that securing the right to vote was absolutely essential to making the women of America a force to be reckoned with. By voting in unison, we could outlaw child labor once and for all and help establish a true industrial democracy, through the enactment of progressive wage and hour legislation. I would speak on these issues before Congress during that very same year.

I had never been to Capitol Hill or walked through the halls of Congress before that occasion. I had visited various state legislatures over the years but ascending those steps and passing beneath that magnificent dome was a thrill that brought a lump to my throat and tears to my eyes.

There I was, a widow whose parents came to America on coffin ships in a desperate search for freedom. I had been called upon to address the subject of a Constitutional Amendment to confer the right to vote upon the women of America. It was Florence Kelley, the head of the National Consumers League, who introduced me to an esteemed panel of congressmen. These remarks are a matter of public record.

"I come to ask you for my right as a citizen, as a producing member of society. To ask for that right, not only for myself, but for the class of people of whom I am a part, the working women and common people of America."

"I know that working women in this country are not receiving a living wage because they have not a vote. The female bookbinders working under this very dome, within this hallowed monument to liberty and the pursuit of happiness are not being paid the same wage as their male counterparts, even now. They are second class citizens in a country whose precepts are liberty and justice for all."

They are the mothers, sisters, wives and daughters of America and they deserve better. They deserve the right to vote."

There were close to two hundred women who had traveled to Washington as part of the National Equal Suffrage Association in 1906 and heard me speak. These were women who had been scorned and imprisoned. Whose sisters here in America and in England had been beaten and even murdered for seeking to become full-fledged citizens by securing the right to vote. That was the occasion when the Women's Trade Union League would become the industrial branch of the Women's Suffrage Movement.

CHAPTER 56

The history of the American labor movement was a history I experienced firsthand. During my early days in Hannibal Missouri I had seen the last of black slavery and the destruction of the American Civil War. Then came the industrial revolution and a deluge of immigrants that combined with the growth of cities to transform America and change the way Americans lived and worked since before the Declaration of Independence.

The banks and the railroads led the way at first, laying the cornerstones for the building of commercial empires fueled by oil, coal and steel. Industry and inventions would on one hand bring Americans closer together, while on the other hand, the wealth and privilege they created would drive them farther apart.

Farms and villages gave way to factories and cities. Skilled artisans and farm hands soon became industrial workers. Those in control of the means of production became industry owners who employed and often exploited their workers, using survival of the fittest and the teachings of John Calvin to justify that exploitation.

Unions came into being to protect and empower many of these workers by organizing them to bargain collectively for better wages and shorter work days. In some instances their political power was used to get legislation passed in various states that would protect the health and safety of the people and make it easier for them to join in unions. Legislation that was

237

most often struck down by the courts under the *"Lochner"* decision of the United States Supreme Court, as unlawful attempts to interfere with the right of businesses to enter into contracts and engage in commerce.

Amid all of this transformation, there was one man whose insights and mastery of the moment were second to none. He was a titan who walked the earth, more powerful than the kings and rulers of ancient history.

I saw him once, while Sam Gompers and I were passing by his residence on Madison Avenue in 1903. At that time he was an imposing physical specimen with enormous shoulders, a broad black mustache and bulbous nose, dressed in a charcoal gray overcoat and hat, with an entourage in tow. His name was John Pierpont Morgan.

He was America's foremost banker and financier, often serving as the architect of many different industries, including the American railway system, Thomas Edison's General Electric, and Andrew Carnegie's United States Steel. In the year of our Lord, 1907, during the worst of times, he was called upon to save the American banking and financial system from outright collapse.

As you may recall, the reason provided for the expansion of American interests into foreign countries was the added markets they would create for American goods. This was one of the reasons for the war with Spain. This we were told would eliminate financial crises or panics like that of 1877 and 1893. Panics that took their toll upon the lives of workers and often upon the banks and the businesses that borrowed from them.

The Panic of 1907 was proof positive that American involvement in foreign countries did not guarantee the prosperity of the American people. Once again, good old fashioned greed brought America to the brink of financial disaster. Had it not been for J.P. Morgan, America as we knew it probably would have gone under the waves for good.

It is not my intention to elaborate to any great degree upon all of the trusts, banks, companies and persons that played a part in the Panic of 1907. It took place over three weeks during that October when the New York Stock Exchange fell almost 50% in value because of a failed attempt to buy up all of the stock of the United Copper Company by a few powerful men.

This failed attempt would cause a run on banks and trust companies throughout America that resulted in a lack of sufficient funds to keep America's financial system in business. That was when J.P. Morgan saw the handwriting on the wall and bailed the entire country out by using his own money and that of those under his control, to keep the Stock Exchange from failing.

The final chapter of this crisis required President Roosevelt to approve the measures that Morgan and his associates had taken in order to avoid a collapse, even though these were against his principles and would make Morgan and his men even more powerful.

Once again greed had reared its ugly head and nearly caused all to be lost. Although certain controls were put in place, they would wither away in the decades to come with the belief that the marketplace would eventually correct itself. The American people would pay a terrible price for this error in thinking in the decades ahead.

In the spring of 1908, while I was sitting on the steps of the apartment house at Dudley Street, watching my children playing on the sidewalk, my boys took off across the street. Mary, the youngest, who was three and a half at the time, suddenly followed after them without looking, directly into the path of an oncoming street car.

My heart was in my throat as I ran to her rescue almost seconds too late. Needless to say, I would never have forgiven myself if my daughter had suffered the same tragic ending as my husband. I resolved there and then to look for a home where my children could be safe. I searched for months for a place near enough to my work, yet suitable for them to grow, with fresh air and room to play.

It was then that I came upon an advertisement for a farm in West Medford, Massachusetts. As I walked up the hill toward that ancient, dilapidated farmhouse on seven acres of land, I swear I heard my beloved Jack's voice whispering to me, "Mary Darling, this is the home we have been waiting for." After it was renovated and ready to move in, I called it "Dunboy", named after the O'Sullivan's castle in Ireland.

It would become the home and refuge I had always hoped for, with spacious living quarters, a study, two meeting rooms for my organizing activities, a breathtaking view of nearby Boston, and ample grounds for the growing of fruits and vegetables. It would allow me and mine to ramble and reflect, as the years passed and America continued to grow in power and stature throughout the world.

This was the time when President Roosevelt's love for nature and the great outdoors caused him to create a national park system where the wilderness and its wildlife could be protected and preserved. It was a time when men like John Muir and Frederick Law Olmstead would help make certain that America the beautiful would never fade from view.

It was a time when the President dispatched The Great White Fleet to circumnavigate the globe on a goodwill mission, signaling to one and all that America was now a formidable naval power. It was also a time when a Michigan farm boy by the name of Henry Ford would develop an affordable automobile and perfect a means of production that would change America forever.

In telling this story I have read through all of the pages of my diaries and sorted through box after box of mementos and memorabilia. When I review what has been written and reflect upon the people and events that played a part in the adventure that was my life upon this earth, I become even more convinced that life is like the tide, a sequence of ebbs and flows, or like day and night, a sequence of light and dark, that leads us toward some greater truth.

In 1909 the light of a new day would shine during a general strike of New York's mostly female shirt waist workers, followed in short order by a strike of its mostly male cloak makers. It would be known to us as *"The Uprising of the Twenty Thousand",* where my cherished friend, Leonora O'Reilly, and our Women's Trade Union League played essential parts. These strikes would reveal how far we of the labor movement had come and how much farther we had to go. They would demonstrate both our strength and our weakness in the quest for equality. They would become a prelude to the darkness of an indelible tragedy, The Triangle Shirt Waist Factory Fire.

CHAPTER 57

THE PRELUDE

Of all the industries that epitomized cut throat capitalism and the exploitation of workers in America, none surpassed that of the garment industry in the City of New York. With the turn of the century, millions were fleeing the oppression of Eastern Europe and drought and devastation in Southern Italy. The boroughs of New York would soon be bursting at their seams with the arrival of these desperate immigrants.

It was a deluge of foreign born whose dire circumstances and difficulty in speaking and reading English would make of them fair game for the predators in charge of the hazardous sweat shops and factories located within the lower East Side. This was where the uprising would begin. This was where the courage and caring of a handful of young women would begin to turn the tide and bring a revelation to America.

So few are known today. So few are even remembered, except by surviving family members and fellow workers who lived through those times and bore witness to the struggle. It was the time of Tammany Hall and the graft and corruption it created. It was the time when an injury to a breadwinner spelled disaster to that breadwinner's family without Tammany's aid.

That was when greed and indifference to the vulnerability of women and children meant the loss of their lives and limbs on a weekly basis. That was when workhouses flourished and were filled with a miserable sea of unfortunates, sentenced there by magistrates without mercy. As part of my story, I must tell their story. For I and they were as one during those times.

Let me tell you their names first and describe, if I can, the circumstances that caused them to be courageous enough to care. They would speak up, organize and for a fleeting period of time prevail against all the odds that were stacked against them. Before a tragedy occurred that America would never forget.

Their names were Clara Lemlich, Rose Schneiderman, Frances Perkins and Anne Morgan to name a few. Their common bonds would be their courage and caring for others and their membership in our Women's Trade Union League. They were my contemporaries and sisters in the cause. Their story is my story as well.

As I mentioned through my involvement with Sam Gompers and my work on behalf of the AF of L, I had walked the streets of the Lower East Side, climbed the stairs of teeming tenement houses where families were housed like captured insects, inspected sweatshops where women and children as young as six worked endless hours until they dropped to the filthy floors of those putrid pigsties from utter exhaustion. Yes their story is my story. I pray that through you, who read these words, it shall not be forgotten.

Clara Lemlich was a women in her twenties when I first met her. We were introduced back in 1906 by Leonora O'Reilly during one of my visits to New York. She was small but muscular with a round face, short hair and an unmistakable fire in her dark brown eyes. At that time she was working at a Manhattan factory, making shirt waists or women's blouses and despised the day to day humiliations that female shirt waist workers endured.

These humiliations included the intrusion of their male overseers into the factory's filthy bathrooms to make sure their charges didn't linger after an inconvenient call of nature. The making of lewd comments or the taking of liberties with a grab or pinch. And finally being lined up like cattle at closing time to be searched at random for a button or a piece of lace that might have been pilfered.

They caused Clara to become a founding member of Local 25 of the International Ladies Garment Workers Union and soon thereafter a card carrying member of our WTUL. Her notoriety in speaking up for what was right had made her the object of frequent threats by constables on patrol and beatings by paid thugs on the payroll of Tammany Hall under the leadership of the taciturn Charlie Murphy. He was a friend to the factory owners in his district, who greased the wheels of his "Operation" and merited his "Protection."

On November 22, 1909 in the great hall of the Cooper Union, Clara would rise to the occasion following a less than inspiring speech by Sam

Gompers, counseling the female rank and file of Local 25 that a strike was folly and their patience was a necessity. Both Leonora and our friend and sister, Mary Drier, were present representing the WTUL and wrote to me afterwards describing Clara's actions at that point.

Hollering in the Yiddish of her Russian ancestry that she wanted to say a few words, she was encouraged by the crowd. As she made her way past her fellow shirt waist workers, she climbed the stairs and shouted,

"I have no further patience for talk, as I am one of those who feels and suffers from the things that have been pictured here tonight. I move that we go on a general strike."

The following day picket lines were set up around the shirt waist factories that populated the East Side. I recall that Leonora and Mary told me the shirt waist workers of Jewish heritage were almost unanimous in joining the strike and they made up about three quarters of the industry. Their ancestry knew oppression well.

The WTUL would enlist its membership to visit the homes of the Italian women and girls who made up the remainder of the blouse makers, encouraging them to join the ranks of their Jewish sisters. Despite a sinister attempt by the factory bosses with the able assistance of Charlie Murphy to enlist priests from Italian parishes to advise that going out on strike was sinful, most of the Italian workers joined in the strike.

The sudden nature of the strike and Clara Lemlich's tireless efforts in addressing meeting after meeting of striking workers and encouraging them to persevere began to bear fruit within a forty eight hour period. Factory after factory decided to give in to the demands of Local 25 for less hours and better wages. In some instances Clara was even able to convince a small number of factories to recognize Local 25 as the exclusive bargaining agent for its workers. That was a concession rarely made in any industry at that time.

These developments shocked Charlie Murphy and alarmed the owners of the bigger shirt waist factories, especially when they learned that wealthy women, like Anne Morgan, the daughter of J.P. Morgan, himself, sympathized with the strikers by joining the ranks of the WTUL.

The harassment of those walking picket lines by the New York City Police soon followed. This resulted in negative editorials being published by William Randolph Hearst's *World* and increased financial support from wealthy women that caused bail bonds to be posted for almost all of the picketers who had been arrested.

In response, a Management Association was organized and added political pressure was applied, causing a crackdown on the striking workers. They were not only being arrested; they were being sentenced to hard labor in workhouses by paid off magistrates.

Leading the charge on behalf of the big factory owners were Max Blanck and Isaac Harris, Russian immigrants who had both been shirt waist workers and had built enormous fortunes from scratch. They were known as the "Shirt Waist Kings" and their factory located on the upper floors of the Asch building, between Washington Place and Green Street in the Lower East Side, was the world renowned Triangle Shirt Waist Factory.

Through their determination to close ranks and hold the line on concessions they were able to weather the strike in the major factories. An offer was finally made by the Management Association to submit the matter to mediation, signaling their willingness to reduce work hours and increase wages in return for labor peace.

On the heels of these developments the mostly male cloak makers followed suit and struck. A Protocol of Peace, brokered by our old friend, Louis Brandeis, would include concessions on both wages and hours of work. *The Uprising of The Twenty Thousand,* as it came to be called, was hailed as a victory for the garment workers and an inspiration to the entire labor movement. It was also a warning signal to Charlie Murphy and Tammany Hall.

Charlie Murphy was wise enough to see the handwriting on the wall and he was not one to back a losing side. The fact that working and wealthy women had joined forces in that instance and those same women were politicking for the right to vote, would not be lost on him and his associates at Tammany Hall.

Whatever optimism these developments created was short lived for the WTUL and for the cause of female equality. On January 2, 1910 there was to be an enormous gathering held at Carnegie Hall to discuss the remaining issues and bring a successful end to the strike. All of the members of Local 25 and the leaders of the WTUL in New York were in attendance. It was meant to be a night to remember, a night of celebration.

Although I had been invited to attend, a blinding snowstorm had prevented trains from leaving Boston's South Station. A telegram expressing my regret and best wishes was sent. Perhaps if I had been there, the outcome may have been different, who is to say?

All I know is that it became a night to remember alright, as Attorney Morris Hillquit, a fiery Socialist, spoke first and insisted that the recognition of Local 25 by the shirt waist factory owners as the exclusive bargaining agent for all workers was essential to any resolution. This position would receive the vigorous vocal support of the workers in attendance.

To make matters worse, he then spoke ardently concerning the necessity of a class struggle against wealth and power in America. Needless to say, this was not well received by the well to do women of the WTUL, whose financial support was a major reason for the success achieved. When Leonora O'Reilly took the stage and unwisely echoed what had been said, Anne Morgan and others of her class decided that they had heard enough and departed.

If that had been the end of it, perhaps reparations could have been made and the rift between the factions of the WTUL closed. Sadly, strong willed females on both sides caused the rift to become even more pronounced.

First, Anne Morgan issued a statement the following day in opposition to "the fanatical doctrines of socialism." Not to be outdone, my friend, Leonora, engaged in a personal attack upon one of the hands that had helped to feed the strikers and support the WTUL, when she stated,

"Perhaps if Miss Morgan had ever been face to face with hunger or eviction, she would understand the way those strikers felt."

Her response made me remember my first reaction to the goodwill of Jane Addams and her associates at Hull House. "Judge not lest ye be judged", should have been the order of the day and the credo of the WTUL, not tit for tat.

This rift would be exploited in turn by the Management Association. The strikers from their factories were forced to settle for much less than the other factories had settled for and for much less than they deserved. In addition, there would be no recognition by the Management Association of Local 25 as their workers' bargaining representative. The shirt waist workers did however win the approval of someone who would soon become well known in our struggle, Bill Haywood, the leader of the IWW, who stated, "For every girl that is slugged in this strike, a cop ought to be sent to the hospital. "

CHAPTER 58

THE CAULDRON

*T*he date was Saturday, March 25, 1911, a seasonably warm, clear spring day, when a match or cigarette butt was dropped into a scrap bin beneath a shirt waist cutter's table on the eighth floor of the Asch building, just before closing time. The Triangle Shirt Waist Factory occupied the 8th, 9th and 10th floors of the building and employed hundreds of workers. Most of them were immigrant girls of Jewish and Italian heritage.

The building had one exit on to Washington Place and one exit on to Green Street. The exits could be reached by one stairway and one elevator for each. There was also a fire escape on the Green Street side of the building, but it did not reach the street. The factory owners, Max Blanck and Isaac Harris, were on the premises at the time that the blaze began. The elevator that led to the exit on Washington Place was reserved for owners and managers whose offices were on the 10th floor.

Fires at the Triangle Shirt Waist Factory occurred regularly. On a handful of prior occasions insurers had paid claims for the loss of inventory at times when the Triangle Factory was closed and no workers were on the premises. Arson for hire was a steady occupation in the garment industry of that time. The payment of large insurance premiums by owners and the prompt payment by insurers after fires struck was a ready means of preventing financial losses when Paris fashions changed.

It was all part of a huge racket and Tammany Hall would stand front and center to receive its cut.

Tenement fires were an all too common occurrence in the Lower East Side at that time, often claiming the lives of poor women and children, crowded into death traps that lacked sufficient exits or fire escapes. The blood curdling screams of these unfortunates about to be suffocated or burned to death was something that witnesses would never, ever forget. The screams of young women and men trapped in The Triangle Shirt Waist Factory Fire would be heard by thousands drawn to the scene by the clanging bells of the fire wagons.

Sprinkler systems to extinguish mill fires had been in place throughout New England since the 1890's. Fire drills to educate workers on proper means and methods of escape were also a part of proper mill management. Edward Croker, the Fire Chief in charge of Engine 33, had warned a few short months before that a fire on the upper floors of the Asch building would be a disaster, if it occurred during work hours, since his ladders could only reach to floor six.

As I mentioned, one of the working conditions that Clara Lemlich detested most was being forced to line up to be searched at closing time. This practice was most often accompanied by the locking of all other exit doors so that workers could not escape these searches. The owners of the Triangle Factory followed this practice. Preventing a loss from pilferage was more important than preventing lost lives.

Floors 8 and 9 of the Triangle Factory were virtual tinder boxes. They were chock full of flammable objects, from fabric to paper to wood to oil soaked rags, that caused the fire to leap from one location to the next. The fire would be fanned by the air that rose like a torrent from the air shafts on each floor, engulfing those floors and their occupants in a cauldron of flame within a matter of minutes.

Leonora O'Reilly was preparing for a lecture at the Cooper Union when she heard the fire bells and ran to the window to see smoke billowing from the upper floors of the Asch building. Hundreds were running toward the scene. Frances Perkins, a disciple of Florence Kelley, was having tea nearby.

Inside the inferno panic reigned, as workers ran wildly from one terrifying trap to the next. Cries of fire and shrieks of mortal fear were everywhere. Acts of courage were common place, as supervisors attempted to bring order to the chaos and usher as many to safety as they could.

Elevator operator, Joseph Zito, was one of these heroic souls. He would make repeated runs between the 8th and 9th floors at the height of the blaze. He repeatedly risked being burned alive in order to rescue hundreds of his fellow workers.

Firemen arrived and lumbered up the stairs on Washington Place with their heavy hoses trailing behind them, as precious minutes passed and hundreds of young women perished. Eventually they would manage to dispense streams of water to try to douse the flames. While inside, young workers franticly huddled together or lined up near stairways that no longer provided escape.

Survivors insisted that the exit door to the 9th floor stairway on Washington Place had been locked and bolted so that workers could be funneled through and searched before exiting down the freight elevator or stairway to Green Street. Fire men would find scores of charred bodies piled next to that thwarted means of escape, like so much lifeless cord wood.

As I mentioned, there was a fire escape on the Green Street side of the building but it was very narrow and did not reach the street. The heat from the blaze was so searing that the metal of it melted within minutes. Those unfortunates who happened to be upon it at the time would plummet to their deaths on the pavement hundreds of feet below.

As a finale to the horror being witnessed by the thousands that had now gathered on the streets below, including both Leonora and Frances, terrified workers began to appear at the factory windows as the flames crept closer to their persons. Then the windows began exploding one by one from the heat and combustion inside. There they now stood at the window sills, terrified and trembling on the brink of eternity, while thousands watched in stunned silence below or attempted to prevent them from what they were about to do, by shouting, "Don't jump. Help is on the way."

With the choice of being burned alive or leaping, they chose to leap and land with a sickening thud below, like bundles of smoldering rags. Some were praying before they made the choice. Some were holding hands, while attempting to land upright as they plummeted. Unforgettably, two young lovers would kiss and embrace before they met their ending.

Hundreds did manage to escape that horrid holocaust of flame. Many made it down the stairways before it was too late. Some shimmied down the elevator cables to safety before others began leaping down the elevator shafts to escape the flames only to be crushed or impaled. Some made it to the roof and were rescued by a class of New York University law students, attending a lecture as the blaze began and lowering a ladder of rescue from the roof above. Among those who escaped by the roof were the owners and nearly all of the factory managers.

There were 146 who died in the Triangle Shirt Waist Factory Fire. Most were immigrant girls who could barely speak the language. They had come to America in search of a better life. What they found was a life of hardship and exploitation. All they left were a few personal effects and distraught family members or friends. They would come by the hundreds to the Charities Pier on Twenty Sixth Street over the next week to identify the charred or crushed remains of their loved ones, and dream the dreams of the lost and the brokenhearted.

CHAPTER 60

THE AFTERMATH

Guilt and grief would cast a pall over New York City and much of the country following the Triangle Factory Fire. The dimensions of the tragedy sparked an examination of the City's conscience and caused many of its leading citizens to take a cold hard look in the mirror.

A mirror that 146 martyrs had helped to fashion. A mirror that showed indifference leading to inhumane working conditions resulting in searing images of sudden death. Illustrious careers in public service would be traced to the pangs of conscience that the Triangle tragedy produced.

The immediate reaction was one of blame. The owners of the Triangle Factory would be indicted on charges of manslaughter, stemming from the locked door on the ninth floor. An infamous trial would follow where hundreds of witnesses testified and kept the tragedy on the front pages of America's newspapers for weeks on end.

Despite a woeful parade of participants and paid experts, the prosecution would fail to prove that the owners knew that the door was locked beyond a reasonable doubt. They would walk free with a windfall of insurance proceeds to smooth their way.

Two young women who could not have been more different in heritage and personality would commence their rise to prominence following the Triangle blaze. They were both beginning their thirtieth year. Rose

Schneiderman and Frances Perkins would soon become my close friends and associates in the cause of female equality.

Rose was born in Poland and poor. Frances was born in Boston and well to do. Rose went to work at an early age in a Lower East Side factory and spoke with a thick Polish accent, while Frances was college educated and articulate. Rose was small and muscular with flowing red hair and light brown eyes. Frances was taller with a shapely figure and chestnut hair. Rose was fiery and fierce in her beliefs while Frances was deliberate and determined to make her mark. I met them both on April 2, 1911.

The occasion was a commemoration of the lives that had been lost, sponsored by the WTUL. A somber crowd filled the magnificent Metropolitan Opera House to capacity. Speaker after speaker addressed the assembled masses with stories of the deceased and the unsafe working conditions that claimed their lives. Not a dry eye could be found as that mournful evening moved sorrowfully onward.

I was seated on the crowded stage between William Walling and Leonora O'Reilly. I had been introduced to Anne Morgan, the regal looking daughter of the titan who had saved the economic system of America four years before. I would meet Rose and Frances later that evening. All of us were card carrying members of the WTUL and Florence Kelley's' National Consumers' League. Almost all of the membership from both organizations was in attendance.

The night would belong to Rose and the ringing address she gave from the depths of her soul. Her words gave testament to the victims and the righteous nature of our cause. A stenographer was present to capture the evening and preserve it for posterity. Truth and outrage were never woven as masterfully together as when that courageous creature commanded the stage and shouted to the rafters.

"I would be a traitor to these poor burned bodies if I came here to talk good fellowship. We have tried you good people of the public and we have found you wanting. The old inquisition had its rack and its thumbscrews and its instruments of torture with iron teeth. We know what these things are today; the iron teeth are our necessities, the thumbscrews are the high powered and swift machinery close to which we must work and the rack is here in the firetrap structures that will destroy us the minute they catch on fire. "

"This is not the first time girls have been burned alive in the city. Every week I must learn of the untimely death of one of my sister workers. Every year thousands of us are maimed. The life of men and women is so cheap and property is so sacred. There are so many of us for one job, it matters little if 146 of us are burned to death. We have tried you citizens. We are trying you still."

"I can't talk fellowship to you who are gathered here. Too much blood has been spilled. I know from my experience, it is up to the working people to save themselves. The only way they can save themselves is by a strong working class movement."

There was no applause or even the hint of congratulation that followed Rose's address; only a grim resolve by those in attendance to rededicate their efforts to bring about drastic change for the better in America. It was a watershed moment like no other and we all knew it. We would move forward relentlessly and together.

Rose, Leonora and Frances would help organize a Committee of Reform. They would petition the legislature of New York to hold hearings and enact laws that would assure workers' safety and protect the lives of women and children. The need for protection from the exploitation of owners, such as Max Blanck and Isaac Harris, was never more apparent.

As I mentioned, Tammany Hall had been watching closely. The tragedy of The Triangle Fire had changed their perspective, like no other occurrence. They would see the light and win a landslide victory at the polls later that year, sweeping the Old Republican Guard from elected office throughout the state on a platform of reform. An indelible tragedy resulting from greed and disregard for the lives and safety of workers would eventually turn Tammany Hall into a positive force to be reckoned with throughout America.

Frances Perkins had become acquainted with Tammany's Thomas McManus as a young social worker, seeking his assistance in helping a constituent's family whose breadwinner had run afoul of the authorities. After the Triangle Fire, Mc Manus would connect her to Charlie Murphy and Charlie Murphy would connect her to an assemblyman by the name of Al Smith and a senator by the name of Robert Wagner. They were two sons of immigrants who knew poverty and the significance of political power, firsthand.

They were known as the "Tammany Twins" and they would advise Frances that unless Tammany was on board with reform, nothing would get through the legislature. That was when the Factory Investigation Commission was created and a brand new day of reform was begun in the State of New York with its millions of soon to be voting immigrants. Leonora O'Reilly and Rose Schneiderman would move to the vanguard of that reform as uncompromising factory inspectors.

I would continue with my lecturing, factory inspecting, property management and organizing activities on behalf of the WTUL, while tending to my three growing children. It would not be long before another dramatic event would require my involvement. It would take its name from a popular union anthem of that time and be known to history as the "Bread and Roses Strike of 1912."

CHAPTER 61

*L*awrence Massachusetts was a textile mill city that hearkened back to the darkest days of the industrial revolution. I was asked to assist in the formation of a strike committee there in December of 1911. Its mills employed at least thirty two thousand workers. Most of them were female immigrants between the ages of fourteen and eighteen years of age who couldn't read, write or speak the language.

Most lived in overcrowded apartments and boarding houses that lacked running water or adequate sanitation. Their wages afforded them little to eat. Their dire working conditions made them old before their time and prone to injury and untimely death from the increased pace of the recently installed two loom system. Once again owners' indifference to the plight of the working poor was the order of the day. That was when the decision was made to call a strike against the textile mills on a freezing cold January 1, 1912.

The reason behind the strike was that the Massachusetts legislature had passed a law to protect working women and children by reducing their work weeks to 54 hours or nine hours per day from Monday through Saturday. The understanding was that this reduction would not result in any reduction in the paltry wages being paid to these unskilled mill workers. The owners resented this interference by the legislature and violated the understanding by vowing to cut wages when the law was set to begin.

The skilled mill workers were mostly represented by the United Textile Workers of the AF of L who refused to join or support the strike, believing that immigrant women and children of different nationalities could not be organized to stick together and persevere in a prolonged strike in the dead of a brutal winter.

Regrettably, the leaders of the WTUL did likewise. That was when Bill Haywood of the IWW, who represented these unskilled mill workers, reached out to me personally with the knowledge that I had faced similar issues in the Fall River cotton workers strike back in 1905. There really was no one I ever met quite like him or for that matter Helen Gurley Flynn, his fellow IWW organizer. We would join forces like never before in that historic episode of labor unrest.

"Big Bill" as he preferred to be called was larger than life itself. At the time of the Lawrence strike he was forty two years of age, standing six foot four inches tall with massive shoulders, dark brown hair and a right eye that was without sight and disfigured from a childhood injury.

He had worked in the mines of Colorado as a boy and had personal experience with the very worst in owner exploitation and hazardous working conditions. It was there that he would rise to become a leader of the Western Federation of Miners during the murderous Colorado labor wars. His fiery temper and his willingness to give a beating or take one in the interests of the workers' cause was legendary.

In 1905 he was kidnapped from Colorado by Pinkerton men under the direction of Joseph McParland, and brought to Idaho to stand trial for the murder of the former governor. A killer by the name of Harry Orchard had confessed to the murder and was promised his freedom if he fingered "Big Bill" and two others as accomplices. Our friend, Clarence Darrow would win him his acquittal.

In 1908 he would become a confidante of Eugene Debs and a member of his inner circle, during his unsuccessful run for President of the United States on the Socialist Party ticket. He called the brand of industrial unionism practiced by the IWW as "socialism with its working clothes on." He was not adverse to violence if capitalist ownership and their governmental allies struck the first blow. He was a very tough and very capable enemy. I considered him my close friend.

I can remember reading a saying attributed to him, "I've never read Marx's capital, but I have the marks of capital all over me." I would disagree with him that workers needed to wrest the means of production from the owners in order to achieve equality. I must say, I admired his courage and his abiding concern for working men and women of all nationalities and races. Besides, he always listened to what I had to say and treated me with the utmost respect. The same wasn't true of the WTUL leadership.

Helen Gurley Flynn was an intelligent and inspiring young spokeswoman for the cause of industrial feminism when I first met her during the early days of the strike. She was in her early twenties at that time, with an attractive oval face, complemented by shimmering black hair, parted in the middle, vivacious dark eyes and a firm womanly figure. She was almost always attired in the latest Gibson girl fashion of that time, a starched white blouse and a flowing skirt of brown or blue.

I first heard her speak in Lawrence to a crowd of immigrant girls in the basement of a Polish Catholic church. Her courage and caring nature shone through her like a radiant light. Her words were translated by a white haired priest and a friend of the workers cause.

"Sisters and workers, in this cause of ours, this is the time to join together and show the world that females of all ages, nationalities, races and creeds can hold on and win victory against oppression and exploitation. History will pass stern judgment on tyrants and vindicates those who fight, suffer, endure imprisonment and die for human freedom against political oppression and economic slavery. We will prevail in this struggle here in Lawrence and in the greater struggle for female equality. "

The strike began in earnest on January 11th when a group of those Polish young women received their paychecks from The Everett Mill. Upon seeing that their pay had been reduced, they had been prepared to chant in unison as they walked out, "short pay, all out."

The next day, females working at the Washington Mill of The American Woolen Company followed suit when they too discovered a reduction in their pay. Picket lines were set up the very next day and all of the unskilled mill workers soon joined in the strike.

That was when the City of Lawrence, under the direction of the mill owners, rang the City's emergency alarm bell and ordered the local militia to turn out and patrol the streets. Shortly after that, the mill owners turned fire hoses upon young women and children on the picket lines on a bitterly cold afternoon.

When the picketers began to pelt the mills with pieces of ice that formed from the frigid temperatures, the police and the militia descended upon them with flailing night sticks, arresting and imprisoning twenty four strikers. In short order they would be sentenced to a year in jail, the severest sentence possible, in an effort to break the strike. Still those girls hung together with the IWW.

A plot would then be hatched where a local undertaker by the name of John Breen planted sticks of dynamite at various locations throughout the City. It was later determined that this was at the behest of William Wood, the multimillionaire owner of the American Woolen Company, in an effort to frame the strike's organizers and encourage the brutality of the police and the militia. After his arrest, Breen was allowed to walk free with the payment of a fine of five hundred dollars.

The pastor of Saint Mary's Church would condemn the strike from his pulpit as the work of atheists and encourage his congregation to take to the City's streets in support of strike breakers. Violent confrontations in frigid temperatures were near daily occurrences between the thousands of strikers and all those who opposed them.

The Governor would call out the National Guard and the State Police as tensions rose steadily. On January 29, 1912 the police would corner a large crowd of strikers at the intersection of Union and Garden Streets when a shot rang out and a young striker by the name of Anna LoPizzo fell dead. Even though the evidence pointed to a trigger happy policemen as the culprit, three immigrant organizers of the IWW were charged with the murder, for spreading the propaganda of violence.

I would concentrate my efforts on raising funds to keep food on the tables and coal in the furnaces where the strikers and their families lived. I would also organize bread lines and soup kitchens and meet with the Committee of Ten, a select group of striking mill workers, whose job was not only to coordinate strike activities but also to formulate proposals for negotiations. It was Helen Gurley Flynn who would come up with a master stroke.

Many of the strikers were mothers with little children to care for during that brutal winter. Helen's idea was to reach out to supporters in other states and enlist them to care for these children during the strike's duration.

In a matter of days hundreds of young mothers brought their children to the Lawrence Central Rail Station to have them chaperoned and transported to safe and secure homes outside of the City until the strike was over. This infuriated the powers that be, since it increased the resolve of the strikers to carry on.

When the police attempted to disperse a congregation of mothers and children attempting to continue this tactic, by attacking them with night sticks for all the world to see, the response against the owners and the City was overwhelming. Soon Congress began an investigation. Hearings were held as strikers told of the conditions in the mills. "The Bread and Roses Strike" would be settled very favorably. It was a great victory for the IWW and the workers of America.

CHAPTER 62

I was relieved that a victory was won for the immigrant girls who made up the majority of the Lawrence textile workers. I remember a jubilant celebration being held at Ford Hall in the center of the City on the evening of April 20th of 1912, after the hard fought increases in wages appeared in their pay envelopes for the first time.

There were so many in attendance whose faces bore the imprint of that terrible ordeal and still they managed to chant and sing in their native tongues, as speaker after speaker addressed them. In spite of our receiving their sincere expressions of gratitude, it was a bittersweet occasion for me and my close friend, Mary Glendower Evans.

Truth be told, we were both terribly disappointed in the AF of L and the leaders of the WTUL during the darkest days of the strike. Their support was conspicuous by its absence. It was the IWW of Bill Haywood and Helen Gurley Flynn that rose to that occasion and won a great victory for working women. Our disappointment would bring the two of us to the same painful realization. It would lead to a joint announcement following a dinner held at my home on the evening of May 1st.

Most of those in attendance had attained notoriety in varied efforts to make America hold true to its promise of liberty and justice for all. Louis Brandeis and his lovely wife, Alice, were the first to arrive, followed by my dear friend and mentor, Florence Kelley, accompanied by Leonora O'Reilly and Frances Perkins. They had taken the afternoon train up from New York City.

Elizabeth Glendower Evans was there along with our mutual friend and confidante, Vida Scudder. Even Bill Haywood and Helen Gurley Flynn appeared later in the evening, much to my astonishment and appreciation. Telegrams expressing their regret at not being able to attend were received and read from Clarence Darrow and Jane Addams.

Before that occasion I had conversed with Elizabeth Evans regarding the matter of our continued involvement with the organizational efforts of the WTUL and it was decided that we would each address the matter at the end of the evening. It was a delightful catered affair with music supplied by a skilled pianist on his night off from the Copley Hotel. My children would be introduced to all and behave politely, before retiring for the evening with the affectionate assistance of their beloved nanny.

When the subject of the Bread and Roses strike was brought up both Elizabeth and I had decided that we would express our relief that it was concluded and that the textile workers of Lawrence should be congratulated.

During the course of the evening, I observed Bill Haywood and Louis Brandeis engaged in a cordial but spirited conversation. I suspect that Louis had merely mentioned that he was a public interest lawyer. "Big Bill", on the other hand, would take that opportunity to educate a new acquaintance on the fine points of the class struggle and the righteous nature of his IWW.

"The capitalist owner will seek to exploit the worker at every turn, unless something or someone prevents it. That something is industrial unionism and workers taking over the means of production. That is the way it is and the way it will always be, Big Bill proclaimed."

"What you're saying is that class warfare is inevitable. What about socialism as a solution?" Brandeis asked.

"With socialism the worker is just trading one master for another, the capitalist owner for a governmental one. At least the capitalist is being true to his nature, like a mountain lion or a bird of prey."

"But Bill, what if man evolves and becomes more considerate of his fellow human beings? What if that evolution brings with it the wisdom of balance? Suppose that owners come to realize that a living wage can be paid and still allow a fair profit to be turned. You say that man must work and that work is the only proper

measurement of his worth. Let's say, I agree. Is enlightened capitalism at least a possibility? "

"Not in my world, sir. There are owners and there are workers and
unless the workers are in charge, the owners will do what it is in
their nature to do, exploit them and discard them when they are
no longer of use."

I intervened at that point and sought to add a different perspective
to their discussion, "Gentlemen, as the mother of three growing
children it is my fervent hope that class warfare is not inevitable,
for their sake. I pray every day that the goodness and order that is
in nature will become the goodness and order that is in mankind.
Where right not might, or class or privilege is the order of things."

"Well, Mary dear, that is why we are here. You are as good as you are
beautiful," Louis declared, "It has been a pleasure meeting you, Bill."

"Likewise," was his reply.

When the chimes of the grandfather clock struck ten, I requested that
all of our guests follow me down the hall and into the study. It was my
favorite location within our home. It was there that Elizabeth and I would
deliver the announcements of the evening. I thought it was better for her to
speak first. She was as regal and refined as she had ever been. She was wearing a silken dress of green and gold, her silver hair and lovely features were
perfectly complemented by her inner beauty. She began with the clinking
of her glass and as always spoke from the heart.

"Dearest friends and guests, it is a privilege to join our sister, Mary
in her lovely home on this special occasion. I wanted to express my
gratitude to each and every one of you for the work you are doing
to make our country a better place for all. I wanted to congratulate
the textile workers of Lawrence on their victory and express my
admiration for their courage and their fighting spirit in the face of
overwhelming adversity."

"Their victory is, I believe, an appropriate time for me to move on
from my involvement with the Women's Trade Union League and
devote my efforts to securing the right to vote and assisting my
brothers and sisters of color in achieving equality. I welcome your
participation and support in these efforts. Now I turn the floor over
to Mary. "

The lengthy applause of those in attendance made me blush. I had contemplated what I was going to say but not prepared my remarks. I remember Florence Kelley, who had taught me to be comfortable when speaking publicly, stood front and center across from me, signaling her support and devotion. I remember observing all those faces and recalling the parts they had each played in my life. I whispered a prayer and once again allowed the spirit within me to speak.

"A lady never wants to reveal her age but I will do so on this occasion, knowing that I am among friends who will not reveal the confidences that we share. I just turned forty eight and it seems like I have been fighting against one form of injustice or another from my early childhood in Hannibal Missouri. "

"When my teacher didn't promote me to the fourth grade for sticking up for a friend that she had treated poorly, I remember storming out of her class and running down the hill to my father's workplace in the pouring rain, with the conviction that I was never going back to that school ever again. That was my first strike I suppose, and I won it, along with the admiration and support of my father, Michael Kenney. "

"He and his best friend, Seamus Egan, were proud members of the Knights of Labor. Some of my earliest memories was accompanying him to Saint Louis to hear Terrence Powderly speak and observing the wounds inflicted upon Seamus, after a run in with company thugs following the Railroad Strike of 1877. Soon after my father would be black listed and forced to forsake his trade as a railroad mechanic. I will never forget how he was required to work at odd jobs into the wee hours, just to make ends meet for his family. "

"These events would lead me to become a bookbinder by trade and a family bread winner at the age of thirteen. When my employer went out of business, I moved to Chicago in the winter of 1887 not long after the Haymarket Massacre."

"It was the beginning of my twenty-fourth year. It was there that I met Lucy Parsons and heard of her suffering and the death of her husband for attempting to organize workers and secure a forty hour work week."

"It was in a Chicago theater on Saint Patrick's night that I heard the inspirational Mother Jones speak. I would meet her on that memorable occasion and a young man who believed in a fair shake for railroad workers, both skilled and unskilled, both native and foreign born. His name was Gene Debs."

"On our way from that theater, we would be attacked by club wielding railroad thugs bent upon terrorizing union supporters and ending an ongoing strike. My companion and landlady, would have her head split wide open on that occasion. Her name was Ida Pudolski. She and her husband had fled the pogroms in her native Poland to make a better life in America. Later, even after her husband was killed at one of Rockefeller's refineries, she refused to give in or give up the struggle. "

"She would treat me like the daughter she never had and teach me that workers must organize and not resort to violence, if they are ever to receive a living wage and a chance at equality in America. I remember her saying that we will win the fight against the greed and the power of the owners through unions and with the truth, because we, the workers of the world, are many and they are few."

"These were words that I have lived by during all of the organizing, all of the strikes and all of the sacrifice of these past twenty or so years. They were never made more evident or more powerful than they were in Lawrence."

"The truth is that those textile factory girls were workers in America and thus deserving of a living wage, whether they were skilled or unskilled."

"There are some who say behind closed doors or by their failure to assist, that this is not the truth. That those workers are less than we. That they are somehow undeserving for not being born in America or speaking like us, living like us or being a different race than we. I say to that, take a look at the photographs of the Lawrence Strike and look into the faces of the women, the girls, the children and let them touch your soul. For we are they and they are we. That is the truth and it always will be. This is the truth that will one day set all of America free."

"Lawrence was my last strike, my last negotiation. My life's work will now become securing worker safety, and winning the suffrage for the women of America. These are the means I will use from this night onward to achieve industrial democracy and female equality. I ask all of you to join with me in these necessary efforts, these noble callings."

CHAPTER 63

efore leaving the occurrences of 1912 and their bearing upon my life to follow, mention must be made of two other historical events during that year. The first involved a dramatic loss of human life that would bring about a dramatic change in safety measures throughout the maritime industry. The second involved the election of a President.

That first event was the sinking of the R.M.S. Titanic on the night of Saturday, April 14, 1912. It was yet another instance where corporate carelessness claimed the lives of more than 1500 men, women and children. Rules of safety are most always derived from the notable deaths of martyrs.

On the next day after Mass, I recall seeing our congregation gathered around a newsboy busily selling the Boston Globe. I would keep a copy of that edition in my memorabilia and I have recently read through the accounts contained within its yellowed pages to refresh my memory of that unforgettable tragedy. There had been a deluge of prior publicity surrounding the Titanic. It was the largest Ocean Liner in the world and it was too big to sink, or so those who designed and commissioned her thought.

It was one and a half times as large as the R.M.S. Lusitania. It could carry almost 3500 passengers and was a modern marvel of speed and luxury, with a first class section of "unrivaled extent and magnificence." Her maiden voyage would commence from Southampton on the morning of April 10th. She would sail to the ports of Cherbourg in France and Queenstown in Ireland first, picking up passengers as she went. By the time she headed across the North Atlantic, she had 892 crew members and 1,320 passengers, split between three classes of travel.

They ranged from millionaires like John Jacob Astor to immigrants seeking the promise and sanctuary of America in third class. It was the third class of passengers that would suffer the greatest loss of life. Telegraphs from other ships at sea warning of the presence of icebergs were either overlooked or disregarded, since the sea at that time was as smooth as glass and the temperatures were unseasonably warm. There were life boats aboard but there were not enough to effect a rescue at sea for all those making that fateful voyage. Perhaps, it was pride in her size and speed that led to her downfall.

At 11:40 P.M., on a moonless night, she plowed into an iceberg that was three times her size flooding five of her starboard compartments in a matter of minutes. She would sink to the bottom in less than three hours. Passenger deaths from drowning and hypothermia would be remembered, recited and recreated in books and magazines for decades to come. It was the most shocking and most memorable of all peacetime sea disasters. It could have been prevented with the foresight of detailed safety measures that would take effect too late for the majority of the unfortunates on board.

The second event taking place in 1912 that would have an impact upon my life to come was the election of Woodrow Wilson as the twenty eighth President of the United States. He had served as the President of Princeton University and ran for the office of Governor of New Jersey as a progressive democrat. He was born and raised in the south and was very proud of his heritage and his Presbyterian faith.

Had I been granted the right to vote at that time, I probably would have voted for him, despite my fondness for Teddy Roosevelt, since Louis Brandeis publicly supported his candidacy and advised him on economic policies. These policies included his stated opposition to monopolies and his support for national banking reform. He also was in favor of women's rights or so he said. It would be his southern roots and his foreign policies however, that would eventually provide cause for concern and condemnation on my part.

I must tell you now about my increased involvement with the suffragists that began with an encounter in January of 1913 with my old friend, Anne Sullivan, and her most prominent pupil, Helen Keller. Helen had returned to Radcliffe College, her alma mater, to deliver a lecture on the challenges and accomplishments of the disabled throughout history.

I had received a formal invitation to attend with an affectionate note penned by the lovely Anne, who had sadly begun to have heart trouble that would soon incapacitate her. It was a cold crisp winter evening under a magnificent full moon. I would be accompanied on that occasion by my cherished friend, Vida Scudder, a professor of English Literature at Wellesley College.

Helen Keller's remarkable writings and speeches had achieved worldwide acclaim by that time, as well as the admiration of notable men and women like Mark Twain, Teddy Roosevelt, Jane Addams and Susan B. Anthony. As I mentioned, her courage had lifted me from the darkness in the past. It was her inspirational commitment to the cause of female equality and suffrage that would light my way in the years that followed.

Following her lecture we would meet for dinner at a Harvard Square restaurant. It was Anne and Helen, Vida and I and our conversation touched upon many of the issues that were facing America and the world at that time. I remember being simply in awe as that lovely creature who was then in her thirties conversed with such wonderful diction and erudition despite her twin afflictions of being deaf and blind.

Her voice was clear and resonant and her eyes shone with the light of a wisdom from within. I do believe she was sent from the Almighty to show us the way and I was blessed to call her my friend and share her insights on our lives and times. She addressed me while looking beyond me.

"Are you aware that a wife and mother in the state where I was born has no rights of personhood? She is to be seen and not heard. She is forbidden and condemned for speaking up or out against her oppression. She can't enter into contracts. She can't protest if her spouse is unfaithful or treats her as if she is a beast in the stable. The female is little more than a slave in America. She is little more than a slave throughout the world."

"As I would have been confined and circumscribed by my disabilities, had I not been taught by Anne to overcome them, so must we teach our sisters to overcome the oppression that makes the female of the species subservient. Self-pity is our worst enemy. If we yield to it, we will never be anything in this world."

"We must join together and do our best to change the world. When we do that we never know what miracle we can bring to our life and the lives of others. Now is the time for all of us to do our best to win the right to vote."

Anne and I have been asked to join in a march on Washington on the day that President Wilson will be inaugurated. Will you come with us and join in the forefront of the suffragist movement? We need your courage. We need your ability to teach and to organize others, so that we can let freedom ring."

I recall returning to my home on that evening and not being able to sleep. I had been called to a new beginning, another opportunity to lift my voice and use the wisdom gained from my experience to join in another fight for a more encompassing freedom, beyond that of the workplace. Just as I had been inspired by an angel in the person of Jane Addams, I had been inspired by another angel in the person of Helen Keller. An angel who had emerged from the darkness of her overwhelming disabilities to bring light into the world. I would join their march in Washington.

The Woman Suffrage Procession was organized by Alice Paul, a small feisty woman in her twenties, and a member of a New Jersey Quaker household. She was a graduate of Swarthmore College who believed that all human beings were equal in the eyes of God. She had lived in a settlement house in the Lower East Side after college and later traveled to Great Britain where she would join in the Women's Suffrage Movement, enduring repeated arrests, and beatings for the cause of female equality.

While under arrest she and her sisters would engage in hunger strikes to protest their confinement, often resulting in a more horrid type of abuse and brutal force feedings. What many suffragists suffered in Great Britain and America is little known or appreciated. While jailed in London, Alice would meet Lucy Burns, a young New York woman, and develop an enduring friendship and commitment to the cause of female suffrage and equality.

I would meet them both on March 3, 1913, before joining in a lengthy parade down Pennsylvania Avenue. Lip service of support was received from both the Democratic and Republican Parties, yet powerful interests behind the scenes were opposed to female suffrage. I had come across these interests many times before in my organizational activities. They were adamantly opposed to equality and liberty for all. That was the way it was. That was the way it always has been in America.

CHAPTER 64

*I*t was announced in the year of our Lord 1913 that John D. Rockefeller was retiring from his life as an industrial capitalist and the founder of Standard Oil Corporation. He would donate one hundred million dollars to the Rockefeller Foundation to foster educational and cultural betterment throughout America.

As such, he was following in the footsteps of another retired industrial capitalist, Andrew Carnegie. They would each be praised on the front pages of almost every metropolitan newspaper in the country for their generosity, thereby winning worldwide adulation.

My father's closest friend, Seamus Egan aka Michael Duffy, once told me that behind every great fortune there exists a great crime. For those who were never taught about the cause of the catastrophe that was the Johnstown Flood or have never been taught about the Ludlow Massacre of 1914, I hope that my story will shine the light of truth upon these matters.

The mining towns of Colorado had been the scene of brutality and bloodshed for decades. That was where Bill Haywood began his career as an organizer for the Western Federation of Miners after working as a breaker boy. As such he witnessed repeated instances of miners losing their limbs and their lives in the darkness and disregard of those infernal depths.

Mining was an industry controlled by companies that cared little for the lives and safety of its workers. The growth of the railroads was fueled by the mining of coal. It and the railroads would make a Captain of Industry of

John D. Rockefeller, whose business interests were too numerous to catalogue here. One of his many companies was the Colorado Fuel & Iron Company, (CF&I), the largest and most ruthless mining company in the country.

The CF&I was acquired by Rockefeller in 1902 and turned over to his son, John D. Rockefeller, Jr. some ten years later. It was run, like so many of their companies, from their offices in New York City. In September of 1913 a strike was begun by the United Mine Workers of America (UMWA) against the coal mine operators in Colorado, seeking better wages, less hours and greater concern for safety.

The UMWA focused their attention squarely upon the CF&I because of its size and its long history of disregard for the health and safety of workers. In addition, their practices of requiring miners to live in company towns policed by convicts and thugs who controlled their comings and goings with curfews and nightly patrols were against every promise of freedom and equality in America. The CF&I had near complete control of their miners' lives and that of their families. A control they were determined to keep, no matter what the costs in human lives.

If a CF&I miner should speak up or seek to organize others to better their working conditions, brutality, eviction, and even murder would be visited upon him and his family. Soon after the strike began, CF&I brought in foreign strike breakers from Mexico and other countries, and hired the notorious Baldwin Phelps Detective Agency to evict the strikers and their families from the company's towns. This forced the strikers into tent cities in the forests and canyons nearby.

The bloodshed would begin when detectives began raiding these tent cities and firing into them with rifles and machine guns, taking the lives of women and children in an effort to spread terror and bring an end to the strike. This would lead the miners to dig pits beneath their tents to provide cover and protection for their families.

On April 20, 1914 during a day of increasing violence between striking miners and an armed militia, hired to do the bidding of CF&I in Ludlow Colorado, Louis Tikas, one of the strike's organizers and two others were captured by company thugs and murdered.

Gun battles would follow and continue to rage into the evening, when the militia descended upon a tent city and began looting it and burning it down. Four women and eleven children, who were huddled in a pit beneath one of these tents, would be trapped and suffocated when it was set ablaze.

In response to the massacre of these women and children, the UMWA called for the taking up of arms. Open warfare raged for the next ten days throughout southern Colorado, until President Wilson sent in Federal troops. At least seventy five men, women and children would die in what became known as the Colorado Coal Field War.

Hearings would be held in Washington and elsewhere following this latest episode of bloodshed. Witnesses were called to give testimony under oath. One of these witnesses was John D. Rockefeller, Jr. When he was asked whether he would have taken action to prevent his hired help from committing the kinds of acts that led to the murder of women and children in Ludlow, he defiantly stated that he would not have taken any action to prevent it.

I remember reading the newspaper accounts of that horrible circumstance and wondering how something like that could occur in a country that was supposed to be Christian. A country that was supposed to be founded upon the principles of the Golden Rule, the source of all of our other laws and principles. This caused me a good deal of soul searching and reflection at that point in my life, as the mother of three children.

I searched for answers in prayer and scripture. I recall returning to the sayings of Lao Tzu, written out so beautifully for me so many years before, by Seamus Egan about virtue being the way to enlightenment. The virtue of loving service to others was the way to a heaven on earth. Besides, as the scripture teaches, what doth it avail a man to gain a fortune and lose his soul

I resolved that for some of those with power, this lesson will never be learned, no matter how privileged or cultured they become. Their conscience will always be a matter of convenience, as opposed to a matter of right and wrong. Like a dog that is trained to keep from barking, so can our conscience be trained to keep from bothering us when we act selfishly, leading, almost without exception, to evil results.

On June 28, 1914 the selfishness and evil of powerful forces would result in a World War that would massacre millions before it was through. It would begin with the assassination of an Austrian duke and lead like a whirlwind to alliances being formed, armaments being manufactured, armies being mobilized and the world as we knew it being divided into two warring camps. It would make much of the European continent a wasteland of destruction, death and desolation.

There were the Allies of Russia, France and Great Britain and they would be opposed by the Central Powers of Germany and Austria/Hungary at the beginning. It was modern warfare of the worst kind where combatants and innocents would be slaughtered like never before.

It would result in four long years of madness, of massive battles and stalemates, of trench warfare and flying squadrons, of poison gas and submarines stalking the seas. It was a war that Woodrow Wilson promised we would never enter. A promise that would be broken and take the lives and break the hearts of tens of thousands throughout America.

CHAPTER 65

I would be remiss in writing this history if I failed to touch upon the issue of racial prejudice in America and how it has continued to deny equal justice under law to our black citizens up through the present time. Even though my life's devotion has been the achievement of female equality, that does not mean that I have turned a blind eye to the bias and hatred that black people have endured and continue to endure in our country.

I was at a dinner party held in the summer of 1916 at the Beacon Hill home of the newly appointed Supreme Court Justice, Louis Brandeis, when I was introduced to the scholar and historian W.E.B. Dubois. This would be after the sinking of the Lusitania and President Wilson's settlement of a nationwide railroad strike. After determining that Mr. Dubois was a man of uncommon insight and decency, I would become a proud card carrying member of the National Association for the Advancement of Colored People or NAACP

It was following this dinner when I began to question whether Woodrow Wilson would prove true to his pronouncements and promises or would seek compromise and create more hardship and inequality for those without privilege and power in America. It was the accomplished Mr. Dubois who gave me a truer picture and a more encompassing view of the State of the American Union at that time.

His was a courageous episode of free speech, given that President Wilson was revered by many of the attendees and had not only nominated Brandeis to the Supreme Court but had vigorously defended him during a recently concluded confirmation battle.

Our conversation touched upon the lynching of black men that was taking place throughout the country at that time and the failure of the President to remedy or even address these horrid incidents. Mr. Dubois had catalogued its prevalence in an article written in the NAACP's monthly magazine entitled *"The Crisis."*

He was a small muscular gentleman in his late forties with coffee colored skin, a nearly hairless head and a waxed mustache that turned up on either end. His gentle manner and winning smile allowed him to be painfully honest and forthright in his convictions, without giving offense.

"Have you heard about the latest motion picture making the rounds," he asked me.

"I haven't had much time for motion pictures," was my candid response.

"It is all the rage. It's called *Birth of a Nation* and it makes heroes and protectors of Klansmen down South. It will increase the incidence of lynching," I fear. "Were you aware that President Wilson has allowed racial segregation to occur in all of the governmental agencies and that commissioned officers of color are no longer the case in our military? "

"I was not aware of that being the case."

"It seems our President's southern roots are beginning to show."

"He has shown support for workers and kept us neutral while Europe is embroiled in war. He seems a fair and decent man with the best interests of the country at heart," I argued. "His appointment of Louis to the Supreme Court and his continued appeals for world peace have won my support for a second term."

"We are not neutrals, Mrs. O'Sullivan. Our armament factories are flourishing like never before and our merchant navy is prospering from supplying arms and munitions to Great Britain and France. We will be fighting in this war sooner than later and make no mistake it is a capitalist war of the highest order, where the lower classes are being killed and the oil and resources of the African continent are among its spoils."

"You really believe that to be true, Mr. Dubois?"

"I do indeed. Just look at what Wilson has done in Mexico, look at Nicaragua and down through South America, propping up tin horn dictators to make it possible for American companies to gain control of foreign markets. I measure his Presidency not by words spoken but deeds done. America is allied with colonialists who are engaged in a war like no other. America will soon become a combatant in this war with our flags flying high and our real objectives hidden from view."

"I'm greatly concerned by what you have to say, and pray it will not be proven true."

"Mrs. O'Sullivan, I hope that you will be of as much assistance in our fight for freedom as you have been for the freedom of female workers."

I would remember what that enlightened gentleman had to say in the weeks and months ahead. For that was the time when the public focus was shifted slowly but surely from American neutrality to America being endangered by the Kaiser and the Central Powers.

When Germany refused to prevent its submarines from sinking American merchant vessels and encouraged Mexico to join them as allies, President Wilson asked Congress to declare war. A war that he promised would end all wars and make the world safe for democracy. A war that allowed America's full participation in the peace process.

As the daughter of Irish Immigrants who had fled their homeland during a famine fostered by British rule, a homeland that was then engaged in a war to end that rule, I was dead set against America intervening on Britain's behalf. That was the overwhelming sentiment in Boston. That was the sentiment of working people throughout America, despite what has been told and taught.

That was the sentiment that caused Congress to pass and Wilson to sign the Espionage Act in June of 1917 making it unlawful to speak out publicly against America's involvement in the war. That was the sentiment behind limited enlistments across the country and the need to institute a draft that would force nearly three million American men and boys into uniform. Foreign markets and entanglements were about to claim the lives of Americans as never before.

Meanwhile many of those who opposed the war, like Gene Debs, Emma Goldman and Bill Haywood, would be tried and imprisoned under the Espionage Act. After Big Bill was sentenced to 20 years in prison, he would jump bail and take up exile in Russia. This would deal a terrible blow to the future of his IWW.

In July of 1918 my sister Annie had written to me expressing her and her husband's views on the need for America to defeat the "Huns" and bring an end to the warfare that had claimed the lives of millions in the mindless slaughter of battles like the Somme and Verdun. They were so proud that their handsome, twenty two year old son, Brian, had enlisted and was on his way to France.

At that time there was a popular song written by George M. Cohan, a patriotic Irish American of the first order. It was called *"Over There"*. It told of how American troops were coming to save the day and it was played and sung at almost all the war bond rallies taking place throughout America.

War bond rallies were the brain child of Bernard Baruch, a financier friend of Woodrow Wilson, who headed up the War Industries Board, and saw to it that America equipped the Allies with men and materials that would make a blood drenched fortune for war profiteers. My nephew, Brian Muldoon, a corporal in New York's Fighting Sixty Ninth Regiment, was one of those men. In September of 1918 Brian would be killed during an artillery barrage in the Argonne Forest. His remains were buried in a French Cemetery along with so many thousands of other American boys who were sent over there.

One of these American boys was the poet, Joyce Kilmer, whose verses speak of the supreme tragedy that was the First World War.

In a wood they call the Rouge Bouquet, there is a new made grave today.
Built by never a spade nor pick. Yet covered with earth ten meters thick.
There lie many fighting men. Never to laugh nor love again.

CHAPTER 66

There were so many consequences of The First World War that it would be impossible for me to catalogue them in this history. One of the foremost was the Russian Revolution of 1917 that John Reed of the New York Times would describe within his book entitled *Ten Days That Shook the World*.

During the slaughter that would follow under Vladimir Lenin's dictatorship, the communism that Marx and Engels had described in theory became a horrid reality in practice for the Russian people. This would indeed send shock waves throughout our country and throughout all of the countries that were combatants on both sides of that World War.

In America, the Sedition and Immigration Acts of 1918 would allow the Department of Justice to arrest and imprison those who were deemed to be working against the war effort as well as their idea of democracy, in violation of the Constitution. Among those in the forefront of this assault on justice was Mitchell Palmer whose tenure as the country's Attorney General would lead to the "Red Scare" where thousands would be rounded up without warrants and a great many deported.

There was an organized effort leading up to the war and during it to spread hatred and distrust of those of German heritage by the government's Committee on Public Information. This would lead to assaults, arson, fear and distrust of otherwise loyal Americans, many of whose ancestors fought and died in the American Civil War.

An unforeseen consequence of this effort was hostility against German owned saloons and beer halls that would add to the rising tide supporting the prohibition of alcohol in America, begun years before by religious groups and the Temperance Union.

I must tell you of an episode that occurred while I was performing an inspection of a munitions factory for safety violations and the presence of child labor during the height of the war effort. I was employed fulltime by the Massachusetts Department of Labor and Industries since the beginning of the war in 1914.

It was in April of 1918 just before American soldiers began to be killed on French battlefields. I will not disclose the name of the factory nor its address since the watchword of that time of conflict and espionage was "loose lips sink ships". It was a foreboding looking three story edifice with few windows located on a dead end street behind a steel fence and gate.

Suffice it to say that a complaint was received in our offices that women and children in large numbers were working in this factory and the Commissioner of Labor had sent its chief investigator in the person of myself to investigate. I recall approaching the uniformed guard at the gate at 7 P.M. on that dark, dreary night. In a surly manner he asked what my business might be and what authority I had to enter. I told him that I was allowed by law to conduct an unannounced inspection since a complaint had been received and it would be unlawful to keep me out. After much delay, the gate was finally opened and I was allowed inside.

Uniformed guards with gold braids, guns and nightsticks were placed on either side of me as I approached the factory floor. I handed one my bag and the other my umbrella and I took the name and address of every young person who was working there, both male and female.

There were nearly one hundred of them and at ten o'clock their work day was over. I took that opportunity to speak with them outside and discovered that most were under fourteen years of age and required to work more than ten hours a day in violation of law.

The next day I spoke with the Commissioner and he told me he had received a call from the owner who wanted me to end my investigation since it was an obstacle to the war effort. The owner also said that he could not guarantee that I wouldn't be thrown from the window if I returned. The Commissioner's reply was, he would like to see them try and authorized my return.

When I arrived that afternoon, there were more uniformed guards on hand. The first one at the gate attempted to restrain me, as I handed him my card and pushed him aside. On the stairs ahead there must have been twelve more. I elbowed my way to the top step where the guard in command simply shook his head and opened the door wearing a broad smile.

I would finish my investigation and write up near to seventy violations of the labor laws. This was a very serious situation where the lives and safety of women and children were being endangered. It resulted in the Commissioner himself going there to meet with the owner and certain members of the Federal Government.

In the end the safety of workers prevailed over the demands of the factory owner. The Commissioner would later call me into his office and tell me that the head guard had spoken to him about me saying, "I didn't think I would live to see the day when as powerful a corporation as this would be outwitted by a woman."

The consequences of the war that were the most heartbreaking was the effect that warfare had upon the sons, husbands and fathers who had witnessed its horror firsthand. Months after an Armistice was declared on November 11, 1918, troop ships brimming with "doughboys" began to arrive back home. Thousands were disabled by wounds and the effects of poison gas while others would suffer from shell shock, a term used to describe the psychological damage that war can cause.

Many who returned had been promised that their jobs would be waiting for them when they came back. Needless to say they were sadly disappointed, even infuriated, when those jobs were denied to them. Now they were in a far different army, the swelling ranks of the unemployed throughout America.

The ill treatment that the damaged and the disabled would later receive from government hospitals and clinics was only surpassed by the disregard of companies and corporations that had continued to prosper while they were making the world safe for democracy. Their resentment would persist and fester. A treaty officially ending the war would be signed in Versailles, France on June 28, 1919. A treaty that sowed seeds of hatred and betrayal in Germany

While the war was grinding on and on and so many men were away from home, women were required to take a greater role in keeping the home fires burning. Believe it or not what had been forbidden and frowned upon, like women speaking up in public or even riding a bicycle, became accepted, even common place occurrences during the war.

There was a change in perceptions gradually taking place, a progressive wisdom that arose from the requirements of necessity and years of struggle and sacrifice by so many stalwart women and girls both in America and Great Britain.

On August 18, 1920 the Nineteenth Amendment to our Constitution was ratified and women were granted the right to vote and to hold public office at long last. Now the stage was set, we believed, for women to join together and take their rightful place as full participants in charting the course for a better America to come.

That was a time of great satisfaction for me. That was a time of great satisfaction for so many of my sisters in the front lines of the labor and suffrage movements. We thought that we could now work in unison as never before and bring a more balanced perspective to a world where, for the first time, Jefferson's Declaration that all men are created equal included the female of the species.

We believed that we were about to embark upon a new age of prosperity and progress in America and in many instances we did, in what would later be called the "Roaring Twenties." But the forces of greed and prejudice in America were by no means defeated. Factions resistant to change would rise and seek to silence freedom's ring, following the war.

They wanted to force their religious beliefs and convictions upon us all. They wanted to tell us what to believe, what to think and what to do, even within the solitude and security of our own homes. They spoke of an America that was lost and loose in its morality. They thought that laws could be passed that would save us from ourselves. These were the forces behind the total prohibition of alcohol in America and the passing of the Volstead Act in January of 1920. It is said that the road to hell can be paved with good intentions and one should be aware of their unintended consequences.

CHAPTER 67

*I*n many ways the "Twenties" were the best of times for me and my family. My three children continued to enjoy good health and received good educations that would allow both Mort and Mary Beth to go on to college, while my middle child, Roger, would go on to become an electrician by trade and succeed in making a good, honest living.

I have been blessed that all three have turned out so well and have raised families of their own that are both a credit to them and to the communities where they now live. I have tried to tell this story of my life truthfully, without belaboring it with too much detail or burdening it with too many tales of woe and wisdom. If I have faltered in this effort, I trust that you will forgive me and as Shakespeare says, "read on."

I began the "Twenties" at age fifty six. Since I showed no signs of ill health, I resolved to work as long as I could. My occupations were that of a full time factory inspector for the Commonwealth, a part-time property manager for The Cabot Real Estate Company, and a guest lecturer at a handful of colleges. From time to time I would even write articles of interest for the Boston Globe.

As I mentioned, I have always loved reading, the game of baseball and that wonderful brand of American music known to the world as Jazz. On evenings and weekends during that decade I would cherish my time with my family and enjoy my leisure pursuits as much as I possibly could.

Chapter 67

Someone once said, just because you're older doesn't mean that you can't be young at heart. That continues to be my belief as I approach this, my eightieth year.

I want to make mention in this part of my story of some memorable people I met and the memorable events I witnessed during that decade when America would spread its wings and become a source of inspiration for much of the civilized world. Let me begin my recollections of the Twenties by telling you of my night spent down in New York City in celebration of Frances Perkins' birthday.

Frances and Florence Kelley had become the best of friends by that time, having met as members of the Consumer's League a decade before. With the invaluable assistance of Tammany Hall and Frances' close association with the "Tammany Twins", Senator Robert Wagner and Representative Al Smith, significant improvements would be made in factory safety and labor relations throughout New York. These would set standards, later adopted by much of the country.

I had frequently traveled to New York and grew to love the energy of Times Square and the Great White Way of Broadway. On that evening a group of us, both male and female, dressed in formal attire, were privileged to spend Frances' birthday within the first row of the first balcony of the plush Warner's Theater. There, Fletcher Henderson's Band entertained us with musical arrangements featuring the masterful trumpeter, Louis *Satchmo* Armstrong, with the finale being his gravel voiced rendition of *Dinah*, amid a dizzying series of high C's on his cornet.

In the years that followed, recordings by Louis Armstrong and Duke Ellington would become my favorites. They became part of a chosen collection that I would play nearly every night on my mahogany Victrola phonograph, along with those of Paul Whiteman's orchestra and the trumpet stylings of Bix Beiderbecke.

My daughter, Mary Beth, and her friends would often dance the "Charleston" to them in their colorful, above the knee flapper dresses, with their fashionable bob hair styles, after graduating from Oberlin College. I must confess that I would often join in the fun and could "cut the rug" with the best of those vivacious young maidens.

The Twenties were also the time when the plays of Eugene O'Neil took Broadway by storm, winning Pulitzer prizes while Bernard Shaw's *Saint Joan* won acclaim and a lengthy run. Meanwhile Scott Fitzgerald's novels captured both the devices and the desolation of what came to be called a "lost generation" with their unforgettable depictions of the well to do and the want to be, as in *The Great Gatsby.*

Songs sung by Al Jolson and those written by music masters like, George Gershwin and Irving Berlin, could be heard on most Saturday evenings on our RCA radio. Maybe my favorite of all time was Gershwin's *Rhapsody in Blue.* It was the "Jazz Age" and I wouldn't have missed it for the world.

Prohibition would make the sale and distribution of illegal liquor a source of enormous wealth and power during those years for some who dared to break the law. I must admit that I became the acquaintance of more than a few, both old and young, who frequented concealed saloons, known as "speakeasies" and carried flasks upon their persons filled with whiskey or gin that was probably mixed in someone's bathtub, but sold as "the genuine article" by bootleggers. Unpopular laws meant to force morality upon the masses oftentimes create immorality among them.

Violent criminals like Al Capone in Chicago and Dutch Shultz in New York would rise from poverty during Prohibition and rule organized, underworld empires with corrupt policemen and judges on their payrolls and an army of leg-breakers and assassins to do their bidding.

A reading of the writings of Damon Runyon in the Hearst newspapers of that time provide vivid descriptions of a host of gamblers and gangsters who resided in an underworld, created by the shortsighted architects and supporters of the Volstead Act.

I must devote some time to a mythic figure of that era whom I had the chance to meet, George Herman Ruth, who would later be known simply as *"The Babe"* or the *"Sultan of Swat."* I would meet *"Babe"* when he was a pitcher and outfielder for my Boston Red Sox who had won the championship the year before by beating the Chicago Cubs in the 1918 World Series.

It was during a game at Fenway Park against Ty Cobb's Detroit Tigers in the summer of 1919. I was sitting along the third base side of that cozy little bandbox in the company of my son, Roger. As *"Babe"* was heading out to the outfield, Roger called to him and he autographed my program of that game with a big smile and a peck on the cheek. That program from July 20th 1919, a contest the Red Sox won by a score of 5 to 1, has been one of my cherished possessions ever since.

That was before the owner of the Red Sox, Harry Frazee, a theatrical agent who was despised by Ban Johnson, the President of the American League, was forced to begin selling off his players to make ends meet. The first was the pitcher, Carl Mays, with others soon to follow. The last and the most notable would be the best pitcher and home run hitter of the Red Sox, Babe Ruth, on January 2nd, 1920.

That trade would quickly turn my home town team from a champion to a cellar dweller and make a fortune and baseball history for the New York Yankees and their owner, Jacob Ruppert. In 1927 I would travel to Yankee Stadium, the magnificent "House that Ruth built".

There I would watch *"The Babe"* with his gigantic personality and unmatched power, clobber three home runs, one more prodigious than the next. He was well on his way to setting an all-time record of 60, that season. I tell you of all the people that made the Twenties so memorable, George Herman Ruth was second to none.

There were so many other notable events that took place during that dizzying decade, I could spend the rest of this story describing them in detail. In speech making and storytelling, however, saying less is often more effective in making a lasting impression, so I will make brief mention of those that continue to stand out in my memory.

Two infamous court cases that revealed an America where bigotry and religious intolerance were still alive and well must be mentioned. There was the Sacco and Vanzetti case where two Italian anarchists were tried and convicted on less than substantial evidence of murdering a guard and paymaster during an armed robbery at a shoe factory in Braintree, Massachusetts. Eventually, they would both be executed.

Next there was the Scopes "monkey trial" case where a high school teacher in Dayton Tennessee was convicted of teaching the theory of evolution to his students in violation of a law that made the Bible's Book of Genesis the only accepted explanation of how mankind came to inhabit the earth.

Both cases would attract worldwide notoriety and touch me personally, since my old friends, Mary Glendower Evans and Clarence Darrow played prominent roles on the losing sides of each, in a vain pursuit of freedom and justice.

Before leaving the darker side of that decade, two violent episodes stemming from the struggle for mine workers' rights should be mentioned.

The first being the massacre in May of 1920 at Matewan, West Virginia between local miners and Baldwin-Felts detectives that left ten people dead. They included the mayor of the town, Cable Testerman and detectives, Albert and Lee Felts.

The second being the Battle of Blair Mountain during the months of August and September of 1921 in Logan County, West Virginia. That was where thousands of armed coal miners engaged in pitched battles with armed lawmen and strikebreakers, despite the pleas of Mother Jones to prevent the violence. More than eighty people would die and scores of others would be wounded in the bloodletting that would nearly spell the end of the United Mine Workers Union.

Not wanting to leave the Twenties just yet, I must make mention of two final events, one that captured the interest and admiration of the world and the other that would capture my interest and admiration as the decade drew to a close.

On May 20th of 1927 a daring young mail pilot by the name of Charles Lindberg would take off from Long Island, New York in the custom designed *Spirit of Saint Louis* and complete the first transatlantic solo flight to Le Bourget Field in Paris. It was a feat of daring and American "know how" that would make us all proud and a shy, soft spoken young American an international hero and sensation.

The other much more personal event was my first purchase of an automobile in the spring of 1928. It was a shiny black Model A Ford which was mass produced by an assembly line in Detroit. It was as its brochure proclaimed "a product of the most up to date design and engineering meant to afford the opportunity of travel to the average American."

Henry Ford was a pioneer in automobile manufacturing and labor relations who had won my admiration for his decent treatment of his employees. He would call it, "enlightened capitalism." It was his means of caring for his workers and making for a better America.

My admiration for both Ford and his automobile would persist, as I slowly learned to drive about my home town of Medford, with my sons, Mort and Roger acting as my guardian angels. Eventually, I would do so all by myself, amid more expanded surroundings. In the years to come I would have the privilege of meeting Henry Ford's wife, Clara, while seeking to have her change her husband's "less enlightened" ways of doing business.

CHAPTER 68

$\mathcal{E}$conomic panics or downturns that resulted in lower wages or unemployment were regular occurrences in America during the course of my life. On Tuesday, October 29, 1929 the darkness of The Great Depression would descend upon our nation with the collapse of the stock market. It was caused by unregulated speculation and a loss of confidence on the part of investors and banks. It would turn out to be the longest, deepest and darkest economic downturn America and the world would ever witness.

Herbert Hoover was President at that time and he believed, like so many well to do advocates of unbridled capitalism, market forces would eventually correct themselves, as they had in the past and prosperity would return. He and his cabinet would be sadly mistaken in these beliefs.

I would bear witness to these hardest of hard times in our country. I would take issue with those who did not appreciate the plight of the hard pressed and the need for drastic measures to preserve our democracy. I believe that I would not fulfill my promise of telling the whole truth of my life, if I did not describe those often dismal years in some particular detail.

The immediate reaction to "the Crash" on the part of those who "played the market" was one of panic. A panic that would spread across the country and result in fortunes being lost and attempts being made at belt tightening by most Americans. These results would sharply reduce the buying and selling of all manner of goods and services. This restricted the flow of money and brought about massive layoffs and unprecedented unemployment. Then began the run on the banks to remove savings and nest eggs. This resulted in bank failures, more panic and a deeper hole for America to climb out of.

I began to see the early effects that this financial disaster was having on our people, while returning from work in the early months of 1930. More and more, you would see haggard, unemployed men of all ages sitting on benches in Boston Common, their glum faces speaking volumes. You would also see formerly well to do young men in business suits and bowler hats, offering to sell their watches, their radios, even their cars for a fraction of their purchase prices, just to pay the rent or put food on the table.

Fear soon became the emotion that marked the lives of those battered and beaten down by the bad news from all around. That was when James Michael Curley became Mayor of Boston once again and Boston became a shining example of drastic public measures taken to combat unemployment and render assistance to the poor.

Curley was one of a kind. His father died in his arms at the age of ten, and his mother would persuade him and his brother, John, to resist the criminal element with whom their father associated and seek a better life for the family and the people who lived in their Roxbury neighborhood. James would show a particular talent for getting things done for others less fortunate from an early age.

He also had the gift of gab and a roguish charm that he turned into political connections and the securing of public office. His talent for public speaking was legendary. So was his support among the powerless. I was invited to hear him speak at the Parker House in September of 1929, just before the crash. He would become the "Mayor of the Poor" and I would become one of his biggest supporters.

The more President Hoover made speeches and assured the people that this economic downturn was a temporary one, the worse it seemed to get. Nothing seemed to work. Nothing seemed to dispel the fear that gripped the country as people began to starve to death, crime began to soar and suicides became common place occurrences. This was particularly true among the well to do who had grown used to luxury and plenty and weren't able to cope with a drastic change in their circumstance.

In Boston and throughout the country members of the Communist party and their sympathizers began to call for the seizure of the means of production and the overthrow of the government to institute "the dictatorship of the proletariat." Their public demonstrations would be dispersed by squads of police on horseback, wielding nightsticks and firing canisters of "tear gas" into their midst.

Mayor Curley's response to this crisis was not the charity of soup kitchens or bread lines to stave off starvation. He would leave those responses to charitable organizations such as the Salvation Army and Traveler's Aid. As a child his family had been offered "the dole" to redeem them from poverty but their pride and their courage had rejected it. He believed, as did I, that the majority of the people wanted to earn their way out of the mess created by the greed and lax regulation of Wall Street and he would provide a helping hand, not a hand out, to assist them.

His immediate response was to grab the bull by the horns and attack the record unemployment produced by the Great Depression with a record expansion of public works projects, including the building of roads, bridges and public parks throughout the city. He would also build Boston City Hospital for the care of the sick and the aged, and a modern airport on an island in Boston Harbor, with an underwater tunnel to reach it.

He would pay for all of this through increased property taxes, increased borrowing from banks and the securing of federal funds through his Washington connections. His efforts garnered the vocal opposition of both Republicans and Democrats alike. His belief was that desperate times required desperate measures. When his people were facing starvation and homelessness due to circumstances beyond their control, he would not let them down.

Following the death of his loving wife and in short order his oldest son, he would take his remaining children to Ireland to mourn and mend through a visit with his relatives. It was on his return from this sojourn when he would, by pure happenstance, meet the Governor of New York and his wife, Franklin and Eleanor Roosevelt.

That meeting would change the course of history as well as the course of my life. That would have been the spring of 1931 and a presidential election was just around the corner. A presidential election where most of the "dyed in the wool" northern democrats were backing Al Smith of New York. Smith had previously been defeated in 1928 by Herbert Hoover and blind prejudice against Roman Catholics. It was Curley's political insight and Smith's biting opposition to Curley that brought him to Roosevelt.

Curley had only gone to the sixth grade but his speech making was that of a seasoned barrister. He had diligently studied elocution in his youth, spending eight of those early years reading the classics of literature and perfecting his tone, his pacing and his diction. He resolved early on in his career to speak from the heart about matters that moved him. He was a master showman skilled at drawing enormous, exuberant crowds. You really had to hear James Michael speak to understand his genius.

Like I said, it was in the ballroom of the Parker House in September of 1929 where we would meet after he delivered his famous "forgotten man speech" about those who had gone off to fight in World War One, only to return home and become jobless, homeless, hapless and forgotten. Having delivered many a speech myself, it was a distinct privilege to watch a master at work.

There he stood in a grey coat and tails, a white shirt complementing a Kelly green tie, his stocky figure with feet astride. At the crescendo of his speech he lifted his right hand over his large, silver haired head, marked by the two fiery sentinels of his piercing brown eyes. He then brought that hand down in a sweeping motion to his knees, while concluding his remarks, much to the delight of the captivated crowd.

To this day, it is my conviction that James Michael Curley's genuine love for the forgotten men and women of America inspired Roosevelt to follow his lead and likewise become a champion of the forgotten during the Great Depression.

Later that evening, upon being introduced to the Mayor, I was quite astonished when he seemed to know all about me. We would soon become fast and famous friends. When Roosevelt was first nominated at the Democratic Convention, Curley would be barred from a Massachusetts delegation filled with Al Smith supporters.

Not to be outdone and determined to always do whatever he could for a friend, Curley managed to work his way into the delegation from "Porto Rico" as "Jaime Miguel" and deliver a short but mesmerizing speech that would help win Franklin the nomination for President of the United States.

It was during a campaign stop in Boston where "Jaime Miguel" would introduce me to Franklin and his charming wife Eleanor. I will speak to you now of Roosevelt's presidency and the passionate commitment of his wife, Eleanor, to causes that were particularly near and dear to me.

CHAPTER 69

ranklin Delano Roosevelt and his wife, Eleanor, were aristocrats from New York state and relatives of the dynamic former President. Despite their privileged upbringing, these distant cousins would share a commitment to public service and to those who lacked the benefits of their wealthy upbringing. Those who bore the brunt of the catastrophe that would be known to history as The Great Depression.

Franklin had been appointed Secretary of the Navy and would later become the Governor of New York in 1928. Stricken with infantile paralysis at the peak of his manhood and losing the function of his legs as a consequence, he would courageously persevere with his devoted Eleanor acting as a source of strength and purpose. To meet Franklin and to receive the warmth of his smiling, reassuring countenance and touch was unforgettable, but it was Eleanor who became my close friend and confidante during those "hard times."

By 1932 unemployment in America was at 25% of the work force. To make matters even worse, a prolonged drought struck many of the southern and western states and turned once productive farm land into what became known as "The Dust Bowl". This would drive thousands of families to the brink of starvation and desperation. Bank foreclosures on farms that could no longer grow or harvest crops soon followed. Alcohol abuse soared and the violence it fostered became almost epidemic, as crimes like armed bank robbery and homicide became weekly occurrences.

This would be followed by the mass migration of thousands of farming families to California and other northwestern states. Highways heading westward would be clogged with the trucks and jalopies of these families, searching for work or hope, loaded with all the belongings they could take with them.

Desperate single men and many women became stowaways on freight trains heading far away from their forlorn lives, taking up residence along the way in hobo camps or shanty towns. Escaping from hopelessness and poverty with the dream of something better was their common bond.

In Washington, D.C. veterans of World War One who had been promised a bonus by the Government for their service and had not received them, took up residence in a makeshift city of shacks across from Hoover's White House, naming it Hooverville. Regiments of Army regulars would eventually be called upon to fix bayonets and evict thousands of these former doughboys and heroes who had fought to make the world safe for democracy and burn their Hooverville to the ground.

That was the dismal state of American affairs when Franklin Delano Roosevelt or FDR assumed the presidency in March of 1933. With a Democratic Congress behind him, he would take the bull by the horns, like Curley before him, instill hope and attack the Great Depression with all his energy, during his first one hundred days in office.

During that period Mayor Curley's speech making encouraged the people of Boston to keep their chins up and to care for each other in a common effort to combat the adverse conditions that surrounded them. Much was made of his supplying long handled mops to the women and girls who scrubbed the floors of City Hall and the nearby State House in order to lift them from their knees while doing their work. It was a heartfelt and symbolic gesture to restore dignity to the lowly.

Roosevelt would use the radio in what would be called "fireside chats" on Sunday evenings to encourage the country to not give into fear and to explain the measures he was taking to restore faith in the banks, reduce unemployment and provide assistance to America's farmers. He would commence with a series of initiatives that began to bear fruit and restore a measure of hope to the people by the end of 1933.

It was Eleanor who insisted that a necessary part of her husband's agenda must be to care for the poor, to better the conditions of miners and working women, to eliminate the scourge of child labor once and for all and to promote the civil rights of racial minorities. It was Eleanor who persuaded Franklin to appoint our friend, Frances Perkins, as the first female cabinet member in history.

Frances would become Secretary of Labor and shortly after her confirmation ask me to travel down to Washington, to share my experience and insights with her and Eleanor. When Mayor Curley heard about this, he insisted that Franklin's son, James, a Harvard Law School student who had been working as the Mayor's personal assistant and a handsome young Boston police officer by the name of Tom Kenney go along as my escorts.

I recall receiving a telephone call from Frances to schedule the time and the place for our meeting. It was then that she asked me to hold the line for just a minute to speak with Mrs. Roosevelt.

"Hello there, Mary, this is Eleanor," she began in that distinctive voice.

"Hello, Mrs. Roosevelt," was my nervous response.

"Frances has told me all about you and she and I are looking forward to meeting with you, down here at the White House. See you soon."

"I am honored to assist in any way I can," was my reply.

I remember Frances returning to the line and discussing the timing of our get together. Truth be told, I was flabbergasted by the entire episode and remained that way on the lengthy train ride into the nation's capital. Along the way, my two escorts became the closest of friends in spite of their different backgrounds.

James seemed less than enthusiastic about his legal studies and more interested in roaming the train and striking up conversations with other passengers. Tom was diligently poring over the questions of the upcoming Sergeant's exam in order to get ahead and to propose marriage to a shop girl from the South End, named Mary Sullivan.

When the chauffer pulled through the gates of the White House, both I and my escort from the Boston Police Department were beside ourselves with nervous expectation. I can remember him saying, "Mrs. O'Sullivan, this will be something we can tell our grandchildren." I recall the thrill of a child at Christmas appearing upon his beaming Irish face. I tell you it was enough to make me shed tears of joy and appreciation. Once again I could hear the whispered voice of my beloved Jack, saying, "Mary, you deserve this."

All the way from Boston I had thought about what I would say, what advice I would give to these refined and accomplished women who were nearly twenty years younger than myself. I was reminded of my first visit to Hull House and the manner in which Jane Addams and Florence Kelley had persuaded me to use my position and my experience to speak up for the downtrodden and the desperate.

I remember praying for guidance once again and recalling the words of Ralph Waldo Trine to be as one with the infinite and have the faith and trust of a little child. When I was shown down a corridor of the White House and into a magnificent room of white and blue with the portraits of past presidents adorning its walls, Frances and Eleanor were waiting to greet me. My heart was nearly in my throat, I must admit. Their gentle manner and solicitude soon put me at ease as we began with small talk and soon undertook a discussion of the pressing matters at hand.

"Mary," I recall Frances saying, "we are each interested in your wisdom as to how we can become most effective in our respective roles."

"You have led a life that is an inspiration to us all," Eleanor remarked. "I feel that the difficulties of these times afford opportunities for meaningful change. Tell us what you think, Mary. That is why we asked you here."

It was as if a more exalted presence took control of me at that point and fashioned my words without the necessity of reflection. I began to expound and to explain with a facility that I had never felt before. I had the distinct feeling that all of my travails, all of my travels and all of my talents, whatever they were, had prepared me for that moment in that momentous place.

"We are sisters in the cause of equality and must serve as spokeswomen of that cause. We must start by speaking up for all our women and children, the most oppressed of us. We shall see that is just the beginning of a more inclusive cause. We must become advocates for the equality of all people in this country and throughout the world in these times of dread and desperation. We must not let fear or the criticism of compromised people deter us or detract from the noble purpose that presents itself through a glass and darkly and then face to face. The opportunity that comes from this crisis will not last. To you Frances and to you Eleanor, the challenge has been delivered. Through courage and God's providence, we will overcome. "

From that day onward I became their advisor and a witness to the remarkable changes that took place in our country through the industry and inspiration of those two historic women. Despite a lack of outer beauty, like Jane Addams before her, or perhaps because of it, Eleanor Roosevelt became an inspired spokesperson for her husband's policies.

Where there was fear, she sowed courage. Where there was hate, she sowed love. Where there was despair she sowed hope. Eleanor Roosevelt would begin as the First Lady of America and become the First Lady of the World.

Holding press conferences that she insisted should have a fair representation of female reporters and correspondents, she shattered the porcelain prison that had confined previous first ladies.

When her husband's duties or disability prevented him from appearances throughout our country, from the coal mines of West Virginia to the dusty plains of Kansas and Oklahoma, she would appear there in his stead. With a smile, a grace, a belief that spoke of a shared suffering and a firm resolve, she set the nation on a new course of hope and promise.

She would tender her particular brand of understanding and confidence to all. In the cities, where bread lines and soup kitchens had given sustenance to the starving, she and our sister Frances would bring the salvation of employment to the able bodied and succor to the sick and the aged.

To our brothers and sisters whose skin color had condemned them to second class citizenship, she gave them the respect and recognition they so richly deserved. This caused them to believe in her sincerity and to leave the Republican Party of Lincoln to join the Democratic Party of the Roosevelts in record numbers. There they would seek to foster and fight for their equality.

During Frances Perkins years as FDR's Secretary of Labor she would become the spokeswoman and champion of policies that would be part of the "New Deal" for America. It would include the creation of the Civilian Conservation Corps where millions of unemployed men were put to work. They would travel throughout the country, planting trees, building roads and bridges and fighting forest fires.

For their labors they would receive a living wage that lifted their spirits and restored a sense of common purpose that those "hard times" had taken away. So that the fine arts would not be forgotten or ground under the weight of the burden of those difficult times, grants were dispensed to promote knowledge and creativity throughout the length and breadth of the country.

Under her administration the Social Security Act would be passed providing unemployment benefits to those without work. Pensions were likewise restored or provided so that the aged could pass their remaining years with dignity. Federal rules for workplace safety and to aid injured workers were enacted that I was honored to assist in formulating.

Through the Fair Labor Standards Act, a minimum wage and a forty hour work week became the law. Child labor of those under the age of fourteen was eliminated. Lastly, labor unions were officially recognized and protected from the political influence of wealth and greed and a Federal Conciliation Service was instituted to reduce the suffering of strikes and work stoppages. The history of America should indeed be rewritten to include the significant part that women played in making America free.

CHAPTER 70

efore leaving the "Thirties" I would like to make mention of the role that two other women played in helping to make America free. One was the wife of a "Captain of Industry" and the other a so called "fallen woman" who would rise like a phoenix from the ashes to become saintly in her love and devotion for those less fortunate among us. Their names were Clara Ford and Dorothy Day. I was privileged to meet them both and to call them sisters in the cause.

As I mentioned, I became an admirer of Henry Ford for his "enlightened capitalism" through the generous wages and benefits he provided for his workers during the "Twenties." When the "Thirties" arrived, bringing with them record unemployment and decreased productivity, the Ford Motor Company would institute changes in their business practices to weather the storm, like so many other companies across America.

By 1937 the economy was on the mend and the worst of the "hard times" seemed to be drawing to a close. Those of us who had engaged in the workers struggle were sadly disappointed when the Ford Motor Company not only failed to return to enlightened capitalism at that time, but became notorious for the cut throat capitalism it was practicing.

It was said that Henry Ford had grown bitter during the Depression and began to believe in the bigotry that was such a sorry chapter of that era. He was quoted as saying that "Jewish Bankers" were to blame for the world's difficulties and labor unions should be rooted out and removed from American industry, lock, stock and barrel.

In practice, he hired Harry Bennett, a former prize fighter to head up his service department with orders to crack down on any organizing efforts on the part of Walter Reuther's United Auto Workers. On May 26, 1937 a pitched battle between armed thugs hired by Bennet and striking workers occurred on a highway overpass leading to the Ford Plant. This would become front page news and signal an alarming return to those dark days of violent labor unrest in America.

When a sit down strike took place at Ford's River Rouge factory, Ford ordered a lockout and threatened to break up his company rather than submit to the UAW's demands and its interference in his business. It was my fervent hope that Henry Ford would see the light somehow and once again pave the way for a better brand of "enlightened capitalism" in America.

It was then that the hand of providence would bestow its blessings upon our country. It was following a lecture in Sanders Theater at Harvard University given by my friend and mentor, Ralph Waldo Trine. It would draw an audience from all over the country, including Clara Ford. As I recall, I didn't know at that time that Henry Ford was a disciple of Trine who made it a practice of dispensing copies of his book, *In Tune with the Infinite* to family, friends and business associates alike.

In fact, Ford attributed much of his great success to the precepts he found in its pages. I suppose that was why his wife, Clara, was there. By happenstance, we were seated in the same row to the right of the stage as that disciple of enlightenment wove a spell of faith and inspiration over the crowd. It was during a reception given after that memorable occasion when Doctor Trine introduced me to Clara.

She was a lovely woman in her middle years, stylish but not ostentatious in dress, with luxurious brown hair, flawless skin, lovely brown eyes and an almost beatific smile that warmed the heart. I was informed later that she had been a student of the dance in her younger years and appeared still capable of performing a demanding routine with strength and agility.

She would advise that it was her husband's belief in Trine that had made her into a disciple as well. When we began to discuss my work and my recent involvement with the latest elements of the "New Deal", she listened attentively. I thought that was a golden opportunity to touch upon the recent unpleasantness at the River Rouge factory and seek to influence her to speak with her husband and have him change for the better.

"Your husband's concern for the welfare of his workers before the "crash," was the very best example of "enlightened capitalism." I am hopeful he can show the way once again and help to bring a balance between the interests of management and labor throughout the country."

"My husband is a good man who wants what is best for America," she replied.

"I know that, Mrs. Ford. I remember a meeting I had with Marshall Field back in Chicago. When I informed him of the true state of his workers he looked into it and soon managed to correct it. He was a great man who also wanted what was best for America. A man, like your husband, who truly believes in what we have heard from Doctor Trine this evening, can move mountains. Please convey my fondest regards."

"I will Mary, and thank you."

Not long afterwards I would receive a letter from Mrs. Ford where she graciously expressed her fondness and her appreciation for my gentility during our conversation. I was puzzled as to what that reference meant and only later discovered that she had given her beloved husband an ultimatum to not break up the family business and sit down and negotiate with the UAW, or she would leave him.

His love for her would result in the Ford Motor Company agreeing to a contract with the UAW whose terms would prove to be the most favorable to date in the entire automobile industry. Such is the power of love, I suppose. A woman whose love for those less fortunate was greater than any love I had ever witnessed was Dorothy Day.

I would meet Dorothy in Boston in August of 1939. She spoke at the Dennison House to raise funds for the country wide publication of *The Catholic Worker*, a magazine that she helped to create to raise awareness of the suffering of the working poor. Her aspiration was to foster direct action through nonviolent, civil disobedience and thus bring about lasting change.

She had been a Communist, a Socialist, an imprisoned suffragette, and a pacifist opposed to America's involvement in World War One. She had lived a Bohemian life style in her youth, engaging in numerous love affairs, and had even arranged for the abortion of her unborn child.

She was on the dark path to a living hell when she turned in desperation to the Catholic Faith for salvation and soon became the devoted mother to a daughter she named Teresa. With little more than the clothes on their backs and Dorothy's new found faith they would set off by train for Los Angeles where Dorothy would get work writing scripts for the Motion Picture Industry.

After the stock market crash and the nationwide suffering that followed it, she would return to New York and become acquainted with Peter Maurin, a French member of the Christian Brothers. Together they would be inspired to publish their magazine and commence a Catholic Worker Movement that was modeled after the teachings of Saint Francis of Assisi. They would create communities throughout the country based upon self-denial and direct interaction with the poor.

There I sat in the second floor meeting room of the Dennison House once more, where I had delivered many a speech and instructions. Where I had heard Anne Sullivan speak and interact with Helen Keller. Where I had gone to hear Dr. Trine at the insistence of Vida Scudder and Elizabeth Evans after the death of my beloved Jack.

On that night I witnessed that frail sandy haired woman in her forties speak to a diverse crowd of men and women. That was Dorothy Day and she was as close as I would come to being in the presence of a saint. On the eve of another heartless World War that would prove even more horrifying and destructive than any war before it. I will never forget the words that she spoke.

"Love and ever more love is the only solution to every problem that comes up. If we love each other enough, we will bear with each other's faults and burdens. If we love enough we are going to light that fire in the hearts of others. It is love that will burn out the sins and hatreds that sadden us. It is love that will make us want to do great things for each other. "

CHAPTER 71

I sit here looking from the window of my home over rolling hills covered by a January snow. It is 1944 and the world is at war. This will be the last and briefest chapter of my story and my life. I feel that I am slowly fading away at this the beginning of my eightieth year. I have lived a life of struggle and sacrifice and would not have had it any other way.

I have loved and been loved, bearing four children who have brought six grandchildren into my life. There have been triumphs and tragedies, joys and sadness, light and darkness. Such are the benefits and burdens of our life in this world.

We must all grow old and pass from this place leaving memories, mementos and loved ones that were part of our journey. As I reflect upon the landscape of my life, beginning and ending with America at war, I bear no regrets, no remorse, just a final resolve to set the record straight. To write with the ink of truth in telling my story and with it, the story of America during my lifetime. I pray that I have done so.

When I first heard my father's friend, Seamus Egan, speak to me of wisdom, I failed to understand what wisdom really was. It took many years of my lifetime to finally understand its meaning. It is an exalted state, beyond the acquisition of knowledge and the realm of understanding.

It is only achieved by the painful bonding of suffering and sacrifice. It is brought forth to us through intuition and insight. It is pure and it is simple, when all is said and done. It is the perception of truth beyond love and beauty. It is a partaking in the blessed oneness of all. It is an entry into the kingdom of the soul and it remains when we have passed into the world eternal.

If you will bear with me just a little bit longer, as the light fades from view, I would like to share with you the lessons I have learned and the hopes I hold for the future.

With love, courage and faith we can live a life that is full. The love begins with love of self and progresses to love of others, to love of all that is. The courage is the courage to stand up for oneself and then for what is right. The faith is faith in oneself and in the order and plan of the divine.

As to my hopes for what is to come. It is my fervent hope that America will soon prevail in this horrid conflict of good and evil and that it will bring Americans closer together than ever before. From this worldwide war, may we gain the wisdom that might never makes right. That power corrupts and greed is never satisfied. That love is truly all we are after and the answer to all of our fears and forebodings. That women will use the wisdom gained from all their suffering and service to others and achieve worldwide equality. Finally, that women will harmlessly lead humanity from the darkness into the light of everlasting life.

Chapter 71

MEMORIAL ADDRESS OF ELEANOR ROOSEVELT, MAY 1ST, 1953.

Mary Kenney O'Sullivan was born in Hannibal Missouri on January 8, 1864. The daughter of Irish immigrants, she received only a fourth grade education. She would begin work as an apprentice dressmaker and later a bookbinder where she would rise to a supervisory position at the age of fifteen. She became the caretaker of her widowed mother and moved to Chicago Illinois. It was there that she began to organize working women and girls into trade unions and gained the attention of Samuel Gompers, The President of the American Federation of Labor. He made her the first female labor organizer in America.

She would marry John O'Sullivan and move to Boston where she would continue to engage in the organization of women workers helping to form the Women's Trade Union League. After her husband's untimely passing, she became the sole support of her three children by becoming a property manager, factory inspector and guest lecturer.

I had the privilege of meeting Mary in 1933 shortly after my husband's election as President of the United States. Through her personal warmth and counsel we were able to formulate and enact legislation that enhanced the equality of women, eliminated child labor and instituted rules and regulations to protect the lives and safety of men and women in the workplace. As a final note, I would like to read from a passage written by her husband to be, in his position as a labor columnist for the Boston Globe in 1892.

"Suddenly she appears in a radiant dress of pink, a woman in her twenties. Her golden hair frames a face of strength and beauty. Her bright blue eyes shine forth across this crowd of working men and boys of all shapes and sizes. They sit there in rapt attention, as if under the spell of an angel. An angel who has risen from the dust of the American workplace to deliver her message, seeking to make their lives better."

Today we honor the memory of this "Angel from the Dust". May she always be remembered by this bust which will remain in this hallowed hallway from this day onward. She was simply the best because she was the first, a pioneer. We shall not see her like again.

Made in the USA
Columbia, SC
16 March 2018